STARRING

Short Stories, Mostly Science Fiction

by

Howard Johnson

FAX: - 904-825-0222

Website: www.HJWriter.com   (May not be available yet)

Email: Senesisword@yahoo.com

Starring-txt-16701W

The Cover:

Photo credit, NASA using the Hubble Space Telescope

Hubble astronomers have uncovered, for the first time, a population of infant stars in the Milky Way satellite galaxy, the Small Magellanic Cloud (SMC), visible to the naked eye in the southern constellation Tucana located 210,000 light-years away.

Hubble's exquisite sharpness plucked out an underlying population of infant stars embedded in the nebula NGC 346 that are still forming from gravitationally collapsing gas clouds. They have not yet ignited their hydrogen fuel to sustain nuclear fusion. The smallest of these infant stars is only half the mass of our Sun.

Although star birth is common within the disk of our galaxy, this smaller companion galaxy is more primeval in that it lacks a large percentage of the heavier elements that are forged in successive generations of stars through nuclear fusion.

Fragmentary galaxies like the SMC are considered primitive building blocks of larger galaxies. Most of these types of galaxies existed far away, when the universe was much younger. The SMC offers a unique nearby laboratory for understanding how stars arose in the early universe. Nestled among other starburst regions with the small galaxy, the nebula NGC 346 alone contains more than 2,500 infant stars.

The Hubble images, taken with the Advanced Camera for Surveys, identify three stellar populations in the SMC and in the region of the NGC 346 nebula — a total of 70,000 stars. The oldest population is 4.5 billion years, roughly the age of our Sun. The younger population arose five million years ago (about the time Earth's first hominids began to walk on two feet). Lower-mass stars take longer to ignite and become full-fledged stars, so the proto stellar population is five million years old. Curiously, the infant stars are strung along two intersecting lanes in the nebula, resembling a "T" pattern in the Hubble plot.

Date 12 January 2005

I DEDICATE THIS COLLECTION TO ALL OF THOSE WITH VIVID AND UNLIMITED IMAGINATIONS, AND ESPECIALLY THOSE WHOSE MINDS ARE LIMITED ONLY BY THE POSSIBLE REALITIES OF EXTRAPOLATED SCIENCE.

I ESPECIALLY APPRECIATE THE WORKS OF JULES VERNE AND ROBERT LOUIS STEVENSON WHOSE WRITINGS FIRST TURNED ME ONTO THE POSSIBILITIES OF THOUGHTS AND IDEAS UNFETTERED BY REALITY YET STILL CONCEIVABLE AND SCIENTIFICALLY POSSIBLE.

Contents

PREFACE

Most of what I write when I write fiction, is *hard science fiction*. *Hard science fiction* is that written which is limited to scientific possibilities—extrapolative science—the unknown technologies of the future. Hard SciFi is quite the opposite of fantasy which has no limits, and uses magic and the stuff of mythology, defying natural laws. If writing is inconceivable by natural laws, those of physics, math and chemistry, it is not *hard science fiction*. Of course, those limits are sometimes stretched a bit as fiction **is** what we are writing. The following is an attempt to describe some of my own chosen concepts and philosophy. Whether they will admit it or not, every writer weaves his or her own beliefs and agenda into their words. They put much of whom they are into their writing be it obvious or cleverly hidden. The soul of the writer is expressed in their writing. Knowing these things about an author should help the reader gain an understanding of the meanings of the writer.

I am no respecter of peer pressures like political correctness. PC is an effort by a few intellectual elitists trying to control others and force them to think and act in conformity to their wishes. Political correctness has come to be an imposed substitute for conscious acts of being considerate of other in speech and actions. I much prefer common courtesy.

I pride myself on being an equal-opportunity supporter or offender though my actual intent is not to offend anyone. I hold much respect for wisdom that can be gleaned from the words of virtually every human being, even those considered far outside the norm. I include those deemed foolish and unwise by the pseudo intellectual know-it-alls who would run the lives of everyone. I believe one should use emotions to enjoy life, friends, family, and community. I also believe decisions should be made using logic and reason, avoiding emotion as much as possible. I believe politics and religion are two sides of the same coin, and are almost certainly driven by pure emotion with virtually no rational component. Politics is only rational to some politicians and religion to some clergy and religious leaders.

Should you enjoy my writing, tell everyone. If you dislike it, tell me so I can learn and become better at the craft of writing.

The Loop

Shaar slowly became more and more aware of herself. "What's happening?" She thought as a wave of unease flowed through her mind just as she realized she had arms and legs. Her mind was so sluggish, like trying to run in a dense gravity field.

Shaar tried to move, but couldn't quite remember how to make a limb respond, or why she should. This whole experience was starting to feel familiar, which was comforting. "It'll be all right," she thought. "I'll figure this out in a moment or two." If only she could remember where she was, or who she was. Then everything came back with a flash, and she screamed.

As the scream died in her throat, and her mind climbed back into sanity, Shaar once more evaluated her circumstances and options. She had lived this same déjà vu so many times. Fear-filled thoughts of insanity again flashed through her mind and were gone. Furiously, she fought for control and immediate action. Her hands scrambled for the computer console as plans and actions found order and demands in her mind.

The time loop reconstituted her body and ship to exactly what and where it was when she began the test. Her memory alone continued in linear time, each rerun starting where the last one had completed. No matter how many physical records she made during a loop, they were all gone when the next one started. Computer memory, logbook, notepads, camera images, voice recordings, even computer programs, all returned to the precise condition they were in when she first reached the point of no escape. The only thing that did not return to the starting point was her memory. Each loop lasted two hours, thirteen minutes, and twelve seconds—the exact time her ship first took to go from the point of no escape to the event horizon of the black hole.

By this time, she knew the drill. She would be mentally alert until about thirty seconds before the end. During those thirty seconds, her senses would grow duller and her mind would *fuzz* out until she lost all mental faculties. She became a consciousness with no input, no memory, and no senses—a mental black hole. The reverse of the process at the start of the next loop brought on a massive surge of incredible fear as her senses and memory returned. Each time, her hands whitened as the surge of fear closed her grip on the console a bit harder. Immortality in an unending cycle of a bit more than two hours at a time promised a maddening future. She often thought of suicide, but feared the outcome when she would be reconstituted in the next cycle.

It is not the same experience each time, just the same point of restarting. She tried countless strategies to break out of the loop using the main jump drives in every conceivable configuration. Frustration gripped her a bit more at each failure. She was frustrated realizing no matter how much power she used, the fuel charge read out always showed 89 percent when a new loop began. She wondered if she was cycling in universal time, and if each new start was the same as the last. If so, how could her memory be linear? Her mind crawled with questions of how and why she could remember actions she took in twenty, fifty, or several hundred previous loops.

She tried sleeping once, but the experience had been an emotional disaster. She was both maddened and frustrated wondering why her memory continued for all of the 274-time circles since the first. Shaar finally decided she didn't need sleep, being in effect rejuvenated every few hours.

She thought about Kiaho and their daughter Minia'i and cried. For Shaar, volunteering for this dangerous mission was her response to the emotional pain of their tragic deaths. The engineers and physicists who designed this entire black hole research project gave her a fifty-fifty chance of survival. Theoretically, her planned trajectory took a *slingshot* around the black hole right at the point of no escape, and then entered a return path to bring her back to Earth. Things do not always go as planned. In the few minutes the calculated path of the ship took to *slingshot* around the black hole while avoiding the event horizon, disaster took control. Unexpected forces overwhelmed everything she did to maintain the calculated trajectory. Instead, she spiraled from the point of no return and into the event horizon in an almost infinite number of circumnavigations, each one a bit faster than the last. The hopelessness of her efforts in this gravity maelstrom ate at her mental control as she spiraled into what she knew would be her doom. The cycle first repeated, and started a growing mix of wonder, incredulity, frustration, fear, and a thousand other emotional blasts which, by this time, ricocheted through her brain, creating stabs of pain at each impact.

At the current moment she fought to control her mind. She had to train herself in setting up the computer to try ways to break the loop. Each time, she managed to be a bit faster, to get a bit farther. Infinitesimal hope grew and overpowered the demons of failure that dogged her as she drove her mind faster and faster. The next time she might succeed. Hope was all she had along with a generous dose of determination and grit. Holding all this information in her memory and planning for the next cycle was all she could do. She continued learning and gaining, but the damning fear of impossibility clawed at her vitals.

She worked at a frenetic pace, knowing the end of the current loop would soon engulf her in the unknown. She memorized what she did so her effort would go faster and farther next time. Still, fear stalked her every step, no matter how she tried to empty the painful fear from her mind. The gnawing fear of continuing in this loop forever kept a real terror hiding just below the surface, ready to engulf her. She would prefer death, but that might prove impossible.

Thoughts of what she might find if ever she broke out of the loop also plagued her. Would her world still exist? Maybe she would come out in a distant time and place. The death that type of scenario ensured would be preferable to living forever in an infinite time trap.

She made gradual headway with her continuing programming and training. If she could time a strong blast from the main control thrusters close to the start of the loop, the blast could move the ship far enough out from the event horizon the main jump drive would work into the originally planned trajectory. Unfortunately, she must complete the entire sequence extremely close to the beginning of a loop. This meant coming out of the state of bare consciousness quick enough to enter the program from memory and execute it within the first minute or so. Each time she missed, she spent the two-plus hours driving herself, training her mind and body to enter the program quickly and without mistakes. She was practicing entering the program when a slight fuzziness heralded the end of the current loop. Shaar wasn't ready for that yet. "Damn!" she cursed as she faded into nothingness and became a bare consciousness once more.

Shaar slowly became more and more aware of herself. "What's happening?" She thought as a wave of unease flowed through her mind just as she realized she had arms and legs. Her mind was so sluggish, like trying to run in a dense gravity field.

Shaar tried to move, but couldn't quite remember how to make a limb respond, or why she should. This whole experience was starting to feel familiar which was comforting. "It'll be all right," she thought. "I'll figure this out in a moment or two." If only she could remember where she was, or who she was. Then everything came back with a flash and she screamed.

The Great One

And the priest said to me, "Pray to the Great One, and he will guide and protect you. In our homeland, he alone withstood the terrible time of destruction." So I prayed to the Great One, to the all-powerful visage of the one standing in the sacred cave temple, and my prayers were answered. Indeed, I walked through battles unscathed. No harm fell upon me or mine. Triumphantly did I walk over my enemies who fell before me.

And the priest said further, "Follow the way of the Great One, and all things will be yours. The land will do your bidding, and all the creatures thereof will be servants unto you."

So I did follow the way of the Great One as ordained by the wise and powerful words of the priests. My land did become fruitful, and the great and the small creatures of the land paid homage to me and did my bidding. My days were full of joyful toil, and my nights did ring with laughter and rest with quiet peace.

One day I asked of the priests, "Why giveth the Great One these things of joy and pleasure to me?"

And the priests answered, "Do not question. Only pray, obey, and follow the way of the Great One, and you will be always happy."

But sadly, my heart was troubled. Question after question bred still more questions, and I became obsessed with finding the answers. I sought among the people, asking of them the answers to my questions.

Even those who had been my friends turned from me, saying, "Do not ask these questions! We are not to know!"

And it came to pass I made the long pilgrimage to the sacred cave of the Great One to ask the questions. Had not he protected me in battle and destroyed my enemies? Had not he done as the priests and the people said and given me more than I asked from the land and the creatures? Surely, the Great One would answer the simple quest of a loyal follower. I entered the sacred cave and walked among the worshipers. As I stood before the Great One in his temple, my knees shook. He stood so tall and powerful in his brilliant reds and quiet blues. His four green eyes shone from his orange forehead, high as the tallest trees in the forest. His upper two powerful arms crossed on his broad chest while his lower arms held the sacred symbols. Cradled in his crossed legs was the pot of plenty with its golden brown cover, gleaming in the dim light. *Surely the all-powerful Great One would be pleased to answer my simple request*, I thought.

Then in quiet, careful tones, I began asking all the questions of my mind and heart and soul. I waited resolutely for the answers. Being patient and obedient, I knelt and meditated while the Great One pondered my questions. After some time, the silence began to weigh heavily on me, and I again asked the troubling questions. Once more, I knelt and patiently waited the answers.

The darkness came and then the light and yet again the darkness, yet still no answering words came from the Great One. I asked and waited again and again with less and less patience each time. *Perhaps the Great One is asleep*, I thought, though his green eyes shone in the dim light of the temple in the cave. I crept up to the altar and thrust my staff to strike the Great One gently on the knee to awaken him. Several times did I tap his knee, each time more vigorously than before.

Growing bold with eagerness and anxiety, I vaulted onto the altar and shouted to the Great One, "Awake! Awake! Your loyal servant seeks of you some answers to his quest!"

The silence bore down on me like an enveloping black cloud of fear, stirring me to more desperate and violent action. I screamed again and again and beat mightily upon the Great One with my staff in growing madness. The people fled from the temple in terror as a thunderous rumble filled the high-walled room and a blinding cloud of reddish dust engulfed me. I realized I had seen my staff pass into the Great One's body at my last savage blow. A large crack shot upward in blackness to his face in the instant before I was blinded by the red-brown cloud. As quickly as the rumble began, it ceased. Had the terrible sound been the Great One's answer? I stood in fear and trembling as the reddish dust settled slowly and quietly to the floor of the temple, my eyes locked closed in fright. Would the Great One destroy me for this insolence?

The silence bore too heavily on my patience so I opened my eyes. A new terror seized and froze my heart; the Great One was gone! My eyes opened wide to survey the frightening scene. In the growing light, I could see the altar clearly, but nothing stood behind it. Glancing down at my feet, I saw potsherds strewn about the altar and the floor of the temple. Behind the altar where the Great One had been was a great pile of broken pottery of many colors. I stood transfixed. In the midst the potsherds, glowing green and unmistakable, was an eye of the Great One. Overcoming my fear, I jumped to the floor behind the altar and picked it up. It was common brown pottery covered with bright green glaze. On the floor, leaning against the back of the altar, was a large brass plaque with words engraved in the ancient and long-forgotten tongue. I had once seen similar words before, but could not understand their meaning:

The largest piece of fired pottery ever created. This piece designed and fabricated by the East Liverpool Pottery Combine, East Liverpool, Ohio. Made for the Great Lakes Exposition, August 23, 1935.

Charles "C" Miller

D r. Charles Botkin dropped his lean frame into the window seat of the 757 as he headed home for a visit. He looked forward to seeing the farm and his family again. As the plane flew east from Los Angeles toward Chicago, the loquacious Charlie became engaged in animated conversation with the young woman in the next seat. The usual exchange of destinations, reasons for traveling, and a little idle chitchat, led to Charlie started telling her about the uncle he was named after.

"I've run across a difficult technical problem I hope my uncle can help solve. That's the main reason for my trip."

"Are you a student? I believe you said you were at Cal Tech."

The youthful-appearing Charlie chuckled. "Actually, I'm sort of a grad student," he replied. Charlie found strangers treated him more openly as a student than as a professor and required much less explaining. "My wonderful uncle "C" has a unique way of thinking about things and may be able to help."

Crazy Charlie, as his friends called him, was sort of a maverick genius. He graduated from Purdue at seventeen with degrees in physics and math. He then went to Cal Tech for his doctorate and has been there ever since. A genuine wild card, an unconventional thinker and personality, and a capable rock musician, his hair and dress make you think of him as anything but a serious scientist. One of the pioneers in the application of quantum physics to cosmology, he was a world-renown leader in his field by the time he reached twenty-seven.

"And you're going clear back to Indiana to visit him? He must be someone special."

"My mother named me for him, and he is definitely special. To all but a handful of people, my uncle Charlie is an eccentric old man with a checkered past, a tendency to tell tall tales, and an unlikely source of unusual knowledge. We all call him C. I was at least seven before I knew his real name. He's my mother's older brother, considered a real maverick by the entire family, except my mom and me. My mom told me many tales about his life before I knew him.

"As a young man, C married a glamorous young woman who left him a year later to pursue a career as a movie actress. Mildly successful, she had small roles in many pictures. *Uncle C* as I called him as a youngster, never tried marriage again although he had several relationships that eventually went sour. He had one long relationship with a lady named Carla. She was something special because whenever C talked about her he would become misty eyed.

"I remember once asking him why he hadn't married her if he cared so much. He stared off trance-like, and said quietly. 'I was young, foolish, and had a severe case of low self esteem. I didn't realize what an incredible person she was or what a beautiful relationship we had. Letting her go and ending that relationship was one of the stupidest things I ever did. I came to my senses and realized the gross mistake I had made far too late.'

"He was light-hearted, thoughtful, and studious. He seemed never to take life too seriously and was always upbeat. Nothing ever seemed to upset him except thoughts about that lady. These were the only times my uncle was ever in a melancholy mood. Everyone in the family suspected he never got over Carla. Afterwards he embarked on a nomadic life of searching. He did so many offbeat things in his life he's hard to describe in a few words. He made a great deal of money on one business venture, only to lose everything on another, ill-fated one. He worked hard to pay his debts and managed to build himself a small fortune of some two hundred thousand dollars. He gave a portion of this to my folks so they could acquire some additional land adjoining their farm. In his late forties, he embarked on a six-year trip through the Far East which exhausted his remaining fortune. When he found himself stranded and out of money in the Philippines, my folks scraped up enough money for his ticket home. With no place to live, he stayed for several months on our farm. I had just started school when he came to live with us."

"My, he sounds like a wild one."

"He is unconventional, but not wild. He's a wanderer, a thinker, and a builder. He built a neat little cabin next to a pond in a wooded area on the farm. The woods and the pond had remained undisturbed since loggers cut all the useable timber during the late eighteen hundreds. I was fascinated and delighted to be helping C build his cabin in 1979. During the next few years, I spent many wonderful times listening to stories of Uncle C's adventures around the world. One of C's passions was his lifelong collection of books, which overflowed the shelves on two walls of the main room of the cabin. There were texts on a wide variety of subjects from astronomy to zoology, several sets of encyclopedias, and quite a bit of fiction, from the classics to Jules Verne and several modern authors. Stacks of *National Geographic, Discover, Smithsonian,* and several other scientific magazines filled the lower shelves on one wall of the room. All had been stored at the farm until he built his cabin. I often read from those books and magazines."

"Sounds like a wonderful experience. He must care for you a lot."

"And I for him. That's for sure," Charlie said, a bit misty-eyed. A momentary pause of wistful remembering and Charlie continued. "C has a well equipped workshop, the largest of the three rooms in the cabin. He has tools fitting many trades. When I was little, he devoted one corner of his workbench to the assembly of one of the new computers that were beginning to hit the electronic hobbyist market. This new gadget fascinated me and I worked on it with C every chance I had. By my ninth birthday I was a bona fide computer whiz."

"Is that what you're studying, computers? I'm fascinated by them, but only use one at work. I haven't a clue how they work. It's all magic to me. Are you going back for help on some computer problem?"

"No, I use computers, but my work is with basic physics."

"Wow! That's another complete mystery to me."

"A lot of physics is still a mystery, even to the experts, but we're learning."

"Is your uncle an expert in physics?"

"Sort of. He's hard to describe. He's done about everything and been all over the world. He spent a year as a preacher for a nearby evangelical, nondenominational Christian church. This led to a short career as a DJ and talk show host on a local radio station. His offbeat views from all over the spectrum earned the animosity of many listeners, so they fired him. This was done in spite of the fact his audience had grown to huge proportions for the local area and in a short time. His short-lived, local-celebrity status was a mixed blessing. This earned him a reputation as *that crazy old coot who lives in a cabin in the woods*. His meager odd-job income barely covered his living expenses, including fuel for the old pickup he drove. I remember many family discussions about C when I would come home from school for a visit."

"When you were in college?"

"No, I was in a military school, a grade school, when this was going on."

"Were you in the military?"

"No, I attended a private school for boys which taught military discipline. I'm not much on that."

"I can tell by your clothes. I'm guessing the military part didn't stick."

"I was grateful for the wonderful education I received there. I endured the military discipline. Truthfully, what I learned about discipline helped my scientific education. There's a lot of discipline required in physics."

"Please go on about your uncle. He sounds like a fascinating person."

"That he is. After I graduated from high school and before leaving for college, C sat me down and shared with me his concern about the unusual knowledge he possessed. There were many things he knew about, but had no idea how he gained the knowledge. Often, when I asked him how he knew so much about so many things, he would answer, 'Just my insatiable curiosity, I guess.' This time was different. He told me he was often frightened and upset when he would explain some strange or unusual phenomenon and realize he had no way of knowing how he knew. I always thought he had picked up all that information reading and from his travels. He explained it was part of his knowledge, but why did he 'know' certain scientific discoveries or theories before anyone made the discovery or published the theory? That's why I'm going to visit him. I always thought he was being modest until one time when I made a new discovery during my research only to realize my uncle C had explained the same thing to me accurately, many years before. The realization startled me."

"I can see why. Are you sure it wasn't one of those *déjà vu* experiences? They can be scary."

"I know what you mean, but no. It wasn't. I had written documentation from years before that I found and compared with my research. They were an exact match. It was a complete mystery to me."

"Well, I hope he can help you out with your new problem."

Her face and body language told Charlie she was through talking, so he settled back and let his mind wander back to when C told him an amazing tale. He had relived that special time almost verbatim, trying to make sense of what C said. This was before he first headed out for college. He was visiting Uncle C at his cabin and helping him repair a TV set. Once more his mind slipped back to that time, and he relived the experience as he asked C the question that started the whole thing.

*   *   *

"You were going to tell me something secret before I went off to college? Well, I'll be leaving in a few days, so how about it? Will you share your big secret now?"

Uncle C leaned back on his stool and looked Charlie in the eyes. "I did promise to, didn't I? I tell you what, let's finish this TV and go sit on the sofa. This story needs a private place with no distractions because I want you to think hard about what I will tell you."

They finished and tested the TV in about fifteen minutes and went into the main room. On the way, C opened the fridge for a pair of cool drinks to accompany the tale. When he sat down on the sofa, C leaned back and stared off into space for a few minutes while Charlie sat and watched him in rapt expectation.

"I'm going to tell you about something that happened to me a long time ago, something I never told your mother or anyone else still alive. This is for your ears only, and I hope it will remain between us. You are the one person on this Earth who will hear this story without prejudice. After you hear, you can ask anything you want. I won't provide many answers for you, but this may explain how so many of our little talks went where they did."

Charlie remembered thinking about his uncle in wonder and amazement. They had spoken of so many things. He couldn't imagine what new marvel was about to be revealed. Enthralled, almost enchanted, he waited, eager and expectant.

C began, "I was walking the few blocks home from grade school for lunch one cold, crisp, blue-skied January day in 1935. WhileI passing the Buhers' house, about halfway home, I happened to glance up and notice a shiny object through the naked branches of a wintering tree. At first I though it to be a new kind of balloon caught in the branches, but as I took a few more steps, I realized the object was above the tree and almost overhead, far from the winter sun hanging low in the southern sky. I was fascinated, for this was an exciting new wonder for an inquisitive second-grader still in the intoxicating time of life when the days are full of new discoveries. I leaned against the concrete wall separating the Buhers' yard from the alley, right where Mrs. Buher would place food for wandering beggars during the Great Depression.

"The object was round and the same apparent size as the full moon in the sky. It was shiny, like a mirror, yet there was no reflection. Transfixed, I watched for a long time, for a small boy—a minute or two. Then it began to move toward the west, accelerated and disappeared over the western horizon a few moments after starting to move. As soon as it was gone, I ran home to tell my mother, and find out from her what I had seen. This was at a time when people ran outside when an airplane flew over, and my favorite was the new Douglas DC-3. This object was not like any airplane I had ever seen before.

"When I arrived home for lunch, my mother was angry with me, and she was rarely angry. 'Where have you been? I've been worried sick!' Her words astonished me. I didn't get a chance to ask her about the marvelous shiny object. She chided me, 'You'll go without lunch young man. Now hurry back, or you'll be late for school.' I didn't understand how I could be late. I had a full hour at least for lunch, and school was five minutes away. I stopped to watch the strange object for just a few minutes. What had happened to the missing time?

"I remember nothing of the rest of the day until I came home and my mother again questioned me about why I was so late. When I asked her about the object I had seen, she thought this was another of the 'stories' I used to invent to liven up my life and amaze others. I had discovered the price you pay and the pain of what happens when you become a 'story' teller, and people learn not to believe you. Every single person who heard my story laughed at me and ridiculed my tale except one, my grandfather. A storyteller himself, he listened to my tale and wondered with me what the object was and what happened to the missing hour.

"I was so humiliated at every attempt made to find out about the object that I gave up. Since then I told no one else about my experience. My grandfather and I discussed the object a number of times over a number of years, often when we were fishing together on the lake. I was around fifteen the last time we talked about our little secret.

"When I was in junior high school, I began to experience a strange phenomenon which has continued unabated to this day. In Mr. Armstrong's science class, I discovered I understood a lot about things I had not read about or had not been explained to me by anyone. For me, this started a fascination for things of science that would last my entire life. I also found I knew the answers to many questions I should not. My classmate and buddy, Fred Hunziker, who sat next to me, was amazed at my knowledge. Even Mr. Armstrong was flabbergasted to the point where he quit letting me answer questions in class. Another classmate, a bright girl, told me she thought I knew more about science than our teacher. They began calling me 'the brain' and not always in a complimentary fashion.

"Your aunt Matty, who was six years older and ahead of me in school, gave me her chemistry book when she finished the course on Chemistry. In my mind, I can still see the diagrams in that book, diagrams of atoms with electrons in circular orbits about a solid, compact nucleus. I knew those diagrams were wrong, but of course, my sister thought I was nuts when I asked her, I was crushed by her dismissal of my questions, but what could I say? She was a high school senior and far wiser than I about everything. Her book piqued my interest in chemistry, which then led to my selection of chemistry for my college studies. It was many years later when I read a similar description of the indefinite *cloud* structure of electrons about a tighter cloud of protons and neutrons, the nucleus, I tried to explain to my sister. It seemed this was the latest concept of atomic structure, developed many years later, long after I tried to explain the very same concept to my sister as a boy of twelve.

"There are many other concepts of our physical world that I know without any idea from where the knowledge came. I keep searching and reading to gain confirmation of many of these things. For example, I 'know,' or at least can conceptualize, an understanding of our universe that has yet to be discovered or explained by anyone. I think the universe has a roughly spherical shape with an irregular, changing surface. At the surface of this shape, all mass would be to one side of any point on the surface. The center of mass of the universe would be near the physical center. Light, warped by this center of mass, does not escape from the universe. The true speed of light is a factor of its distance from this center of mass. Our measurement of light speed is a function of our own distance from this center of mass. Light passing near or through this center of mass is moving much faster than when passing us. Likewise, light, on reaching the limit of the universe where all of the mass is to one direction or side, slows and finally *falls* back in the same way one celestial body orbits another, controlled by the force of gravity. The gravitationally limiting surface of the universe acts to return light and hold it within the gravitational grasp of the universe.

"The first time I heard a flying saucer story, I thought of my childhood experience. My story was so similar to the descriptions of many of these tales. The ridicule heaped on those who said they had seen a UFO caused me to rethink my experience and continue not to talk about it to anyone. The first time I heard an *abduction* story, I thought about the missing hour so long ago and of the things I know that I really shouldn't.

"I came to no conclusions, nor do I make any claims other than those I described. The mystery to me is now greater than ever, and I am sure I will not find an answer in my lifetime. I search and ask in every way I can, yet the mystery continues to deepen. If there are others with similar experiences I would like to meet them, yet I hesitate to admit what I experienced. I am still a bit apprehensive about any ridicule that might come and destroy my own knowledge. I tell you this now because you understand me. besides, I am nearing the end of my life and have so much less to fear than when I was younger. You can decide for yourself if the story is for real or the ravings of a crackpot. A discovery confirming the view of the universe I know and described would change the acceptance of my story now, wouldn't it?"

"Would it ever!" Charlie replied, then asked, "What do you think it was?" Charlie was amazed, grasping the implications of the story, but never doubting a single word his uncle spoke.

"I gave up speculating on that years ago," C replied. "I only know what I told you. No more than that, but no less either. Many years later, when the first UFO stories began appearing, I thought I might find an answer, but soon realized all I would do would be to make a fool of myself if I came forward with my story. It's clear to me that whatever or whoever they are, they have a purpose to their activities. I've wondered for years what their purpose might be without ever coming up with anything logical. I can't determine if it bodes good or bad for humanity and is a real mystery. Why would they imbue a small child with advanced knowledge? I'm convinced that is what happened to me so long ago. There must be others who received similar treatment. Though I've searched my whole life, I've never found another person who shared my experience. I've met and spoken with people who reported sightings and abductions, but none were anything like mine. In fact, I find myself doubting the truth of their stories like everyone else."

"The truth is like the proverbial needle in the haystack, isn't it?"

"That's almost an understatement. Over the years, I've had many incidents where the announcement of a discovery was something I already *knew*. Did I actually know, or was it a trick of the mind, a déjà vu experience? I've pondered that question many times. Once, while talking with a group of engineers about a particular metallurgical problem, I posed a solution to them. The solution was one I didn't need to think about. I just 'knew' it. Several months later, the specific problem was solved by the method I proposed. One of the engineers from the group contacted me and asked how I had come up with the exact solution. He knew I was not a metallurgist and wondered how I knew the particular solution to a problem no one else was able to solve. I was at a complete loss to explain. Had my lack of knowledge in the field let me think outside the limits imposed by an expert understanding? Was my solution one of those serendipitous 'aha' happenings we all experience occasion, or had I *known* the answer? I don't have a clue as to how, and would not claim to understand where the answer came from.

"There are two concepts I feel certain came into in my mind by an extraordinary process. The understanding of the true nature of the particles in the atom is one. The general makeup of the universe with the gravitational effect on light and other electromagnetic waves or particles, is the other. The first was postulated by particle physicists many years after I knew and described the atom exactly as it is. The second seems to be a theory in my mind alone. No theory I ever read about is remotely similar. I don't know if it's correct, and I certainly don't know how to prove it."

Charlie determined he would set that as one of his goals, to prove or disprove C's theory about the universe. It would prove to be a daunting task.

＊　　＊　　＊

Charlie came back to reality as the woman next to him shook his arm.

"Wake up! Raise your seat back and fasten your safety belt."

"What? Oh yes! Thanks! I guess I went to sleep."

"You certainly did. You've been sound asleep for at least an hour. Never moved a muscle."

It took him a few minutes to reorient from the where-am-I, what-time-is-it daze. By the time the plane arrived at the gate he was wide awake. He walked through O'Hare Terminal toward his next flight still thinking about his Uncle C. One more quick jaunt in the small commuter airplane to South Bend and his folks would be there to pick him up. He hoped C would be with them.

＊　　＊　　＊

Charlie walked down the steps from the small plane that brought him from Chicago to South Bend, and realized his folks were not waiting there. This was unusual. He hoped nothing was wrong. He walked to the baggage carousel, waited for, and picked up his luggage. Still, no one appeared even as he walked outside. His folks were never late, so visions of accidents or other calamities stalked his mind. After waiting about ten minutes, he turned to go inside and call home using his cell phone. He started to go back in when his mother's car came around the corner and pulled up to the curb. She was the only one in the car.

"Where's everyone?" he asked as he placed his bags on the rear seat. When he sat in the front seat, his mother stared straight ahead and said not a thing. "What's wrong, Mom?" he asked again, sensing something was wrong.

"It's your uncle C." she said through tears. "He's disappeared. We drove out to his cabin to find if he wanted to come with us to pick you up, and he was nowhere to be found. His door was standing open, and last night's supper was still sitting on the table, uneaten. Ralph was sitting on the porch, whining, and he always takes his little dog with him wherever he goes. I'm afraid something terrible has happened."

"I'm sure he'll turn up. Maybe he walked somewhere."

"No! He just disappeared. His pickup was still there, and with Ralph on the porch, something strange surely happened. Your dad stayed there to search for him while I came to pick you up. Maybe he'll find him by the time we are back."

On the way home, Edith drove much faster than usual. "Slow down, Mom! I know you're in a hurry to be back, but let's not add an accident to today's problems."

"I'm sorry! I didn't realize I was driving so fast. I'm worried to death about C."

"I'm concerned myself. Does he usually go off without telling you?"

"Never! Even when we're away, he'll leave a note on the door about where he's going and when he'll be back. He's really good about that."

"I'm sure it's something simple. Possibly a friend of his came over and picked him up."

"Not a chance. Anyone driving would go right by on the driveway. We'd hear them no matter when they went by. Besides, how do you explain the uneaten meal on the table? C would never leave the place like that under ordinary circumstances. He eats at about dark this time of year, so he left last evening between six-thirty and seven."

"What were you doing about then? Were you home?"

"We were eating dinner about then ourselves. There was one strange thing, the lightning flash. It was a bright, sustained flash of lightning. You know how sometimes, at night in the dark, a lightning flash lights up the whole sky for almost a second and you can see everything, even in the pitch-black?"

"Yes, I know what you mean. You must have had a thunderstorm last evening."

"No, we didn't! After the bright flash, your dad and I went outside to close the windows on the car and the sky was crystal clear. That's when we heard Ralph barking. Also, there was no thunder. We decided the light was a bright flash of lightning so far in the distance we couldn't hear the thunder. We thought Ralph was barking at some strange dog or critter. You know how he carries on when something's around the cabin. What else could we think?"

"It sounds strange to me. As soon as I am home, I'm going to check the neighbors to find out if anyone else remembers that flash," Charlie commented. A dark cloud of silence hung in the car during the rest of the trip home. Charlie was hoping C would be there waiting when they arrived.

As they crested the rise in the road north of the farm, they could see two sheriff cars parked in the driveway. Ray was standing in the backyard with two deputies, and they were all staring back toward the woods where C's cabin was hidden. The two deputies were friends of the Botkins and longtime members of the local sheriff's department. His mother parked the car. She and Charlie stepped out and walked to where the men were standing.

"What did you find?" Charlie asked as soon as he joined them.

"Nothing," his dad replied in obvious distress. "I called Pete and John here to see if they could find anything I missed."

"We checked over everything and couldn't find anything suspicious," Pete said. "Wherever he went, C didn't leave a trace. We don't make missing person reports until the individual has been missing for at least twenty-four hours, but this seemed unusual. We hightailed it out here as soon as Ray called. John and I combed the area for more than an hour and found nothing, nothing at all."

"We called for some dogs to come out to track him in case he walked off somewhere and can't make it back," John added. "They'll soon be here. Pete is going to stay and work with the dogs. I've got to go back right away, but I leave you in good hands. If he's here, those dogs will find him."

After John drove away, Charlie took his bags up to his room. When he came down, his Mom, Dad, and Pete were sitting in the living room and talking about C's possible whereabouts. Before long until a truck drove up in the driveway. The dogs and their handler, Tara Bailey had arrived. Tara was a popular dog trainer and breeder who had two hounds often used by law enforcement all over the northern part of the state. Ken Bailey, her husband, was a veterinarian. Together they had an animal hospital, training center, and boarding kennel in the next county about thirty miles away. All four of them went outside to greet her.

After talking to Tara for a few minutes, Pete said, "She asks that none of you go with us to the cabin. The less people around, the better the dogs work. We'll drive the truck back to the cabin and release the dogs there. Is there any article of clothing you can remember him wearing recently? We'll need something to give them his scent."

Edith thought for a moment and then said, "He puts his dirty clothes in a hamper in his bathroom closet. He hasn't brought them up to wash for a while, so there should be plenty in the hamper."

"That's perfect. I'm sure the hounds can obtain a good scent from those clothes," Pete answered.

"Where did you leave Ralph?" Edith asked her husband.

"I think we left him inside the cabin," Ray answered then added, "You'd best leave his little dog inside. He'll be friendly enough to you folks, but he wouldn't take kindly to a couple of hounds poking around his property."

"We'll make sure he's okay and kept out of the way," Pete remarked as he stepped into the truck with Tara.

— The Dogs Are Buffaloed —

"How about some details, Pete? When John called, all he said was someone disappeared and asked me to bring the hounds here as soon as I could," Tara said as she guided the truck down the bumpy lane toward the cabin.

"The missing man is Charles Miller. Everyone calls him C around here. He's an unusual, somewhat eccentric old man about seventy-five, the brother of the woman who lives here. I'll say one thing about him. The man can build or repair about anything. You'll see what I mean when we are at his cabin. He built the place all by himself about sixteen years ago, a neat little place, perfect for a man living alone."

"Sounds like an interesting man," Tara commented. "Do we turn here?" She asked as they reached the end of the lane where they crossed a small, dry streambed.

"Just follow the stream right into the woods. You can see where he's driven his truck over the years. It's a bit bumpy but high enough above the streambed to be out of the water in the spring and early summer when the stream runs full of water."

After they entered the woods, the trail made an abrupt right turn and led about fifty feet to a cleared area by the cabin. As they stepped out of the truck, they heard Ralph inside, barking furiously. He knew there were strangers outside and was giving them what for. While they walked up to the door, Tara asked, "He's not a biter, is he?"

"He was quite friendly when we were out here an hour or so ago. I'm sure he'll be okay."

Tara crouched down as she entered and extended her hand along the floor, palm up in a friendly gesture. The little dog stopped barking, came over, and sniffed her hand, his tail wagging furiously. He did not like to be left alone and was genuinely happy to see them."That's a good boy," Tara said as she gave him some soft pats. She was rewarded with several doggie kisses. Ralph was a typical affectionate pooch. With the little guy now at ease, she retrieved several shirts from the hamper to use for the scent. "Why don't you stay inside and keep Ralph company while I work my dogs? If he can be kept from barking, he won't distract the hounds. It will make my job easier."

"Okay! Give me a call if you find anything. Use your two-way. Set it to our standard frequency."

Tara closed the door behind her and headed for the rear of the truck. She opened the small door and released the two hounds who bounded around exuberantly for a few moments, glad to be out of their confinement. Soon they were back at her side, knowing full well what their job was. They sniffed the shirt Tara held out, then sat down to announce they were ready. Her hounds were well trained. She didn't need to run them on leashes as they knew not to outrun their handler. They waited for her at times so she could catch up. She directed them to the porch where she wanted to start the search. Hand signals were her method of directing the dogs who worked in relative silence.

As soon as she gave them the signal to begin, they headed off the porch, trailed about fifty feet to the center of the clearing where they began circling. Several times, they started off on a track only to stop and return after going twenty or thirty feet. Obviously these were old, cold tracks. After returning to the porch several times and sniffing for other tracks, the dogs returned to the center of the clearing and sat down. There was no ambiguity to their message. The track ended right there in the center of the clearing, the only fresh track the dogs could find. She had them try several more times with the same result indicating several things. There was no way of determining which direction the short track was laid down. It could have been from the house to the clearing or the reverse. C had either walked from a vehicle parked in the clearing to the cabin or walked the other way, from the cabin to a vehicle. There was no other possibility. Tara examined the ground for tire tracks or other markings around where the track ended. Other than what appeared to be a single faint set of footprints in the softer ground, she found nothing. She took a marker flag from the truck and stuck it in the earth to mark the spot. Knowing they would stay nearby, she let the dogs roam as she headed for the cabin to tell Pete what she found.

"Did you forget something?" Pete asked as she reentered the cabin so soon.

"No, but the dogs did find the end of a short trail in the middle of the clearing," Tara replied.

"What do we do now?" Pete asked.

"I marked the spot where the track ends. I let the dogs roam to try to find something else. When we drive back to the house, I'll let them search the way back and around the house. They might find something. I think we should take this little guy with us. He'll not be happy if we leave him alone; I can tell." She called Ralph over to her. When she picked him up, he gave a low growl to tell her he didn't like being held. He would endure the indignity without complaint after she reassured him with soft words and a gentle touch and headed for the door. Tara was a master at handling dogs.

As soon as she walked outside, the two hounds romped over to investigate this little pooch their master held. A few words and a hand command and the two hounds sat still while Tara took Ralph and placed him in an empty kennel in the back of the truck. Signaling them to begin tracking again, Tara got in the truck with Pete, and they headed back, following the dogs as they searched back and forth across the stream side driveway and then the lane. When they reached the house, the dogs crisscrossed the entire yard, pausing several times by C's pickup where there was an obvious, but weak scent. Several days had passed since C drove the pickup and he last walked to the house on Friday, so all the tracks were old and weak. The dogs followed tracks up to the house and the truck, but it was apparent these too were old tracks. Tara retrieved Ralph from his cage in the truck and carried him into the house. He never made a sound, resting peacefully in her arms.

"I didn't think this little guy should be left alone in the cabin. Can I bring him in?" She asked Edith as she stood in the doorway.

"Certainly," Edith answered with a smile as she opened the door for them. "C brought him here often. He knows his way around. We keep a bed for him and food and water bowls. He can stay with us 'til we find C. Incidentally, what did your dogs find?"

As they walked into the living room, Tara relayed what happened with the dogs and how she marked the end of the scent trail in the clearing. "That's in case anyone else wants to search for signs of what happened. I couldn't find any indication of tire tracks or anything other than the single set of faint footprints. There were tire tracks near the cabin where cars parked and from there to the drive, but nowhere else in the clearing. If your brother walked anywhere other than the one scent trail, the dogs would find it. There's been no rain to wash the scent away, and the one scent track we did find was fresh and definite. He walked that track one direction or the other within the last twenty-four hours. The dogs told me so in no uncertain terms."

Ray was puzzled. "That's strange, almost like he disappeared into thin air, right at that spot. Since that is impossible, we must try to come up with something else, something that makes sense."

"I have no idea what that could be," Pete commented. "No wheeled vehicle could possibly make the clearing to take him without being seen, so it had to be a helicopter. Unfortunately, no chopper could possibly set down in the clearing."

Charlie replied, "The only way a chopper could pick him up would be on the end of a cable lift dropped down from above the trees."

"We would hear any chopper hovering over the trees at that time of night," Ray commented.

"I don't know about that," Pete said. "Some military birds can hover almost silently. They make some noise when they fly fast, but at slow speeds, and while hovering, they are silent. You wouldn't hear them from here. The cabin is nearly half a mile away, isn't it?"

"At least," Charlie answered. "But what would the military want with C? He's never been in the service as far as I know. He traveled all over the Pacific Rim for a number of years, and he's done some contract work with the navy out there, but that was twenty years ago. I can't imagine what the military would want with him. Anyway, they could drive up in a car and pick him up."

"A good point," Pete replied. "It's a real mystery. The only way anyone could take him away was by lifting him into a helicopter. There was no sign of a scuffle anywhere. I searched for those signs, particularly where the scent trail and footprints ended. Those footprints were hard to see. Tara found them when the dogs sniffed at them. They were slight indentations spaced as normal walking prints would be. We couldn't be sure which direction they headed. Then we found one complete print in some softer ground toward the porch. The print showed he was headed away from the cabin. We checked around but found no other prints within ten or twelve feet of the end near the marker Tara placed."

"What about your own footprints?" Ray asked. "Couldn't they cover or obliterate other footprints?"

"A good point," Pete replied. "One of the most important aspects about inspecting a crime scene is how to do so without destroying evidence. Extensive training and practice on how to walk so as to avoid areas we believe may contain clues is part of our forensic discipline. I can assure you there were no other footprints around that marker. We can't consider that a crime scene, but we did use the same procedures in the same careful manner."

"My dogs were the only ones who walked in the area, and the ground is quite hard, so I doubt they left much of a mark," Tara commented. "It would take a person weighing more than a hundred pounds to leave any mark on the ground. I'm a hundred and forty, and I barely left a print where I walked."

"So that leaves us without a clue," Charlie said. "Your dogs found significant information, but it merely added to the mystery. C couldn't just evaporate into thin air, but that's what it seems like so far. Where do we go from here?"

"Well, I need to go write my report," Pete said resignedly. "I don't relish doing so, seeing as we came to no conclusions with any merit to write down. I hate to leave things so unresolved, but I think we all need to move on. I'll do some checking in a couple of areas including the nearest military bases, but I am at a loss as to how to proceed from here. So far we generated a lot of questions and no answers. I'm sorry folks, but that's the reality. If you think of anything else, please call me."

Tara stood up. "I'm sorry we didn't find more, but I must gather up my wandering hounds and head for the barn. I hope you find him and soon. I'd like to know the answer, so please call me when you learn anything new. I'll leave my card for you."

After Pete and Tara left, Charlie and his folks sat in the living room and talked about the last twenty-four hours. The last time either of his folks had seen C was on Friday evening when he joined them for dinner. He usually walked up to the house two or three times a week and stopped in whenever he went off in his pickup. Charlie thought the meal left on C's table could be from Saturday until he asked his dad.

"No, the meal couldn't be from Saturday or the meat would have smelled. In this warm weather, it would be okay for about eighteen hours. Another twenty-four, and the meat would smell bad," his dad explained. "It was the first thing I checked. He fixed his dinner Sunday evening and never ate. There is no doubt about that."

"Did he seem worried or preoccupied Friday during dinner?" Charlie asked. "Was anything bothering him, anything at all?"

"No, nothing. He was his usual happy self. He talked about your coming visit which made him quite excited. He thinks you are the greatest scientist in the world" his mother told him.

"And I think he's about the greatest uncle and friend a young man could have," Charlie said with worry in his voice. "I hope and pray nothing's happened to him. Run through Sunday evening again. Try to remember the slightest thing out of the ordinary that happened no matter how insignificant."

They talked about the strange lightning flash and Ralph barking, but that was all they could remember that was unusual in any way. Then his mother said, "We missed our favorite Sunday evening TV show. The satellite signal was probably messed up. Remember, Ray, you tried adjusting the dish? No matter where you searched, there was no signal. You shut it off to silence that awful hiss, so we could eat our meal in peace. Then there was the unusual lightning flash with no thunder. Half hour later we tried the TV again, and everything was okay."

"That's significant," Charlie said. "Was there anything else strange that evening? Think! It's important. Dad, do you remember anything at all unusual when you went outside?"

"Yes, the dead quiet. The only sound I heard was Ralph barking. If I hadn't gone outside, I wouldn't have heard him. I didn't find anything unusual, at least nothing I remember. After I went in to eat, everything seemed normal. We watched TV for a while and went to bed. We discovered C was missing when we stopped out to find out if he wanted to go with us to meet your plane. You've heard all the rest."

"I've got to call Matty and tell her about C," Edith said. "She'll be worried sick. I think I'll ask her to come over. I'd like to tell her in person what we know. Her whole family will take the news hard. What will we do when this hits the news? I hate to think of how some of the local news people will treat it. I hope they don't come out and want to go over C's cabin."

When his mother mentioned C's cabin, Charlie remembered the new portable PC his uncle showed him during their last visit. He wondered if C had entered anything that might throw some light on what happened. He explained to his folks he was going to check the computer from C's cabin and try to find anything that might help.

Charlie grabbed a flashlight as he left to walk out to the cabin. He called Ralph to join him for the trek. Ralph bounded eagerly out the door and trotted along in front of Charlie as he made his way to the cabin. When they entered the clearing, Ralph put his nose to the ground, found the end of the old scent trail, sat down next to the yellow marker Tara had placed in the ground, and began to howl. Charlie flashed the light all around the clearing and nearby woods but nothing showed up. He called Ralph who stopped howling, but stayed where he sat. "Okay, little buddy, you stay there. I'm going inside," he said to the dog as he turned and headed into the cabin.

Once inside, he went straight to the workshop for the PC. When he turned on the lights, he realized it was not on the desk where C had shown it to him. The printer and scanner were there with their cables among the organized clutter of the workshop, but the PC was gone. Maybe C had taken it with him. He continued searching back in the main room. The PC was nowhere to be seen. He next went into the tiny bedroom where he opened the closet located in one entire wall. There were many things in the closet, but no computer. As he started to leave the bedroom, he found C's briefcase on the floor behind the open door. Next to the briefcase was a shipping box all sealed and ready for shipment. The box was about twice the size of the briefcase and had a label with Charlie Botkin written in C's printing. He picked up the box and examined it. There was nothing else written on the box, no address, just his name. He placed it on the bed, took out the pocketknife C had given him many years before, and cut the box open.

It contained the computer and a note in C's handwriting dated Sunday, September 23, 2001. He sat down on the bed and read the note.

✳　　✳　　✳

Dear Charlie,

It is early Sunday morning as I write this note. Since you are reading it, I am either gone or dead as I plan to destroy it if I'm still okay when you arrive. Some strange things happened the last few days. I've been having dreams about the past like I never had before. They've been almost like TV shows where I am reliving the experience when I was seven and saw that strange object. I've had that same dream at least four times in the last few days. I never dreamed about that before in my entire life. I wonder why now. During the same time I felt weird at times. I told you about those spells I used to experience once or twice a year where bright, twinkling purple and orange lines like C-shaped battlements would interfere with my sight. Well, in recent weeks, they came more and more often. When they did, I felt dizzy and lightheaded, and my heart beat erratically for a few minutes. Then things would go back to normal. A couple of times I thought I might be having a heart attack but then it would go away, and I would feel fine again. I have an appointment with Doc Markley for a physical next week, but until then I plan on taking things easy. Ralph must be noticing something as well. He follows me around and stays right by me when we're outside. That's unusual as he usually heads off for a jaunt in the woods when we go out. This morning, I had one of those *spells*. When I sat down on the couch, Ralph sat down on the floor facing me and let out a howl. He has never done that before! He must sense something. I have no idea what is happening, but it is strange.

I logged those spells once I realized they were coming with increasing frequency and intensity. The results startled me as the time between spells has been decreasing regularly by about one-third each cycle. Projecting this forward, the time between spells will disappear at about seven this evening. I certainly don't know what this means, but there must be some significance. I'm not in fear, but a strange, sad feeling about this keeps coming over me. Each time a spell comes, I experience an overpowering feeling of sadness which makes no sense at all. I glance at Ralph and almost burst into tears as he looks back at me. I may have an unusual hormone imbalance. Hopefully this will pass, and things will return to normal.

I want you to take the computer, as a gift. Take the briefcase too. Tell your mother and dad and your aunt Matty I love them and thank them for being such a wonderful part of my life. Share with them whatever of this note you feel is appropriate. I love you very much. You are the son I never had. I am so proud of you, what you've done, and of the man you became. Keep your spirit of adventure and hunger for knowledge alive throughout your life. I hope you will live a full one.

In the briefcase and also in the *Charlie* directory on the computer, you will find a collection of sayings, poetry, essays, letters, and miscellaneous quotes and writings I saved over the years. These are ideas, happenings, experiences, and concepts that are of great value to me and tell about the man I tried to be. I hate to give advice so consider this collection of words as a sharing for you to use as you see fit. I will end this note with a quote from Alfred Adler that I applied liberally to my life. It may explain a lot. "There is only one danger I find in life. One may take too many precautions."

✳   ✳   ✳

The note was signed, "With love and respect, C."

Charlie finished reading the note and sat there on the bed, tears streaming down his face. He felt certain he would never see his uncle again. He sat on C's bed for a long time, staring into space and recalling memories of times with his uncle. He missed C terribly, and now there was a big empty place in his heart. This would hurt for a long time. It was the first loss of someone close Charlie had ever experienced, and he wasn't handling it very well. Sharing the note with his folks and Matty would be a painful necessity. Convincing them C was not coming back would be difficult. The troubling thing was wondering what had happened? Not having the answer would be maddening, but he believed they would never have it.

It was past ten when Charlie heard the door to the cabin open. It was his father. "Are you okay, son?" Ray asked. "We were beginning to worry when you didn't come back. When Ralph showed up at our door, we thought something else happened, so I came to find out."

"I found this note from C," Charlie replied, holding the paper in his hand. "I don't think we'll ever find him. He's gone, and not under his own power. Right now I feel tired. Let's return to the house. It's late, so let's hold off examining and talking about the note until tomorrow."

Charlie left the computer and briefcase where they sat and headed out the door. He put his arm around his dad, and the two of them headed home. For once his dad didn't stiffen at his touch, but responded by placing his arm around Charlie. It was a powerful, loving message that warmed Charlie's heart.

When they reached the house, his mom opened the door, saying, "Is everything all right? We were worried."

"Yes, everything's okay," Ray answered as they went inside. Neither of them mentioned the note to Edith. They would tell her about the note tomorrow.

The Mask

*A*lexis *carefully slid the package into her leather purse, slung its strap over her shoulder, and casually walked around the corner into the heart of the space port and up to the customs desk. The fat albino behind the desk looked up from his monitor to stare at her. She noticed his right hand sliding slowly out of sight and down by his side.*

"Ah, Ms. Stereo, back so soon?"

From behind her, a familiar voice shouted, "Alexis! Don't!"

Alexis spun around, "Schad! Where have you been? I've been worried something had happened to abort our trip. Were you afraid I was about to retrieve my stuff from customs and cancel our flight?"

"Something like that. I... I... took the wrong shuttle and had a frantic time getting back as soon as I did. My communicator quit working, so I couldn't contact you."

Ignoring Schad's lame comment, Alexis turned back and glared at the albino as she spit out, "Touch the alarm button, and you'll be in more trouble than you can imagine."

The albino raised both hands, palms forward. "Why did you think I was going to hit the alarm, Ms. Snotty?"

"Enough of the swazzo crap you fat slob! I'm not blind. I gave you enough cash to cover any contingency, and you took it. I recorded everything right here." Alexis snarled, patting her AV. "One wrong move on your part, and you'll spend a long time rotting in the Ranko penal colony."

The albino's pink eyes morphed from arrogance to radiated fear. A bit of drool ran down his chin from a loose, shivering lower lip. "I'm sorry. I'll do as you told me. It's just that I didn't expect you back so soon. You told me you were leaving on the two-ten, and it's past three."

"So you figured something went wrong and started to turn me in and keep the cash. Definitely not a good thought!"

Whirling back to face Schad, Alexis narrowed her eyes. Something was not right, and she knew it. Two obvious security cops started moving toward them, trying to appear casual. "How in hell could you take the wrong shuttle?" She snapped, trying to decide, run, fight, or wait for a better opportunity. Reality hit her like an LK blast. "You bastard!" she shouted at Schad. "You pulled a switch and turned me in for the reward."

As one of the cops pulled his Galbo blaster, she dove at Schad. In a single motion she pulled him in front of her, grabbed the LK from her leg, and rolled into firing position. The Galbo cut Schad in two as the stutter from her tiny LK knocked down the cop who had fired and leveled the other one before he could raise his weapon.

Back on her feet and running at the end of her move, Alexis headed for the neutral zone at the end of the terminal. Galbos didn't work within the force field there, but her LK did. She would be safe for the moment. The two cops would take about an hour to recover, and by that time, she would be long gone. Fortunately, running in the Ranko space port was quite common and drew little attention. The bloody mess that had been Schad and the two unconscious cops drew all of the attention. People paid no attention to a small woman in a dark-blue Cirec suit running from the mayhem. Many others nearby did the same when the excitement hit. The tiny LK, unseen in her palm, didn't signal any threat.

Alexis approached the neutral zone, slowed down to a trot, and chanced a glance back. No one was paying her any attention. A police shuttle streaked toward the gathering crowd, ordering people out of the way with a blaring PA. Numerous guards on foot were hustling toward the scene and moving gawkers out of the way.

So far so good, she muttered under her breath. *Now, if I can step aboard one of the outbound shuttles before that damned albino spills his guts.*

She scanned outbound flights and chose the one headed for Stentor 7. The gate was about two hundred yards from the neutral zone. She was sure she could make the gate before all hell broke loose in the main port. If her fake ID chip cleared the security scanner, she would be home free. The ancient Telurian mask contraband in her purse was another matter. The mask was the reason for the whole setup with Schad. Worth several hundred million on the open artifact market, the mask was her ticket to freedom. She was to split with Schad after he smuggled it through security, his specialty.

How in hell am I going to take this past security? Alexis wondered as she neared the gate. A smile crossed her face as a brilliant plan popped into her mind. She stopped for a few moments in one of the Icom booths, made an adjustment to her purse and threw the now-empty mask packaging into the trash vac.

As she entered the security scanner, the operator, an attractive young blonde, commented, "What an unusual purse. Where did you find it?" as she opened the purse and examined the contents.

Alexis tried to appear casual as the inspector closed the purse and put it on the *passed* counter. "It was a gift from a dear friend," she commented sweetly. "I have no idea where he got it, but I do like it." Then she had another idea. "Incidentally, would you be a dear? His wife is a vindictive bitch and may have found out about it. If anyone comes asking for me, tell them I'm on the flight to Aldebaran Three, over there. Her brother is a security cop, and I don't need the hassle."

"I know what you mean," she answered with a wink. "Angry wives can be a real bummer."

As soon as her ID chip cleared, Alexis picked up the purse and headed for the flight at a rapid walk. *So far so good* she thought. Once the boarding shuttle cleared the terminal, she would be home free.

Taking a window seat, she kept an eye on the security gate she had just cleared. Two security cops ran up to the blonde, pointing and talking rapidly. "Good girl!" she said out loud as the blonde pointed to the other boarding shuttle and the cops took off at a run. The shuttle doors spun shut just before they got there. The blonde turned toward her shuttle and gave a thumbs-up. *Sometimes you need a little impromptu luck to complete a good plan,* Alexis thought as she leaned back in her seat for the short hop to the IS craft.

As the shuttle lifted off, she began dreaming of happy times on Stentor 7 with the fortune the mask would bring on the open market. She wouldn't need to share it with Schad as planned. The Telurian mask stared up at her and seemed almost to smile in spite of the Zepok fasteners holding it seamlessly and flush on the front of her purse.

The Switch

*T*imothy O'Brien never expected to find himself in such circumstances. Whoever would? He paused on the narrow path on the side of the grey granite mountain, the wind pressing on his backside as if it wished to push him to his death on the ragged rocks a kilometer below. A sound caught his attention over the rush of wind.

A sound heightened my fear responses and made me shudder. "How could they have found me?"

The sound was unmistakable. Vordanay thrusters make a unique noise and the only units that use these old but effective thrusters are Old Earth military police RG vehicles. hard to handle in Earth gravity, RG vehicles would be fast and quite maneuverable in the light gravity of Stentor seven where I had hidden for seven years.

I searched for a place to hide, but found none. In a panic I started running down the path as fast as I could. The light gravity stretched my running steps to ten meters, but I had to plan a landing place for every huge step. One misstep and I would be off the path with a kilometer of air between me and the rocks at the base of the huge cliff. My mind raced trying to find an answer, but none was forthcoming. Then I came to a slight curvature to the right on the almost flat and vertical granite face of the mountain. I shortened my paces to stay on the path.

On my third giant step, I misjudged and missed the path by a meter. I was hurtling away from the cliff at a slight angle and beginning to drop. In the low gravity of Stentor Seven I would still be falling fast enough to be killed after falling a kilometer. For a moment I wondered if terminal velocity would be low enough to let me land without a major injury. Considering it a possibility, I spread my arms and loosened my shirt to slow my descent.

The sound of the Vordanays grew louder. "They've spotted me." I muttered to myself as I tried to locate the direction of the sound. "Shit! Even if I survive the fall, they'll catch me." They were coming from my blind spot above and to my rear. Then something flat and heavy hit me with considerable force and everything went black and silent.

As dazed consciousness returned, I realized I was out of the wind and in the vehicle with the Vordanay thrusters. Then I opened my eyes and stared into the face of my bride of six weeks, Enid. She had her finger to her lips, so I complied by lying still and quiet. Enid pulled out and leveled a Gleary laser pistol at my head and said, "He's coming to. I've got him covered," to the pilot. Turning to me she snarled, "Lie still and don't move."

I was devastated! Had my sweet lady sold me out in order to collect the 400,000-credit reward for my capture? Something was not right. This was impossible. Then I noticed her little finger was waving in front of the pistol. The safety switch, right where her finger was pointing, was on. With the safety on, the Gleary was as harmless as a toy.

The pilot said, "Lady, I don't know what you have against this guy, but I do appreciate your help. We'd never have caught him without your tip. He's in for some rough treatment when we take him back to Earth. I'd rather we blasted him when we found him and only had to deal with the body. Now he'll receive prisoner treatment, and that means a lot more work for me."

"My reasons for wanting him alive are my own. You can't know why." Enid said, winking at me. "I'm sure not going to tell you, Jack."

"I can say one thing," Jack remarked, smiling. "I'm glad you're on my side. I'd hate for you to be working against me."

I had no idea what was going on, but the safety and Enids's wink were reassuring.

Jack glanced over his shoulder. "Keep your eye on him. He's the only one ever to escape our holding center. I must report his capture and send him on his way to Earth within the next five days, or those charges against him will expire. He'll no longer be a fugitive."

"Incidentally, how are you going to sneak us past security here at the terminal? He destroyed his ID chip and mine's specific. Tim's popular with the locals and until I am cleared of some legal crap, I'm not."

"You leave that up to me. I've got connections." Enid said, smiling.

"Well, you got me in, so I suppose you can get me out OK. We're approaching the terminal."

"Remember what I told you." Enid ordered. "Set her down outside the confinement zone so you two can change clothes. When we walk into the zone, security will think Tim's covering you, the renegade Earth agent, and let all of us through. Once through security we'll be in International territory and your jurisdiction will take precedence. Then you can process him, we can split the reward, you can retire here as you planned, and I'll have my revenge. Tim will be shipped back to Earth, and after that, who cares."

"Lady, I wouldn't want you working against me. Your mind is devious."

"If he only knew." Enid whispered to me as the set down sequence began.

As soon as we landed, Enid ordered, "Come back and cuff him to the hand rail. Then you'll be able to change clothes without danger. I'll sit back here and cover you." Then she moved to a seat in the rear of the vehicle. We needed about ten minutes to change clothes, everything including underwear, which I thought a bit much.

Jack turned around and went to the front to retrieve his own pistol before getting out. Enid released the safety and cranked the control on her pistol up to max. Jack turned around and caught the blast from her pistol center chest. He was dead before hitting the floor. In an instant, Enid handed me her pistol, took a knife out of her pocket and began slicing Jack's chest open.

"What the hell?" I shouted. "He's already dead!"

With a flourish Enid held up a small, bloody ID chip and tossed it to me. "This is the key to the success of our mission. You are a free man with a new identity no one can crack. Stick it in your pocket. It will cover you for the five days until those charges expire. After they expire, you're free and clear of those trumped-up charges."

She took the pistol out of my hand, cut the power to half, and seared the open wound on Jack's chest closed. Then she hit his face with enough wide laser spray to make him unrecognizable. She handed me the pistol as sirens of approaching security announced a tense visit shortly. In a single motion Enid grabbed Jack's pistol, set the control on low, and blasted my left shoulder enough to burn Jack's uniform and sear my skin a bit.

"Damn it, Enid, that hurt!"

"Sorry!" she muttered as she replaced the pistol in his hand.

As soon as she stepped back, the door flew open and two uniformed officers of Stentor Seven security entered, pistols drawn. "Don't anyone move. Touch the trigger on that pistol and you'll be fried," one of them said to me. I dropped it on the floor.

"He's a security agent from Earth." Enid panted, feigning fright. "His prisoner managed to grab one of his pistols and burned him. Jack had no choice but to terminate him. Scan Jack with your reader and you'll read his ID. That one doesn't show an ID, but check him anyway."

"Both of you stay still while we check this out. You realize you're on sovereign Stentor soil, and your special privileges don't amount to anything." He said to me.

He activated his scanner and read the ID chip in my breast pocket. "Jack Evans, EAPD 17685 it says. It also says you're retired. What's this all about?"

"He's a bit dazed after flat-face there popped him with a laser pistol. This was his last assignment planned to bring him here to Stentor Seven to end his stint where he planned to retire. I'm his fiancé and can answer most of your questions."

The other officer turned to me and sneered, "If you're the Jack Evans we have on record, you're in some trouble here."

Enid snapped back, "Not anymore. That's the guy who caused all the trouble and he's dead. Now, can't you get Jack some medical attention?"

Getting into the act and thinking about the bloody ID chip in my pocket I protested, "I don't need a medic. It's just a slight burn. He shot before turning up the power and grazed me. I didn't miss him."

"You sure didn't" the second officer muttered. "His mother wouldn't recognize him now. How are we going to be sure of whom he was?"

"The word of a field agent of the Earth Allied Police Department should be good enough. Besides, Jack will ship the body back to Earth on the next flight to complete his mission." Enid remarked. "That will save you a whole lot of paperwork. All you need to do is move us inside the zone and out of your jurisdiction. We can do the rest."

"You're right about that. It would save us a lot of grief."

"I'll reassign this old RG vehicle to you." I said with a sudden inspiration. "I don't need it anymore, and an RG vehicle is sure to be worth something."

The two officers turned toward each other, nodded their heads, and in unison said, "Deal!"

✳ ✳ ✳

By nightfall of Stentor's thirty-hour day, Enid and I were sitting at the table in her apartment. Enid explained the entire plan and how she had arranged so much.

"My position at Nebson Security Research gave me not only the information, but enabled me to pull this off. You knew Jack Evans was the one who offed your brother and faked those charges against you, didn't you?"

"I was quite certain he was the one."

"That's why he wanted you so badly, that and the reward the EAPD paid us for terminating one Timothy O'Brien. Poetic justice don't you think?"

"I must make one comment."

"Oh? What?"

"To quote one Jack Evans, 'I'm glad you're on my side. I'd hate for you to be working against me.'"

Enid grinned.

No Bomb Needed

Abdu Rahman answered the door to his small rented Chicago house. FedEx came with a package from Germany. He grinned as he signed the papers for the lanky, hawk-nosed deliveryman. The package contents were the essentials for his project and the only item he couldn't purchase locally. Shaking with excitement, he took the package into the bathroom and placed it on the counter next to the sink. Thoughts of the next steps in his project and the deadline four weeks away raced through his mind. *At last, I can do my part,* he thought as he headed for the kitchen.

He opened the refrigerator and removed several of the five-pound packages of hamburger which filled the inside. *How proud my father will be,* he thought as he picked up the large, heavy-gauge plastic trash bag from the kitchen counter, tucked it under his arm and headed back for the bathroom. Placing the bag and the packages of hamburger on the counter, he directed his attention to the bathtub. After checking the silicon sealant he used to seal the drain closed, he turned on the hot water. When the tub was about half full, he unfolded the trash bag into the tub and ran several gallons of water into it. Next, he opened one of the packages of meat and emptied the contents into the trash bag with the water. The pungent smell of the warmed meat assailed his nose. Ten days in the frig and the meat was beginning to spoil. *Excellent,* he thought as he picked up and dumped a second package into the bag.

A few trips to the kitchen and all one hundred pounds of meat were in the bag, supported by the water in the tub. To keep the top free and away from the slurry of meat inside, he secured the bag to the wall above the tub with duct tape. The next step would be tricky. Abdu opened the FedEx package and removed the plastic bottle from the bubble wrap. He glanced at the short piece of garden hose he had placed on the floor by the tub, checking to make sure it would be within reach. Then he carried the bottle filled with a thick greyish brown liquid to the tub. To calm his jumpy nerves, he paused, holding the bottle above the bag opening. *Now for the tricky part,* he thought as he unscrewed the bottle cap and removed the seal. He lowered the bottle into the bag, inverted it, and dumped the contents into the meat slurry. Then he dropped the empty bottle into the bag.

Abdu turned to the sink and washed his hands with disinfectant soap. He breathed a sigh of relief as he dried his hands to prepare for the next step. Picking up the seven-foot section of garden hose cut from the one he had purchased, he thrust the cut end slightly inside the bag opening. Holding the hose there, he wrapped the bag tightly around the end. Then he used duct tape to seal the bag to the hose so the only opening would be the other end of the hose. Raising the open end of the hose near the vent above the bathtub, he fastened the hose to the wall with duct tape in many places. The vent fan would remove the noxious fumes soon to be generated in the bag as the meat decomposed. He then turned on the new vent fan he had installed in the ceiling. There would be four weeks of waiting as the evil brew cooked and ripened.

During this period, Abdu did a bit more shopping at the local plumbing supply store. He purchased two six-foot pieces of metal-covered, high-pressure hose with standard female hose connections on each end and two tap-in saddle-valves with hose connections. These saddle valves were the kind which cut their own entry hole into the pipe with a sharp hardened point on the tip of the valve stem. He also bought a small high-pressure pump, the kind that powers the water jets used to strip paint. Abdu smiled as he paid the bill. "Only $486," he commented smugly to himself. "Add that to the twenty dollars at the hardware store and rent for three months, and it comes to about $2,000. Who says weapons must cost billions?" He was quite pleased.

Once back at the house, he went about connecting and testing the new equipment. He replaced the aerator on the bathroom sink faucet with a hose adapter and connected the high-pressure hose between the adapter and the pump on the floor. A short suction hose cut from the other end of the garden hose was also attached to the pump. The open end of the garden hose was placed in a bucket of water Abdu had placed on the floor. "Now to try it out," he said as he opened the cold-water faucet of the sink. The sound of the sudden flow of water into the high-pressure hose stopped as soon as the hose filled. The positive displacement pump acted like a closed valve and prevented the water from flowing through the suction hose.

"So far so good," he mumbled as he reached to plug the power cable of the pump into the wall socket. The pump whirred into life, then objected loudly and strenuously as the check valve in the meter stopped the back flow. He immediately pulled the plug to stop the pump and headed for the basement with the other metal hose and the two saddle valves. "Now to bypass the meter and the check valve," he murmured under his breath as he walked down the stairs.

Abdu turned on the naked light bulb and lay the hose and valves on the floor next to the water meter. *How simple,* he thought as he fastened the first valve upstream from the water meter. When the valve was securely in place, he twisted the valve handle, driving the point through the pipe wall. He held his breath as he cracked the valve open. A trickle of water brought a lusty "Allah be praised" from his lips. Then he installed and tested the downstream valve, connected the metal hose between the two valves and opened them. When he found there were no leaks, he headed back to the bathroom.

"Now it should work," he remarked to himself as he once again plugged the power cable of the pump into the wall socket. The pump spun once more, groaning a bit noisily as its pressure fought the system pressure. Soon, the higher pressure of the pump drove the water from the bucket into the faucet and then into the water system. "Praises be to Allah! it works!" Abdu shouted as the bucket emptied. He pulled the plug, refilled the bucket, and tried it again. Several tests later, he shut off the faucet, disconnected the hoses, and moved pump and hoses to the end of the room. Now all he could do was wait.

As he sat checking the TV news for any signal that would cancel his project, he thought of how easy it had been to gain access to the details of the Chicago water system. It pleased him that it took only three months to find and rent a small house fed directly by the main water line near the treatment plant. He was particularly pleased since he was allowed six months by his cell leader at the cell meeting where the project was given to the members. At the meeting, all members had been forbidden any further contact with any member of the cell until the project was completed. For the rest of the project, Abdu was on his own.

As he continued observing, the news shifted to a panel of defense experts discussing the costs associated with the Star Wars missile defense system. When the spokesman stated, "Only about a hundred billion dollars to keep America safe," Abdu laughed out loud. "Stupid American infidels with your useless expensive toys," he snarled at the TV. "Wait until you learn what we have in store for you."

On the appointed day, Abdu awoke early. He was so excited he could not sleep. His hands trembled as he put on his clothes. It was Wednesday, November 21, 2001, the day before America's Thanksgiving Day. On this date, many others of his jihad cell would be doing exactly what Abdu was doing, hidden inside small unobtrusive homes in quiet neighborhoods. They were acting in large cities all over the United States. He hated having to wait until eleven o'clock. The time went excruciatingly slow. To help pass the time, he again checked everything: the bypass hose in the basement, then the rig in the bathroom, the pump to the faucet. Once more he stuck the suction hose into the water-filled bucket, and repeated the test done earlier. When everything worked, he went to the living room, sat in front of the TV to catch any signal in the news. He jumped from channel to channel, listening for an interview with the code words which would abort the project. "Allah! Don't let those words come," he said repeatedly.

When the clock reached eleven and with no words to abort, he headed for the bathroom, placing a disinfectant-soaked face mask securely over his face. He opened the door. Moving swiftly, he took a knife, slit the plastic bag, and emptied the contents into the tub with the water. The putrid smell of the reddish brown foamy mass assailed his nostrils through the mask, almost driving him out of the room. He held his breath as he lifted the now-empty, dripping bag from the tub and placed it in the bucket on the floor. He secured the suction hose in the tub, turned on the pump, and waited as the pump groaned and began to pump the foul mess into the water system. Before shutting the door, he made certain everything was working properly. All that remained to be done was to check the pump periodically to be certain it continued to pump. With the suction side restricted, it took several hours to empty the tub. As soon as the tub was empty, Abdu shut off the pump, closed the bathroom door, took his belongings, and headed for the international terminal at O'Hare Airport. As he boarded the international flight, the first leg of his trip home to Yemen, he smiled smugly to himself. He was certain his efforts would help destroy America.

Epilog

The Next Few Days - The evil biological soup flowed through the house pipes, the street junction, and into the large main under the street which served a major section of Chicago. Mixing with the flow downstream from the treatment plant, the reddish brown color disappeared as it was diluted by the large amounts of water flowing in the main.

A mile or so downstream on the tainted main, Beth Sosa drew some water to mix formula for her two-month-old daughter, Maria. It was early Thanksgiving Day, and many of her family would be coming for dinner. Not far away, Alan Black drew water to make coffee for himself and his brother Carl who lived with him. Across the street, Adrian Melchior mixed concentrated orange juice with tap water for his family's breakfast. Months wold pass before the deadly prions in their blood would complete their relentless rage of doom.

May 2007 - In May the CDC first realized something was wrong. Reports of a strange neurological disorder of small children began coming in from all over the country. Slowly at first, but then in growing number, infants and small children were losing control of their limbs and those walking were starting to fall down. In July, ten-month-old Maria Sosa of Chicago died of the disease. By September, the death toll was rising, and the first older children and adults were beginning to show signs of the disease. In November, Beth Sosa, the two Black brothers, and Adrian Melchior died. They would be the first victims of a mysterious neurologic disease which was soon claiming thousands in large cities all over the nation. Then came a sobering announcement from the CDC.

The symptoms of this new disease are the same as for variant Creutzfeldt-Jakob disease (vCJD), a type of bovine spongiform encephalopathy (BSE). BSE is a transmissible, neurodegenerative, fatal brain disease of cattle. The disease has a long incubation period, but ultimately is fatal within weeks to months of onset. BSE, commonly called mad cow disease, first came to the attention of the scientific community in November 1986. At that time, the appearance in cattle of a newly recognized form of neurological disease appeared in the United Kingdom (UK).

BSE is associated with a transmissible agent. The agent affects the brain and spinal cord of cattle and lesions are characterized by sponge-like changes visible with an ordinary microscope. The agent is highly stable, and resists freezing, drying and heating at normal cooking temperatures, even those temperatures used for pasteurization and sterilization.

vCJD was first reported in March 1996 in the UK. In contrast to the classical forms of CJD, vCJD has affected younger patients, has a relatively longer duration of illness (median of 14 months as opposed to 4.5 months) and is strongly linked to exposure, through food, to BSE. Recent studies confirmed that vCJD is distinct from sporadic and acquired CJD.

The larger the infected person, the slower the disease progresses. As of this date, there is no known cure once the agent has been ingested. The disease is always fatal.

2008 and 2009 - By mid-2008, the disease had decimated the United States and spread to Canada and Mexico. More than a hundred million were dead, and the disease showed no sign of slowing. Deaths soon overwhelmed disposal facilities, and city streets became littered with the dead and dying. All warm-blooded life was affected, which added more decaying flesh to the streets and fields everywhere as birds and small mammals succumbed. Then began a series of events unforeseen by the terrorists. The disease began appearing in isolated areas all over the globe, first in Europe then Africa, Asia, South America, and Australia. It seemed to be transmitted in bottled drinks, then foods, and finally by air. During the year 2009, the disease appeared in every corner of the globe, and no one was left to try to stop it. Decaying birds and mammals covered every continent. The sea was littered with bloated decaying cetaceans as porpoises and finally the whales began to succumb. Reptiles, sharks, bony fishes, and other cold-blooded life-forms did not contract the disease.

Final Note - On July 8, 2013, the last human died. Mammals larger than humans lasted a bit longer, but by 2015, the last whale died, and the Earth was free of all bird and mammalian life. All warm blooded creatures were extinct.

A Doctor from Detroit

D r. Francis Lane drank in the lovely view before him. Lush tropical plants crowded the edge of the pond both on land and in the water. Several Hawaiian geese, or nenes, glided across the surface, along with many ducks. White wading birds dotted the edge wherever the vegetation was sparse. The pond was fed by a small stream which flowed in at one end and out over a concrete spillway at the other. The stream continued into a large culvert under the main road and then meandered off on the other side. To the east of the pond and the bordering street was a small hillside where their home merged into the lush vegetation. In the early evening Dr. Lane sat quietly on his patio with his wife, Oona, enjoying an after-dinner drink and gazing down across the pond in front of their home in Hilo, Hawaii.

Though the house was rather large, it didn't stand out but merged into and became part of the hillside. Up the slope from the street, all that could be seen was the edge of the hipped roof and the upper part of some huge picture windows. The area seemed almost a wilderness, undisturbed by human invasion. From the cul-de-sac in front of the house, the driveway curved to the right and upward, disappearing behind the sloping front yard as it turned toward the three-car garage beneath the house and hidden by the slope of the yard. There was a doorway to the right of the garage doors and a stone walkway climbing lazily up a slope between the garage and the mound which hid the building. Walls on both sides of the walkway were faced with flat, casually stacked lava slabs. Plants grew profusely, drooping down the irregular stone walls and nearly closing the view to the sky above. At the top of the walkway, there was a surprisingly large patio overlooking the yard, pond, and cul-de-sac. The patio and main entrance to the house could not be seen from the street or driveway below. Line of sight from the street made the house roof appear to come to the ground at the edge of the patio. The view west from the patio was breathtakingly beautiful.

The main entrance to the house consisted of two huge glass doors centered between two equally large glass windows—a wall of clear glass. When the doors slid apart, the house opened itself and became part of the outdoors.

Beyond the patio, hidden by a wall of vines growing on a broad trellis, was a lanai with a pool. Entrance to the pool was through a two-gated arch in the trellis which almost hid the pool from view. The poolside lanai was ideal for casual entertaining with several wrought-iron tables and chairs mixed in with beach loungers. Like the entrance patio, it could not be seen from the road below. A glass wall opened from the large recreation room to the pool area exactly like the patio wall. On the far wall of the room was a huge picture of a football running back, exploding through a group of would-be tacklers.

Beyond the recreation room, the house tumbled up a gentle slope, half a floor at a time for a total of four levels, including the garage. The home was as spectacular inside as out with the clever, tasteful blending of art and decorations reflecting the four cultures of the owners with a local Hawaiian flavor.

Dr. Lane continued staring silently to the west. Oona followed her husband's gaze toward the pond. The sun was beginning to drop behind the mountain. She finally remarked, "It's such a beautiful scene. I am never tired of it. I can't imagine a lovelier place to live."

"Yes, our place is lovely, spectacular in fact. A far cry from where I originally lived," Francis commented as he thought of how he came to be here at this point in his life.

✳   ✳   ✳

Francis Lane had not always been so fortunate. He grew up in the inner city of Detroit during the late fifties and early sixties. His father, an ethnic Chinese, had been a math teacher in Beijing, China, who escaped to the West from Czechoslovakia while on a cultural exchange there. He waited a long time in England and then Canada. Finally, he was admitted into the United States as Charles Chang. He came to live with relatives in Detroit and worked as a cook in a Chinese restaurant in the city. His mother, Louanne, an inner city African American, was a waitress in the restaurant. Less than a year after his birth, both parents died horribly when the restaurant was firebombed one evening shortly after closing.

Francis, named by his mother, was brought up by his maternal grandmother, Annabel Lane. She lived in a neat, clean little house which stood in contrast to the row of dilapidated old houses populationg the rest of the block. Annabel worked as a cleaning lady for an office building downtown to supplement the small pension she received as the widow of a soldier killed in World War II. There were five other family members living in Annabel's house: her brother and his wife, two daughters, and an elderly uncle. Annabel ruled the household with a firm, but gentle hand. Everyone was expected to do their part in keeping the house clean, neat, and in good repair. Theirs was the only yard on the block with grass and a neat flower garden in front. There was a productive vegetable garden in the back.

Under Annabel's firm guidance, Francis grew into an honest, capable young man and an excellent student at school. With a lot of effort, she finally convinced his Chinese relatives to accept him and teach him something of their different culture. He spent each Saturday with the family of a cousin of his father who lived in a Chinese neighborhood not far from Annabel's home. The blending of the two cultures gave Francis a unique vantage point for growth and learning which fed his insatiable appetite for knowledge. This blending also created inner conflicts which led to growing problems as he matured. Knowing both cultures, yet not accepted by either outside of his two families, Francis felt isolated in spite of his happy, outgoing personality. A brilliant student in a difficult school, he was frequently involved in scuffles over name-calling. A week after his high school graduation, he was seriously injured in a brawl with several gang members. After a short hospital stay, he completed his recovery at home where Annabel nursed him back to health.

"Now, Francis, you'd best tell your grandma Annabel what this is all about," she asked repeatedly as she tended his injuries. "I know somethin' o' what goes on in the streets 'round here, and I don't want you dead. Who was it, and why'd they beat you?"

"Grandma, you don't want to know."

"I've lived in this house for almost fifty years and seen some bad things goin' on in the neighborhood. Grandma Annabel knows how to keep her yap shut when it needs to be . . . Tell me what this is all about and maybe I can help . . . I won't do anythin' without your okay . . . I can't help if'n I don't know what you're up against . . . Talk to me, chile . . . they were Ahmed and his bunch, weren't they? I hear the rumors. Why'd they beat you?"

Francis finally opened up. "They beat me because I refused to be a runner for their drugs, wanted me to hook up with some people in the Chinese community. They figured I might be able to connect with people they couldn't."

"Did you talk to any relations in Chinatown?"

"Nah! I don't want to be involved. Sooner or later, I'd be caught or killed."

"Won't they come after you again? Why don' you go to the police?"

"They're sure to kill me if they think I ever talked to the police. I've got to be out of Detroit as soon as possible. They'll kill me if I stay and refuse to run drugs for them. My choices are absolutely zero."

"Where you gonna go, an' how you gonna live? What about that scholarship to college? Wouldn't you be safe away at school?"

"If I take the scholarship, they'll learn where I am and come after me sooner or later. I can't take the chance. If I head to the West Coast and hide my tracks, they'll never find me. Hopefully, they'll give up after a while."

"You crazy! I'm afraid you'll get into trouble what with no friends, no money, and all. How you gonna live?"

"Grandma, you taught me to always try to be a decent person. You did a good job. I won't do anything to get into trouble. You can believe me."

"Bless you, chile. I am so very proud of you. I still don' want you to go, but where you thinkin' 'bout?"

"I thought I might try Chinatown in San Francisco. I'm obviously part Chinese and speak enough of the language to pass. I'll make out okay. I'll keep in touch somehow."

"I still don' like your plan. You heal up an' we'll talk some mo' 'bout Ahmed and his gang."

Several weeks after he recovered from the beating, Annabel found a long, loving goodbye note on her grandson's pillow. He left during the night with a plan that started a chain of events leading to many changes in his life.

Francis was both frightened and fiercely angry with the three who had beaten him. His passion for revenge and intended flight west were combined in his plan. The leader and local drug boss, Ahmed, had been a classmate of Francis. Ahmed made quite a bit of money in a short period of time and was building his organization with relentless force. Those who opposed him either disappeared or were found beaten to death. Francis was alive only because Ahmed believed he could still recruit him as a courier. The group had taken over an abandoned house several miles away from Annabel's. There were seven of them in the house who drove around in two fast cars kept in the backyard. Around the yard was a six-foot high chain-link fence with a locked gate. There were always at least two members on guard, one in an upper front window, the other in the rear.

Word among students at the high school was that the drugs were kept in the basement near the front of the house. Ahmed supposedly kept most of his cash in his favorite of the two cars, a high-performance black Camaro. He frequently bragged about his car, once telling Francis about the hidden ignition lock beneath the shifter cover. With this sketchy knowledge, Francis made his plan.

About four in the morning, dressed completely in black, he crept up to the fence in the back, lugging a suitcase filled with clothing and a satchel filled with tools. He took a large bolt cutter from the satchel and opened the fence with a hole big enough for him to move through. He then crawled through the hole and crept silently up to the Camaro. Remembering about the door wiring from his auto shop training in school, he slid under the car to a position beneath the front of the driver's door where he could reach the inside lighting wire harness. Using small diagonal cutters, he snipped the wire to the door switch, opened the door, reached inside, and felt for the ignition lock under the shifter cover. His heart stopped as he heard the loud click of the solenoid as it snapped into place. The car was ready to roll. Next he felt for and found the starter button which replaced the key switch in the dash. He would need to learn the exact location of the switch for later. He placed the suitcase on the back seat of the Camaro, left the door unlatched, and crept toward the fence.

The bolt cutter made quick work of the fence, creating a hole directly in front of the Camaro and big enough for the car to drive through. He hoped the hole would give him room to run in, start the car, and drive away with a minimum of problems. Next, he headed for the front of the house, pleased that the front sentinel had not seen or heard anything. As he approached the side of the porch, he heard snoring. One of the gang was sleeping on a couch right under the open window to the porch so he must be extremely quiet. Taking the gallon jug of kerosene he brought, he poured the fluid across the edge of the wooden porch floor, hoping it would spread evenly across the porch. By the dim light of the one streetlight at the end of the block, he saw the reflection on the shiny surface of the kerosene as it ran to the middle of the porch and began to puddle there. *Perfect*, he thought to himself. *The porch sags in the middle.* Taking a large rag from the satchel, he spread it out on the porch in the kerosene. He then placed a dozen shotgun shells on the rag, spreading them evenly and facing the porch wall. After pouring the rest of the kerosene over the rag and shells, he closed the satchel, grasped it tightly in his left hand, and prepared for a rapid, silent escape to the rear. With his right hand, he took a lighter from his pocket and started to light the rag.

Before he could snap the lighter, a car spun around the corner and sped up the street toward the house. His heart pounded as he moved away from the porch and flattened himself against the ground. The lights shone brightly on the side of the house as the car approached. Thankfully, it sped on past the house into the night. The sentry on the second floor leaned out the window and cursed the car as it sped by. Francis watched him by the light of the nearby streetlight. He hugged the ground, remaining immobile until the sentinel withdrew from the window. He thought he would never leave. When he finally disappeared inside, Francis crept back to the edge of the porch and again prepared to light the rag. The porch roof hid the entire porch from the sentry, but as soon as the fire was lit, the light and reflections would be seen.

He lighted the corner of the rag, moved away to the rear to be out of the light, and paused for a moment to make sure the rag caught fire. Seeing the porch corner post glow orange from the light of the burning rag, he moved silently back toward the opening in the fence where he paused to try to catch a glimpse of the rear sentinel. By then the nearby house was glowing in the light of the expanding flames. Next he heard the front sentinel shout "fire!" By now the rear sentinel peered intently in his direction. As the light of the fire on nearby houses brightened the area, he remained motionless while wondering, *Did they see me?*

The loud bang of the first shell to explode took the sentinel out of the window toward the sound of the explosion. The sentinel gone, Francis headed straight for the Camaro. Showtime! He seemed to take forever to cover the thirty or so feet from the hole in the fence to the door of the Camaro. Several more of the shells went off before he reached the door. Throwing the satchel in the back, he jumped into the driver's seat and pushed the starter button. *Damn!* Nothing happened! He pressed it several times more. Absolute silence! By now he could hear shouts from the house. *Did they see me?* he wondered once more as his mind screamed for action. *Try the ignition lock again.* He felt under the cover for the lock switch and snapped it off and back on. Still, the starter button produced silence. Possibly the ignition lock was sticking. Holding down the starter button, he flipped the switch off and on. Each time he did so, the starter jumped and fell silent. Then reality dawned on him. *The damned lock was left on for a fast start, and I was turning it off!* As soon as he flipped the switch once and pressed the starter button, the Camaro's engine exploded into life. He slammed the car into gear, turned on the headlights, and vaulted toward the fence. As he zipped through the fence, the crack-crack of bullets hitting the Camaro's rear window sounded. *Why didn't the glass break?* he thought for an instant.

By the time he hit the end of the quarter mile alley, a pair of headlights sprung up behind him near the growing glow of the now-blazing house. They were in pursuit. He had planned his escape route well. At the end of the alley he took a left, then three blocks and a right, three more blocks, and a left would take him to Livernois. A right turn on Livernois and about a mile of main thoroughfare would take him past a police station. If they were still behind him as he went down Livernois, he would drive normally by the station, hoping they would not. If he could get the police in the chase, he should be able to get away. Just beyond the station was a short side street curving to the left and ending at another where you could head back to Livernois or go in the opposite direction. There was a narrow, enclosed alleyway off that street which led to a doorway in the rear of a small manufacturing plant. With the windowless building above and on both sides of the alleyway, it seemed to be a hole in the building not large enough for a car. It was a footpath to the rear door and was just wide enough for a car. In the daylight, it was dark and hidden. At night, it would be the perfect hiding place for a black car.

When he reached Livernois and headed for the station, his pursuers were a good half mile behind. There were more cars than he expected on the road. He slowed to normal speed to approach and pass the station. His pursuers moved at high speed once on the straight, wide road and began gaining on him rapidly,.

It took forever to reach the station. As he passed, several policemen were outside on the station steps. In a sudden inspiration, he honked and waved as he passed. During the time he took to drive the single block to the side street, the other car covered the distance to the station. They were only a block away when he turned off and headed for the alley. At the speed they were traveling, they would not be able to negotiate the turn into the side street. That should give him time to dive into his hiding spot. As he approached the alley, he heard the loud screech of tires as brakes were applied in a panic stop. As he drove into the alley and up to the door, he turned off the lights, killed the ignition, and stepped out of the car into the pitch-blackness. The sound of tires spinning in reverse told him they had indeed missed the corner. More burning rubber as the car spun into the side street and accelerated past the alley. They missed his hiding place and continued. He could hear their engine as the car accelerated away on the next street. His plan worked. As he turned to examine the Camaro more closely, the wail of sirens filled the night air. Two police cruisers sped past the alley, chasing his pursuers. He smiled to himself at the astonishing success of his plans.

Taking a small flashlight out of his satchel, he stepped to the rear to inspect the trunk of the car. As he turned the light on the back of the car, he found several bullet holes in the trunk. There were also several marks on the rear window where bullets hit and glanced off. *Bulletproof glass,* he thought to himself with a smile. Shining the light on one of the holes, he found something behind the hole. The bullet had penetrated the sheet metal of the rear only to be stopped by a heavy steel plate behind the sheet metal. The Camaro was an armored car! There was no place for a key to the trunk which must be opened by a latch on the inside. He remembered how several boys had worked on hidden trunk latches in auto shop class at school. He spent fifteen fruitless minutes trying to find the latch.

The rear seat upholstery had four large upholstered buttons, two on each side. After fruitlessly examining the floor, roof, and sides both inside and out for a pull ring or lever, Francis began feeling around the buttons. The upper ones did not move as easily and freely as the others. He pulled and pushed one button and finally twisted it and heard a loud *click*. The trunk latch advertised its opening. Stepping to the back, he took hold of the trunk lid and tried to move it. Nothing happened. Could be that wasn't the latch after all. Going back inside, he reached for the button to twist it again. It was then he realized the seat back was loose. An easy pull and the left seat back came down, revealing a compartment more than a foot deep behind the seat. A repeat effort on the other side revealed a similar compartment. Both were empty.

Obviously there was a space several feet deep between the back of these two compartments and the rear of the trunk. He couldn't find a single seam in either one. He wondered how to open the space? The money had to be hidden there. As he closed the compartments, he realized the rear seat was split to match the backs. It, too, had the large buttons on the front panel of each side. Twisting one brought the same *click* he heard from the seat back buttons. Lifting the seat revealed a thin black briefcase in a compartment just large enough to hold it. Under the other seat was another identical briefcase.

He gasped as he opened the first briefcase. It was packed with neat bundles of one-hundred-dollar bills—a lot of money. Opening the other revealed about half as many bills. *The rumors among students at school had been correct. Apparently, Ahmed couldn't keep things to himself and had to brag about them,* he thought as he placed the cases back in their compartments and closed the seat. The next few moments he sat in the car, trying to decide his next course of action. He had planned to drive the car west to Chicago, and if he found the money, dump it there and buy another plain, older car to drive onto the West Coast. San Francisco was his goal. Although he was rather dark for Chinese, he did have strong Chinese features and planned to get lost in Chinatown. The problem was the bullet holes in the trunk. A high-performance, late-model Camaro with bullet holes in the trunk driven by a young black man would be an invitation for every policeman he passed. How could he hide the holes?

A quick realization and he dove under the dash. With his flashlight, he spotted several wiring harnesses held together with shiny black electrical tape. He took about ten minutes to peel off six short strips of tape and place them over the bullet holes. The trunk was not noticeably damaged, rather it seemed to show a few scratches on an otherwise smooth black surface. He waited, deciding when to leave his hiding place. He turned on the ignition lock and then the radio to listen for any news. It wasn't an ordinary radio, but a police band radio set to the local police frequency. He was startled to hear reports about the end of a chase where five black teenagers were killed. Their car went through a filling station and struck a parked dump truck at high speed while trying to elude police. This happened about ten miles away. The driver of the car was identified as a local drug dealer named Ahmed.

What a waste, Francis thought. *Ahmed had been such a bright kid in grade school with me. Too bad he turned that good mind into the wrong direction.* Relieved of the fear of being chased across the country, Francis headed west, deciding to drive the Camaro all the way to San Francisco.

By the end of the week he took to make the trip, many things happened. A number of Detroit charities received anonymous cash donations of ten thousand dollars in boxes sent by first-class mail. The Chinese community received a donation of fifty thousand for their proposed youth center. Annabel's church received a fifty-thousand-dollar donation earmarked to be used for youth programs. Annabel was the treasurer of her church and would administer the donation. She had no idea about the source of the funds. A string of five-thousand and ten-thousand-dollar donations were received by youth charities in inner cities across the country.

There were many bank accounts opened in small town banks from west of Chicago to Reno, Nevada, by one Charles Chang. Francis explained he would be moving there soon and wanted to keep a local account. Francis Lane, as Charles Chang, was using his dead father's social security number on all these bank accounts. He was accepted as Chinese without question when he gave his name as Chang. The forty or so bank accounts totaled in excess of one hundred thousand dollars. Annabel had taught him well about bank accounts and squirreling away money.

In Cheyenne, he stayed long enough to find a repair shop to fix the holes in the rear of the car and paint the car metallic silver. He paid cash to the repair shop. He explained the holes saying some hunters were shooting at a billboard, not realizing his car was behind. His explanation was greeted with, "Those kinds of problems with crazy city hunters happen all the time." To avoid obvious questions, he asked them to fill the holes from the outside, smooth and then paint them. He didn't want anyone poking around and trying to open the trunk. When asked about the steel plate in the trunk, he explained he added the steel to provide two hundred pounds in the rear to balance the power of the engine for slippery streets during Michigan winters. That made sense to the body man.

When he reached San Francisco, there was about fifty-thousand dollars left in one of the briefcases. Once there, he found a small furnished apartment above an import store and moved in. He asked about a job at the import store when he found a posting on the back of the front door. The owner, who was his landlord, said he was holding the job for a relative coming from China. When he asked if he could fill the job temporarily until the relative arrived, he was put off for a few days. He tried again, asking to be able to work enough to earn his rent.

After a lengthy discussion in Chinese with his wife, he turned to Francis, saying, "You start job next Monday. I pay you five dolla' an hour. You pay me rent as usual, okay?"

Francis agreed with a broad smile. Apparently his persistence paid off. Francis decided to do something about the car soon. He wanted to find out what was in the space between the rear seat compartments and the steel plate at the back. Opening both compartments, he searched for a way to open the space behind them. While banging on the back of the compartment, he realized there was a steel plate there as well. There was more than two feet of space between the two steel plates. Apparently, access was only possible through the bottom of the trunk. He lay on the ground and examined the trunk bottom. He found a tire well on one side and gas tank on the other, but missed something.

He went back inside and opened the rear compartments. Examining them, he discovered a one-quarter-inch threaded hole at the top outside edge of the rear panel, flush with the carpet covering the back of the compartment. Francis remembered the two wing-screws in the glove compartment. He reached over and removed them, screwing one into this threaded hole. He tightened the wing-screw which went in all the way and kept on turning. As he continued to turn the screw, he realized it was beginning to come out, bringing out a three-eighths-inch round rod. Withdrawn, the rod was about twenty inches long. Checking the other side, he discovered the same threaded hole at the extreme left top. Again, screwing in the wing-screws brought out the three-eighths-inch rod. With both rods withdrawn, the trunk lid was free. Stepping out of the car, he took hold of the edge of the trunk lid which moved a little. Then he remembered the other objects in the glove compartment, two heavy plastic handles. From their shape, it was obvious they were used to lift the trunk lid. Taking the two handles and placing them on either side of the trunk and engaging the thin graspers with the side edges of the trunk, he lifted the lid straight up, the only way it would move. As he raised the lid, he found four more steel rods protruding down from the lid. He lifted the heavy trunk lid until the rods came free from their guide holes and placed it on the ground.

Peering down into the now-open trunk, he found two soft brown leather zippered bags. As he lifted the bags from the trunk, he realized one was empty. Opening the other one, he found several plastic bags with white powder. He had been transporting a large quantity of drugs! After a moment of panic, he wished he had dumped the car a long time ago. Leaving the two bags on the ground, he replaced the trunk lid and closed it with the locking rods. After the seats were back in place, he picked up the two brown bags and headed for his apartment where he flushed the contents of the plastic bags down the toilet. He then went to the Dumpster behind the restaurant next door where he dumped the brown bags and covered them with trash hoping no one had seen him.

He decided to get rid of the car as soon as possible. Such a liability might put him in jeopardy. Simply abandoning it was not an option as it could be traced back to him through the body shop where it was painted. Francis had to find a way to obliterate the car with no trace. It had to be done with no help from another person. I thought, *dump the car in the ocean in a secluded spot where it would never be found.* After studying maps, he found several promising spots. Checking each of them out, he selected one not far from the Golden Gate Bridge. Roadway construction of some kind had made a narrow dirt road sloping down to the edge of a cliff which dropped straight into the water. Late one night, he removed the temporary wooden barrier and stood on the dirt road while the Camaro rolled over the cliff into oblivion. Taking a branch from a nearby brush pile, he obliterated the Camaro's tracks from the edge of the cliff to well beyond where he replaced the barrier. He then walked a mile or more to where he caught a bus to make his way back to Chinatown.

Francis Lane, now Charles Chang, would work hard to establish himself in Chinatown, away from the dangers of Detroit gangs. He called Annabel to tell her he was safe and would talk to her often in the coming years. He did not tell her about the car, the money, or what happened the night he left. She told him Ahmed and his friends died in an accident, but several others had asked about him. She told them she had no idea where he was but suggested he might have gone to New York. Annabel was no fool and would keep his whereabouts to herself. Francis was grateful he had such a grandmother.

It took him nearly a year to be accepted into the Chinese community. By his twentieth birthday, he was given a party by the family who owned the import store where he worked. Then a job opened up working in a local hospital. There he took training as a medical technician. After several years, he became an emergency room technician in the hospital. He stayed there, enjoying the work and the people for the next five years.

Francis thought hard about his future and finally decided to go back to school and try to earn a college degree. He phoned Annabel to ask her help in getting his records for college entrance. She was thrilled when he said the University of Michigan would be his best bet. With her assistance, Francis enrolled at Ann Arbor the following fall under his own name. The decade since his departure gave him a good separation from the past. No one had asked about him for at least five years.

Francis finished his undergraduate work in three years, graduating with honors. Accepted into the U of M Medical School, he worked hard, and by his thirty-sixth birthday, he had begun his internship at Detroit City Hospital. During his education, the many Charles Chang accounts across the country had been transferred one-by-one to a bank in Ann Arbor and used to pay for his schooling. By the time his internship was completed, there were three accounts left totaling less than ten thousand dollars. The drug money had been put to good use. About this time, Annabel grew gravely ill.

She smiled proudly at Francis from her bed on her last day. "Dr. Francis Lane! What a glorious sound for a name. I am so proud of you!" she said softly.

Francis was losing his greatest life asset. With Annabel gone and his Chinese cousins moved away from Detroit, he decided to make a major move. The one cousin with whom he kept contact over the years lived in Hilo, Hawaii. On a hunch, he called her to ask about coming out for a visit. Dee Chang was a jolly woman of about forty who never married. Yes, she would be delighted by his visit. Francis sold his car and other possessions, arranged for Annabel's house to be titled to her church for use as a youth hostel, and left for Hilo with all his remaining things packed in two suitcases.

With no openings for new doctors available anywhere on the islands, Francis applied for an EMT position at the University Hospital Trauma Center in Hilo. Two years later, he was given the next opening as staff physician. During that time, he met and married Oona Lee, a nurse at the center. He would remain there for many years, earning a reputation as an excellent physician. He also gained the community's respect as an active supporter and promoter of youth programs aimed at troubled young people.

Time Trap

*A*lexis *carefully slid the package into her leather purse, slung its strap over her shoulder, and casually walked around the corner into the heart of the space port and up to the customs desk. The fat albino behind the desk looked up from his monitor to stare at her. She noticed his right hand sliding slowly out of sight and down by his side.*

"Ah, Ms. Stereo, back so soon?"

From behind her, a familiar voice shouted, "Alexis! Don't!"

Turning she heard Dr. Stanford out of breath from running to catch her. "What do you mean, don't?"

"Just don't!" Dr. Stanford stammered through gasping breaths as he almost stumbled up to her side.

"You said so yourself, I must go back twenty-four hours to stop the release of the RESO virus or the whole planet will be dead, and . . . and as soon as possible."

"They were . . . wrong! The RESO virus is . . . harmless and didn't cause the deaths . . . another experimental virus the two women . . . had in their bodies was triggered by the RESO . . . The medical team found and destroyed it . . . easily before there were any more deaths. . . . but the TCD is **not** harmless . . . There are some unusual side effects if used on a large scale," Dr. Stanford blurted out between gasps for air.

Alexis paled. "What's wrong with the time collapse driver anyway? I already triggered it before slipping the package into my purse. It's set to cycle twenty-four hours back at precisely eleven o'clock, a few moments from now, and it can't be stopped."

The albino pulled up what he had been reaching for and leveled a Galbo blaster at Alexis. "I've been waiting for you to return with that gadget. It showed up in the security scan and I wanted it. That box will be my ticket out of this hell hole."

"You jerk!" Alexis snarled. "The damned thing will be useless to you. The start mechanism requires my hand print before it will fire."

"Hand over the purse and I'll not worry a bit. Those scabs in the Telurian black market think they can reverse engineer anything. They pay highly for any new or unusual device."

"You have no idea what you're getting into." Alexis stalled and held her purse tightly.

"And I don't give a crap! Give it to me or I might pop the trigger on this Galbo and you know what it can do."

"Let him keep it, Alexis, the damned thing doesn't work right anyway."

"What do you mean by doesn't work right?"

"Ms. Stereo, give me the damned purse NOW! Otherwise, you and the doctor here will be splattered all over the customs office and I'll take your purse out of your dead hand."

Reluctantly Alexis handed over the purse. The albino took it and disappeared through a door into the bowels of the space port.

"Okay, Doctor. What's wrong with that expensive little gadget?"

Dr. Stanford finally caught his breath and explained, "We had only tested the unit on small bursts of power—ten or twenty seconds' worth. We didn't have any problems, and it only warped a small section of space. Gravity waves from such a small disturbance leveled out, and no harm was done. We decided upping the power to warp enough space for a person would work the same"

Alexis was puzzled. "So what's the big deal? We'll cause a little blip, and everything will be okay."

"That's not exactly correct."

"So what does happen?"

"We theorized that a large-enough gravitational disturbance could cause a cascading G-wave effect creating a major rift in the space-time continuum. The entire universe could be pulled through that rift in an instant and revert back to whatever time it was set to."

"That little box could do the whole universe?" Alexis shuddered as she said it.

"Yes . . . theoretically."

*   *   *

Then there was an instantaneous physical change, absent of sensory information.

*   *   *

Alexis checked the clock on her desk. It was precisely 11:00 a.m., and she needed to hurry to get to the meeting on time. The meeting at the Stanford Gravitation Field Experimental Station was to discuss results of the testing of the new portable TCD unit.

At about the same time in the university hospital research facility nearby, the RESO virus was about to be tested on human volunteers. The Replicating Exchanging Self-Organizing virus would search out all nonstandard DNA cells in a person's body and replace the faulty DNA with the correctly sequenced DNA. It was a cure not only for cancer but for many other diseases caused by aberrations in cell DNA. The promise and possibilities were staggering in their depth and breadth. Two women with advanced cancers were selected from thousands of volunteers. Its creator, Dr. Chan Ling, estimated it would take thirteen hours for the virus to convert all nonstandard DNA. Once done, it would disappear when all nonstandard DNA, its food in effect, disappeared. No trace of the virus would survive. One volunteer was injected with one type of RESO virus. The other with a slightly different strain.

"Now all we need to do is wait," Dr. Chan murmured as the two women got up to return to their rooms in the hospital section.

Three hours later both women were dead, their bodies riddled with a rapidly developing cancer. Seemingly, the RESO virus had not destroyed itself but had invaded every living cell in or touching the women. Near panic gripped the staff when they realized the gravity of the situation. The entire wing of the hospital was sealed off.

Searching frantically for a viable solution, Dr. Chan remembered his friend, Dr. James Stanford, had been working on a time-warping device using gravity waves. "Get me Dr. Stanford at the Stanford Gravitation Field Experimental Station," he shouted at one of his assistants as they rushed toward the office.

In less than half an hour, he had explained the situation to Dr. Stanford who promised to find out if his equipment might be useful in providing a solution. Soon he was explaining how the new and powerful TCD could send someone back twenty-four hours. This might enable them to stop the release of the RESO virus.

Dr. Stanford was coaching one of his assistants, Alexis. "Set this digital readout to 24.00, indicate hours and then press your hand against the actuator. The nuclear distorter will start building up G-pressure, and in about ten minutes, it will fire a monstrous G-wave that should bang you back twenty-four hours instantaneously."

Alexis thought for a moment. As Dr. Stanford's assistant, she knew there were some special location and time constraints. "When and where do I do this?"

Dr. Stanford took out a map. "The best place is inside the space port . . . here, in this open area." He pointed as he spoke.

"I must go through security. What do you suppose they'll do when I try to check this device through?"

"Tell them it's a new medical device using nuclear power. Dr. Chan would confirm that should they get testy."

"I suppose I'd better get going."

"The sooner the better."

Half an hour later, she stood by the security scanner and waited as the TCD unit was put through without incident. "That was easy," she muttered to herself as she picked up the TCD unit, hand printed the actuator, and slipped it back into its protective package.

Alexis carefully slid the package into her leather purse, slung its strap over her shoulder, and casually walked around the corner into the heart of the space port and up to the customs desk. The fat albino behind the desk looked up from his monitor to stare at her. She noticed his right hand sliding slowly out of sight and down by his side.

"Ah, Ms. Stereo, back so soon?"

From behind her, a familiar voice shouted, "Alexis! Don't!"

Toys Are U.S.

March 11, 2002

Corporal Lance Mugambi sat studying the color display screen in front of him. His hands were on the keyboard of a Gunslinger remote controller. He and about a hundred other newly trained weapon operators, dubbed gunslingers from the weapon they used, were aboard a refitted AWACS plane high above the mountains of Afghanistan. He was deeply engrossed in the scene on the display. In one window was a video taken by a tiny Sky Eye TV camera mounted on a small Super Chopper deployed from a much-modified Tomahawk cruise missile far below them. In another window, a photo map of the mountainous terrain was displayed. A bright yellow dot moved over the map, indicating the exact position of the tiny helicopter as it was taking the video being shown.

"Damn! There's the camp," shouted the corporal as an Al-Qaeda training camp appeared on the display. It was in a canyon among the mountains. "Look at those guys running for cover. They must think it's an attack," he reported to his group of four as they watched the scene unfolding on their screens.

"Now, they're firing," another gunslinger remarked as bright flashes appeared on their screens. "They waste lots of ammo shooting at tiny things barely visible. I wonder what they think is happening."

"There's one with a Stinger missile," another remarked. "Is he going to fire at our choppers? This should be interesting."

"Wasting a $20,000 missile to attack a $300 drone helicopter is wonderful for our side," the corporal commented. "Shoot, damn you, shoot."

They all cheered as a bright flash and smoke trail erupted when the Stinger burst into action. "Anyone hit?" Someone asked. There was no answer. A moment later, another one was fired from the camp.

"They got mine," another called out when his screen went black. "No . . . wait . . . I might be okay." The scene on his screen reappeared, tumbled wildly before it slowed, and then stabilized. "My bird is still going down. The ground's coming up too fast." Indeed the ground rushed up to meet the camera and the screen went blank. He switched to an alternate camera on another Super

Chopper in his assigned group of four. One of the four green active camera indicator lights on his screen was red.

"Anyone else get a red light?" the corporal asked. Silence indicated a negative response. "Terrific! So far the score is our $300 to their $40,000. At this rate, we'll bankrupt them in a hurry. Let's go on with the mission. We need at least three head counts to plan tonight's attack. Also, use your cursors to pinpoint any possible military target. Don't forget objects like buildings, vehicles, gun emplacements, caves, deep ravines, or any place they can hide. We don't want to miss anything. Don't worry about major roads or bridges. We've already got a handle on them, and they should be destroyed by smart bombs within an hour or so. First we isolate them in their camps, then we eliminate them."

✳　　✳　　✳

Zalmi glanced up at the sound of the Tomahawk missile as it blasted by the camp and then disappeared over the hill to the north. No one had time to raise a gun toward the missile. "Wakil! Wakil!" Zalmi shouted to his partner in the lookout station. "The Americans! They are coming, and we must repel them."

Wakil cranked the ancient siren to arouse the camp which immediately burst into action. Soldiers with weapons poured out of buildings and took positions among the rocks. The fifty or so trainees were rushed from the conditioning field into a deep cave in the rocky hill to the east of the camp. Some were given weapons and posted in the rocks outside the cave entrance. Unseen were sixteen tiny helicopters dropped from the Tomahawk far down the valley to the south of the camp.

"I don't like the silence," Zalmi said to his partner. "It could have been a single missile headed north. If we were the target, they missed."

"The stupid Americans. They'll blow up some mountainside. That's all there is north of us where it headed."

They both laughed. Zalmi cupped his hand to his ear. "Listen! Do you hear? Sounds like a swarm of bees far in the distance."

Wakil frowned. "I don't hear a thing . . . Wait! Now I hear, and it does sound like bees. I wonder what it could be."

After about five minutes, the sound level jumped as the flight of tiny helicopters topped the rise a mile or so to the south and descended toward the camp. Zalmi grabbed an ancient pair of binoculars and pointed them toward the growing, high-pitched din.

"What is it?" Wakil asked. "What do you see?"

"Nothing at all. Clear sky and no dust on the ground."

The tiny low-flying helicopters were impossible to see at this distance, even with binoculars. Their sound, enhanced deliberately to create confusion, grew to an intense, almost-painful level as they neared the camp.

"You must be blind! Give me those so I can find our enemy." Wakil grabbed the binoculars from Zalmi as the noisy choppers passed over their outpost a few hundred feet above their heads. The size of a small bird, the tiny choppers were still nearly impossible to see. This was especially so when most of them reached their observation area with the sun directly behind them.

Zalmi sat on the grounded as wild gunfire erupted from the many automatic weapons in the hands of his fellow Afghans. A few took aim, most simply fired at random into the air. Like Zalmi, many of these hardened fighters were confused and disorganized. "In the name of Allah, what is this?" he shouted to Wakil as panic distorted his face.

Wakil was angrily emptying his AK-47 into the air and couldn't hear. The unmistakable flash and roar of a handheld Stinger missile rent the air blasting off from a few feet away. Zalmi followed its corkscrew smoke-defined path as it disappeared high in the sky. A second missile was fired only to explode almost immediately a few hundred feet in the air. Zalmi watched a tiny black dot descend from the area of the explosion. It fell slowly at first and then picked up speed as it headed for the rocks about thirty feet from his post. It struck the ground and exploded with much less force than a hand grenade. The self-destruct mechanism in the fragile tiny chopper blew it to thousands of tiny bits when it hit the ground.

Zalmi climbed down from the observation tower and rushed over to examine the site of the explosion. He picked up a tiny piece of green plastic and showed it to Wakil who followed him to help in the inspection. "What could this be?" he said, turning the tiny flat object over in his palm. "This tiny piece of plastic is all I can find. Search for yourself."

Wakil examined the ground and came up with two tiny metal screws, the type used to fasten to plastic. "This is all I've found so far. What can it be?"

While the unearthly din roared above them, Zalmi left to check with Colonel Mustapha, the camp commander. Wakil climbed back up the ladder to man the observation post. Zalmi went in person as once more the ancient telephone connection failed to work. As he arrived at the headquarters building, Colonel Mustapha ordered a cease-fire and sent a boy to check the camp for casualties.

"What can you report?" the colonel asked of Zalmi.

"Here's all we could find from the site, sir," he said as he handed the small piece of plastic and the two screws to the colonel. "There was a small explosion when the object hit. It was the size of a blackbird and fell quite slowly, so it was small and light. Do you have any idea what this is all about?"

At this point a young boy ran up impatient with news for the colonel. "Spit it out, child. What did you discover?"

"There are no casualties, sir," he answered. "No one was killed. No one was injured except a few who fell on the rocks while rushing to their posts. Sir, what is that terrible noise?"

"We'll tell everyone when we find all the details. Go, spread the word to search for any unusual objects on the ground and bring them here to the headquarters building. Go!" Turning back to Zalmi, he said, "Continue your report."

"Wakil and I examined the spot where the object exploded and found nothing but the three objects I gave you. That was not a bomb and was much less powerful than a hand grenade. I doubt it would cause injury unless it exploded in contact with a person. We were less than thirty feet from the explosion and nothing reached our post."

Colonel Mustapha was puzzled. "That is strange. Return to your post and try to find more pieces."

Zalmi was returning to his post when he realized the sound seemed to be dying down. Reaching the observation post, he found Wakil searching the sky with the binoculars.

"They're definitely moving away," Wakil said as he put down the glasses. "I can no longer see the tiny black dots. The source of the sound is moving north toward the mountains."

They checked their northern view for some time after the buzzing faded away. There were a number of tiny bright flashes high in the mountains. They heard no sounds from the distant explosions.

✳   ✳   ✳

"Let's take them out of there," Corporal Mugambi ordered. "Head them for a high mountain peak and destroy them so no one can get their hands on them. We've got thousands more waiting to be used."

"I almost hate to destroy them," an eighteen-year-old gunslinger said as he headed his four Super Choppers north into the mountains.

At twenty thousand feet above raged peaks, the remaining fifteen tiny Super Choppers were deliberately blown into thousands of indistinguishable pieces the size of sand grains which rained down over a broad area of the deserted mountains.

✳   ✳   ✳

It had been many hours since the tiny Super Choppers surveyed the terrorist camps, the sun had set and it was quite dark. Wakil and Zalmi were observing from their posts in the windswept silence. Two large explosions created a flash from several miles to the south, and the camp went dark as the explosions cut the power. The flashes and resulting smoke were clearly visible from their post. Twenty seconds later the unmistakable rumble of the distant explosions reached the camp. Zalmi reached for the battered phone to report to the colonel as the generator kicked in and the emergency lighting came up.

"Praise to Allah!" Zalmi uttered as the phone worked. When Sergeant Mahkmud, the colonel's aid answered, Zalmi reported, "Two explosions about two miles south of us, sir. We saw the flashes, and lots of flames and smoke. They appear to be at the camp entrance in the valley below us."

"I'll check with the guard post," the sergeant replied.

A few minutes later the phone buzzed. It was the sergeant. "We've lost contact with the guard post. The phone is dead. I'm sending a weapon carrier and men to discover what's happened. I'm also sending all men to their defense positions. Keep your eyes open for anything unusual. This may be the Americans."

They saw the lights of the weapon carrier as it wound its way down toward the guard post until going out of sight. About twenty minutes later, it returned. Zalmi could tell by the outside lights there were only four men on board as the carrier returned to the headquarters building. He waited tense and expectant until the phone rang.

"They've destroyed the bridge and a large portion of the roadway above the bridge. The guard post has disappeared with the roadway collapse. All direct communications lines were severed as well as the power lines. Our only means of communication is now by radio, and we're having problems with that. Many radio stations are now silent. We expect an air attack, so the lookouts will be doubled at the next changeover."

✳   ✳   ✳

Far out of sight and missile range of those below, the modified AWACS plane was at fifty thousand feet for the entire operation. As the plane turned toward home base, the mission leader, Captain John Mook, rose to speak to the entire group. "That was a job well done. If phases two and three go as well, our terrorist enemies will lose about half of their members. The twenty battle groups of between four and five men on this aircraft used the Super Choppers for phase one of project WellCo. This one aircraft holds all airborne members of phase one surveillance. The entire project depended on the success of our mission, and you all performed well. Members of the entire WellCo project were branded WellCo Warriors. At this point in time, there is talk your existence will be kept secret permanently. Though your exploits remain unknown and unexplained, the results of your efforts will be a major historical event." At this point, an aide handed Captain Mook several papers.

"Here's a report on the last part of phase one. Laser-guided and other smart bombs destroyed most of their communications network, at least the major installations, and isolated most of the training camps. The cruise missiles that delivered our choppers then struck at hardened targets. Damage assessment will come in about two hours from pictures taken by Eye Spy aircraft dropped with the smart bombs and from the cruise missiles. So far, the news is better than we hoped."

A cheer went up from the men.

"There's more," Mook said. "Here are the results of your efforts. Of the twenty possible camps we surveyed, four were small seemingly peaceful villages, three had been training camps in the past, but were abandoned sometime before our mission. We took detailed pictures and plots of the other thirteen, including personnel counts and weapon assessments. As the result of your efforts, phase two will start at about midnight local time. Fortunately, the weather is staying clear."

As the men began to celebrate, Captain Mook held up his hand for silence.

"Hold on for a minute while I give you the numbers and the response from our enemies. You can celebrate as long as you want, just don't damage the aircraft. Now for the numbers. Eight modified Tomahawk cruise missiles deployed 324 Super Choppers at twenty locations over literally thousands of square miles of rugged terrain. Seven of the choppers failed to respond and we assumed were damaged in the drop and self-destroyed. During the mission, five of the choppers were damaged by ground fire and six destroyed themselves, we assume from hitting an object like a hill or building. The enemy fired a total of forty-one Stinger missiles at them, destroying only eighteen. Apparently one Stinger took out two choppers and twenty-four missed. As far as we can tell, all Super Choppers were then destroyed by their fail-safe self-destruct mechanism after completing their mission. In our operation, the enemy spent about $820,000 in Stinger missiles to destroy $5,400 in our hardware that would self-destruct later anyway. The total cost of the hardware expended in our mission was only about $96,000. Who says a high-tech war has to be expensive?

"Now, the news. These are the first reports from the Taliban in Kabul, which, incidentally, has not yet been attacked, at least not by us. The report read, 'Armed forces of the evil satanic Americans attacked the peaceful citizens of Afghanistan with bombs and troops. Raining death and destruction on Kabul and other cities, the Americans killed and maimed thousands of innocent civilians including women and children. Their soldiers attacked many of our peaceful youth camps killing mostly civilians. Brave Afghan soldiers repulsed the Americans, inflicting massive losses. Cowardly American blood flowed deep in the streets at these camps as our fighters defended Islam. All attacks were repulsed, and not a single American soldier is left alive on our soil.' At least the last statement is true," he added with a smile. "Okay, men, we can relax and wait for the second wave."

❋   ❋   ❋

Zalmi was awakened by the sound of a series of small explosions quite different from gunfire. Vaulting from his cot fully clothed, he grabbed his AK-47 and headed for his post. He was running toward the observation tower when a huge explosion came from the cave. The whole camp lighted by the billowing flames as fuel stored in the cave burned, amplifying the explosion. Frozen in place for the moment, he saw the headquarters building disintegrate, and the white blast knocked him flat on the ground. As he crawled to retrieve his weapon, his barracks went the way of the headquarters. During the time he took to crawl to the ditch beneath his post, all the rest of the buildings in the camp exploded. As he dropped into the ditch, a ball of fire erupted above his head. He huddled deep, covering his head with his AK-47 as debris from the exploding observation tower rained down all around him.

"Praise Allah!" he remarked as the rain of debris stopped and he found himself unhurt.

The silence after the final explosion was interrupted at first by moans and cries of the wounded, then by shouted commands, "Go to the rocks! Go to the rocks!"

Zalmi vaulted out of the ditch and headed for the rocky hillside east of the camp where the rocky terrain would provide excellent cover. At the top of the ditch, he stumbled over another soldier. It was his friend, Wakil, who had not been so lucky. A large timber from the tower had impaled his chest. Zalmi hesitated for a moment; then realizing Wakil was beyond help, he ran for the rocks. As he ran, he saw many others heading the same way, black figures outlined in smoky silhouettes against the yellow flames. Some ran alone; some were helping wounded comrades. He finally dropped into the shadow of a large rock and leaned against it while regaining his breath. After a few minutes, he concentrated on staying hidden while listening for commands. All he could hear was the crackling of the flames and the moans and cries of the wounded. Then he heard a high-pitched buzz from above. The buzz grew louder and louder until finally a voice from the sky spoke in his own tongue, Pushto.

"Lay down your weapons and come to the center of the camp. Anyone who does not obey will be killed." The voice was answered with several bursts of AK-47 fire from the rocks to his south. This was followed by a number of streaks of fire high overhead. The streaks went straight to where the AK-47 fire originated and were followed by several small explosions.

A few moments' silence, and the voice spoke again, "Resistance is futile. Throw down your weapons, and gather in the center of the camp. Those who do not will be killed. Bring your wounded comrades with you, and they will be cared for."

Another round of gunfire from the rocks was followed by the same small streaks in the sky and then the small explosions. The same scenario repeated three more times until there was no more AK-47 fire. Everyone stayed where they were in the rocks.

Another five minutes of silence and the voice spoke again, "All who remain hidden in the rocks will be killed. We will start killing in ten minutes if you do not throw down your weapons and move to the center of the camp."

Zalmi was quite unnerved by this voice in the sky. His thoughts raced wildly about. *Should I follow their order? Will I be killed if I don't? Will others shoot me if I do? How can they know where I am?* For the moment, he chose to stay put and wait.

The voice again boomed out, "We can see all of you clearly. We have the means to search out each of you and kill you if you hold a weapon. Each one of your soldiers that fired on us was killed. If you do not throw down your weapon and head for the camp as directed, we will start killing in five minutes. Any soldier raising a weapon against those who choose to surrender will be killed before he can fire."

Zalmi saw two soldiers walking toward the center of the camp. Almost as soon as they appeared, several small explosions burst in the rocks.

Again came the voice, "The three who raised their weapons to fire at those surrendering were killed. In three minutes, all who hold weapons will be killed. We can and will do what we say."

Hearing this, Zalmi threw his AK-47 out from his hiding place. Many more soldiers walked toward the center of the camp, empty arms held high above their heads. Zalmi soon followed. Despite the Islamic fundamentalist promise of instant paradise, Zalmi wanted to live.

✳   ✳   ✳

Far above the camp, the mission command plane circled. Twenty gunslingers worked their keyboards to control eighty attack Super Choppers. Each little helicopter carried eight RATTLER antipersonnel rockets the size of a pocket pen as well as a tiny Sky Eye TV camera. The camp below was displayed in twenty sections, each section controlled by a single gunslinger keyboard. Mission commander, Captain Wesley Charron, spoke in Pushto over the speaker in a Super Chopper hovering several hundred feet over the targeted camp. As he spoke, the gunslingers used their screens as bright green images of men moved in their fields of view. When an image raised and fired his weapon, the gunslinger clicked on the image, sending a RAP rocket on a body-heat detecting path to terminate the enemy soldier with a small shaped charge.

"I count eighty-three without weapons gathered in the middle of the camp," Captain Charron announced. "I don't think any more are coming in, so you know the routine. Don't target any man unless you're certain he's holding a weapon. Okay, fire!"

✳   ✳   ✳

As the group waited in the middle of the camp, a number of small explosions among the rocks were followed by an eerie calm. The sounds from the still-burning buildings, the steady buzz from the sky, and the low rumble of voices of the soldiers were all that could be heard.

The voice in the sky boomed out, "Thank you for following our directions. Now please face east and sit on the ground. A rescue mission is on the way to carry you out and treat your wounded. You will not be harmed if you follow our orders."

In about half an hour, the sound of fast-moving helicopters came from the south. Within a few minutes, two attack helicopters disgorged twenty armed troops who secured the camp. Soon after, two more large troop carrier helicopters set down. A contingent of five men approached the prisoners and stopped about thirty feet away, while armed guards flanked them on both sides.

Once again, the voice boomed from the hovering chopper. "Form a single line and approach our delegation one at a time. The first to be processed will be provided with stretchers to bring in the wounded. You will not be harmed if you cooperate and do as you are told. Any sign of resistance will be met with lethal force."

The careful processing of the eighty or so prisoners through metal detectors and onto the troop carriers took three hours. When told to give up all knives and metal objects before going through the detector, many argued they were valuable family heirlooms. In spite of promises they would be returned later, a few scuffles broke out. They were subdued and the resistors placed in handcuffs and leg irons. One zealot broke for the interrogators with a raised knife. He was cut down before getting within ten feet of his intended victims. After the excitement cooled down, a ground search of the area found eleven wounded men who were loaded on stretchers and placed aboard the helicopter with the medical team.

For the last time, Captain Charron's voice boomed from above the camp. Speaking in English, he said, "The mission is complete. Let's head for home."

* * *

In a secret meeting room at Andrews Air Force Base, five men waited at a table. As Andy Wells approached to take his seat, the men all stood up and applauded. This was the same group he met in this same room at the beginning of the project on September 13, 2001. He knew only one of the men, his old friend and partner in the project, Dusty Adams. The other four included two men in uniform and two civilian representatives of the president. As always, no one wore a name tag, decorations, emblems of rank, or service branch identifications. When finally the applause quieted, one of the uniformed men spoke, "Welcome, Andrew. Please be seated."

One of the two civilians arose to speak. "The president and his cabinet are positively ecstatic. Accordingly, I bring congratulations to you all. The results of our first attack on world terrorism are better than we had hoped. All objectives were met. Other than those who were in the camps, there was not one civilian casualty. The only casualties we suffered were three minor injuries caused by falls as our men exited their aircraft in the dark after the mission. The mission was so successful, the president has ordered a hold on the second attack until the effects on the terrorist organizations and their supporters can be assessed. because of our success at destroying their communications infrastructure, the news from Afghanistan is slow coming in, so we adopted a wait-and-see attitude for the present."

Turning to Andy, he said, "Before we begin, here is a letter from the president of the United States, thanking you for your help. I believe you will be quite pleased with what it says."

Everyone waited silently as Andy read the letter.

Dear Mr. Wells:

Thanks to your unique talent and the unprecedented success you helped us achieve, we earned an outstanding initial victory over the terrorists and their supporters. When your original project was cancelled eight years ago, you left government service to start your own company. Who would guess that in a few months, your reinstated project could produce unique weapons invaluable in this new kind of war. Your country has a friend of mine to thank for telling me about your cancelled project. That was a most fortunate bit of information from a trusted friend. You took your weapons technology and converted it into peaceful civilian use building an extremely successful toy company in a competitive business. This gave testimony to your talents.

Unfortunately, your specific efforts and the many useful products you provided will go unheralded for security reasons. Rest assured, however, the nation will hear about the results of your efforts and you will be accordingly rewarded. I counted on you, your country counted on you, the entire free world counted on you; you let no one down. We all thank you from the bottom of our hearts.

It's positively amazing that the thousands of young people who grew up playing electronic games using Welco Toy Company gunslinger keyboards would become so effective in actual combat? They used those skills to control the military versions of America's most popular toys in one of the nation's most successful military operations.

The President of the United States.

The Hike

*T*imothy O'Brien never expected to find himself in such circumstances. Whoever would? He paused on the narrow path on the side of the grey granite mountain, the wind pressing on his backside as if it wished to push him to his death on the ragged rocks two thousand feet below. A sound caught his attention over the rush of wind.

At first he thought he knew what the sound was, a small animal moving through the bushes on the ledge below where he stood, but as the sound grew louder, he realized it was coming from much farther above. Soon the sound was like many irregular hoof beats, the sound a herd of horses or buffalo would make running in a stampede. He leaned harder against the rock away from the sheer drop on the other side of the path as the sound grew louder and louder. He was horrified when he realized the cause of the sound. An avalanche of rock was plummeting down the mountainside above him.

Tim realized how exposed he was on the narrow ledge with no protection above. Thinking quickly in that time-slowing pace of near panic, Tim remembered passing a deep indent in the path with a substantial protective overhang. He hurried back toward the safe haven as quickly as he dared on the narrow path. *If only I can reach the place in time.* Small rocks, dislodged by the vibrations from the approaching mass of plummeting rock, began pelting him as he ran. *God! How far back was that spot?* he thought as he rounded bend after bend without seeing the safe haven.

Finally! There it was on the opposite side of a deep ravine that cut back into the mountain. The safe place was much too far to reach in time. Then he found a narrow break in the rocks beneath the path about fifteen feet ahead. By then the small rocks dislodged by the earthshaking deluge far above were falling more often and getting bigger. One hit his arm and drew blood, then another. He ran to the edge above the break, searching for a way to move himself into the crack. Moving into the break seemed impossible. One slip and he would drop to the jagged rocks below. A huge boulder bounced on the path a few feet from where he clung, and he realized the main part of the avalanche would soon be smashing into him.

Grabbing a small rock handhold on the edge of the path, he rolled over the edge and into the crack. He was dangling in space inside the crack, supported only by the handhold. He searched the sides of the crack for another handhold or foot support. The sides of the crack were smooth. Then he realized the crack narrowed both downward and inward. If he could swing far enough in, he would be able to jam himself into the crack and hold himself there by pressing against the sides. After swinging several times to gain momentum, he prayed and let go as he swung inward.

As he let go, a huge piece of rock smashed the ledge he had just been holding, smashing a section of the path into small pieces, and showering the area with small jagged projectiles. He was deep inside the crack, but slipping downward. After dropping at least twenty feet, he was able to stem his fall by jamming his legs against one wall and his back the other. About ten feet inside the crack and under the path he hung on tightly as the massive avalanche crashed onto the path where he stood moments before.

The mountain shook, dust filled the air, and the sound was deafening as the main part of the avalanche thundered by a few feet from his refuge. Then he couldn't breathe because of dust whirled at him by the air blast from the avalanche. He used his free hand to pull his shirt out and over his face as a filter to keep the dust out of his lungs and eyes. Breathing was difficult, but possible, and the shirt kept the choking dust out. *How long would the thundering continue?* he wondered. Then he felt himself slipping and pressed harder with his legs, jamming himself tighter in the crack.

He wondered, *will the thundering never stop?* Then everything began quieting down. The thundering was rapidly moving down the mountain, and the dust was settling. Tim eased his shirt off his face and surveyed the scene before him. There was still a pall of fine dust in the air and an occasional small rock plunged off the shelf above him, but at least he was still alive. Glancing up about thirty feet, he realized the crack was now open at the top. The avalanche had obliterated the path that capped the crack. He wondered how much of the path still traversed the mountainside and if he could use what remained to go down the mountain.

His legs were beginning to ache from pressing so hard against the sides of the crack. He would soon need to move into the narrower section of the crack and jam himself in so he could rest his legs or they would eventually give out. He took about fifteen minutes to move far enough into the crack so he could wedge his hips and rest his legs. As he relaxed a bit, he began examining his body. Blood oozed from several cuts on his arms and legs, and when he wiped his forehead, his hand came away quite bloody. Fortunately he was not losing much blood, just a bloody mess of small cuts and abrasions.

As he rested, Tim considered his predicament and options. *At least Alicia wasn't with me, so she was safe. By now she would be frantic and asking for help. Surely the avalanche was noisy enough and near enough to alert people back at the lodge. Alicia would be driving everyone to find me. Well, I might as well start finding a way out. Any help is surely hours away.*

With that thought, Tim decided he should work his way up the crack, keeping to the narrowest part so he could rest periodically. After about an hour, he was only five feet below the open top of the crack. Unfortunately the crack narrowed at that point in such a way that his only way up was out beneath an overhang with a long drop below. One slip and he would fall at least a hundred feet. He decided to rest for a while to prepare for the exertion he was about to make.

Fortunately his hiking boots were strong, so he decided to use them to grip the narrow portion of the crack as he worked his way out almost upside down. He jammed one boot into the crack and swung the other around and jammed that boot into the crack about three feet ahead of the other. Four maneuvers like that and he should be able to reach the top with his hands and pull himself up. The effort would be difficult, but doable. Each maneuver took him farther away from the wall hanging above a huge drop. If he missed—well—he couldn't. After the fourth maneuver, his feet were jammed into the crack a foot from the top. He would rest again for the final move where he would fold his body forward and reach for the top with his right hand. Once he had a hold, he could release his farthest foot and pull himself onto the path. He had taken nearly three hours to get this far, and he wasn't taking any more chances than he had to.

After resting for about fifteen minutes, Tim started making his move, bending forward as far as he could and reaching for the edge which stayed a few inches out of his grasp. He repositioned his feet to move a bit closer. Once more he bent up and reached for the edge. A third try provided a precarious hold as his fingers finally caught the edge. He worked his hand around the edge until he found a decent hold and began to release his left foot for the final move. Once he released, there was no way to put it back. He would be holding on by one foot jammed into the crack and a precarious hold on rather smooth rock with his right hand. He couldn't move far enough into the narrow part of the crack to jam his torso without releasing his other foot. That would leave him dangling with but one tenuous handhold as he swung his other hand up for another hold. If there wasn't one, he was done for and he couldn't see where he had to reach.

Finally Tim took a deep breath, released his other foothold and reached over the edge of the crack with his left hand searching with his fingers for any projection or small opening he could catch with one finger. With his elbows over the edge of the crack, he held for an instant, but knew he must find a hold or he would slip off the edge. Frantically his fingers probed the smooth surface searching in vain for anything to hold. His right hand began losing grip and started to slide toward the edge. He was losing his hold. "Damn" he said out loud. In a few seconds, he would be waiting for that crushing pain as his body hit the rocks below. He thought of Alicia. "Damn I hate losing!"

As his hand slipped slowly and agonizingly toward the edge, it seemed as if time was slowing. was he imagining things, or had he heard a voice from above him? His left arm slipped off, and he hung for a moment with one hand. As his right hand began to lose its grip and ever so slowly slip toward the edge, he knew it was all over. Astonished when he didn't fall, Tim felt something snap around his wrist before his hand could slip over the side. A feeling of relief came over hin when he realized there were two friendly faces above him. Jack had grabbed Tim's hand. The rope in his hands was secured to others on the path.

"Hang on there, ole buddy," Jack said as he reached down with his other hand and grabbed Tim's left. They pulled him up over the edge to safety. As soon as he was safely on the ledge Alicia was sobbing and holding him like she would never let go.

✻   ✻   ✻

Back at the lodge, showered, cleaned, and patched up, Tim sat with Alicia and his friends and ran through the day's adventure. Alicia wouldn't let him out of her arms.

Jack reported, "This gal of yours was a whirlwind when we heard the avalanche, less than a mile from the lodge. When we heard the horrible sound, she shouted 'Tim!' and got us going right away. We were headed up the mountain before the avalanche stopped, I swear."

Rory added, "She ran up that mountain like a mountain goat. We had a hard time keeping up with her."

"Don't you ever go anywhere like that without me?" Alicia ordered, her dark eyes flashing.

"I don't plan to." Tim smiled to think what an unbelievably lucky guy he was in several ways.

The Gold Feather

From force of habit I deliberately studied each passenger who came through security and into the waiting area for the shuttle. The years working on various highly sensitive projects taught and trained me to check carefully for anything unusual. On my first vacation in years, I was headed back to my favorite place in this quadrant of the galaxy. Officially "on vacation" I remained, as always, an active though relaxed member of the Eegis project.

My relaxation ceased and my mind sprung to attention when a tall, and beautiful redhead strode catlike into the waiting area and flowed into a seat. From the feline way she moved I was sure she was a Scentar, a rare, homo variant. I'd heard about this advanced human subspecies, but had never seen one. Her simple dress clung to her like a second skin, moving enough to show the cloth was not attached. An unusual color, her dress was a deep red with amber overtones, almost Titian.

As she sat, our eyes met and locked for a moment. A sudden, intense feeling of pleasure ran through my body as I imagined her moving sinuously against me. The sensation was more emotion than thought and caught me off guard. I am **never** caught off guard. The thought, *something is not right*, sent a chill through me for an instant and was gone.

When they called my group to board, she stood and walked toward the gate right in front of me. She was so slender, almost fragile, as she moved fluidly up the steps and into the shuttle. I never remember seeing anyone whose body moved so smoothly. She almost seemed to have extra joints in her limbs.

This is one lucky day. I thought to myself as she slithered into her assigned seat next to mine. She turned and looked directly into my eyes.

"I'm Leura Clauson. Who are you please?"

Her directness and the musical sound of her voice surprised me more than her exotic appearance. "Uh Draxel, Draxel Syl—call me Drax." I was uncomfortable and ill at ease—certain that my voice betrayed my discomfort.

"Have you been to Stentor Seven before? This is my first visit to the Vegan star system."

"Been there several times," I struggled to say. Her breath held the faint aroma of warm milk. She wore a perfume that hung on the edge of awareness. The fragrance was there, but as soon as I thought, the scent was gone. I was in uncomfortable territory without a secure mental foot hold.

"I'm going on my first vacation in years and this is my favorite place to visit. Are you on vacation?"

"No, I'm a botanist on a research project. I plan to study plants growing in the low gravity and artificially controlled atmosphere."

The lilt of her speech was enthralling. Not an accent, just different and quite musical. "A scientist! I'm impressed!" I smiled as I spoke thinking that was a huge understatement. "How long will you stay, on your project, I mean?"

"At least one stellar year. My grant may be renewed for an additional year. This is my first major assignment. . . . What was that little smile about?"

"A little private joke—on me." Her perception was amazing.

"A secret?"

"No, just a laugh at myself." Her directness, too, was a surprise.

"Tell me."

Now I was getting irritated. "Let's say it's something I'd rather not tell someone I've just met."

Disregarding my irritation, she switched the subject. "What's your profession?"

"I'm a gravity propulsion engineer. Do design work on the propulsion systems on craft like this one we're on."

"That must be interesting. Gravity propulsion is a highly complex technology, is it not? It takes a lot of education. Tell me about it, please."

"You want those boring details?"

"Absolutely! And where did you get your education?"

"I took advanced gravity propulsion at the AGP center on Earth."

"And how long did that take?"

"On top of a basic engineering degree, state licensing requirements include two more years of advanced schooling with lots of math and physics. Then we spend a year training on the equipment, two more of working in the field and finally, passage of an examination before the state grants a license."

"That's five years. Botanists have it much easier."

"I don't know. Biochemistry is an intricate and demanding science involving complex living systems. That must demand a lot of effort."

"It is also fascinating and rewarding."

"I'll bet it is."

"So you are vacationing here?"

"Yep! This vacation is long overdue and Stentor Seven's my favorite place to visit."

"Tell me about it. I've seen the digirecords, but those are quite bland. No beauty or poetry. You said you've been there?"

"Yes, and it is beautiful, so spectacularly beautiful it must be experienced."

The shuttle's engine hum increased and it rose from the pad to start the four-hour trip. The motion was apparent, but would disappear as soon as we cleared the atmosphere and the main drive kicked in.

"How did it come to be? The records were sketchy about the planet's origins; they mention it was artificially created with no explanation. What does that mean?"

I was becoming more comfortable because I was on familiar territory. "It was once a small, sterile planet a bit smaller than Mars and about two thirds its mass. It lies the right distance from the red dwarf star, Stentor, for a life supporting environment. Focused gravity beams were used to tow huge ice planetesimals in from the Stentor Oort cloud. They melted and became the oceans and created the atmosphere, mostly carbon dioxide. Special vegetation was introduced to consume the Carbon dioxide and add oxygen to the atmosphere, but you should know all about that, don't you?"

"Yes, I studied, the conversion of primordial atmospheres. All botanists study that early in their schooling since it has been used to modify many planets."

"Then you should also know about the biota from earth-like environments and that it took almost six-hundred years for the growth of these plants on the land and plankton in the seas to bring the atmosphere to its present mixture. It's much like earth's. Am I right?"

"The introduction of the biota, yes, but the six hundred years it took? I don't remember being taught about that."

"That's because the exact time for the change varied from place to place. Temperatures, pressures and everything else were adjusted for human habitation and the biota thrived. Since then, many larger life forms were introduced and flourished. The combination of optimal rotation rate and distance from Stentor, along with lots of work over the years gave us a semitropical paradise covering the entire surface."

"It sounds wonderful."

"Because of the low gravity, plants grow to immense size and spectacular proportions. That, I trust will be the focus of your research project."

"You are correct. Please tell me more."

"Better yet, I can show you. When we come in to land, you'll learn what is possible in this light gravity. You'll see mountains that rise seventy thousand feet with sheer cliffs and unbelievable waterfalls. You should be able to see a lot of unusual geology and geography. It's quite spectacular from above."

"Point those things out to me, will you?"

"Gladly! Once on the ground be sure to take in how water behaves. It's quite different from Earth. The muted sounds of the slow waterfalls and of the unusual rivers are like a chorus of musical mumbles. Waves on the oceans can grow huge, yet they seem to roll in slow motion. The surf amazes everyone with spectacular thirty foot breakers tumbling slowly and gently onto the sand."

"I can see why it's such a popular vacation spot. How about the weather?"

"The weather is marvelous, sunny and warm with fractal-like white clouds moving across hazy, pale blue sky. In order to preserve adequate surface pressure, the atmosphere is kept many times deeper than on your home planet. because of this, no stars can be seen at night and the central star, Stentor appears bright red. Clouds can rise as high as a hundred miles and the winds always drift by gently."

"That's amazing, quite different from Earth."

"Then there's the rain, the unbelievable warm rain. because of the low gravity, raindrops fall slowly, congealing into large blobs which grow to near tennis ball size before they blow apart by the air as they fall through it. The soft pelting of large blobs of warm water feels marvelous."

"I heard about the rain. I can hardly wait to experience it. I want to run through it—without clothes."

I would like to see that, ran through my mind, but I didn't mention it. Her next comment drew vivid mental pictures in my mind.

"If the chance comes up, could we run through the rain together? I'd like that."

It was said so innocently, so matter-of-factly, she caught me speechless. I paused to calm my imagination and struggle for composure. "Uh—yeah—sure. That sounds like a great idea."

"It sounds like true paradise. I hope I can spend my leisure time enjoying a few of the things you describe. Would you show me around some while you're on vacation? I don't mean to interfere with your plans, but I know no one else here."

I was beginning to believe my good fortune might overwhelm me. "Why, yes! I would enjoy it. I made no specific plans, none at all."

"Wonderful. My schedule is very light for the first few weeks so I want to move around a lot. I'm certain to find many new things to experience. It all sounds so exciting," she said as the main drive took over and the hum and vibrations ceased. We soon cleared the atmosphere and were on our way.

Over the next hour I relaxed as we spoke about families and friends. She drew pleasant experiences out of my memory and shared her experiences as a child and about growing up. There was an unusual quality to her stories. They were softly emotional. Incredibly, I could almost feel her joys and pains as she described them.

A long pause in our conversation and I realized she had fallen asleep. Her head against my shoulder brought on pleasant sensations, as did her snuggling down against me several times during the flight. I examined her closely. Her hair was extremely fine with individual hairs growing unusually close together. It was the same dark red as her dress with no hint of a color change near the roots. If it was dyed, it was an absolutely perfect job. She turned a bit and put her hand ever so gently on my right arm. Her pale amber skin was baby-soft and unflawed. When I touched her hand, it felt like satin, almost frictionless. She was far too perfect for a normal human. Scentar were reported to possess unusual emotional abilities. She certainly seemed to exhibit those.

She wore a gold pin high on her dress, the only adornment she wore of any kind. It was a feather, about an inch long and quite fragile. It appeared to be like a real feather, but tiny and clearly gold. When it moved, it displayed faintly the many colors of the spectrum. One moment it seemed to be gold, another to flash color, and another to catch and reflect any light source like a diffraction grating. Colors flashed so vibrantly it seemed almost alive.

A slight bump was followed by vibrations and the hum of the landing drive. Leura sat upright without the slightest hint she had been asleep. "We must be arriving."

"Check out the scene below. Like I described earlier, it's spectacular."

She leaned toward the window. "It is amazing. The mountains—everything you said—they're so different."

When she sat back from the window, I turned to her. "You slept the last hour of our trip almost without moving. I wish I could do that."

"Concentrate on pleasant thoughts and close your eyes. You'll go right to sleep."

I smiled at her easy answer, still concentrating on the lovely gold feather pin. "What's that pin your wearing? it changes, sparkles with colors that seem to vibrate."

"A gift. My mother gave it to me when I completed my studies. It's the only jewelry I ever wear. It's supposed to signify fidelity."

"That's one I never heard before."

"Actually it's a special kind of fidelity. Fidelity to a common, usually treasured experience with someone you love. My mother loved me, and I her. It's about the wonderful life we spent together before I left home. Specifically, it's commemorating our last day together. That experience will never happen again."

"That tears me up, it's sad, but beautiful." I felt undeniably and intensely morose for a moment as she spoke. That nagging wariness of unknown origin again troubled me.

"Yes, I gave her a similar pin. It's a family custom. We both knew we would never see each other again."

I'm sure my shock showed. "Why not?"

Her voice had changed almost painfully. "It's a bit complicated. We just knew our paths would never cross again."

The sorrow within me became almost overpowering. "How can you be so sure?"

Leura had the tiniest hint of melancholy for an instant. "Please, I'd rather not talk about it anymore."

I experienced a sudden intense change to terrible anxiety. It was almost overwhelming. Then it was gone and I felt fine. "What was that all about?" I said out loud in reaction.

"What was what all about?" her clear, silky voice had returned.

"Sorry. I had a strange feeling for an instant and it startled me."

Once more Leura shifted mental gears without hesitation. "Would you be able to help me to my hotel? This is all so new to me and I'm a bit nervous about going there alone."

With my luggage scheduled to be delivered, I was free to go where I wished. "Certainly!"

"You're sure it won't be an inconvenience?"

"Positively. I'd love to go with you to your hotel." Once again I could hardly believe my good fortune. By this time I was beginning to grow accustomed to her soft, musical speech.

As we approached the hotel I remarked, "Buildings like this hotel are constructed in ways unimaginable on planets with normal gravity. Giant overhangs, huge spans, delightfully fragile overhead structures with plazas, walkways and open spaces."

"Yes, it is quite extraordinary," she said as the air car dropped us at level 196 of the hotel. It landed smoothly on the cantilevered plaza. Leura picked up the one small bag she carried and danced across the plaza right to the edge. She was a little girl spinning with excitement from one side of the outside walkway to the other as I led her to her room.

"I've never been up this high in the hotel. How'd you manage such a room? I thought the upper floors were reserved for foreign dignitaries?"

"And foreign botanists," she quipped as she flipped her hair and, with a flourish, hand-printed the key pad. The door slid soundlessly into the wall and then closed silently behind us after we walked inside.

I was dumbfounded. The room was decorated in shades of the exact same colors as Leura's dress and hair. "This can't be accidental. How'd you get your room decorated to match—you?"

Her appearance and demeanor changed and she laughed in that sensuous, lyrical way, no longer the little girl. Her voice also changed its timbre and now sounded almost like a flute or muted violin, terribly emotional.

"I plan on being here for at least a year so they let me choose my decoration. Do you like it?"

"It takes some getting used to, but it is beautiful." Once more I smiled as an intense feeling of warmth and pleasure flowed through my entire body. "Wow!" came out of my mouth as an involuntary expression.

Leura stepped lightly to the entertainment console and turned on music I had never experienced. In its unusual tones and mixed rhythms I sensed more than heard the plaintiff cry of a loon, the rustle of pine trees in the wind, the crashing of waves on a rocky shore and even the sounds of passion. It bordered on being visual and was pleasant to hear. Leura smiled as she switched the glass outside wall from clear to one way. We could see the beauty of Stentor Seven stretched out before us, but no one outside could look in.

Once more I became aware of her delicate perfume, on the edge of my senses as she walked to face me closely. Her eyes were fixed directly onto my eyes. The warm milk-like fragrance of her breath was erotically stimulating—emotionally intoxicating. She reached up and gently placed her wrists on my shoulders. Her hands hung loosely, barely touching my back. I hated the shirt that lay between her hands and my skin.

"Now, Mr. Syl, I want us to dance together. Would you like that?"

Completely out of my element and on the edge of losing any hint of control, I replied lamely, "Yes, I would."

I was totally beyond rational control. She slipped her slender fingers around my neck, took my hand and moved to the music. My eyes fastened directly onto her eyes. They were a dark blue with a hint of red to the black of her huge pupils.

"Pull the little ring at the back of my collar," her soft voice commanded.

With a slight pull her dress changed from the dark red-amber to an iridescent blue-green. She began moving rhythmically against me to the hypnotic beat and sound of the strange music. The sensation penetrated my whole body which flushed with warmth.

"Now, dear Drax, I want to show you my appreciation for what you are going to do for me."

She pulled me gently into the bed where cool satin sheets caressed my skin. I could hardly tell the difference between those sheets, her skin and her satiny dress. Something akin to fear, surged through my being. I was perceiving everything with intensely heightened senses and enjoying every delicious moment.

"Lie on your stomach. I want to give you a massage," she urged.

Ecstatic, I complied. Her long, slender fingers were working up and down my spine, around my shoulder blades and neck and finally down the back of my legs. I never felt so good, so totally aware, not in my entire life. Just when my body had turned to jelly, she stopped the massage and began dragging her fingers lightly over my bare arms. I felt her lips moving up and down the back of my neck. The stimulation to my skin was ecstatic. She stopped and lay down on her stomach beside me.

"My turn."

I was overcome with passion and amazement. "What do you want me to do?"

"Do to me what I did to you. Don't you think that's fair?"

I remembered a line from the distant past and uttered it under my breath, "Resistance is futile."

I began in the middle of her back. The fabric of her dress seemed like a second skin. Unbelievably soft and satiny, it moved smoothly to my touch. She had no taut muscles. After I massaged her for a while she rolled over on her back and looked up at me, those dark eyes boring into my essence.

"Tickle me please. Slide your fingertips slowly and gently over my skin. Barely touch me. Just like I did you. You liked that didn't you?"

"I prayed you'd never stop."

"Do it until I can't stand it anymore. Then we can weep together."

"Weep? What do you mean, weep?"

"Weep for joy. Ultimate joy."

"I'm game. Joy sounds wonderful right now."

"You're being fantastic. Then, when both of us are overwhelmed with joy—then we will weep."

I felt as if I would explode. Every touch of my fingertips on her silky body drove me to new heights of ecstatic pressure. It seemed like hours later Leura rose, slid over beside me and began brushing my hands and arms with her fingers as I continued touching her. When I could stand it no longer, I stopped moving my hands.

She sensed the change and rolled ever so slowly onto her back pulling me down with her.

Those dark blue eyes continued to bore into my soul while her soft voice hummed quietly, "Weep my love. Weep for all time,"—her voice trailed off into silence.

My mind and senses virtually exploded, one long explosion of complete and delicious abandon. I lost my sense of gravity and seemed to float in the midst of continuing soundless reverberations. I had never before felt such intense pleasure. The center of my being separated from my head and floated through my body. Intense feelings ricocheted between joy and melancholy, then pleasure and despondency, never remaining for long in any single state.

Leura's near whisper floated through my head. "Thanks dear Drax. Thanks for life and love." I opened my eyes and saw her face for an instant. I was surprised to see narrow streams of tears running from the corners of her eyes. Once more, I drifted in complete, all-engulfing, feeling-filled silence.

Things changed—suddenly and drastically. Normal gravity had returned. When I reached for her, all my grasping hands found was a slightly damp, rumpled cotton sheet. *What the*... I thought as I opened my eyes to the shock of a bright, sunlit window in a beige room. I was alone and in a different bed in a different hotel. Outside, the sun was rising over the unmistakable skyline of Cleveland Ohio. "My God!" I said out loud incredulously. "I never . . . almost forgot who I was," came stumbling out of my mouth.

A flash of realization made me check my watch. There was barely enough time to reach my breakfast meeting with Arlo Trippy, the engineer who was my NASA contact. He was working with me on their part of the Eegis project. I dressed, grabbed my suit coat and headed for the dining room. Arlo was waiting as I walked in.

"Right on time. I like people who are punctual."

"I almost wasn't. You wouldn't believe the wild dream I had last night or rather this morning. At least, I think it was a dream. It was so unbelievably—real."

"Sometimes dreams can seem very real."

"This one sure was." I shook my head. Still, bewildered. "Well, let's get down to far out physics. That's reality."

"Certainly." Arlo paused and gazed intently at my coat lapel. "What's that pin in your lapel? You weren't wearing it yesterday."

I glanced at my lapel. Firmly attached was a tiny gold feather.

Lyriel's Decision

A threat and a menace are not the same thing. A threat is the mere possibility of danger or something without danger that may have the appearance of danger for a time. It can usually be dealt with or avoided by clever counteraction. A menace, on the other hand, is a real danger that must be dealt with and is as certain as the rising of the sun. Though empty threat it may seem, beware the true menace that hides under the cunning mask of a threat.

Lyriel, leader and the oldest of the five in the control group at Far Station 322, was alone in her quarters and deep in troubled thought. The New Life Project she headed had gone terribly wrong. As usual, she would make the final decision to try one last time to redirect the project or terminate it and start over. The other four were divided, two on a side as usual. The project that seemed so promising now posed a terrible threat. It had burgeoned into a serious menace to her sector and possibly the entire galaxy.

A Muerr, Lyriel was by far the largest of the group and the farthest from her home planet. Despite her large size, Lyriel did not dominate the group, but worked diligently, almost gently, at leadership. The other four included two Fallons: Farcos, and the only other female in the group, Shremon: Stagus, a Thrack: and Llalimeno, a Torbun. The Fallons usually took positions opposing each other, rarely agreeing on anything and arguing constantly. Stagus was loud, aggressive, and stubborn while Llalimeno was almost the opposite: quiet, thoughtful, and open-minded, but not easily swayed once he took a position. Now the four were deeply entrenched, two to a position, leaving Lyriel to resolve the situation.

Finally deciding on an action, Lyriel stood up and popped her communicator. "Everyone to the observation deck. Let's make one more try at a solution we can all live with." She belted her tunic, pushed back her long reddish hair, and headed for the meeting. The door to the lift swished open to reveal Farcos and Shremon standing opposite each other, staring in cold silence. Their black eyes and grey faces were tightly framed by their straight black hair. As she stepped silently onto the lift, Lyriel smiled as she thought of these two having sex and wondered how they did it. They were like clones with no obvious differences showing through the skin-tight coverings that could hardly be called clothes. Their ID patches were the only method of telling them apart. Even their voices were identical.

"After you," Lyriel said softly when the door of the lift opened, extending her hand to indicate the door. Usually talkative, the Fallons stalked off the lift, side-by-side in cold steely silence. As she followed them down the hall, Lyriel thought to herself, *This is going to be a difficult meeting.*

They took their seats in front of ULDI's display screen and waited for the others. Almost a sixth member of the group, the computer was an interactive, free-thinking entity called by the acronym for its unlimited logic database interface. Lyriel knew there was no point in trying conversation, so she set up project simulations on her input console. Before it swished open, the muffled sound of a loud angry voice penetrated the door. Stagus was about to enter.

"What the hell are we doing now?" The small but burly Thrack bellowed as he entered. "I say terminate the damned project so we can start again with a clean slate. We've wasted far too much time in endless bickering already. I see no reason to waste any more time." Stagus had a loud, booming voice despite his small body. He plopped his compact frame firmly in his seat, crossing his arms defiantly. His long scraggly white hair hung over the back of the seat, completing the caricature of the stubborn, bellicose diehard—an immovable object.

"Now, Stagus, try to accept another viewpoint," Llalimeno said quietly, but firmly. The tall slender Torbun constantly tried to persuade his companion to be more open, usually without success. He almost slithered into his seat, his body flexing as he adjusted to the seat's contour. The pale blue skin of his hairless head was in contrast to the ample hair of the other four. His pale blue head turned brilliant blue on those rare occasions when his emotions got hold of him. As usual, it was quite pale, indicating he was in control.

Lyriel gazed up at the information on the display. "Let's go over this once more to try to find a way to avoid termination."

"Damned waste of time!" Stagus muttered.

Lyriel stood up, turned, and towered threateningly over the smaller Thrack. She was quite angry. "I've had my fill of your closed-minded, non helpful attitude and comments. If you've nothing constructive to offer, keep silent!" she demanded. "And don't answer!" Though physical violence was not her way, the threat was there, and at three times Stagus' size, the threat worked. The rest of the group registered surprise and submission at this unusual, for Lyriel, display. She returned to her console and the business at hand.

"Let me review the situation. As I do, listen thoughtfully for anything we may have missed in our previous efforts. Try an open-minded approach. I know this is difficult for some of you, but do it anyway. I would like your acknowledgment that you will at least try to put aside any strong feelings and consider things objectively. Rather than answer by voice, please stand to show your agreement to this simple request."

To Lyriel's surprise, Farcos stood up immediately, followed by Llalimeno. Shremon, surprised at Farcos' quick move, glared steadily at him for a moment before finally rising. It was several tense, suspense-filled moments later when Stagus got out of his seat.

Lyriel smiled when Stagus rose. "Thank you all, now let's proceed. Please resume sitting, and I will review the situation. When we found this planet, we discovered it had been seeded with life by natural processes. The life was quite normal in every respect, save one. The evolution of new life-forms was quite rapid, about a thousand times faster than on any other known planet. We knew it was only a matter of time before intelligent life evolved, so we waited. After several species with dawning intelligence were wiped out by rapidly evolving microscopic forms, we decided to try intervention and the New Life Project was created."

"We understand all that. I think we would be better off if we let things take their natural course," Farcos commented in his shrill voice. "Our interference created the problem in the first place. We should terminate it before it gets beyond our control."

"I agree, do it now," Stagus added in an uncommonly subdued, almost-reticent comment as he looked directly at Lyriel. Her threat had dampened his usual fervor.

Lyriel was livid, but gave a controlled response. "None of that. You both agreed to keep an open mind, and I intend to hold you to that agreement."

"Let's hear the rest of the review. We might have missed something. It might trigger an idea in someone so we can solve the problem," thoughtful Llalimeno commented. Shremon remained silent, staring blankly at the display.

"Please don't interrupt unless you have something constructive to say," Lyriel said firmly then resumed the review, following the outline on the display in front of them. "The next time a reasonably intelligent form appeared, we created this project and helped evolution by tinkering with the DNA of several of the most intelligent creatures. The end result was a bipedal creature, quite similar to us physically. A bipedal omnivore and tool user that stumbled along for a while before it learned the skills of an effective predator and exploded over most of the planet. Tool use, language, clothing, and growing intelligence rapidly changed the creature into a highly organized pack animal living in family groups that steadily grew in size and power. When written language and then the tools of science appeared, we moved our station from its orbit around the planet and tethered it on the edge of their moon to hide it, yet permit our direct observations. I arrived at Far Station 322 shortly after it was moved to the moon. With me came two more scout craft, and the station complement was increased from three to five. Llalimeno and I are the only two remaining from that first contingent of five. We increased our surveillance with the new scout craft and stopped all direct contact. About this same time, we began calling them the Leutra from the extinct inhabitants of that planet. The Leutra were beginning to search the sky with better and better telescopes, and it would not be long before we must move the station again."

"That's about the time we two Fallons came aboard relieving those horrid Kleps," Shremon commented. She was clearly repulsed by the hairy Kleps with their ugly eating habits. The Fallons were almost antiseptic with their personal habits, even eating in private. They avoided any gathering where food or drink was available. "Our first scouting mission analyzed the Leutra's preoccupation with reproduction. That was when the problem we are facing now was first predicted."

"Correct!" Lyriel said, regaining control of the review. "Their knowledge and technology grew at an unbelievable rate. We believe that their short lives and rapid development were one effect of the high rate of evolution. It took a long time for us to realize everything about life on this planet was moving at an unbelievable rate of change. They had terrible wars, plagues, and were set upon by rapidly evolving microscopic life-forms, but still their numbers steadily increased. When they began conquering the diseases that were holding their numbers to a slow rate of growth, the rate exploded unbelievably. That caught us off guard, and we instigated a number of control factors, primarily new diseases they had trouble fighting and were specific to the Leutra. It wasn't difficult considering the rapid normal rate of evolution of the planet's tiniest life-forms. We tweaked the DNA of a few bacteria and viruses, thinking we could use that to keep a balance of populations of the many interesting life-forms that had evolved. We had slowed the explosive growth of their population, but only for a short period. With amazing speed and efficiency, they found cures and preventive measures for these diseases while engaging in several major wars. They developed machines that flew, created fission and fusion weapons, and had the beginnings of space travel. About the time they began flying rockets, we moved the station away from their moon and placed it in its present position, matching the planet's own orbit and hiding behind its star, 180 degrees away."

"It's their damned preoccupation with procreation that is the problem," Stagus boomed, finally unable to hold back. "As intelligent as they are, and with the knowledge they have, why can't they control their population growth? Their technology would enable them to do so. They've already far outstripped all other large animal species in numbers, and the creature mix has become terribly lopsided. They recently reached the limit of growth of their food supply and now starve by the millions. Yet, they remain so passionately involved in reproduction they can't understand, or won't consider, it will ultimately lead to their destruction, and to the destruction of all other large animals as well. Any Thrack with half a brain would know that and insist that such madness be stopped. The Leutra evolved into a high-enough intelligence level to be considered for contact and possible membership in the union, but they are still controlled far too much by instincts. Loosed on the union as they are now with their present knowledge, and particularly with their unusually rapid life processes, they might reproduce themselves into numeric control of the entire galaxy. I can't permit it to happen. It would be genocide for all other intelligent species."

"Stagus is right," Shremon began. "Consider those few planets with dominant intelligent species whose uncontrolled population growth created similar problems. Animal life on every single one I studied eventually lost diversity, leaving only a few species which eventually went extinct. There was one planet where the intelligent species, a pure predator, eventually became its only remaining food supply. Horror stories of the resulting cannibalism are legion. Thankfully, they didn't achieve hyper–space travel or gain membership in the union before going extinct."

Lyriel was pleased the group was loosening their entrenched minds and beginning to open up a bit. "Good points, but are there any new ideas of what we can do to turn around the direction the Leutra are headed? They will surely learn the means of hyper–space travel and Trias Teleportation in the near future. We cannot let them expand beyond their planet as they are. In their hands, TT technology would create a huge menace. We need a means to change them, and soon. The alternative is to annihilate the species and start over. That would be a terrible setback to the project, not to mention the elimination of a promising species."

Llalimeno unfolded his sinuous form from his seat and stood up. Torbuns use so much body language with their long lithe bodies, they rarely spoke while seated. "Unfortunately, legal limitations on our actions prevent us from using some methods directly. Couldn't we develop a means to persuade them to take action themselves? What they need is a major cultural, emotional shift. Are their decisions so instinctively controlled, so emotionally charged, so illogical that we cannot find a method to cause them to overcome their passionate, illogical preoccupation with reproduction?"

"It seems to me, their tremendous drive is what caused their rapid development in the first place," Farcos brought up. "If we can't find a way to cause them to reduce or eliminate that reproductive drive without reducing it in other areas, the whole reason for the project will be lost. So far, we haven't a clue as to how that can be accomplished legally. We pushed the legal envelope long ago when our first DNA tweak resulted in the Leutra. There's no reason we can't push the legal envelope again. Can't we bypass a few of those bureaucratic limitations to obtain the results we seek?"

In a rare moment of harmony with her fellow, Shremon agreed, "A little legal latitude and we might find a workable answer. For such an advanced intelligence, they are still almost totally controlled by instincts. This is unusual. Most advanced, intelligent species learn to think logically rather than emotionally. The Leutra think they are so far above the other species on their planet and that they alone overcame instincts, replacing emotion with rationality for decision making. How wrong they are."

"They are less rational than some of the species that live in their oceans," Lyriel remarked as she again took control of the discussion. "We must be wary of ignoring our legal limitations. If we find a method that 'pushes the legal envelope' as you've said, we had best examine it thoroughly and have immutable evidence of its effectiveness. With that caveat, I'm open to new and innovative ideas."

Stagus stood up smiling. "Let's merely inform them by using their visual communication system that unless they limit their population, they will be destroyed. Llalimeno could be our spokesperson. One glace at that bald blue head would scare them into compliance."

Most of us laughed. Llalimeno, his head a brilliant blue, stood up and glared at Stagus. "I doubt my visage could instill one-quarter the fear as would one glance at your ugly pink face and scraggly white hair."

After several moments of accusations, shouts, and curses, Lyriel stood and raised her hands in a command of silence. "I believe we just demonstrated we, too, are subject to instinctive, emotional behavior at times. Let's not condemn a species that exhibits similar lack of control in a different behavioral arena. Now, I am going to demand effort. Stagus and Shremon will work together as will Farcos and Llalimeno. Go wherever you wish to work. I'll give you forty hours to come up with one or more new concepts for possible development into a solution. Push the envelope if necessary, but thoughtfully. Whatever we do, we had better gather unimpeachable reasons behind it. We will be judged by results, not effort. I will work on one of my own, so when we reassemble here there should be at least three new concepts. It's 11.0710 now, so I will expect you all back here at 12.1310. That gives you the full forty hours to leave, do as you wish about developing a solution, and return with a full report. Now, go to it."

Lyriel left no room for questions or argument. With some shuffling about and a few grumbles, the two teams arranged for their places to work and left the room. Lyriel remained on the observation deck, her favorite place on the station. For a few moments she sat in silence, staring at the huge display screen. "ULDI! Show me the current full view of Leutra."

A view of the planet from the observation camera in another part of the planet's orbit filled the display. She marveled at its beauty. A bit larger than her home, Muerr, it was bright blue with patches of tan, green, and white. Muerr had more than twice the land area and about a third of the oceans. There was much less greenery on Muerr since most of the planet was desiccated deserts. Located closer to the center of the galaxy and at the trailing edge of the next arm, Her home planet orbited a star almost identical to this one and at about the same distance away. The two planets were near twins with similar atmospheres, temperatures, and life-forms. Life on Muerr was limited to the oceans, the islands in the oceans, and the edges of the three continents where rain fell. Unlike Leutra, there were vast areas of Muerr in the continental interiors where no rain ever fell and no life existed. She knew the Leutra well from data gathered by their manned research vessels and unmanned scout craft over many years. Once the Leutra developed electronic communication, including video transmission, the bulk of their knowledge was obtained from the Leutra themselves.

She continued musing about the focus of the project. Forbidden from having direct contact of any kind once the Leutra developed written records, they became observers only. Persistent reminders of earlier contacts were part of the lore of many Leutra cultures, coming from oral records repeated through many generations. Lyriel was amused every time a Leutran reference was made to the grossly changed, but unmistakable information about those contacts. No harm had been done. Sightings of their research and scout craft was another matter. Though there were few actual sightings, the Leutra expanded those with creative imagination and outright fabrication into a discredited phenomenon. The research craft, used to examine and experiment with Leutra individuals directly, created the most problems. Their use was discontinued some twenty years earlier when it was feared the sophistication of Leutra weapons and surveillance technology might result in confirmed detection or capture of one. The much smaller, faster, and more maneuverable scout craft continued in use. Her reflections of the past completed, Lyriel set to work on another possible answer to their dilemma.

When ULDI reminded her at 0920, she had less than twenty minutes to gather her thoughts for the meeting. She expanded on an unusual idea that passed through her mind on several different earlier occasions. Pleased with the results when it was provisionally approved by ULDI's legal program, she thought. *This might work.* Usually quite punctual, the other four would begin returning about 0935.

Lyriel commanded the computer, "ULDI! Clear the display. Access none of my latest Leutra project without my voice activation." She was prepared. If any new proposal seemed superior to hers, she would not reveal her work, but support one of the others. Smiling to herself, she thought, *There are some privileges of command.*

As usual, the rumble of Stagus's voice announced his arrival before the door opened. "I still say the only thing that will work is to change their culture. Any plague or other partial annihilation will only put off the inevitable, and we're running out of time," Stagus argued as he and Shremon entered.

"Let's find out what the rest think," Shremon replied. "Your idea will not pass the legality test." A moment's delay and she took her seat, the other two entered and seated themselves without comment. Llalimeno's head was quite blue.

Lyriel rose and faced the group. "I'm sure you've transferred your work to ULDI, but let's hear verbal reports first. Shremon, from what I heard as you and Stagus entered, I take it you did not come to an agreement. What a surprise," she remarked sarcastically. "Tell us what you think."

Shremon seldom agreed with Stagus, or anyone else for that matter, including her fellow Fallon. "The Thrack has no idea how hard it would be to change their culture, even if we could find a way to skirt the legalities of such action. ULDI! Display SF22 statistics."

A table of items and related numbers appeared on the screen.

"This list of Leutra diseases includes all those the Leutra currently hold in their arsenals of biological weapons. It lists the lethal effectiveness as a percent of the total population, the probable rate of growth for outbreaks under several conditions, and the probable time before the Leutra could stop an outbreak. After selection of the best prospect, we could modify some of our supply of the selected organism and use them to reduce the population to an acceptable level. This would buy us time to find a way to cause them to regulate their own population and restore balance to the planet's life-forms. A reduction to about half a billion Leutra would be the most practical."

Lyriel commanded, "ULDI! What is the probable length of time after activation of SF22 that the Leutra would develop hyper–space capabilities?"

ULDI answered while displaying the same information at the bottom of the display. "Roughly two hundred standard years if the disease terminated scientists likely to be in that field in the same proportion as the general populace. It is more likely that particular group's termination rate would be closer to one third of that of the general populace resulting in a projection of only eighty standard years."

"That's far too short a time for us to do anything indirectly about their culture," Stagus commented, sneering. "If we create a controlled decrease in their food supply, the resulting starvation would reduce the population substantially and teach them how important it is to control their numbers. Combine that with efforts to directly change their culture, so they themselves would stabilize the population at some desired level where the balance of life-forms on the planet would be more stable and in accord with Union standards."

"Your interference in their cultures would not pass a legality test," Shremon countered.

"Let's find out how illegal it is. Stagus, ask ULDI the legality question," Lyriel requested.

Stagus was hesitant, but finally did as he was asked. "ULDI! Test the legality of ST279."

ULDI replied, "In its present form, ST279 is too vague for a legal opinion. It is necessary for you to define the level and method of changes to their cultures to obtain an opinion."

"Damned, stupid machine!" Stagus muttered. "I thought working together we could come up with an acceptable method."

"Possibly," Lyriel replied. "ULDI! How long would a major culture change, as proposed in ST279, take to be accomplished by the Leutra, given we found an acceptable method to trigger it?"

"Approximately two hundred standard years."

"ULDI! Could we reduce that to fifty standard years?" Stagus asked.

In a few minutes, ULDI replied, "No answer to that question is possible without additional data about the method and application."

"You knew that was coming," Lyriel commented. She turned to Farcos and Llalimeno. "How about you? Did you come to any consensus?"

Nodding to Llalimeno, Farcos stood up to announce their results. "We feel another genetic tweak to the Leutra would be the best solution. We could introduce a modified virus or bacteria that would reduce their numbers to an acceptable level while modifying the remaining Leutra to more tolerable levels of reproductive drive. I believe it is a hormone they call testosterone that drives their reproductive excesses. A substantial reduction in their ability to produce testosterone should have the desired effect. One beneficial side effect would be modifying their aggressive nature as well."

Stagus butted in. "That would never pass the legality test!"

Llalimeno, his head only slightly bluer than usual, sneered at Stagus, "Is the Thrack substituting his legal expertise for ULDI's? ULDI! Please provide an opinion of the legality and viability of FL229."

Farcos and Llalimeno both smiled in satisfaction as ULDI reported, "FL229 in its present form is barely legal. I would need more details to be certain. Genetic manipulation is not an exact science and never will be. The results of this procedure could result in the extinction of the Leutra."

Noting the dissatisfaction of Stagus and Shremon, Lyriel stood and addressed them all quite formally. "You heard three proposals, all of which use various methods to reduce their numbers. One proposal would use genetic modification to reduce their reproductive drive, a questionable and risky process. According to ULDI, each one has questionable legality as proposed. Now, before we discuss and vote, I would like to present a proposal of my own."

Stagus stood angrily. "Don't the articles of our charter specifically state a leader cannot make a proposal? How can we legally listen to a proposal from you?"

Lyriel smiled as she gazed patronizingly at Stagus. "ULDI! Under what circumstance is it permissible for a leader to make a proposal? Please display all references."

"Should the members of the New Life Project fail to agree upon the solution to a problem, and be hopelessly deadlocked, the leader may make a proposal. Article four, section three," ULDI spat out, displaying the reference on the screen.

Greatly chagrined, Stagus muttered a few expletives as he sat down, then remarked sarcastically, "All right, let's hear this proposal from our glorious leader."

"Thank you, Stagus," Lyriel replied, ignoring the sarcasm. "I propose we give them a history book."

There was a long silence as the four displayed baffled faces. Llalimeno spoke, "A history book? What kind of history book?"

"That's crazy! How could a book accomplish anything?" Farcos asked with a still puzzled demeanor.

Lyriel laughed. "Let me explain my proposal. In our archives are the complete records of this planet since the first promising creatures evolved. ULDI could convert those records using the languages and style of the Leutra into a book entitled *The True History of Planet Earth*. The history could be extrapolated through their extinction. We could plant it in the form of a manuscript by a famous, but deceased writer. ULDI could create such a book using the literary style of the famous author. We could then TT it to an appropriate place where it would be found and then published."

Stagus was soon back complaining. "That's ridiculous. Such a book would never produce the desired effect. The Leutra would consider it fiction, ignoring the obvious."

Llalimeno slithered to a stand, his visage a pale blue indicating satisfaction as he stabbed at Stagus verbally. "I can't understand how an individual with so little insight or imagination could become a member of this project. I imagine such a book could be a truly innovative solution. I'm certain we could devise a way to word it so it would be believed. My only question is, would it produce the desired effect?"

Lyriel had anticipated this type of question. "ULDI! Please report on the efficacy and legality of proposal LY83."

"The book proposed in LY38 is quite legal as described. Since I would be creating the book, the legality of the entire proposal would be assured. Analysis of the psychological effect and resulting action of the Leutra show a probable success of 70 to 90 percent."

Shremon stood and questioned, "How can we ensure the book's message will be taken seriously?"

"You all know about Supernova EMX356 that caused a major evacuation in nearby sector eight of the galaxy," Lyriel reported to heads nodding in agreement. "Its light will arrive here in about two years. We will place the precise location, date, and time of the explosion in the book. That, together with the many other confirmable facts, should make them patently aware of its accuracy. Then if they don't change their current course and control their population, we will terminate them and start over."

A four-hour deliberation of the details continued during which time all came to agreement except Stagus who doggedly stood his ground.

Finally, he struggled to his feet, hands held high in resignation and spoke softly, almost apologetically. "I hate to admit it, but that may be the only realistic, workable option. Let's start on it right away. Remember, the book is Lyriel's idea and should be recorded in the record books as her decision. If it works, she'll receive the credit."

Lyriel smiled triumphantly at Stagus' desperate attempt not to appear totally defeated. "And if it doesn't, I'll be blamed, right?"

A Matter of Dedication

Onas awoke to the warmth of sunlight on his face and animal noises some distance away. He was half-hanging, half-lying, and almost upside down in a tree, about twenty feet above the ground. He had no memory of how he had gotten there, but imagined it was painful. Trailing away from him up into the higher branches were several parallel lines of nanocord, and far above him in the forest canopy, the remnants of his gliderchute.

A drop of sweat formed at his chin and ran the length of his jaw toward his ear. His right cheek burned, which was not a good sign, and his right eye was half-stuck shut. His right foot was tangled in the cord, and when he exerted himself to free his leg, an intense pain shot up his back and nearly caused him to black out. It was all coming back to him: the sharp crack, his momentary panic at the collapsing wing, and then his GC folded and helicoptered him down to a soft crash into the forest. He was at least two miles from the long river sandbar he and Eyalon were supposed to land on and set up the geo-research station.

A sudden lurch downward and Onas realized the GC was beginning to slip from its hold in the branches of the canopy. He watched fascinated and unable to do anything as the branch holding the GC bent and then finally broke, dropping him the last few feet to the ground. Before he could move, the GC broke free and headed straight down at him from at least a hundred feet up. He raised his arms instinctively to ward off the blow as the broken wing caught the air and spun away from him at the last minute.

Damn! That was close! he remarked to himself as he tried to stand up. When it didn't hurt too much, he rolled over and got to his hands and knees. The GC wreckage was right in front of him and it was a shocker. The main composite member had been cut apart neatly, like with a knife. The secondary member had unexploded red primer cord wrapped around it. *Some son of a bitch tried to kill me!* He thought as he traced the primer cord to a tiny device taped to the composite brace. About three inches of the broken primer cord dangled nearby, broken away from the switch before it could be fired. That had doubtless saved his life. The device was a simple pressure switch set to fire the primer cord well below the drop height and at least half a mile above the jungle. If all the primer cord had fired, the GC would have blown apart and he would be lying dead on the ground. The loud crack was the primer cord going off and cutting the main member in half. All things considered, the gods had been kind to Onas.

He sat there for a while amidst his scattered test equipment and tried to decide who would want him dead. Mentally he replayed the last crew meeting aboard Mother, searching for clues.

84

Captain Fogarty, the flight commander in charge of everything except the research station itself, was nearing retirement, and their relationship had been jovial from the start. Kropa, the young flight engineer and second in command of the ship, was on his first deep-space assignment. Reserved and seeming a bit self-absorbed, he still didn't impress Onas as the kind to indulge in any intrigue. He was too intent on furthering his career at this point. Greg, the data manager, about fifty, was rather a geeky, reserved man. Like most people who manage and record numbers, he could be curt in conversation and strongly opinionated when on a subject he knew, and he knew numbers and data tracking. Adriana, the assistant data tracker, was not friendly with anyone. A plain and introverted woman of about thirty-five, she rarely spoke to anyone unless it was absolutely necessary. She made it plain that anything other than business in which she was involved was strictly off-limits. During the meeting, her only participation was to ask for direct authority to download and record all data from the research station once it was in place. At that meeting, everyone else had lots to say, even Greg.

Eyalon was the only one who had crossed swords with Onas. They had often been at odds since the project began. Second in command of the research station to Onas, Eyalon was overtly envious. They had several clashes over minor things in the configuration and operation of the research station. The last was an angry exchange about the division of actions and responsibilities during the two-month operation of the station on the sandbar. It ended with Onas putting his leadership stamp on the situation by telling Eyalon, "That's the way it is going to be." Eyalon stomped out of the meeting, grumbling unintelligibly. That was less than two hours before their scheduled drop. There were two more in the crew of eight, Salus, a grumpy old guy in charge of ship maintenance and Pirie, the steward, cook, and comedian of the group, also handled communications. Pirie always had something to say, usually a joke, but his cooking was definitely first-class. He didn't get on too well with Salus, but then Salus didn't get on too well with anyone.

Onas knew Eyalon had the time, the knowledge, and even the anger to rig the GC for his demise. Since neither he nor Eyalon knew which GC they would be taking until drop time, he could have rigged both GCs and easily disabled the one he was using long before the pressure switch fired the primer cord. Onas thought since Eyalon needed to retrieve his part of the equipment to set up the geo-station, he was probably searching for his body right now.

Before standing, Onas took out the emergency medical kit and applied self-sealing aid packs to his hip and his cheek. A cold crush-pack relieved his swollen right eye, but it would be a while before he would be able to see clearly. When standing didn't bring on any searing pain, he decided he was okay to gather the equipment for the geo-station and head for the sandbar.

He had been walking for half an hour when he found the unmistakable yellow and red of Eyalon's GC wing on the ground up ahead. Before he got to the wing, he had to take back his suspicions about Eyalon whose crumpled body lay on the ground still attached by nanocord to the remains of the GC. It was obvious from the wreckage that the primer cord on his GC had all fired and ripped it apart.

"Sorry for the bad things I thought about you, old man," he said quietly. "Whoever did you is still alive and aboard Mother. They also think I'm dead, and that's to our advantage. I promise to make that bastard pay."

Onas changed plans. He began setting up the research station and rain canopy on the bank of the river under the trees, not out on the sandbar. He wasn't about to let anyone on Mother learn he was still alive. He could conduct the experiments and take all the readings just as well in safety from prying eyes. Onas grinned as he mused, *The first com reports are due in two hours, before sunset. I wonder what will happen when their call goes unanswered.*

Onas began thinking about the planet and the project. Raza Three was an unusual planet. About 20 percent larger than Earth, it nonetheless had only about 80 percent of the Earth's mass and gravity. This was because it had a tiny iron core inside a huge mass of much lighter rocky material. There was no evidence of tectonic movements of the surface. It was smooth and quite level. About 90 percent of the surface was covered with a shallow ocean at most a few hundred feet deep. The land was flat as well, and because of the warm temperatures, it was very wet. Broken rain clouds moved, constantly bringing alternating rain and sunshine in irregular periods. It rained constantly at the highest elevations—about five hundred feet above sea level. The only things that sculpted the landscape were huge slow-moving rivers running from the highlands to the sea. Their flood plains were the only land not covered with a dense jungle canopy of trees. Virtually no sunlight reached the jungle floor, so it was smooth and easily traversed on foot.

Raza three rotated once every twenty-seven hours and thirteen minutes, approximately. For this reason, the program clock reset every twenty-seven hours and thirteen minutes at about midnight, Raza 3 time. This kept ground station time in sync with the planet's natural rhythm. The ship's clock remained on Earth time, so there were two reference clocks on the bridge, one for each kind of time. The planet had a huge moon about a third its size. The two rotated around a point somewhere between them but much closer to Raza three. The research project was to determine if gravitational distortion—tides in the rocks—was generating the heat that kept the planet warm. It was much warmer than their research indicated it should be, considering its atmosphere, surface conditions, and distance from the star, Raza.

Its atmosphere, twice the depth of Earth's, held a much higher percentage of carbon dioxide, 1.5%, and oxygen, 23.2%. Nitrogen, argon, and the other rarer gases were each a lower percentage of the total than Earth's. There was also a measurable portion of methane. The carbon dioxide was strong enough to make it noticeable with a slight, sharp stinging sensation when one breathed in. The surface air pressure was a bit more than Earth's at sea level. He had to know all this to properly set up the instruments. By the time for check in, Onas had everything up and running and plugged into the data storage banks. He did not connect the data relay as that would give him away.

Suddenly the speaker on the com unit barked out, "Baby one, are you there? This is Mother. Come in."

The message was repeated several times, each repeat a bit more urgent than the last. The voice on the other end was that of Pirie, the communications guy. Finally, almost pleading, he said, "You guys aren't fooling around, are you? Please respond."

"Onas? . . . Eyalon? . . . This is your captain speaking. Report back . . . now!"

Onas wished he could see their faces at the moment. The guilty party would stand out like a neon sign on a dark night. They would send someone down to find out what was going on, but that couldn't be done until morning. Onas wondered if the killer would be the one to come down. He settled down in his sleeper for the night, knowing he would be ready in the morning.

Almost hourly through the night, the com unit broke the silence with, "Baby 1, are you okay? This is Mother. Please respond." Onas couldn't shut it off as that would be a dead giveaway that someone was alive. He did turn the volume all the way down.

At eight in the morning, the message changed. "We're dropping out of orbit. We will fly by and release a rescue party to find out what's been going on. He should be on the sandbar in about two hours. Make sure your com units are on so we can find you." Onas wondered if this flight would be blown apart as were the first two. Only now, everyone would be attentive. Also, this would be a military GC, not a civilian one and launched from a secure spot on the ship. He checked his com unit, carried it back into the forest, and set it on the ground some distance away. He wondered about the rescue mission. Would the killer be on it? Surely they would bring a new pickup rig, balloon and all, to lift the nanocord to where Mother could catch it as she flew by and lift whatever was attached to the end of the cord up into her belly as she flew away.

He camouflaged the research setup with branches and leaves as best he could and waited, hidden from sight in a small hollow of an old tree stump. Mother flew slowly by, wings fully extended at about twenty thousand feet and released the GC. He followed the mottled green glider as it circled and descended to the sandbar. Who was piloting the craft but Lieutenant by-the-book Kropa himself. Well, of course. That would be his job. He tied down the GC and spoke on his com unit. It came through softly, but clearly on his unit, "I'm on the sandbar, and there is absolutely nothing here. What do I do now?"

"Start a search pattern of semicircles on the windward side of the river, you idiot, just like I explained before we dropped you." Captain Fogarty always said it like it was.

"Yes, sir!" Kropa clipped off as he turned and waded through the shallow river to the shore about two hundred yards downstream from where the setup was hidden.

After about forty minutes, his voice came on the com a bit unsteady. "I found Eyalon, sir. He's dead!"

"Dead? Where? How'd it happen?" Fogarty was obviously quite shocked, at least as shocked as one with so many years of military service can become.

"I don't know, sir! it appears he crashed into the treetops and fell to his death from there. It's a hundred-foot drop at least."

"Is there anything strange or out of place at the crash site?"

"I'm examining the wreckage right now. I'll send images . . . It is awfully broken up."

Damn! Please don't look at those broken members too closely. I thought.

"He hit the trees going fast," Kropa told him. "I can't believe how broken up the GC is."

As Onas was congratulating himself, Kropa added, "There is something strange though."

"What's that?" the captain queried.

"It's just that I can't find the research equipment, or his com unit. They are all gone."

Damn! Damn! Damn! Onas cursed under his breath.

"I know it was attached to his GC right on the main member. Wait a minute. Most of that piece was destroyed in the crash. That stuff's likely to be anywhere within a few hundred feet."

"Well, find it. Damn it, and tell me when you do."

"Yes, sir!"

Now much relieved, Onas worked his way to near where Kropa stood examining the wreckage. Setting his LK on stun, he placed his finger on his lips to indicate silence and stepped into view, leveling the weapon. Kropa froze, started to speak, and then stopped as Onas waved his weapon at his lips with the universal sign for silence.

"Turn off the mike on your com unit—carefully and moving slowly," Onas whispered.

A slight click on his unit and Onas knew he had complied. He then stepped over to Kropa and relieved him of both of his weapons, holstered his LK, and said, "Welcome to the deadly forest."

"What in hell is going on here?" Kropa asked when he felt free to speak.

"That's what I would like to know. Let me tell you what I do know."

As he led Kropa back to the setup, Onas explained most of what happened. When he finished, Kropa sat dumbfounded.

"Who in hell would want both of you dead?"

"That's precisely what I'd like to know, and I hope it isn't you. Incidentally, you'd better call in and report you found the missing equipment in working order and my dead body like Eyalon's. I don't want anyone on Mother to find out I'm alive yet. That would be too helpful to our killer. So far it seems like an accident. Only you, I, and the killer know otherwise. That should be a great help in catching him."

After Kropa's report, the captain asked him, "Do you think you could set up that station and take those readings? The instructions are all there in the computer."

"I don't know, sir." After Onas' emphatic affirmative head shaking, he added, "But I'd like to give it a try."

"Good boy!" Onas muttered softly.

"I'll give you all the help I can from here, Lieutenant. I'm sure we can pull it off and make this mission a success. I'd hate to lose two of my crew and go home with nothing for it," Captain Fogarty said before clicking off the com unit.

Kropa was at least sharp enough to understand the realities of the situation. Now they had to take and record all the readings while finding and catching a murderer who, for all, they knew, was fully capable of killing both of them, possibly by leaving them to starve to death.

At this point Onas returned the weapons to Kropa who stared at them curiously then to him, and said, "Sir?"

"Hell, Kropa, that wasn't being too risky. I shorted out the charge on both weapons before giving them to you. If you were the killer, you would try to use at least one of them and I would know."

"I could suspected that and wait for them to be recharged to use later," he remarked with a broad grin.

"Not a chance! Your eyes would betray you to this old one-time psychologist. I concentrated on them when I handed you your weapons. They would give you away instantly. Now, Let's give Eyalon a proper burial. One due a dedicated man killed doing his job."

Kropa heaved a sigh of relief as they returned from Eyalon's burial. Onas was beginning to genuinely like this young man. Something about him struck a chord.

"How about we do a little rundown on the five remaining crew? Let's rate them as possible murderers and consider motive," Onas suggested.

An hour later, they had made little progress but had the following list of facts:

1. It was not personal, but rather was directed at the project. This was quite obvious from the fact that both science officers were to be killed.

2. Captain Fogarty was placed at the bottom of the suspect list for lack of motive. The other four were equal possibilities, but nowhere was there a shred of evidence as to a motive.

3. All had roughly equal ability to obtain the primer cord, pressure gauge, and tape used on both GCs.

4. All had equal access to the staging area where the GCs were fixed to crash and kill their fliers.

5. No one of the suspects knew Onas was alive. That was their biggest asset.

"It's not much to go on, sir," Kropa said, appearing dejected.

"No, but it is a start. Now we'll try to develop a plan. We scheduled almost sixty days to finish the project and can use all that time to do that **and** find our killer."

✳   ✳   ✳

The first few weeks went without incident. When it came time to send the collected data, Onas coached Kropa. "You'll convert the data to a transmission format on your own. If I did it, I'm sure those data geeks would realize it was not the work of a junior military officer."

"How am I going to do that?"

"Tell me what you're doing and I'll tell you if it will be okay."

"It seems kinda like an inventory report. I've done lots of those."

"You'll do fine." Onas smiled as he kept to himself that he was storing all the raw data on digicards just in case. If one or both of the data geeks wanted to sabotage the project, he would still keep a backup.

✻   ✻   ✻

The end of the seventh week, Onas called Kropa over. "We're almost done here, so we'd better prepare things for pickup. It's fortunate that the balloon pickup systems on the badly damaged GCs were intact. That means we will need Mother to make three runs, each one protected against sabotage. As we decided, you'll go up on the first lift. It's definitely the safest. You'll tell them you are sending the instruments up first along with some fragile samples. Call for the pickup now."

"Won't they be suspicious when I show up in place of the equipment?" Kropa asked as he contacted Mother on the com unit.

"I'm counting on you disrupting their plans. If we sent the equipment up first I'm sure there would be a fatal failure on your lift. Make sure you note as much as you can how everyone reacts. Tell them you must make a military report to Captain Fogarty and then ask Fogarty to take you to his cabin for a private talk. You know what to tell him."

The com unit barked, "Are you ready for pickup?"

"Soon as I send the balloon up," Kropa replied. "This will be the equipment and some fragile samples, so treat them gently."

"We'll be there in about forty minutes. We're already out of orbit and flying."

"Wasn't that Greg, the data geek?" Kropa asked.

"Wonder why he's manning the com?" Onas questioned, "I thought Pirie would be doing that."

"He should be, especially during flight operations. I hope this isn't an indicator of trouble."

"Too late to worry about that now. Be sure you go to the captain as soon as you're aboard."

"What about the others while I'm talking to the captain?"

"There's not much they could do at that point. Fogarty will be conducting a wide circle to make the second pickup pass. Ask him to secure the rest of the crew in quarters so you and he can make the pickups without interruption. We don't want any of them to gain access to any part of the pickup system or loading bay until I'm aboard."

With the balloon carrying the pickup line high above him, Kropa got ready to crouch into lift position in the pickup capsule while Onas stood behind the equipment, ready to duck under the cover as Mother flew by.

As the hum of Mother's air drives picked up, she showed up above the horizon over the river. As Kropa crouched for pickup, Onas shouted, "Pray man! Pray the lift gets you to Mother."

The catcher fork extending from Mother's belly picked up the balloon line which stretched, drew tight, and then snatched the capsule containing Kropa up into the air to be retrieved by the recovery winch. Onas was pleased to see the capsule taken aboard without incident before Mother flew out of sight.

Aboard Mother, Greg and Adriana were manning the retrieval equipment. When Kropa stepped out of the capsule, both registered extreme surprise.

"I thought you were sending the equipment up first," Greg remarked. "Why the switch?"

"Last-minute change of plans," Kropa reported. "Right now I must report to Captain Fogarty. Military protocol, you know."

"This is a scientific expedition, Kropa," Greg remarked. "First order of business is the data. Where is it?"

"Coming on the next pickup."

"How can there be another pickup? You're up here!" Adriana asked in her most sarcastic tone of voice.

"I rigged the other pickup balloons to deploy as soon as the previous one is picked up. It was quite simple. Now I must report to the captain." That said, he stepped into the lift before they could complain and headed for the bridge.

Captain Fogarty was incredulous at the tale Kropa unfolded. "That Onas is both lucky and resourceful. I doubt I can confine everyone to quarters without a known emergency. In the mean time, let's start Mother into another pickup turn."

"Why were the two data processors manning the catch lift? Where is the rest of the crew?" Kropa was puzzled.

"They offered to do it, and I saw no reason not to allow it. Now it is an obviously different situation. My bet is on those two as the culprits. That Adriana will do about anything Greg orders, so he's got to be the man behind the plot. I'd like to know what it's all about. Makes no sense to me."

"Me either, but Eyalon's death was definitely murder, so it must be serious."

"We'll be lined up to recover the equipment in about ten minutes. I'll send Salus down with you to the recovery bay and try locking the others in quarters. Go!"

"Yes, sir!"

When Salus arrived at the bay, they were about two minutes out. Kropa moved one of the mobile cargo cranes against the lift door just in case.

"What the hell's that about?" Salus asked.

"We don't need any unwanted company. I'll explain after this pickup."

"Okay, Lieutenant."

"Drop the catcher now," Kropa ordered.

Salus pulled down the lever and the winch lowered the catcher.

Kropa tapped his com unit and said, "Captain, the catcher is down and locked."

Some ten minutes later, the captain said, "Got it! . . . Raise it up . . . I'll start a new circle. The third capsule should be picked up in about twenty minutes."

It took about five minutes for the winch to bring the equipment capsule aboard. As soon as it was tied down, Salus lowered the pickup cable catch for the next pass.

Once more Kropa used his com to speak to the captain. "The catcher is down and locked."

And again after ten minutes, the captain said, "Got him! Pull him aboard. Then all of you report to the bridge. We still have a serious problem to deal with."

"Roger, Captain. We'll bring him aboard in about three minutes."

Before Onas was up, the door to the lift opened, and Greg and Adriana tried to move the crane that blocked them. Somehow they managed to release the lock on the crane wheels, push the crane aside, and step into the recovery bay.

"What's going on here?" Greg asked curtly. "Why were you trying to keep us out?"

"Captain's orders!" Kropa answered lamely, positioning himself between Greg and the winch controls as the two moved between him and the lift winch. "This is now a military project and you are to return to your quarters."

Greg replied, "Not while I'm here. This is a scientific project, and in the absence of the leader and his second in command, I am in charge."

Kropa tapped his com unit on and hoped Onas could hear him. "Greg, you are no longer in charge. There's been a murder, and until that is solved, military law prevails and you are under the captain's command."

With that Adriana pulled out a Galbo blaster and leveled it at Kropa.

Greg was surprised. "Adriana! Put that away! That's a dangerous weapon."

"Shut up, Greg. This is a whole lot bigger than any of your petty little data thefts. I'm running this show and don't you forget it."

Kropa inched his hand toward his LK holster, but she could cut him in two before he could raise it, and he was quite sure she would. "What the hell are you two up to?" he asked. Behind them, the capsule holding Onas was coming aboard.

"Saving our planet," Adriana shouted. "Saving our planet from alien invasion. Our organization is dedicated to preventing any material from any alien planet from reaching Earth. My assignment was to scuttle this project by any means possible."

"What the hell are you talking about?" Greg asked as bewilderment twisted his face.

Salus grabbed for his weapon, but before he could aim it, Adriana cut him in half with a blast from her Galbo. Kropa took this opportunity to dive behind a bulkhead. The last thing he saw before he dropped to the floor was Onas stepping out of the capsule, holding his LK at the ready.

Onas stepped out of the capsule as Salus was blown apart. He was out in the open with no cover nearby. He hit both data geeks with a wide spread from his LK. That would stun them for only a moment. In the instant, he ran and dove behind the loading dock bulkhead, putting three feet of steel between he and the deadly Galbo. Finding one of the round barrel covers, he hurled it toward the opening in the bulkhead where it was vaporized by a blast from Adriana's Galbo. In that same instant, Kropa rose and knocked Adriana down with his LK. Her Galbo clattered to the floor. Before he could fire off another shot, she rolled over, grabbed the Galbo, and grabbed Greg, holding the Galbo against his neck.

"Drop your weapons and step out or I'll blast Greg," she shouted.

Onas called out, "We're not that stupid, you damned bitch. Go ahead, kill him. While you're doing that, we'll both hit you with our LKs—at full power."

After a short silence, Adriana began moving toward the door to the lift. Kropa was out of her line of sight, and Onas couldn't fire without hitting Greg. He tapped his com. "Captain! Adriana killed Salus and is using Greg as a shield so she can reach the lift. She's not inside yet. Can you do a complete lockdown—right now?"

Almost instantly the lock down siren went off, and all doors locked and the lift was immobilized. Unfortunately Adriana and Greg got inside the lift before lock down occurred. The lift doors were not blaster proof. Thinking quickly, Kropa rolled a heavy mobile cargo crane up against the lift door and locked it in place. It left enough room for a thin person to squeeze between the crane and the door frame. He positioned himself right beside the door.

Onas ran over to the other side of the lift door, took the same position there, and asked, "Captain, reverse the lock down—right now and be prepared to lock it again on my word. Now!"

As the door opened, Adriana pushed Greg out in front of her. Onas shouted "now!" grabbed Greg, and jerked him through the narrow space. Adriana burned a hole in the crane, but missed Greg then pulled back inside the lift. The door closed with her inside.

"Captain? I got Greg, and Adriana's back locked inside the lift."

Behind the crane, the door to the lift began to turn red, then yellow, then almost white. Adriana's Galbo was at work. Then the door melted away. A badly burned Adriana fell through the doorway, incinerated by the intense heat from the Galbo in such a confined space. She was dead before she hit the floor.

A few minutes later they informed the captain what happened. They heard the captain say resignedly, "Use the walkway and both of you come up here right away and tell me what in the hell is going on. I hate being totally ignorant about what's happening on my ship."

Onas replied, "Right away, Captain, but first let me say your Lieutenant is one helluva second in command. I'd recommend a promotion for this man, and I plan to put that in writing."

Kropa blushed!

Purple World

The change was as unnerving as it was subtle. Each time she looked away and back, she knew her view had somehow changed, but she couldn't figure out how. Caroloona checked her pouch. *Empty! Blast it!* With urgent need, she scanned around her. Where was Jeff when she needed him the most? Then she realized what had been changing. Her gaze rested on a dark form that moved only when she looked away. The only way she knew it had moved was that each time she looked away and then back the form was in a slightly different position against the background of purple vegetation. Still, its shape was hard to discern, and that was frightening. That it was absolutely immobile when she looked at it was quite disconcerting. Those who indoctrinated her and Jeff for this expedition had no knowledge of animal life on Koola except they suspected it had evolved from the same root as animals on Earth. That meant plant eaters and carnivores—maybe intelligent life, but no technology. Of that they seemed sure.

The deep maroon-purple of the vegetation on Koola combined with the long slender shape of the huge leaves gave forest vistas a different appearance from Earth. It also made the forest dark, in the midday light of Koola's sun. It was difficult to believe Koola's plant life had evolved from the same plants as the green ones on Earth and used the same photosynthesis. Then she remembered the oxalis hanging in the planter at her mother's. That plant was the same dark purple and had tiny white flowers. The colors of the forest flowers amazed her. White was common, but so was pale green, dark blue, dark yellow, and blood orange. Virtually every imaginable hue was present among them. Some of the flowers were huge and were suspected of being carnivorous. That dark form was no plant as it was definitely mobile and headed toward her position. *Why couldn't she ever see it move?*

Where in hell is Jeff? He'd been gone far too long and was almost an hour overdue on his com check in. She popped her com for him several times and received no response—a bad sign. Then there was her missing Galbo blaster. It had been nestled between two meal packets in her now-empty pouch. It and the food packets were missing. How could that be? She did not remember doing anything with the Galbo and the spare meal packets when she took out the food for her and Jeff to eat as they rested during their first foray into the forest.

They had secured the Gonga III, their explorer shuttle, and walked about twelve kilometers due planet north. *Could she have set them aside while they ate and forgotten to put her weapon and remaining food packets back in her pouch?* That was extremely unlikely, but possible. Her food and only weapon for protection had vanished, and she was alone on an unknown planet with an unknown creature of some sort approaching with unknown intent and purpose. She checked the autonav unit and tried to bring up where they had stopped to eat so she could backtrack to find the missing items. The autonav unit didn't seem to be working properly and would not provide the location.

A flickering pale purple light emanated from the form which she guessed was about fifteen meters from her position. An answering flicker came from far to her left where she now became aware of another form. The flickering appeared then ceased, first from the form nearby then from the other. There were subtle color changes in the flickers. She guessed these were intelligent beings communicating.

A bright purple flash exploded in her eyes, silently. She was transfixed as the light held her gaze, and she could neither shut her eyes nor turn them away. Her mind became confused as memories, pictures, and a few sounds from her past life flashed through her consciousness then vanished. After what seemed like an hour, three words started and then kept repeating in her head, *No hurt, learning*. They repeated several times, *No hurt, learning. No hurt, learning.* The words were clear enough, hesitant at first, but definite and clear by the third repeat. *Learning what?* Caroloona thought out loud. The answering words came into her head clear as a bell, *Communicate you. Learning language. Know soon.*

As suddenly as it had begun, the purple light went out. It took a moment for her eyes to adjust back to the darkness of the forest floor. As they did, Caroloona realized the two forms were standing directly in front of her. They did not appear to be threatening in any way, so she assessed them visually. Four long legs topped with a short heavy body, they were unlike any creature she had ever learned about. The body and legs reminded her a bit of a small, black, smooth-skinned giraffe. About a foot taller than she, the height difference was all in the long legs. The head and other appendages were alien. Two "arms" were mounted, one on each side of the body and resembled the legs much as our arms do our legs. The ends of the arms were different. Their "hands" were seven "tentacles" ranging in size from about ten inches to no more than three. The head was larger and more oblong than ours and topped a short, thick, flexible neck. Between the wide-set eyes was a round organ about two inches in diameter—the light emitter. Beneath the eyes and centered, were what must be nostrils, pairs of small holes surrounded by cup-shaped depressions. The mouth was a large, thin slit at the forward end of what could be called a blunt snout, much like that of a frog. There were no other openings on the snout.

There was a long silence before Caroloona blurted out in frustration, "What do you want?"

A brief flicker from the light organ from one of them and the words, *Come with us. Your friend is hurt*, came into her mind much like a recalled memory. This was going to be interesting—and a bit frightening. As they turned to lead her, she realized the two had a third member, a tiny replica of the two, no more than eighteen inches tall with short legs. The tiny one scampered ahead, leading the way. "Search and discover" had been the bywords of this expedition, and she was doing so. Unfortunately it was not on her terms, but on those of her newfound "friends."

They walked approximately planet west for more than an hour in complete silence. The silence! That's what was so different. There were no animal sounds of any kinds, nor did she see any other creatures—ever! Only the deep purple vegetation broken occasionally with bright flowers. Then she touched the trunk of one of the trees as they passed. It was soft, smooth, and wet. Her hand was purple where the wetness clung to her skin. As she stared at her hand, now itching, one of her companions pulled a yellow cloth or skin from somewhere and proceeded to wipe the purple from her hand thoroughly. A slight flicker from its light organ and the words *bad, poison,* and *do not touch* came quite clearly from her memory. It pointed to several other trees nearby with the slick, wet purple trunks like the one she had touched.

"Okay! So I'll not touch them anymore," she said out loud. *Correct!* was its immediate unspoken reply. After several of these strange conversations, she realized that only when she could see their light organ did the words come into or from her memory. Clearly their communication was coming from that organ and reaching her mind through her eyes. All she had to do to stop information transfer was to close her eyes. That they had gained access to her memory and thoughts via her eyes also became obvious.

She became aware of a soft *clicking* in her head as she walked. It was getting steadily louder as they approached a wide clearing. When she shut her eyes, the clicking stopped. One of the creatures turned toward her, its light organ flickering. *Danger ahead. Stay close to us,* popped into her thoughts. The two drew close together on either side of her, and the tiny one got in between the front legs of one of them as they approached the clearing.

The clicking stopped, and an actual whirring sound came from above in the clearing. As she glanced up, bright red flashes and streaks tore through the air at and from about half a dozen flying creatures descending toward them. It was over in a few seconds as the six bodies plummeted to the ground with resounding "thunks" and lay still. Not unlike her friends, they were the size of a large dog, but with wings in place of the *arms* and front pair of legs. The rear pair of legs ended in the same type of tentacles as the "hands" of the others. There were also three small tentacles at the end of each wing. One of the huge open mouths was amazingly similar to the mouth of terrestrial sharks. *Parallel evolution,* she thought.

Immediately into her mind came, *Carnivores. Dangerous, but not intelligent. Safe now.* She wondered if that large slit of a mouth of her friends was armed with equipment similar to the flying creatures.

As they walked past the dead creatures, rustling in the debris on the forest floor near one of the bodies caught her attention. It was a fat, snakelike creature, about a foot long and its business end was obviously trying to bite its way into the dead animal.

Scavenger, no danger. She learned. *It will grow to many times its length while eating its way through the dead.*

Name? she asked mentally.

We use no names as in your language. Evolutionary classification replaces names. Very complex. May be impossible to convert to your understanding.

"How do I call you?"

After a long pause, *Call me Blue, my friend Red, and the little one Black. Not accurate, but it should fill your need.*

It was obvious at least Blue had learned a lot about our language and was able to convey complex meanings and concepts. I still wondered what their mouth slits hid. Were they also carnivores?

Like you, we are omnivores. Told me my thoughts had been read through my open eyes. It was obvious they knew a whole lot more about me than I did about them.

We came upon a large clearing. It appeared to be several kilometers wide in each direction. In the center stood a large building seemingly made of grey stone with many large glass windows. We were quite obviously headed for the building. "What is that building?"

Hospital in your language. Your friend is there.

"How badly is he hurt?"

That's why we need you. Your anatomy is quite unfamiliar.

"How did you find him?"

He probably tried to climb one of our "trees." The "tree" didn't like it and threw him out. We "heard" the EMF disturbance and arrived in time to prevent the flying carnivores from attacking him. They would have received a nasty surprise. We believe your flesh to be toxic to all life here. Though the chemistry is similar, the subtle differences are quite major.

"So we're toxic to you guys. That's comforting."

But you would be dead before the carnivores realized that.

Small comfort, that. I thought as we entered the building through a large transparent door.

Your friend is down this way came as we headed down a short hall and into a small, brightly lit room. Jeff lay there on a soft table, a bit bloody, but still conscious.

"Jeff, where do you hurt?"

"Everywhere, damn it! These geeks weren't gentle moving me, and I'd guess I've a broken leg and arm. They wouldn't do a damned thing to help me."

"No? They brought you to this hospital and brought me here to help. I'd say they saved your life. Let's check out your arm and leg."

A cursory examination and I determined his leg and arm were bruised, but not broken. "Hell! You're sore from bruises. Nothing's broken. A little painkiller, some rest, and you'll be good as new." I gave him a couple of pills from my aid kit and dressed his small, but numerous wounds.

I massaged his arms and legs with painkilling cream for about fifteen minutes. He then seemed much better.

"There! . . . You should be feeling a bit better."

"Easy for you to say. How are we going to escape from these four-legged monstrosities and back to the shuttle craft?"

"First of all, they are not monstrosities. They are intelligent beings who are taking major risks to help us."

"How can you say that? They don't talk."

Blue's words came through to my mind loud and clear. *He has resisted all our attempts at communication. We were quite surprised when you responded so well to our efforts. It appears your "brains" are, as you say, wired quite differently from each other. He reacted quite differently from you. We didn't learn much from him.*

"Too much testosterone addles the brain, I guess. but it sure helps out in the quick decision-making process."

"Who the hell are you talking to?" Jeff commented.

"Blue here was telling me our brains are quite different."

"Blue? Who the hell is Blue, and how is he telling you about brains anyway?"

"Blue is this one right here, and he reads your mind through your eyes with light. I haven't a clue how, but he does. He also makes words and thoughts appear in my mind—almost like remembering, but different. We communicate in English!"

"That's bullshit!

"Incidentally, how is it that you are able to communicate so well with me, yet can't with him? You seem to exhibit an excellent grasp of our language."

I believe with the knowledge we gained from you, we could now reach his mind, provided he doesn't fight our efforts. Try to persuade him to relax, look at my face, and try understanding what he remembers. That's the best way I can describe it.

"Who in hell are you talking to? Your words make no sense to me."

"Stare directly at the organ in the center of his face, relax, and think what you remember."

"That's nonsense!"

"Just do it! That's an order!"

Greetings, Jeff. Your commanding officer knows what she's talking about.

"Wow! Wow!" was all Jeff could manage. "I heard or should I say, thought all those crazy thoughts before. Never realized where they were coming from."

"It will take a while to learn how, but it will become almost like talking."

"Great! We can ask them to help us go back to the shuttle so we can get the hell off this purple hell."

Caroloona turned to Blue. "Will you help us? I need to find a tool and some food I lost. It's important. Without that food, we won't last more than three days."

With that Blue retrieved several items from somewhere on his person and showed them to her. He held the Galbo and the two food packets. *You may take the food packets, but the weapon we will keep* came through clearly.

Caroloona closed her eyes and began thinking furiously. "Jeff! Don't think or question, but close your eyes and tell me when they're closed."

"Okay! They're closed."

"As long as our eyes are open, they can read our thoughts. I don't believe their hearing is well developed, so they are unable to detect our speech or read our thoughts as long as our eyes are closed."

"Wow! I'll keep them closed."

"Good! I learned that they somehow took our food packets and my Galbo back when we stopped to eat. They returned the food to me but will not return the Galbo. I'm beginning to smell a rat. It could be a security measure on their part, or it could indicate something a bit more sinister."

"Oh? What would that be?"

"I'm not sure, but I am going to open my eyes and avoid thinking about it while I inquire a bit more. Keep yours closed."

"How about using the words *shut down* whenever either of us wants to talk to the other in private? That should keep them out of our heads."

"Good idea! I'm opening my eyes." I continued talking as if none of my secretive words had been said. "Why won't you give me my weapon back?"

"Mine too!" chimed in Jeff.

*We allow no weapons other than those that evolved. In your home worlds, you developed technology outside of yourself. We **evolved** our technology.*

"Then we'll need to go back to our shuttle craft immediately." Caroloona said to Jeff.

"We'd better start right away. It will take us several hours to get there," Jeff commented.

We cannot let you leave came through clearly to both of them.

"I'm sorry, Blue, but we must get back to our food source or we'll die of starvation. Your water tests fine for us, but the local plant and animal life is definitely not compatible with our chemistry."

We cannot let you leave came through clearly once more to both of them.

"Sounds as though he's stuck in a verbal loop," Jeff remarked and then said, "Shut down."

She closed her eyes and said, "What's up?"

"I realized we each kept a deadly weapon we can use if necessary."

"What's that?"

"You still have that machete strapped to your leg, don't you?"

"Damn! I never thought of them as a weapon, but they are good ones. They must not view them as weapons either, or they'd be gone like our Galbos. I'm going to open my eyes and push them to learn what happens."

With that she opened her eyes and said, "What will you do if we try to leave?"

Her thoughts caused Blue to stand alert and soon Red was in the room with them. *Restrain you* was his answer.

"What if we fight?"

You will be restrained.

"How will you restrain us?"

With light energy from our light organs. You learned what they can do when we were attacked by those carnivores we encountered.

"In other words, we're dead! Shut down!"

She spoke quickly and emphatically to Jeff. "Since we're going to die anyway, let's do some damage. Offense is the best defense. Loosen your machete and keep it ready for use. Do you still have your UV-block sun visor?"

"I sure do."

"Then put it on now. Then when I say go, you take the one on the right closest to you and I'll take old Blue. I'd go for a chop right through that light organ. Hit its head with all your strength. Then let's head out the same way we came in. I managed to keep my com unit, and with that, we should be able to find our way back to old Gonga baby. Hopefully, they haven't set a guard around it. No need with both of us in custody."

She found her UV visor and put it on. "Is your visor on?"

"Check!"

"Ready, go!"

The attack caught the two off guard. It was like there was no bone in their heads, necks, or upper bodies, and they were split in two down to where their arms attached. They dropped like stones. She and Jeff bolted for the doorway, ran down the short hallway and out the entrance. They hadn't seen another Koolan anywhere.

"That was way too easy! Something's not as we think it is," Jeff muttered as he ran.

"I hope you're wrong!" Caroloona replied. "My com unit shows Gonga to be about five kilometers that way." She pointed across the clearing to a spot at the edge of the forest.

As they entered the forest, she warned, "Don't touch any of those trees with the slick, wet trunks, they're deadly. Most of them seem to be near the clearing."

"Gotcha, boss!"

They ran until they were exhausted. "My com unit says one more kilometer. We should be blasting off this purple pit in less than an hour. Thankfully, the higher percentage of oxygen in Koola's atmosphere makes catching our breath a short experience. Let's take a five-minute rest and approach Gonga from downwind. I sense trouble when we are there."

Jeff started to lean against a tree and realized it was one of the wet poison ones. "Wow! That was close." He said as he moved away. A familiar whirring sound came from above.

"Nasty big carnivores coming. Use your machete!" she screamed. Again, their large knives sliced through the nasty critters like a hot knife through butter. In five minutes, it was all over. Five mutilated bodies lay on the ground, and the rest had retreated out of sight and sound.

"Well, how's that for a nice rest? Let's head for the shuttle before we run into any more trouble."

In about half an hour, they were in the clearing where the shuttle craft, Gonga III, awaited them. Unfortunately it appeared that a small forest of young poison trees had grown up around it.

"How in hell are we gonna pass through that?" Caroloona commented. "Those poison trees aren't there by accident. Our friends probably planted them shortly after we arrived."

"Machete time," Jeff joked.

"Be careful not to let any of those branches touch us as they fall."

"Our hazard protection gear is in Gonga, but I happened to stash the gloves in my pouch," he said, reaching for them and then displaying them gleefully. "These should protect me, so I'll chop at 'em. You stand back just in case."

After a few minutes of cutting the two-meter tall trees so they wouldn't strike him when they fell, it became apparent it would take hours to cut a path to Gonga.

"I wonder if these suckers will burn."

That said, Jeff took out an igniter pack, crushed it to start the reaction, and threw it into the pile of trees he had cut down. The flames grew so quickly it surprised them both.

"That slick material on the trees must be an organic oil of some sort. Those trees burn like they were doused in kerosene."

The conflagration grew rapidly, and they both drew back, driven away by the intense heat of the fire.

"Great idea, Jeff. I only hope Gonga doesn't become so hot we can't touch the hatch to open it."

It took two hours for the fire to burn out and the hatch door to cool so they could enter Gonga. Once inside they ran the prep sequence for takeoff, and in another ten minutes, Gonga was heading back to Big Mom. Their ship, affectionately called Big Mom, had been orbiting Koola since they left in the shuttle to explore. It would take them at least three hours to rendezvous, so they settled back for a well-earned rest. As they did so, Jeff switched on the spec display to check fuel and rendezvous time.

"Uh-oh!" he exclaimed as he viewed the spec report. "The ship shows 120 kilograms more weight on board than should be aboard. Where the hell is all that mass?"

"Could it be something stuck to the hull?" Caroloona wondered aloud.

"How could this be. I didn't find anything when I did the preflight."

"We'd better check the cargo compartment."

A short weightless traverse to the cargo door, and she grasped the handle. "The damned handle is stuck."

"Try the electronic release."

"Nothing!"

"Let's check with the cargo camera."

As the display came on, they were greeted with the sight of one of the Koolans like Blue grasping the inside of the hatch with its hands, and with its four feet planted securely against the surrounding bulkhead.

"We have an unwelcome stowaway. We don't want him aboard Big Mom. How are we going to handle that?"

"Well, we must figure that out in just three hours."

About an hour into the flight, Jeff asked, "All cargo hatches can be opened from inside, but couldn't we weld that one shut from outside? Then we could leave him in there, and let the experts deal with him when we are back to Earth."

"I don't see why not. Of course, we'll drop the shuttle at the decon base on the moon, but that's no problem."

"There's a welder among the repair tools in the tool compartment. It's a small one, but it might do the job."

"Do you suppose he'd live through the trip? I wonder if he brought any food?"

"Well, if he didn't, he may be reduced to a pile of goo when we arrive."

Some things didn't add up to Caroloona, and the more she thought about it, the more it troubled her. *Why had our escape been so easy? it seemed the Koolans wanted us to escape, but why? And why would one of them stow away on the shuttle since that meant almost certain death?*

She shared her concerns with Jeff. "I think we should send the shuttle back down to Koola as soon as we are picked up by Big Mom. Then our worries about contamination will be gone."

"Old Pam will be mighty pissed if we do. That's a valuable piece of equipment to toss away."

"Yes, but that's the only sure way we can prevent contamination of any kind."

"How long would it take to send a permission message through on the Q-com?"

"I don't think we have enough time. At this distance, it would take about a week for a two-way response—three days for the questions and three more for the answer, if we get one."

"Why don't we weld the door and decide what to do about our passenger when we reach home? We could always dump the shuttle into a sun trajectory before we set down."

"That'll work. See if you can get that door welded before we rendezvous with Big Mom."

"You de boss!" Jeff said with a grin as he headed for the tool locker.

They outlined the situation to mission head, Pam, when they arrived in Earth orbit about two months later. Her decision? Drop the shuttle at the moon decon base. They could wait there until the decontamination squad did their job and then come home with the shuttle only slightly damaged. Pam was a stickler for not wasting anything that cost money. The decon squad took a full week to do their job.

"She's all yours. Clean as a whistle," Mac, the head of the decon squad, reported. "We found no sign of the critter you said was in there. All we found was about 120 kilograms of dark sand spread all over the cargo compartment."

"Sand? What kind of sand?" Caroloona asked.

"Our guys stuck it all in a sealed decon isolation pack. We should receive a complete analysis for you in a day or so."

"I'd be careful of that stuff," Caroloona warned. "Koola was a weird place with some strange life-forms. Are you sure you got every grain of that sand?"

"Every single one! We removed everything but the paint on the storage shelves. Standard decon procedures."

"Paint? What paint?"

"Just the standard paint used on most storage racks. It's a thick plastic coating, hard and tough and contamination proof."

"I hope you got everything. Be sure to tell me as soon as you analyze that sand."

"The weight of the empty shuttle matches its exact tare weight to a hundredth of a kilogram, so we got everything. We are thorough."

By the time Big Mom took them home, they had been gone for almost two years. There were lots of records to go through, so they stayed in Big Mom for eight more days while all the samples went through standard cataloging and storage procedures. Funny thing about that sand. Decon reported it analyzed as organics with some unusual silicon compounds. The day before they were to head for home, the two researchers went into Gonga III to pick up the hard copy of the trip log and check for anything they left behind. Caroloona was in the cargo compartment when she realized something was wrong.

"Jeff! Call security in here instantly!" she shouted over the com unit.

"What's wrong?' he asked as he rushed into the compartment."

"Did you call security?"

"On their way! What's cooking?"

"Look around? Is anything wrong?"

Jeff looked all around and shook his head. "I don't see any problem."

"The shelves."

"Clean metal shelves are all."

"Where's the paint? That heavy plastic paint. I thought it strange when decon mentioned it."

"Damn!"

"Damn is an understatement. We've been invaded."

Epilog

For ten years, there was no sign of any Koolan life. Security decided it probably perished in an environment that was chemically hostile. Then reports began coming in about strange purple flashes in the night. It took ten more years for expanding Koolan life to reproduce enough from the "seed" that had been the "paint" on the shuttle shelves to come out of hiding. The effects of Koolan micro biota were devastating to virtually all Earth life. In another decade larger, Koolan life-forms took control of the Earth. While the Koolan life-forms were poisonous to Earth life, they easily digested Earth life as nourishment. In another three years, purple vegetation had largely replaced green as the alien life overwhelmed the native green plants. Evolution trumped technology. About fifty more years and all Earth life had been eradicated in the now-purple world.

The Hygienist

I later found out her name was Barbara LeFang. I met her last week in—well, you know—one of those bars. Business had been profitable, and I wanted to celebrate. Honestly, I had only had a couple of drinks when she walked by my table. Little did I know she would drastically alter my life when she sat down at the bar near me.

Most of the women in this remote outpost on Apodia 5 were missing a tooth or two from fights in bars like this one. I oughta know, I'm the only dentist in this section of the galaxy, and I've seen some horrible mouths—especially on women. Why women get into so many bar fights here is a mystery, but they do, at least ten times as many as men, according to the stats. The news junkies here are big on stats. Go figure!

And yes, I was celebrating. Lately I'd had a run of major rebuilds on mouths busted up in local bar fights, and my cash box was overflowing. Yes, cash! Mostly hard cash at that. No CCs or DCs here, no credit or credits of any kind and no checks or IOUs. Paper money, registered Centars, are discounted by at least 50 percent. Coin of the realm, gold, platinum, or diamonds for major purchases is the rule. Sure, it's a bit archaic, but this far from civilization, no one trusts anyone. Everyone carries a Waxtal analyzer to check on coin quality and value, a small price to pay to prevent being cheated.

My little sign, "Dentist, Reasonable Fees," sat on the table in front of me. It was about the best way I had found to advertise my services. After she eyed my sign, she took her fresh drink from the bar and ambled over to my table. Barbara was different. Her revealing blouse competed for my focus with her perfectly formed face framed with lots of tousled black hair in that just-hopped-out-of-bed style. Her pearly whites were neat and straight.

"May I join you?"

"Of course. Any particular reason?"

"I read your sign and thought you might be interested in what I do."

"Yea? What's that?"

"Let's say I'm a dental hygienist searching for a dentist to hire me."

"A dental hygienist? Lady, most of my clients are lucky to have teeth, especially the females. About all I do is rebuild busted mouths. My operating room hasn't seen a prophy in fifteen years."

"I'm a special kind of dental hygienist. Do preventive care, you might say. I can help your *clients* keep their teeth, bright and straight in the first place."

"If my clients don't lose their teeth, I'm out of business. Right off the top, I don't like your preventive care."

"How much do you think you could charge if you promised—no, guaranteed—their teeth would be perfect permanently, and you would never need to rebuild their mouth again?"

"Aw, c'mon. No one would believe that."

"Even if we could prove it to them . . . convincingly?"

"How in hell could you do that?"

"Easily! I can do it right away if you're game."

"Lady, I can't figure what kind of con you're trying to pull, but I'm not buying."

"Even if I took one of your patients and made their smile beautiful and indestructible?"

By this time I was getting tired of her little game, yet I was still curious. "What's it gonna cost me?"

"You provide me with your worst patient in your office, and I will do a single demo for absolutely nothing. Free!"

"If I fall for it . . . and if it actually works?"

"I want 50 percent of all your fees my services provide."

I couldn't believe I was going to let her work on one of my patients. "Okay! I'll let you do a demonstration, and if I like it, it's a deal."

"How soon can we start?"

"How about tomorrow morning at nine? I have a patient in mind, Lowiece Grenby. She has already had three rebuilds and needs a fourth scheduled for that time. She only has about five real teeth in her mouth. The rest are all bridges and crowns, a shaky situation."

"I'll be at your office at seven as it will take me some time to set up my equipment. Is that okay?"

"No problem!"

I'm not a bad looking guy, but when I propositioned her she laughed. It didn't take long for me to find out she liked sex, but with the same gender I did so it was back to the dental business. As soon as we agreed, she left. I was wondering what kind of scam I had gotten myself into. I had to find out. Curiosity killed more than cats.

Next morning at seven, she was at my office with a small truck and a large black piece of equipment that seemed ominous. It took us fifteen minutes to muscle it into the building and into my spare treatment room.

"What do we do now? Where's the power cord?"

"It has its own power supply. Doesn't need a cord."

"Okay! How do we work this thing?"

"We don't! . . . I do!"

"Okay! So how do you work it?"

When she opened the front bottom-hinged panel, a chair appeared. There was also a gadget that resembled a space helmet with a large cable attached to the rear of the device. The cable led to a box under the chair.

"Now! All we need is your patient."

"I figure the helmet thing goes over the patient's head, but what's inside?"

She picked it up, turned it over, and pulled out what appeared to be like one of those form-fitting mouth guards attached to the back of the helmet with another stout cable. She smiled as she told me, "This is the business end of my system. The patient places it in their mouth and holds it firmly. I place the helmet over their head, fasten the straps, and turn it on. In about half an hour, they ir mouth contains a nice new set of indestructible teeth."

"That's all there is to it? You've got to be kidding."

"That's it! . . . Job over . . . I receive payment. Once this demo is finished, and I use my machine . . . I receive payment. Every time."

"How do I know it will work?"

"Simple! . . . Try to damage or remove one of her new teeth."

"Ha! One crunch with my forceps, and your job will be wrecked."

"Ha yourself. More likely your forceps will be wrecked."

"We'll find out soon enough. Ms. Grenby should be here shortly."

I introduced Barbara to Ms. Grenby as my new *hygienist.* Lowiece's answering smile showed that about half of her teeth were missing. When we ushered her into the room, she stared a bit apprehensively at the strange chair we asked her to occupy.

"Don't worry! It's a new technique I'm sure you will like . . . a lot!" I assured her.

Barbara explained, "Here! Put this piece in your mouth and bite down hard. It will reshape to fit your mouth and existing teeth. and don't worry! This will not hurt a bit . . . Really!"

"Go ahead, Lowiece! It's okay!"

Once she bit down on the mouth piece, she relaxed. She did not move or utter a sound as Barbara placed the helmet over her head and fastened the straps. She sat motionless and uncomplaining, without exhibiting her usual stream of nonstop questions and idle chatter.

"The system uses a powerful tranquilizing system," Barbara explained as she stepped back. "Now, let's leave the room. Consider that as an X-ray machine and stay away from it as it does its job."

"What about Lowiece? Isn't it dangerous to her?"

"Like X-rays, emanations from the machine are perfectly harmless at low doses, but can accumulate and do considerable damage during repeated and long-term exposure."

"That I can understand, but what kind of emanations?"

"If you were a particle physicist, it would still be difficult to explain it to you. Let's say it's doing some serious quantum gyrations and leave it at that. It's called quantum repolarization."

With that, I began to worry a bit. What in hell was I putting my patient through?

"You're sure, absolutely sure, that this will not harm Ms. Grenby?"

"Not in the least. In fact, she will feel better than she has in her entire life."

"I'm still quite skeptical."

"In about half an hour, you will be both surprised and reassured. Why don't we just sit back and relax 'til it's over? Just remember our bargain."

The emphasis she placed on those last words concerned me a bit. In fact, I was getting more nervous as each minute ticked by. By the time the treatment was over I was almost a basket case.

As Barbara headed for the patient, she grinned broadly and remarked "Bargain time!" as she pressed the remote control and turned the machine off.

Lowiece began to move in the chair as Barbara lifted the helmet off. She was bright eyed and animated as the cable was unplugged from the mouthpiece.

Barbara explained, "The mouthpiece has formed closely around her teeth as you can tell. I will peel it off, and you will find a new and indestructible set of teeth."

I was amazed as was Lowiece when she looked in the mirror. "I can't believe it!" she exclaimed with a broad smile. "My teeth were never so beautiful!"

I shared several minutes of disbelief with Ms. Granby before I checked her mouth. It was flawless.

"Now for the acid test," Barbara said, smiling as she led us into the other treatment room and motioned for Lowiece to sit in the chair. "Dr. Dunning will demonstrate the indestructibility of your teeth."

"What do you want me to do?"

"Forceps, you idiot. Try to pull one of her teeth."

"I couldn't do that."

"You will, or I will. Take your pick. I said this was a demo, so try to prove me wrong."

Reluctantly I took out a set of forceps and proceeded to try to remove an upper central. I was gentle at first, but when Lowiece said she was feeling no pain, I tried harder and harder. I did literally thousands of extractions, and when I braced my other arm against her forehead and wrenched with all my might, not only did it not budge, but Lowiece said it didn't hurt a bit.

"Now, do you believe me?" Barbara said with a smile. "Let me show you something."

With that she took the forceps from my hand and belted Lowiece directly in the mouth with all the force in her considerably strong arms. Other than her head snapping back a bit from the blow, and Barbara's hand holding the forceps bouncing back like a rubber ball, it was as if nothing happened. No blood! No broken teeth! No pain! This was far more than I had bargained for. Lowiece was delighted as she began realizing what this meant.

"Wow! Doc, your new machine is a marvel. I can't wait to tell everyone of my friends. My enemies will find out about it soon enough."

"Now, Lowiece, don't be too hasty," I said, sounding like an old-school teacher.

"It will take some time for you to become used to your new mouth, so be cautious," Barbara warned.

Several days later and after we had *repolarized* numerous other patients, we learned that Lowiece had nearly killed a woman in a bar fight when the woman hit her in the mouth with a beer bottle. The news announcer expressed amazement at her lack of injury from the bottle and the fight that ensued. When interviewed, Lowiece gave me a plug.

With that publicity, my practice grew by leaps and bounds. Although I raised my fees to triple what I had been charging, my office was overwhelmed with new patients. or should I say Barbara was overwhelmed. All I had to do was rake in the loot. When a patient asked her last name, I realized I had never done so. I was not surprised by LeFang, the big tooth, as she made it big in the tooth business.

Six months later, most of the personnel at the outpost on Apodia 5, about nine hundred individuals, had been made indestructible. Oh yes, once treated, their entire bodies became indestructible, not just their mouths. I, of course, was among those treated. Barbara finally admitted to me that her machine not only regenerated mouth and tooth tissue, nerves, dentin, enamel, and all. It also changed the atomic structure of each atom in the body. *Quantum repolarization,* she called it. Roughly the energy expended in a blow is reversed or *bounced* back into the matter of the striking object. That's about all I could fathom, but the result is obvious—indestructibility.

Then the ship arrived. It was a small ship, with room for no more than a few hundred individuals and a crew of five. When they disembarked, we received a shock. The five armed crew members reported to Barbara, saluted (at least that's what it seemed) and proceeded with her to Outpost Commander Quelter's quarters. We were all escorted by the armed crew to the

Commander's quarters for an announcement. The announcement was made by Commander Quelter, who was obviously under duress.

"To every member of Apodia 5. All but a few of us are *repolarized*. The rest will soon be given the same treatment. I have been informed that in spite of what it may seem, we are not indestructible. I repeat, we are not indestructible. The weapon each of the crew of the ship *Freedom* holds will instantly depolarize anyone struck by its Q-ray. The repaired parts of our bodies will remain, but they will no longer be indestructible. We are all to be trained as an armed force that will, according to the crew, begin systematically conquering the entire galaxy. Those who are willing to join this force will be accepted as comrades. Those who do not will be eliminated. Do I make myself clear?"

Commander Quelter was visibly shaken as he spoke. The resounding yes throughout the compound was obviously driven by fear, not enthusiasm.

"Great!" Quelter continued. "About half of us will board *Freedom* in ten hours. The rest will remain here for the second ship which will arrive a few days after the first one leaves. Don't take anything with you as everything needed will be provided aboard ship. Now, those of you who are notified to be in the first group, do what you will, but be at the ship at 0200 sharp. We intend to leave at 0300 on the dot. See you aboard."

It took me almost an hour, but I managed to talk to Barbara.

"Can you tell me what this is all about?"

"Well, I suppose since you were so helpful, I'll give you a special job. You can repolarize the remaining members of the outpost. That means you'll be on the second ship."

"But why? What's it all about, conquering the entire galaxy?"

"Doc, don't concern yourself about it. Being indestructible, I doubt we'll run into much real combat. It should be a piece of cake."

"But your guys have those depolarizing weapons. Suppose some others do as well?"

"Impossible! I've got to go. Conquests to plan and all that rot. You understand."

"I guess," was all I got out before she turned and hurried off toward the commander's building.

By the time I had finished *depolarizing* the rest of our little army—these were for free—it was a half hour before *Freedom* was to lift off. I walked around my office and gazed longingly one final time at the store of precious metals in my safe. *I could have lived like a king*, passed through my wistful mind. *Oh well, easy come, easy go.* I locked my safe—yea, stupid, useless effort that it was—and stepped out my door for the last time to head for the launch pad where I was to board the second ship with the remainder of our group. As I walked down the deserted street, a shadow fell over me. It was far too early for the second ship, and the first one wasn't to leave for at least fifteen minutes, but that shadow was definitely caused by something big—something very big.

One blinding, silent red flash then another, and I stumbled to the ground. My knee started bleeding. For me at least, physical normalcy had returned.

✱   ✱   ✱

It was about six months later, and I was entertaining friends at that same bar—I was the new owner, all that gold and platinum. We were discussing how wrong Barbara had been about the invincibility of depolarization. It seems the commander of the federation starship was an old girlfriend Barbara had dumped. Hell hath no fury, remember? The crew of the federation starship turned us all back to normal, destroyed the *repolarization* machine, and hauled Barbara and her buddies off to the hoosegow—all without a single fatality. I defended my being the only one to profit from the venture by reminding them that the whole incident had put Apodia 5 on the galactic map. The resulting inundation of tourists meant huge profits for the locals. We even got a federation bank and useable credit cards. The bar fights between women ceased, and the new dentist—I sold him my practice—wasn't making out so well. Civilization had tamed Apodia 5.

There went the neighborhood.

A Repair Mission

33.64.21.0600 (Stardate/time)

Captain Woolgah headed his starship, the Gelwah, away from the Vega sector at maximum welt. A sudden peace following millennia of constant warfare with the Scentar caused Captain Woolgah to struggle with his new peacetime role. The peace treaty between the Segwah and the Scentar had held for eight years after millennia of bitter and deadly fighting. Negotiated cleverly by his human friend Draxel Syl, the peace was extremely beneficial for all parties.

33.64.23.0600 - Two days at max welt speed behind them, first officer Jemrah reported, "Sir, there is a Scentar ship following us. It left from near the Vega system about twelve hours after we left. At first they were vectored substantially away from our path, but recently they shifted heading and are now on an intercept course."

"Did you identify the ship?"

"No sir, they are running without a transponder or ID code. According to their Iway pattern, their ship is a Delfro class warship."

"Their ship might be faster, but the Gelwah could easily out maneuver it in virtually any combat situation. I wonder why they are chasing us? I'd like to talk to them as soon as they are within hailing distance. Set navigation control for course change of one hundred-twenty degree Y, forty degree Z, and 0 degree X. Then be prepared to execute."

"Yes sir!"

A few moments later Jemrah said, "I estimate hailing and active combat contact in about three hours."

"Hail them as soon as they are within range and be prepared to make that course change on my command. I don't want to give them much of a chance to fire on us just in case."

33.64.23.0900 - "Hailing, Captain."

A minute later the Captain said, "They don't want to answer our hail. Change course—now!"

"Done Captain."

A few minutes after the course change Jemrah remarked, "Our move surprised them. I estimate it will take them thirty to forty hours to be back within combat range."

"Thank you, Jemrah. We will continue on course. That will take us to eighty degrees Y, sixty degrees Z, and ninety degrees X. Then in fifteen minutes, reverse the procedure minus five degrees in each plane."

33.64.24.1500 - Jemrah reports. "Sir, the Scentar ship will be coming within combat distance in about fifteen minutes."

"This time, on my command, repeat the last maneuver with a plus five degree correction instead of minus five. Then, in five minutes, put us back on our original course."

"May I ask why the same maneuver we did the last time?"

"That's because they won't expect it. They will be set up for the opposite maneuver and overrun our position by several hours. By the time they figure out where we've gone we will again be at least thirty hours beyond them."

"Do you want me to try hailing them when they come close enough?"

"Not this time. They didn't respond last time so let's find out if they will hail us if we remain silent."

"Yes Captain. Uh, May I speak freely sir?"

"Certainly! What's on your mind my friend?"

"I've been considering our situation—this critical mission to try to stabilize a growing tear in the space time continuum. This tear was started by crude gravity wave experiments conducted by humans."

"Yes, Jemrah, what are you getting at?"

"The Segwah technology in the form of our new gravity-based defensive energy shield may be the only system available that can repair that tear and stop its propagation, correct?"

"Damn! Jemrah. That is an unproven theory. The Scentar, with their understanding of inter dimensional rifts, admit they are guessing, albeit intelligently. They do know if that rift continues to propagate at an accelerating rate the Scentar universe and the human universe will eventually fold into each other through the rift and be annihilated. Our mission is to try to repair the rift and stop any possible collapse."

"I realize that, Captain, but such being true, it escapes my understanding why a Scentar ship would follow us in such a threatening manner."

"Mine as well, Jemrah, but so far they are only a nuisance. The times they were within combat range they did not fire anything, and they could. We must make certain they do not come within combat range again until we've placed and engaged the shield."

"If they are desperate enough they might portal to where the rift is and wait for us there in spite of the risk. They must know as we do that using a portal near the rift could trigger the same gravitational collapse we are trying to prevent."

"Surely they're not that stupid. Should that happen we would all be annihilated. I wish I knew what their game was."

Jemrah, first officer of the starship Gelwah ex-captain of the starship Remlah had been demoted when he made a foolish move in a fleet battle with Scentar starships almost twenty years ago. His ship, the Remlah was destroyed, he lost half of his crew, and he was disgraced. Captain Grala Woolgah took him on as first officer, the position he held earlier. Since that time, Jemrah distinguished himself in a fierce battle with renegade Segwah on the Scentar base on Vega Five. At great personal risk, he had attacked a large group of renegade warriors trying to assassinate two humans and restart the war between the Scentar and Segwah. For this action, he was awarded the highest military honor, the order of Cheemah, reinstated in the military, and offered a new ship as captain. He refused the commission and chose to stay as Captain Woolgah's first officer.

33.64.24.1515 - "Captain! The maneuver is complete. The Scentar ship is far off our course. It will take them at least 30 hours to catch us."

"Thank you, Jemrah. One more course change to lose them again, and we will almost be there. We should be in position to deploy the shield in about forty-two hours."

"Sir! I hope my gravity shield theory is correct, and the shield stops the rift when we operate it? My original idea was based on my understanding of standing gravity waves used to generate and maintain the shield. That seemed logical to me. My gravity wave expertise is self acquired."

"Jemrah, you know much more about that than anyone else here. All I know is that the Scentar scientists confirmed your basic idea. They think that it will reverse the tear if we operate the shield at the end of the tear where it is coming apart. They told me the tear had much in common with unzipping a zipper, and that use of the shield would be like zipping it back up. That is, of course, a loose example. Unfortunately, if it doesn't work or if we miss the targeted area, the Gelwah with us in it will not survive."

"Then we had better not miss."

Captain Woolgah smiled. "That, my good friend, is imperative. Now let's check the shield generators to make sure they will be fully functional when we need them."

33.64.25.2209 - Jemrah shouted, "Captain! The Scentar ship is within half an hour of reaching active combat contact. but that's impossible with rational action."

"They used their portal. That's the only way they could reach their present position so quickly."

"We're lucky that didn't trigger the collapse."

"They must be in maximum welt drive. An instant before they reach combat range, reverse course, and they will blast right past us. When they do, reset course for the end of the rift. That should give us the ten hours we need to reach the end of the rift using welt drive. Once we operate the shield they won't be able to touch us."

"Yes Captain! Course changes entered as ordered."

As the Scentar ship reached combat range, Jemrah executed the changes, and the ship flew past them as expected.

33.64.26.0802 - Captain Woolgah from the bridge. "Jemrah! Cut the engines, and prepare to engage the shield generators in seven minutes. At that time we will be at the optimum point to engage the shield around the rift."

"Yes sir!"and a few seconds later, "Captain, the Scentar ship is directly in our path. Four minutes to impact."

Suddenly the com system lit up with incoming on screen. "Captain Woolgah, this is Captain Raoul Saras of the Scentar starship Intreba. You are ordered to stand down. Abort the mission. I repeat. Abort the mission."

"And on whose authority do I abort this mission?" As he spoke he signaled Officer Jemrah to be ready to activate the shield control.

"On my authority, and because we are ready with massive disrupters powered and trained on your ship. If you do not do so we will obliterate you."

"Give me two minutes to shut down the deployment series. It will take that long."

"Granted. but not a second longer, Captain."

With that Captain Woolgah shut down the com unit and issued rapid fire orders to Jemrah. "Set sensors to activate the shield generator the instant they fire anything, not before. Set the envelope to include the Gelwah, no more. The shield should not only stop anything they fire at us, but should brush their ship aside like a toy when we impact them. They've never faced our shield before and don't realize what it can do. Any kind of energy poured into the shield is absorbed by the shield and strengthens it. When we hit them, they will bounce off the shield like a rubber ball. I doubt anyone on their ship will survive."

"Yes sir!" Jemrah said with a smile. "What about the rift?"

"As soon as we clear their ship, shut down the shield and reset it to the original pattern. We should be in contact with the rift in less than five minutes."

"They're firing sir." Jemrah announced as the sensors activated the shield.

The screens went black, No impact was felt, and there was no sound for two minutes.

Then Jemrah reported, "The shield is off and reset as you requested, sir. We are fifty seconds from optimum position."

"Fine work, Jemrah. I see no sign of the Scentar ship. I wonder what happened to it?"

"Prepare for shield activation, Captain." Jemrah said as he brought the coasting ship to a halt with a retro burst and in line with the end of the rift.

Once more the screens went black as Jemrah activated the shields. "Now what do we do, Captain?" Jemrah said as he looked at the Captain with a big grin on his face.

"We park here for fifty hours and hope it works. Our fuel supply is enough to power the shield for at least seventy more hours, but you estimate fifty will definitely do the job." Captain Woolgah said, grinning. "I don't know about you my friend, but I am going to take this opportunity to catch up on my sleep. I suggest you do the same. We've earned our rest, and we can't go anywhere or do anything anyway."

33.64.28.1009 - Captain Woolgah and First Officer Jemrah finished their two hour workout on the exercise machine and stepped off the platform. Then they showered, dressed, and walked together toward the bridge.

"Jemrah! It's about time. If the shield hasn't done its job by now it never will. Let's power it down and visit where and when we are."

"When? Captain?"

"Yes, my friend, when. We are dealing with unknowns here, unknowns based on sketchy theories of a bunch of scientists who deal with gravity and gravitational rifts using their expertise and super computer simulations. We're the ones who risk life and limb to test those theories in reality. I'm betting we will be in for a few surprises when we drop the shield."

"Is that why you insisted the entire crew stay behind?"

"No need to risk lives unnecessarily. You and I are enough crew to handle this mission. I thank you for volunteering."

"Every man aboard ship volunteered. They are quite loyal. Thank you for choosing me. It is a great honor."

"The honor is mine to have such a man as yourself by my side."

"Thank you sir."

"Here we are. Let's see what happened. Shut down the shield."

"Yes sir!"

In seconds the shield was gone. All they could see in the display was blackness. Not a single light, star, galaxy or other visible object could be seen.

"Well, Jemrah, where could we be? Activate the position search system."

Several tense moments of waiting and the system reported "location unavailable."

"Captain. I don't like the sound of that."

"I don't either. Prepare the basic portal for transport to a known position in the human universe. That is where we were."

"Yes sir!" A few minutes at his console and Jemrah reported, "Ready sir."

"Execute."

The blue glow gradually engulfed the bridge then died away. It was not a good sign.

"Well, Jemrah, the portal couldn't find the destination coordinates. At least we are fairly sure we are not in the human universe. Let's try our own. Set a search for home base."

After a few minutes Jemrah reported, "Ready sir."

"Do it!"

The blue glow grew bright in the viewer and then died away.

"That leaves only the Scentar universe. I hope this is it."

Once more the blue glow intensified then died away.

"Damn it, Jemrah, we seem to be outside of any known universe. We may need to use the universe portal, and I don't want to use the power that will require. Check our power reserves."

A few moments at the console and Jemrah reported. "Welt drive power is down only 20 percent, sir, steady at 60 percent. We used much less than we thought we would to generate the shield. Portal power is maximum since we didn't use the portals. System power is only 22 percent. Weapon power was never used and is at max."

"That's good news. Check the transfer conduits to make sure we can transfer power if necessary."

"Yes sir."

It took Jemrah no more than ten minutes to set up the tests, execute them and report. "All tests are positive, sir."

"Good. Let's run a forward impact weapons fire test on visual with trajectory analysis."

"Sir? The purpose?"

"It's a strange request, but I want to check out one of my suspicions. Fire as soon as you can."

Within seconds Jemrah fired the forward impact guns with tracer rounds. The tracers did not go straight, but curved sharply up and to port, and went out of sight.

Captain Woolgah barked an order. "Set courses for a 90.30.150 turns and give me full Welt drive as quickly as possible. We're in the grip of a massive gravitational force and quite close to its event horizon."

There was a sizable jolt of the ship as the welt engines powered up. This was followed by surging vibrations. The ship groaned and creaked as if it were being twisted and stressed physically. He watched the display for any sign of light.

"Repeat the forward weapons test, now!"

This time the tracers made a much wider curve directly upward.

"Change course minus 45.00.00 and maintain full welt."

"Yes sir! - - - Done!"

"Repeat the weapons test."

"Done."

This time the tracers went straight ahead with no curvature until they burned out.

"Thank you, Captain. That was close. We were about to fall into some kind of event horizon, weren't we?"

"Right you are my friend. Check out the display, the view outside. That's a beautiful sight, all those points of light. Let's do a position check."

"Yes sir." Jemrah said with a smile, "Yes sir indeed."

A few motions at the console, and Jemrah reported, "It still indicates the location is unavailable, sir."

"All right my friend, let's repeat the same jump sequences as before with the portal and see what that gets us. Before we do that, shut down the welt engines. No sense in wasting fuel."

"Yes sir."

Engines were cut off and the sequences run. The result was the same as before.

Jemrah turned to his Captain and said, "We must be in another universe in a still different dimension from the three we tried."

"More likely we are still in the human universe but at another, later time."

"Of course. The result would be the same, wouldn't it?"

"Yes! Out of curiosity, do a search for solid objects, million kilometer range. We might pick up something."

Jemrah executed the search command and the image of a ship appeared on the screen. It was the Intreba and she was badly distorted.

"Distance?"

"About fifty thousand kilometers, Captain, and we are approaching. She's within hailing distance."

"I doubt anyone is alive, but hail them anyway, Jemrah."

"Yes sir."

The display flickered, but there was no answer.

"She's derelict, sir, seems to be badly damaged."

"Yes, Jemrah she's quite misshapen, and with all those pok marks on her outer hull. She's been here a long time and received many meteor strikes after her impact shields quit working."

"Captain, it would take more than a hundred years to produce so many meteor impacts. I think you were right about another time."

"All Scentar ships carry flight recorders as do ours. Those recorders also use permanent atomic clocks that run virtually forever. I wonder if we could find theirs and remove it?"

"Sir, if we could obtain that recorder it would tell us a lot about what happened and even where we are."

"Our current trajectory will take us within about ten-thousand kilometers. When we reach that position, set a corrected course to bring us alongside Intreba. Find out how long that will take."

Jemrah adjusted the controls and did a few calculations. "At minimum power use it will take about five hours. I assume you don't want to use any more power than necessary."

"Correct. Until we learn more about our situation, we have a lot more time to spare than power. We have no idea when or how we might go home."

33.64.28.1525 - "Captain, We are in sync with Intreba about a quarter of a kilometer off her starboard bow."

"Thank you, Jemrah. Well done. Let's see if that atomic clock is still working. Set the energy scan for the lowest emission and scan Intreba. If we find anything, we'll then figure out how to remove it."

"Sir, there are three small energy sources that showed on the scan. From its emission signature I can tell the forward one is the atomic clock. I have no idea what the others are. There are no life signs, and there is no air in the ship, only the vacuum of outer space."

"Is there a hatch forward near the clock?"

"Better than that, sir. The flight recorder is in its own easy access tube that can be opened from the outside. The Scentar at Vega Five showed me when I took a tour of their ship. I can put on a vacuum suit and take a scooter over to remove the recorder. I'll need a Darium cutter to open the tube because we are without a key."

"Do it! I'll keep watch in case something goes wrong. Check to make sure our com units are working before you leave the airlock."

"On my way, Captain."

As Jemrah prepared to go for the flight recorder, Captain Woolgah started searching Scentar ship schematics to try and find out what the other small sources of energy could be. He had examined energy sources on three Scentar ship plans when Jemrah clicked his com unit.

"All set, Captain. The air lock is open, and I'm ready to go."

"Good luck my friend. Don't take any chances. I can't afford for you to be injured. Return to the ship the instant something doesn't seem right."

"Yes, Captain. I'm out of the airlock and on my way."

Captain Woolgah went back to his searching for energy sources. Every few minutes he checked the display focused on Jemrah and the scooter. The bright white flashes of the Darium cutter told him Jemrah had found the flight recorder tube and was working to extract it. About an hour later the com unit signaled.

"I've reached the recorder." Jemrah reported. "It's going to take a while to cut it out. Both the outer and inner hull shells are crushed in, the tube is badly mangled, and the recorder itself is jammed into the bulkhead it was attached to. I would say I'm about half way finished with the cutting. That means another hour at least to free it and carry it back."

"No hurry, Jemrah. Make clean cuts and don't leave any jagged edges that could catch and puncture your vacuum suit. While you are doing that, I'm searching Scentar ship plans to try to find those other energy sources. They must be significant sources or they wouldn't still be active."

"Yes captain. I'll contact you when the recorder is free."

With that Captain Woolgah went back to studying Scentar ship plans. True to his estimate, Jemrah called about an hour later.

"Captain, I'm about to cut what seems to be the main power cable to the recorder. I don't understand why it is so thick, about the size of my wrist. Once I cut through that, the recorder is easily removed."

"Jemrah, be careful. There is no reason why the recorder would need a power cable. They always contain their own separate power source inside the box. Maybe it's a security lock or hold down. Wait a minute. Here is a diagram of a flight recorder installation just as you describe. I think I also discovered those two power sources."

"Captain, I'm cutting that cable. It's hollow."

Immediately the display of the energy sensor lit up with a brilliant display. At the same instant, the Captain realized what they were.

"Fusion Bombs! Jemrah get out of there!" He shouted over the com unit.

As he watched the display, Jemrah mounted the scooter and headed back toward the Gelwah. In one fluid movement the captain set the shield to include Jemrah and turned it on. In the instant before the shield was deployed, the hull of the Intreba turned white hot.

"Jemrah!" the captain screamed into the com unit. There was no answer. As the captain bolted for the door to head for the airlock, his com unit popped, and Jemrah's calm voice stopped the him in his tracks.

"Yes Captain? What happened? I was half way to the airlock when everything turned dark. I had a hard time locating the com unit in the darkness. Could you turn on the airlock navigation lights so I can come back into the ship?"

Captain Woolgah slumped into the nearest operations chair on the bridge in immense soul-wrenching relief. "I'm sorry, Jemrah. The lights are on. Please come aboard and come directly to the bridge. We were both extremely lucky."

"Yes? How's that, sir? And why did you turn on the shield. I assume that's what happened."

"I'll explain when you reach the bridge."

Half an hour later Jemrah walked onto the bridge carrying a large metal cylinder with at least a meter of large diameter tube hanging out of one end.

"What happened, captain? I had started the scooter back toward the ship when everything went black. Why did you turn on the shield?"

"Those two energy sources I couldn't identify? They were two fusion bombs connected to the flight recorder with a wave guide trigger. They used a similar long-lived atomic power source like the one in the flight recorder. When you cut that waveguide, it triggered the bombs to go off. I realized what was happening when the energy sensor display lit up when the firing mechanisms energized and set the bombs to explode. I tried to tell you what was happening, but apparently your com unit was turned off. As soon as you were clear of the Intrepid I set the shield to include the space you were in and turned it on."

"Was it that close?"

"Here's how close it was. The hull of the Intrepid turned white hot no more than a nanosecond before the shield deployed. Which reminds me, Why didn't you respond when I shouted *fusion bombs* over the com system?"

"I had to turn off and stow the com system in order to extract the recorder from the ship, it was that tight. As soon as I boarded the scooter I turned it on and heard you screaming for me. I was only a few meters away from the Intreba when all light disappeared."

"That was much too close. I'll wager we benefitted from those bombs when their energy fed the shield and filled storage."

"I'll check power storage." Jemrah punched a query into his console. "You were right. All energy storage systems report full."

"Good! Turn off the shield and then let's examine that flight recorder clock and see what it tells us."

"Damn! Captain, check the display. All those incandescent objects must be the remains of the Intreba. They're all rapidly receding from us."

"The advantage of being at the center of a huge explosion while protected from it."

33.64.28.1735 - It took almost two hours to remove the flight recorder from its heavy protective cylinder. The record showed that the ship had jumped three times since leaving Vega Five. It had then sustained a sudden acceleration of almost forty G's. There was nothing after that. The recording continued until the space filled. No living being could survive that much sudden acceleration.

Captain Woolgah said. "Whatever those Scentar wanted, whatever their mission or purpose, we will never know. The impact with our shield killed all of them instantly. Whatever records they had were incinerated when those bombs went off. There's another shocker. The atomic clock shows we jumped 126 years into the future. That's why the locator can't tell us where we are. The data base of celestial objects is that much out of date. Those objects all moved."

Jemrah entered some information on the console and queried the locator once more. "I've updated the data base with the known movements of those baseline objects. That should provide us with a fix. There! At last we know where we are."

"And when!" the Captain added. "We're slightly more than ten million kilometers away from where we sealed that tear. We're also about fifty days from the current position of Vega Five"

"Do a dimensional gravity scan to see if the tear is there."

After a few moments, Jemrah said, "No sign of any disturbance, sir."

"I guess that means we should head back to the base on Vega Five. Set the return heading to the new coordinates, and let's go. I'm wondering what we'll find after being gone more than a hundred years. It should be interesting."

Jemrah grinned. "At least we'll carry a clean slate. No one there will know us."

33.66.18.1735 - Approaching Vega Five orbit, Captain Woolgah speaks. "Jemrah, open up a direct channel and see what we can find out."

"Yes sir, Captain."

The display held a background full screen shot of Vega Five from the Gelwah forward cameras.

"There seems to be no response to our signal. Send out a frequency pattern call and zoom the camera in close on the base location."

"Yes, Captain." The display filled with an expanse of green vegetation with a huge, black tower. Atop the tower was a fairly detailed model of a space ship. "What the hell is that?"

"Unless I miss my guess, that is a model of our ship, the Gelwah. Are you getting any confirmation of our signals?"

"Not yet, sir. Wait, there's something digital coming in. It's in human English requesting we identify ourselves. They do not recognize our ID signal."

"Switch the display and communications to their frequency."

A disturbed and obviously human face displayed on the screen. "Please identify yourself. Your ID signal is unknown to us."

"This is Captain Grala Woolgah of the Segwah starship Gelwah. Aboard with me is First Officer Der Jemrah. There is no one else on board. We left the Scentar base on this planet more than a hundred years ago on a critical mission which has been accomplished."

"One moment, please" was followed by a long silence as the face on the screen looked off to his left. At least fifteen minutes later the face on the screen turned to the camera. "Please enter security orbit D for David and wait for further instructions."

The Captain smiled. "If you will provide me with the vector and coordinates for security orbit D, I will comply. Who are you, please?"

"One moment, Captain. We're not accustomed to providing such information as it should be in your ship's navigation data banks. My name is Charles Sung. I'm a security officer on Vega Five."

"Our navigation data banks have not been updated in more than a hundred years so it's no wonder they are out of date. If you put our ship on visual, you will note it is exactly like the one atop that huge black tower near your base. That is no coincidence. Please provide us with the requested navigation guides so we can comply with your request."

The display went blank for a few moments and then a different and smiling face appeared. "I am Grace Shelbourne, governor of the Vega Five territory, the oldest human outpost in the galaxy. I want to take this opportunity to welcome you back, Captain Woolgah, and to apologize for your earlier treatment. Your return is miraculous and quite unexpected."

"Thank you, Governor Shelbourne. It is good to be back."

"Is your ship capable of landing on the surface without assistance?"

"Tell us where we can land, and we will do so unassisted."

It took less than an hour to land the Gelwah on the broad grassy area near the tower and next to the road that circled it about a third of a kilometer from the tower itself. It took another hour to shut down all flight equipment and prepare the Gelwah for ground access and control before they could exit for any length of time.

By the time they lowered the entrance ramp a large crowd had gathered from all directions, running across the grass and along the road. A military detachment had surrounded the legs of the Gelwah and held the crowd back. As the entrance ramp lowered from the nose of the ship a group of small busses or "porters" pulled down the road, through the crowd, and stopped nearby. Two women and three men stepped out of the first bus and walked over to the staircase as Captain Woolgah and First Officer Jemrah came down the ramp. Media cameramen and reporters tumbled out of the other busses and literally fell over each other getting positioned and set up. It was a historic occasion.

As the two Segwah officers stepped on the grass, the taller of the two women spoke. "As Governor of Vega Five it my great honor to welcome two historic figures from the past. but for their courage and daring in a successful mission of great danger, none of us or our universe would exist. Welcome, Captain Woolgah and First Officer Jemrah. Welcome back to your adopted home. We all read, in our history books, about two dedicated soldiers, Segwah soldiers, who risked their ship and their lives to save both the Scentar and Human universes from annihilation. All the more amazing is that their home universe was not threatened, and they could have gone back there and lived out their lives without danger."

With that the crowd applauded and stomped their feet in approval. They also called for Captain Woolgah to speak.

The Captain faced his First Officer, smiled, turned and addressed the crowd. "Madam Governor, citizens of Vega Five: believe me when I say we are extremely pleased to be here. We are especially pleased that you chose the Segwah foot stomp to honor us. According to our clocks, it was sixty-six days ago we left this same spot on our mission. During that same time, you experienced more than a hundred years. That will take some getting used to on our part. I'm sure we will have much to share with each other in the future. Right now we are exhausted from the rigors of flight deceleration and orbital maneuvering."

After much hand shaking and greeting of members of the crowd who responded with a few Segwah stomps, Governor Shelbourne turned to the two travelers with a big smile. "We thought you would be exhausted from your ordeal so we arranged for you to stay in the VIP suite at our finest hotel. We will hold any debriefing and celebration until you are refreshed and ready to enjoy our hospitality."

At this time Captain Woolgah took and raised the hand of his First Officer and said, "We may be tired, but before we go to the hotel, I want to say something important about First Officer Jemrah, something the history books may not mention. I publicly acknowledge that First Officer Jemrah was the one who conceived the possibility that our gravity-powered shield might repair the damaged space/time fabric. He conceived of this entire mission. True, Scentar theoretical physicists confirmed Jemrah's concept and calculated the details of the mission, but this man initiated the entire project. That such a man would choose to remain my first officer when offered a command of his own was the greatest compliment, honor and reward I ever received. No man had a better or truer friend."

Jemrah was a bit embarrassed. "Thank you, Captain. To hear such words from you brings me great joy. You will always be my friend, my mentor, and my captain. I'm not good with words, but we both lost all of our friends, save each other. True, we will make new friends, but to lose all one's friends and family in two months brings sadness to my heart, and I'm sure to my captain's as well. Thank you all for being so kind."

Governor Shelbourne responded. "There were momentous new revelations today, happy and pleasant revelations. Let's take you two travelers to your hotel for some rest. This will also give us the opportunity to prepare a proper welcome along with a few surprises for you."

A few more handshakes, cheers, and foot stomps, and the group headed off to the hotel in the porters.

It was afternoon about a week later when Governor Shelbourne and a larger group of officials picked them up in several porters. They entered the porter with the governor and her aide. The governor spoke. "Now we would like to take you to a reception in your honor. It is being held at our life research facility which incidentally was funded by generous gifts from Humans, Scentar and Segwah alike in memory of the two brave adventurers who saved two universes. The full name of the building is, The Woolgah-Jemrah Life Science Research Facility."

"Thank you for the opportunity to rest. I assure you Jemrah and I appreciated your thoughtfulness." Captain Woolgah said. "It is wonderful to meet new people and make new friends."

The Governor responded, "Do you remember the friends who said good-bye when you left? Our historical records indicated there were many at your departure. Those who were there to send you off included the crew of your ship and a wedding party gathered for the marriage of two close human friends."

"Of course we do. We will miss each and every one of them." Captain Woolgah replied as the porter pulled up to the Life Sciences Research building.

As they walked inside, Governor Shelbourne guided them to a large reception room where the trappings of a major reception celebration were laid out, and a large number of people were gathered. The Governor walked to the podium to address the crowd.

"Welcome ladies and gentlemen and thanks for coming to celebrate the miraculous return of two of our most cherished heroes."

The governor continued recounting their departure, realization, and acknowledgment that their efforts had succeeded, and the long wait not knowing when or if they would return. She then described the purpose and mission of the research facility.

"Some important and successful research has been accomplished in this establishment and the fine people who worked here over the years. One major accomplishment happened after our travelers left on their mission. This success was in the Life Stasis project. This project was to develop the means to suspend life activity for long periods, mainly for those with incurable, fatal diseases. It was hoped that once a treatment was perfected, those suspended could be awakened and cured. I would like to introduce a group that chose to be suspended, not for health reasons, but for another that should be obvious. Let me introduce this group who went through the process of rejuvenation and were awakened during the last week. This was done carefully so they could be here at this reception today."

At that point the doors at the end of the room opened, and a group of people walked into the room. The Governor announced, "Captain Woolgah and First Officer Jemrah, I give you your friends, Draxel and Maria Syl, the newlyweds, and most of your original crew of the Gelwah. These loyal friends and comrades chose to go into stasis to wait for your return."

The New Job

Mary lifted the pen from the old desk. Sounds of sirens came through the open window. *Had David called the police to try and stop me,* she wondered? *Would I be able to finish writing the goodbye note? Would anyone believe the contents of the note?*

Aerlo waited in the bedroom beside the open door of the stargate, an aperture that occupied much of the wall where her plasma TV hung. "Hurry!" he urged, knowing that the siren might mean trouble.

"I told my son I am leaving and why. He doesn't believe me, of course, and thinks I am losing it. Hopefully he'll believe what I said about not coming back and that he should not consider searching for me. It will only take a minute to finish writing the note," she called from the study.

"We must be through the gate and close it before anyone enters the room."

Mary's thoughts ran through the startling events that had begun three hours earlier.

*   *   *

She awoke at six and turned on the TV to view the morning news, her normal routine. As she was thinking about the breakfast she would soon prepare for her and her son, David, the news program was unexpectedly interrupted. A strange man's face appeared on the screen and spoke directly to her.

"Mary Carlisle, you have been chosen for a special privilege. I am speaking directly to you, and you can answer as if I were there in the room with you."

A bit startled, Mary sat upright and clutched the covers to her.

"Can you . . . See me?" She asked haltingly.

"The same as if I were there in the room with you," the man answered.

"What is this? . . . How? . . . Are you serious?" She asked as she arranged the covers closer.

"My name is Aerlo, and I am speaking to you from a craft that is orbiting your planet. I came here from another planet in your galaxy. I am quite familiar with your Earth, having spent several years among you during my training. My species is closely related to yours. We are virtually another race of *Homo Sapiens*. In fact, both of our species came from the same ancestors. Please do not be frightened as I will not harm you in any way. Ask any question you wish, and I will reply truthfully."

"I don't know what to say . . . Why are you speaking to me? What do you want?"

"In a way, I am offering you a job. It will be yours to accept or reject. Should you reject my offer, I will leave and not trouble you again."

"A job? What kind of job? I already have a fantastic job I love."

"That is precisely why we would like to hire you, your expertise on cetaceans."

"I'm a marine biologist—a specialist on cetaceans. I work with them every day here at the Oceanic Research Center. It's the foremost research installation of its kind in the world."

"That's precisely why we want you. We started an interesting research project involving cetaceans on another planet quite far from here."

"This isn't some kind of weird promotion, is it? You can't be for real. How do I know you aren't some con artist? it is hard for me to believe you."

"Tell me what I must do to convince you this is all true and proper. I will do whatever you say unless you ask something impossible or that will reveal my presence to others."

"Anything?"

"Anything!"

"Let me think."

"Mom!" called a voice from elsewhere in the house. "Who are you talking to?"

"The TV news. I always talk back when they say something I don't like." And as an aside to Aerlo, "That's my son, David. He's staying with me while his group is trying to free some beached whales nearby." it was a lame explanation to David, but it worked.

"Well, I must go to the beach in less than an hour, so if you're going to fix breakfast, please hurry up," came from the far end of the hall.

"Attend to your son. I can return after he has gone," Aerlo said.

"I am not due at the center until noon, so can we talk in, say, an hour?"

"That's okay with me. Incidentally, if you turn off the TV, it will cut off our connection. I will not be able to contact you, so be sure it is on in one hour. Also, there are only about three hours before my departure window closes. I must leave by then and will be unable to return here for about eight years."

"I can't leave in three hours, that's impossible!"

"Wait until you hear what I have to say, please."

"Okay! In an hour then. Now I will turn you off so I can dress."

"Goodbye!"

During breakfast, she told her son nothing about the visit, only that a new job opportunity had come up. "I must make a decision now and will leave before noon if I accept."

"That's unbelievable!" David remarked. "Are you crazy? Who are they? Why you? And why so suddenly?"

"Whoa there, son! One question at a time. No, I'm not crazy. besides, I am already eligible for retirement, and you are my logical successor. You've been with me at the center for fifteen years and understand more about what I do than anyone. You could take over in a heartbeat. We've already discussed that."

David was almost in a panic. "Can't this hold until after I finish at the beach? We should be finished by dark. Why don't we discuss it then?"

"If—and that's a big if—if I take the job, I'll be gone before noon. Also, I'll be out of the country and unable to communicate with you for some time, so if I decide to go, please don't worry."

"Mom, I'm going to cancel my work at the beach, stay with you, and find out what this is all about. I'll call Denise, and she can take over for me."

"No, David, you'll do no such thing. I insist! That project is quite important and will not wait for another time. Denise is smart, but she hasn't done this before. Those beached whales will be dead by nightfall, and that must not happen."

"But, Mom!"

"Hush! If you won't talk sensibly and rationally, I'll end this conversation and run you out of the house."

"Look who's talking about sense and rationality? You sure don't make either."

"Please, David. I have been searching for something different to do ever since your father died six years ago, and I think I found it. Let me do something crazy with my life if I decide to. Now, go take care of those poor beached creatures."

"I still think it's crazy, but have it your way. Call me on my cell phone when you decide."

With a shake of his head, he hugged her and left with the admonition, "Don't do anything stupid, please!"

"I assure you that I won't."

She cleaned up the dishes and headed back to the bedroom to turn on the TV. The eight o'clock news was starting. Before it had been on five minutes, the screen went blank, and once more Aerlo appeared.

"Did you decide on a test of my veracity?"

"How about showing me pictures of your ship, inside and out, your home planet, and the place where the research project is located."

"Your wish is my command."

With that, a picture of a large vessel appeared. It was sitting on what was obviously a launch and retrieval platform with open countryside in the background. People and loading carts or carriers were moving in and out of numerous hatches on several levels.

Aerlo narrated, "That's the *Curex* as she was being loaded for this trip. She carries a crew of sixty and provisions for trips of up to four million light years. Right now she's orbiting Earth about six hundred of your miles above the surface. EMF shields are on, so she is invisible to light, radio, radar, and any other kind of EMF radiation sensors or detectors."

The picture changed to what was obviously living quarters not too unlike the cabins on cruise ships Mary had been on, but a bit larger.

"Nice room," she commented.

"There's one like it waiting for you," he added. "Both the bridge and the residence areas use artificial gravity systems and inertia neutralizers as do all passageways and lifts."

"How can I be sure those aren't fakes?"

"Would you like a personal tour?"

"Come on."

"Seriously, I can transport you there in a second through this portal."

With that, an opening appeared in the wall near the TV screen. It appeared to be an open window to the ship's interior, a salon or recreation area. Aerlo stood on the other side.

"My god!"

"No, just advanced technology. Your own technology is not many years behind all of this."

"How can I be assured you won't whisk me away once I'm aboard?"

"That's a risk you must take unless . . . wait a minute." He walked away from the window and reappeared carrying a small furry animal about the size of a squirrel, but with no tail.

"This is an oolabit. It's what you would call a pet, a small version of, say, a cat on your planet. Take her! She won't bite."

Mary held the little critter which curled around her hand and held on softly with padded feet, but no claws. "She's cute and cuddly."

"Does that convince you that I am from another planet?"

"Absolutely! How about that tour."

Aerlo helped her step through the portal into another world . . . literally.

"It's lovely," she remarked as she walked through the room toward the windows in the side. What Mary saw through that window blew her mind. There was her beautiful blue Earth from six hundred miles up. "That is spectacular!"

"A nice view, yes. Any more tests?"

"Tell me about this job. I'd like to see pictures of the lab and where the animals are kept."

"Don't be shocked please, but your lab is an entire planet with deep oceans."

"An entire planet?"

"Yes! It's called Stentor Seven and is a planet orbiting the star Stentor near the star you call Vega. We call this area the Vegan sector of the galaxy. It's an artificially *enlivened* planet about halfway in size between your Earth and its moon. All the water, the ocean-river systems, the plants, and animals were transported to the planet to create what you might call a recreational world—a place for R and R as your people say."

"Are you serious?"

"Very! We want to transfer some cetaceans from your planet to Stentor Seven, and would need to provide them with an environment fully stocked with appropriate food and support systems so they would live as naturally as they do here."

"That's a tall order!"

"And one we understand quite well. You posses the mental tools and experience to accomplish what we need—tools which we lack."

"All the records of my work, my research, are in the center's computer system . . ."

Aerlo interrupted. "And in our data banks as well."

"Then why do you need me?"

"For the immense store of knowledge and experience in your brain that is not in those data banks."

"You think of everything, don't you?"

"We try. Let's send you back to your home so you can make your decision in a free environment—and soon, I hope."

This is incredible! Mary thought as she headed back to the portal with Aerlo. "I'd like to do it, but there are so many unasked questions in my head. Will I ever be able to come back here?"

"Not for slightly more than eight years. Space travel over such long distances is only possible under certain conditions and at certain times. That's a limit our scientists and engineers are trying to overcome. The temporary window we are experiencing lasts only a few days and ends in a bit more than one of your hours. We have no time to waste."

"You mean that if I go, I'll only be back for a few days after eight years?"

"No! This window was a short one. Some of them are much longer. The one open about five years ago was almost six months. That's when I trained for this project. The one in eight years is at least a year, or even a bit longer. I must look it up to be exact."

As they stepped through the portal into her bedroom, Mary decided she was going to go. "What do I do if I decide yes?"

"Just step aboard. Everything else has already been taken care of. Your clothes, books, medications, records, everything. We've prepared a cover story and arranged legal access for David to all of your records and property."

"Everything?"

"You will be able to veto anything about David's legal access that makes you nervous."

"No! David can be trusted, but the thought of eight years with no communication is disturbing."

"I don't mean to press you, but it is less than an hour before I must leave, with or without you."

Mary turned and walked into the study and sat down at her old desk. "I'll do it! I must write a letter of resignation to the center and recommend David as my replacement. I've already talked with the board about that, and they are in agreement. What can I say to all my friends and other relatives? An hour is such a short time."

"We use a contact and control person here who will be able to help David handle all that for you. His Earth name is Ralph Gora, and you and David already know him."

"Dr. Gora? Our dentist? He's been our dentist for more than fifteen years."

"He was my contact when I trained and has committed to living his life here on Earth with his family. He is a good one."

"You seem to think of everything."

"We've been planning this for at least twenty years, but had to fill in all the blanks."

"What would happen if I said no?"

"It would have set our project back the eight years until the next window. By that time, we would line up several other prospects and a full year to find and select one. Incidentally, that's when we plan to pick up the whales and dolphins."

"No animals for eight years? What will I be doing?"

"You will use those eight years to prepare their home. At least to design their home and prepare to transfer all the required life forms. We are carrying a rather large amount of seawater from several of your oceans where the whales and dolphins roam. Those will provide at least part of the required biota for designing Stentor Seven's oceans."

"You do plan well. I hope you didn't miss anything."

"If we did, it will be eight years before we can correct it."

With that, Mary sat down to tell David the story of her new adventure. When Aerlo suggested she tell him the truth, Mary replied, "He'll never believe it."

She was almost finished when the sirens startled her. When they stopped in front of her house, Mary panicked. "That boy of mine must probably had second thoughts and called the authorities."

"We must leave now!"

"As soon as I finish this last sentence for David. It will take them some time to come in if I answer and say I'm dressing and will soon be at the door." As she finished, she walked into her bedroom and was greeted with a room empty except for her desk, chair, and the TV hanging on the wall.

"We are taking all your things as I explained earlier. My people came and moved them into your quarters on the ship while you were writing your note. Your house is virtually empty."

"My god, you move fast!"

"We must. There is little time to spare."

As he said that, the doorbell rang and the intercom sprung to life. "Mrs. Carlisle? Are you all right?"

"Quite all right, thank you. What do you want?"

"Your son, David, asked us to check on you. Would you please come to the door?"

"Wait 'til I put on my robe."

Two men climbed through the portal and headed for the study. "I assumed you would like to take your desk and chair?" Aerlo said with a broad smile. "Please follow me through the portal while they bring the desk."

"What about the note?"

"David will find it on the floor where your desk once stood. Now, let's hurry."

After Mary had stepped through the portal, the men came through with her desk, chair, lamp, and remaining items from her study. As they did, she heard a loud crash. The police were coming in.

The sounds of their shouts were silenced as Aerlo turned off the portal.

"All they'll find is a plasma screen TV hanging on the wall. Let's head for the Vegan system."

"Well, Mary Carlisle is off on a wild adventure. I certainly hope this was no mistake."

"I think you will find it more rewarding than you can imagine. Stentor Seven is a marvelous place."

The Ultranet

*T*his introduction is information describing some new ideas and technology that will soon affect much of the world. The devices and concepts described are quite startling, but they are all in use or in the R&D stages as this is written. Many will be available surprisingly soon along with the worldwide systems they serve and require. Understandably, this may seem a bit fanciful to those an arm's length from digital technology, but wouldn't the Internet have seemed so in 1980, a few years ago?

*RFID or Radio Frequency ID, tags identify a great many details about the package or item to which they are attached. They are read by **RFID** readers (handheld computers) that can instantly read and extract the information, pages of information. These tags have been in use for several years! They are one reason for the success of marketers like Wal-Mart.*

*The **FMID**, or FM Input Device, is already a reality. The Blackberry, iphone, and ipad are handheld wireless devices that can access the Internet and so much more. They have been popular for several years. One version can be used as a wireless access device for a computer and the Internet as well as a cell phone and digital camera. With available verbal commands, an advanced **FMID** would combine all these features and also replace the mouse and keyboard.*

*PUAIs, or personal universal access interface devices, will replace FMIDs in the near future. They are like thick credit cards with a viewing screen filling one side. There are no buttons and they require no manual entries. All commands are voice or mind actuated and keyed to the owner. Right now **PUAIs** are merely wireless interface devices for the Internet with far more power and functionality than complete computer systems of a few years ago. They carry no programs or data since that is all stored in multiple digital storage banks serving the Internet. **PUAIs** can also serve as credit or debit cards and as a telecom system. They can hold personal ID information, including an ID code that positively identifies the owner including a picture, fingerprints, and an iris scan. They also carry a GPS device so they can be positively located. They contain an internal power source that needs recharging only once every few months, and they are always on and active. Any function that needs to be turned off for any reason can be turned off by a simple mental command as can the entire system. The GPS signal cannot.*

*The **IBI**, or intra brain interface, is being researched and tested at several universities. Types of IBI are being developed by our military for pilots to use to control their aircraft. These devices could replace other access devices in the next ten or twenty years. The IBI, a link between the brain and the owner's **PUAI**, will be part of the next quantum leap for the digital world. Look at the screen and a cursor appears and moves wherever the eyes focused. In discussion mode, whatever anyone says comes out from speakers at the workstation of each member of the discussion group or class. Sometimes those discussions* become quite animated. *All the subtle and not so subtle actions of any group e-meeting, e-class, or e-conference will be available to every member of the group attending the e-meeting. This will be accomplished either directly by the* **PUAI** *or by its being connected to a screen and speakers.*

In text mode, words or commands, spoken or mentally imaged, are digitized and converted to text on the screen in the format of the program being used. Graphics entry, a bit more complicated, requires some fairly intense training. The entry of programming code is almost as simple as spoken or mental, SM, commands, converting directly into code. Editing is quite simple and direct using SM commands. The **IBI** *device is a tiny chip or several chips inserted surgically under the scalp and near the speech, visual, and other thought centers of the brain. The chips pick up brain activity and turn it into digital input read directly by the individual's personal universal access interface device -* **PUAI.**

These "Star Trek" technologies either are a reality already or will be in a few years. Fact seems to be outrunning fiction. The story that follows is an extrapolation of the preceding—it is science fiction. Today's science fiction is tomorrow's real science and technology. The same thing has happened many times before. The time span for that conversion is shrinking from centuries to years to months to weeks to days.

The story begins:

I am Leon Moon of Fort Wayne, Indiana, the first member of a training research group here at CDI Fort Wayne. Mara Singleton of CDI Mexico City was assigned as the second member of my group, and Vivek Piloto of CDI Rome was the third. Brought up on a Hoosier farm, I dove into the exploding world of Internet technology like a hog after a bucket of Indiana corn. We are IBI development engineers at CDI currently assigned to develop a training program for our own people to use the latest development from CDI, the Intra Brain Interface, or IBI.

The IBI is a set of small chips, highly miniaturized and compacted digital devices combined into a high-speed, wireless interface between a person's brain activities and existing Personal Universal Access Interface devices, or PUAIs, pronounced "pooies" by all in the trade.

Our introduction to each other was by Gregory Stilling at a meeting in the Inet conference room. Stilling, a stuffy, balding, slightly pudgy man, is vice president of the IC technology section here in Fort Wayne. It was eight-thirty in the morning, local time, when we met. We often speculated that Stilling either inherited a major portion of the local organization or had something on someone high up in CDI. He never seemed to say anything intelligent or be doing anything productive we knew about. However, whenever Chinese big shots visited, the ones from China especially, Gregory squired them around, and they seemed to like him a lot. CDI or China Data Industry is headquartered in Dalian, China and has hundreds of research centers around the globe. Fort Wayne is one of eight in the United States. Like the other seven, it is located in a small city not known for high technology or digital expertise. For some reason, the Chinese think it safer, less costly, and just as efficient.

Stilling made sure all three of us were on line, then launched his inspiring introductions. "This is . . ." until all three of us had verbally shaken hands via the conference room TC setup. "Now that introductions are over, let us begin."

I was already bored. I examined the other two. We had no chance to speak to each other beyond the short greetings of introduction before Stilling launched his inspiring lecture. Vivek seemed like the typical Italian geek—tall, skinny, and awkward—but don't all geeks look like that? On the other hand, Mara was a real dish, so I studied her carefully. It was hard to tell how tall she was. TC screens often distort the vertical. She looked good to me, but not the least bit Mexican.

What was she doing in Mexico? I wondered. *She is more like a Swede or Hungarian than a Mexican? Singleton, that certainly wasn't a Mexican name.*

"Mr. Moon? . . . Mr. Moon?" it finally registered that those words were coming from Stilling.

"Yes!" I answered, pretending to know what was happening and not appear startled.

"You agree then to being group leader for this project?"

Damn! I thought. *I should have paid some attention to what Stilling had been saying.* All three faces stared directly at me, and I didn't feel any warm fuzzies.

"Yes, Mr. Stilling. I'll be pleased to be group leader." I had put on my best loyal-and-cooperative-employee attitude along with a friendly smile.

Stilling didn't seem too happy at this point. "For a moment I thought you weren't on the same page with the rest of us. I seem to be mistaken."

Had I missed something? I was suspicious. I definitely missed something, something important at that. No problem, I'd pick it up on the transcript after the meeting. Stilling always provided transcripts.

Stilling continued, "Ms. Singleton, you will handle the editing of all reports from Mr. Moon. Mr. Piloto, you will be the coordinator of all data for the group."

As they both agreed, I realized I had missed something important. *Damn!* I said to myself once more. *Damn! I'd best check that transcript over ASAP!*

"Mr. Moon will create a complete outline of the work to be done by the group and provide you with a finished copy by tomorrow at 2200 GMT. Is that all right with you, Mr. Moon, or will you need a bit more time?" There was a sarcastic smile on Stilling's face as he finished.

Something was amiss, so I fired back my cleverest response. "Let me go over the scope of the project thoroughly. I'll tell you if I will need more time."

It was not the response Stilling had hoped for. "I hope you will not disappoint us, Mr. Moon."

"I'll find a way not to do so," I answered quite honestly as I picked up the card with the project code he left me. That pompous ass was not going to trap me.

As soon as the meeting was over, I headed for my office to examine the transcript. It was then I realized he left no transcript of the meeting. *Shit! That bastard set me up. I'll download the meeting record, and it will all be there.* I had started to look for it when my phone clicked. I glanced at the screen of my PUAI and there was the lovely Ms. Singleton's smile. *What's this all about?* I wondered.

"Hello, Ms. Singleton. What can I do for you?"

"Mr. Moon! I don't know what kind of problem you have with Stilling, but get over it or we'll all look bad. I can't afford to appear even a tiny bit bad on this project. Also, call me Mara. I'm not one for formalities."

Obviously Ms. Singleton, in addition to being informal, was not one to mince words or practice diplomacy. "Okay, Mara. Call me Leon, or Moon for that matter. I'm no stickler on formality either, not like old Stilling. Incidentally, I don't see any real problem with him. It's just that he's so stuffy."

"Unless you want a problem with me, try to treat him with a bit more respect. He may be stuffy, but his standing with CDI bigwigs trumps his personality."

"Okay! You made your point. I'm sure that's not what you want to talk to me about, so go on with it. I've a ton of work to do on this outline, and Stilling's information is fairly sketchy. At least the part I've been able to check out thus far."

"Here's a question for you: How long have your implants been in place, and what version are you running?"

"Getting rather personal, aren't you?"

"Grow up, Moon, we're both at the same clearance level and working on the same project. Mine are now operational for fifteen months and are updated to version 1.02."

"Sorry, Mara. I find it hard not to pull your chain. I'll try being a bit more serious if you will try lightening up a bit. Mine are operational now for almost eighteen months. I'm up to revision 1.01. I'm supposed to receive the 1.03 upgrade tomorrow. I didn't see the need to upgrade to 1.02 when the other one was almost ready."

"I guess I did come off a bit caustic, but I'm bucking for a big promotion and need this little project to go extremely well. What I wanted to confer with you about is something I've been experiencing lately. It's been happening since I was updated to 1.02."

"Oh! What's that?"

"I seem to be occasionally having some unusual interference between my IBI and PUAI. It's as though I am having hallucinations—at least they seem like hallucinations—both visual and verbal. I find at times I am *remembering* things which are not in my memory. I thought since you worked on the revisions, you might be able to help me out."

"I haven't a clue! Never ran into anything like that in any of our tests and research on that upgrade or on the whole project for that matter. It could be a chip failure, but that's extremely rare anymore. How many received that upgrade? Do you know?"

"I'm the only one here in Mexico. I don't know about the rest of CDI. I thought you would, having worked on it."

"Nope! Not my concern. I leave that up to the statisticians. but there has to be some kind of record."

"I couldn't find any. Lots of info about the initial few hundred insertions, but nothing about the upgrades."

"I guess no one thinks that is important. Those first two upgrades were minor changes. This new one, 1.03, is a significant advance and is a lot more sensitive. I'm supposed to conduct a series of tests as soon as the four of us here are upgraded, and that is scheduled for tomorrow. We also scheduled installation of more than two thousand IBIs here at the university during the next few weeks. If I'm not mistaken, CDI has several million IBIs ready to go. They are waiting for the okay to be given as soon as our training program is ready. The training program will be made available to the public so all those customers can use them. It's like teaching people to walk or talk, and I'm still learning. My guess is that will be a never-ending project."

"Let me know how it goes with the upgrade. I can't help but think the IBI/PUAI system is doing something it was never intended to do. I hope it's nothing harmful."

"Likewise! In fact, CDI is planning on selling two billion of these things in the next few years, so there had better not be any problems."

"That's for certain! There's a lot of money, betting these will be a fantastic success. There will be hell to pay if they aren't for any reason."

"You can say that again . . . I'd best be getting on with this project outline, or Stilling won't be happy. I'll say goodbye. See you later."

"Okay! Just don't forget to tell me about 1.03."

"Willco! Out!"

The screen went blank, and I went to work on the project outline.

Two days later, after my update to version 1.03, I knew exactly what Mara had been describing. Fleeting thoughts and images, unfamiliar ones, came into my head and then were gone.

It happened when I was relaxing, not when I was reading, talking, or concentrating on any mental task. It became obvious that concentrating on moving a cursor, writing, drawing a graphic, or accessing any program or data, swept these mental aberrations away.

※ ※ ※

By the end of the six months it took to complete our project, Mara and I became good friends as well as colleagues. She also received the next upgrade, and we both continued having the strange images and thoughts. It didn't take us long to learn to push them out of our minds like unwanted thoughts.

※ ※ ※

During the next few months, CDI delivered hundreds of millions of IBIs. They had become the standard system for interacting with the Internet—fast, accurate, easy, inexpensive, and quite reliable. CDI was unable to keep up with the demand and waiting time for customers grew to months.

During this time, something unprecedented happened.

Out of nowhere it was there. It took some time before anyone realized what was happening. The reality sneaked up on everyone. It was a wholly new concept, entity, system, whatever one could think of to call it. One day it didn't exist, the next it did. Talk about a paradigm shift, this was the paradigm shift of all paradigm shifts—and no one created it. Hell, no one knew what or how it was, just that it was. With this sudden appearance, everything changed—instantly.

※ ※ ※

My first inkling of this happened one day when I was thinking about contacting Mara, her voice was in my head. *Moon, is that you?* came through clearly with a strong feeling of amazement.

The thought and feeling of incredulity coursed through my mind. It was a strange experience. *What? . . . How? . . . Mara?* The words crossed through my mind and were soon answered.

Am I hallucinating, or is that really you? came into my mind directly from Mara—of that there was no doubt.

I hear you in my head loud and clear. That is, it seems I hear you, but how can that be? Mara's thoughts as well as her disbelief rang in my head.

From knowledge I had from my work on the IBI, I began to realize what was happening—what those "hallucinations" were. It was an awesome realization. *Mara? Hear and listen to my thoughts. I know what is happening, and now you do as well.*

I'm listening, came into my head crystal clear.

The IBI/PUAI system is a bidirectional communication system, right?

Yes, I'm beginning to understand. Your thoughts are coming to me clear as a bell. Somehow your thought patterns are being picked up by your IBI, transferred to your PUAI, to the Internet, to my PUAI, to my IBI, and thence directly into my thoughts, virtually instantly. It's digital telepathy on a grand scale.

We realized we were thinking together. It was so much faster and clearer than talking. Then came the visual—I could see clearly the image from Mara's eyes, and she saw the image from mine. Our minds were linked.

This may pose some problems we'll need to learn how to handle soon, I thought.

It certainly does. I can think of one glaring example. I must close my eyes or turn off my PUAI when I'm getting dressed or looking in my mirror.

Never thought of that. There goes privacy. Hell, we both know what we think of each other, and I like what you think.

I do too. That sure cut out a whole lot of thoughtful speculation and planning, didn't it? . . . You're right. We must try to be together soon. Of course, we're thinking about when and how.

Mara, this is going to take a whole lot of learning—other minds, strangers, people we don't like as well as those we do, may gain access to our thoughts unless we can learn to block them. It's getting quite scary. Yes, I can think that again . . .

Then Mara contributed an insightful thought, *Our two minds seem almost to be as one, communicating is almost exactly like remembering. That is going to take a great deal of adapting and learning.*

In the ensuing months, we learned a lot about how to communicate over what became known and came to be called the "Ultranet." Our plans to meet brought on growing and shared excitement.

✳   ✳   ✳

Mara! My lovely Mara. Where in this electronic maelstrom are you? buzzed in my mind as I tried finding hers. She couldn't be asleep at this time of day—not even dozing. After several months of Ultranet thought sharing, I was finally going to meet her in person. Our lunch date at the CDI salad bar was set for eleven-thirty, two hours away, but why couldn't I find her? For some reason she was off-u.

Starting Ultranet contact is much like trying to remember a name or recognize a face: trying to make a connection with someone, *remembering* their pattern, connecting with that one thought process among the billions out there. There are hazy images, mumbled words, whispers, all in the mind. Unintelligible visual patterns like remembering the face of someone you met in the past. They all flash through your mind like experiencing a changing mental collage. It is hard to describe as every part is a new and unstudied experience for anyone who goes, *on-u*. Using the Ultranet, being *on-u*, is almost like silently talking with yourself, but you know it's another person, not you. You can also know with whom it is you are connected.

This direct mind-to-mind connection ability was dubbed the *Ultranet* by some unknown person soon after its reality was recognized. It was nothing like the telepathy of science fiction and charlatans. It was sometimes hard to do. After a year of learning this new means of communication, most people had just scratched the surface. Being specialists in developing the intra brain interface, Mara and I were in the forefront of that learning process. We continued working closely together at CDI. Understanding this amazing thing that had happened was a daunting challenge. We were collaborating on trying to learn its use and capabilities and teach others—she in Mexico City and me in Fort Wayne. We were among the early ones to recognize the existence of the unimaginable soon after IBIs came into common use. and we were among the few who had a fairly good idea of how and why it worked.

During the months of working together, our feeling for each other grew from that first sharing of thoughts. We realized we had a special personal *connection*. There was no point in denying it as we each had access to the other's innermost thoughts and feelings.

There you are! Mara cued in that sweet, warm tone of thought that always melted me away. *I accidently shut down my PUAI while searching for lip gloss in my purse. Sorry. I knew you cued me when I realized I had shut it down.*

When I cued and you weren't there, I wondered if you had gone to sleep on the plane, I responded.

I cannot sleep on planes. Too much mental noise with all those high-profile minds working in such tight quarters. Evidently few people learned an effective blocking technique as yet. Many never learn to turn their PUAIs off, she cued as she exited the plane.

I suppose they don't think anyone can reach into their thoughts without their noticing. I could make out the hairy neck of a short, fat man walking in front of her. *That guy in front of you sure has a hairy neck*, I cued and laughed out loud.

Yeah! So I noticed. The view shifted to the floor and her carry-on case as she checked it out.

When those hazy visual images from another's eyes first registered on my mind, and I realized what they were, it blew me away. It was unnerving. *Remembering* in visual context what another person was seeing and sorting a single *vision* from the multitude of competing mental images took a long time to learn.

My first clear picture of Mara from her eyes happened about a month after we started Ultranet communicating together. The vision came clear as can be as she stepped out of the shower in front of her full-length mirror. We were both startled, and she immediately closed her eyes—show over. She gave me a hard time over that, but realized it was unintentional. Though we were several thousand miles apart at the time, we could just as easily been in adjacent rooms. While *on-u*, one learns not to look at what one doesn't want another to see. Of course, going *off-u* by shutting down one's PUAI makes a complete disconnect, so there is that option.

After eight months of trying, Mara managed to wrangle a temporary assignment to CDI Fort Wayne from her boss at CDI Mexico City. A year working closely together long distance almost every day, and we were soon going to be together for real for the first time off-u. We were both excited as the last minutes ticked by. CDI Mexico City was finally going to meet CDI Fort Wayne, in person.

It was late June when *I see you* rang through my mind from hers as her rental car pulled up to the door where I was to meet her. *You're much taller than you seemed to be in the conferences,* followed.

I opened the passenger door to climb in and direct her to the parking lot. I was not prepared for my reaction when we met in person. "You're much more beautiful in person." I said out loud without exaggeration. After one long awkward moment, I began directing her to the parking lot. "Wow! . . . Wow," was about all I could convince my mouth to say. At the same time, our minds were speaking in an entirely different language and on an entirely different level.

This was a strange situation for both of us. Our personal, direct visual and vocal contact was as awkward as any first meeting of strangers. Our continuing intimate mental contact did not affect our new, physical meeting. We were, in effect, on a first date—awkward. We were two different couples, one with intimate and close personal contact, the other, two strangers who met in person after having corresponded for some time over long distances. In person we were both shy and reserved.

"I can't believe we find it so difficult to talk," Mara said.

"I feel the same," I replied.

At the same time our minds were locked in a battle. *Why can't we verbalize? Should we kiss? I'd love to hold you,* flicked through my mind. I didn't know if they were my thoughts or Mara's. They were almost in images rather than words—like memories. It's quite difficult to describe.

How do we handle this? Our unison thought was like two people saying the same thing at the same time, only more intense. The disconnect between our thoughts and our physical actions and voices was utterly amazing—weird.

Our thoughts came virtually in unison, *Shut off our PUAIs!*

The resulting mental quiet was wonderfully relaxing, quite similar to turning off a too-loud radio or blaring TV. That was the last time we ever let our PUAIs remain on when we were together. This worked beautifully; our minds may commune well when we are apart, but are a strong source of distraction when we are together. We are now together in new and unknown territory. It is quite strange.

We had to become acquainted with each other the old-fashioned way. Our work together in the electronic conferences did not prepare us for direct contact. All of our senses were in play, not just sight and sound. The subtleties of face-to-face contact: the interplay of all of the senses: the power of direct three-dimensional eye contact: and especially the actual presence with all those powerful pheremones in play, overpowered the mental aspects of the familiar Ultranet memories, images, and sounds. This was heady stuff. Our Ultranet communion had only intensified all of these sensory experiences and emotional connections as they occurred.

We both remained silent as I guided her car to a spot in the parking lot. As soon as we got out of the car, Mara walked up to me, smiled, stuck out her hand and said, "It's nice to meet you, Mr. Moon. I'm Mara Singleton from Mexico City."

The ice was broken. We stood laughing almost to the point of tears. It was a special moment. I took her hand in mine and as formally as possible said, "Pleased to meet you, Ms. Singleton," whereupon we had another laugh.

The bright dance of her eyes could only be appreciated in person. "I'm glad we thought to turn off our PUAIs. We are now in a much more real situation. I did not expect this kind of first meeting."

"Nor I," Mara said as we walked hand in hand toward the lunchroom across the parking lot deserted of other pedestrians.

At the sight of someone exiting the building, we self-consciously dropped each other's hand. We were truly like two kids on a first date—self-conscious and unsure of what to do or how to act.

By the time we had finished our meal from the salad bar, we were much more relaxed and talking quite freely. "I think I'm beginning to like you, Moon." Mara's grin and downcast eyes when she said it indicated the ice was not only broken but rapidly melting away.

My response, "I know I really like you—in fact, all those thoughts and feelings we shared are running through my mind—WOW," was followed by a meaningful silence.

✳   ✳   ✳

It was late Friday afternoon when we finished our tour of CDI and the meeting with Stilling. We scheduled her visit to start on a Friday so we could spend the weekend together free of the concerns of our professional lives. That evening, after she checked in at her hotel and freshened up, I led her to the Riverwalk.

"It's quite beautiful, cool, and friendly." Mara commented as we wound our way along the shore of the river past shops, art displays, numerous restaurants, clubs, a few small theaters, and a movie house, all under the early evening sun.

"This is one of my favorite spots in town," I explained. "When I was little, this was a stinking, dirty river lined with old buildings—mostly abandoned warehouses and manufacturing plants. It was not a pleasant place. During the economic recession of 2008 to 2015, Chinese-American companies made a huge investment in the city, putting lots of people to work. One of their projects resulted in this beautiful Riverwalk in the downtown of the city. The river was cleaned up, most of the old buildings were leveled, and what is now here came to be. It took four years and lots of investment to prepare and then build it. Since then it has grown tremendously and repaid the investors many times over."

"What's that?" Mara asked as a small tour boat rounded the nearby bend and headed toward us with about forty people on board.

"That's a boat we can ride if you like. It takes about an hour to go around the city loop of the river all along the Riverwalk."

"I'd love to."

"Done! But not until after we eat. I'm starved, and the Riverwalk Grille is right there ahead. They serve some of the best Italian food in town."

"How do you know I like Italian food?"

"I'm a mind reader," I answered with a broad grin.

"I forgot we already shared that information."

After dinner—ahi tuna, a green salad, focaccia bread, all topped off with freshly made cannoli—Mara was emphatic. "That was one of the best meals I ever had. The tuna was absolutely fantastic."

"No disagreement from me. Now, how about that boat ride?"

By the time the boat tour was ending, it was almost nine-thirty. The sun had slipped below the horizon. "It is so beautiful," Mara said, almost misty-eyed. "The clear water, fresh smells, orange sky, and fireflies everywhere. It's hard to believe we are in the center of a city and a small one at that. It's much like Venice, but without the unpleasant smells."

"You've been to Venice?"

"Went there during a visit to Italy with my parents when I was about twelve."

"Awesome! Then you've traveled quite a bit?"

"With my parents when I was quite young."

"That's right. I seem to recall your father was a diplomat of some sort. One that moved around quite a bit."

"Still is!"

The slight bump as the boat nudged the landing dock interrupted our conversation. We joined the passengers as they exited the boat and dispersed down the Riverwalk on their separate ways.

"You've had a long day, starting out in Mexico City. I suppose you'd like to get some sleep?"

"Not quite yet. I'd like to walk some more if you don't mind, but thanks for your consideration."

A few minutes later when we walked through a particularly dark arch of trees and bushes, Mara turned, grabbed my hands and turned her face up. "Kiss me right now before I drag you off into the bushes and attack you."

After a long silence interrupted only by heavy breathing, my only comment was, "WOW! . . . WOW!" All those close-shared thoughts and feelings of the last year overpowered us as they rushed into our consciousness. We were definitely in love—a state I had never experienced so intensely before.

We turned and purposefully started for her hotel. Anticipation and swelling passion soon overcame us. Our steps quickened so that we were running by the time we turned onto the street where her hotel waited. We barely controlled our wild physical contacts as the elevator lifted us toward her floor. Mara could hardly slip the key card into its slot, her hands were shaking so. The door closing, the total darkness of her room, and her body hard against mine, was the last thing I remembered.

✳   ✳   ✳

I was laying face down on something hard, rough, and cold. When I tried to push myself up, I found my face was glued to the concrete by dried blood. Pain blasted through my face when I tried to pull free. I struggled to open my eyes but could see nothing in the pitch blackness. Something hard and heavy lay on top of me. I freed my left hand from beneath my body and dug in my pocket for the knife that was always there. Cutting at the dried blood to free my cheek took forever. My face must have been in that position for many hours for the blood to dry so hard. My mind snapped into reality and screamed for answers with a mix of anger, wonder and fear. Mara! What had happened to my Mara?

My face freed from the grip of the dried blood, I tried once more to rise up. The heavy thing that weighed me down finally fell over with a bang, and I arose to my knees. On the surface, a few feet away was a thin slice of light. It was coming under the bottom of a large door, a roll up overhead door. Groping my way toward the faint light, I felt for the vertical surface above and found the narrow metal strips of a commercial truck door or loading dock. I tried standing, but dizziness and pain in my head kept me on all fours. I followed the door to its right side and felt for any lever, switch, or other opening device. Nothing!

Once more I tried to stand, this time I succeeded in spite of the pain and dizziness. I felt around on the wall for something to open the door. A switch! I flipped it and was assailed with light as the bare, overhead lightbulb illuminated what I decided was a small warehouse. There were no windows or man doors in the grey room that was my prison. The only way in or out was the overhead door. Then I knew where I was. It was an empty storage space, the kind people rent to store cars and other belongings when they lack space available in their homes. On the left side of the door, I found a red handle—it was an emergency door opener to be used by anyone stupid enough to close the door while inside.

One pull down on the lever and the door raised about an inch, letting more light under the door. It was daylight outside. Another crank was unsuccessful. It was apparent the door had been locked or at least latched on the outside. I searched for something to try to pry up the door. There was nothing but the heavy door that had been on top of me. Other than that door, the room was clean. There was not so much as a splinter of wood or metal. There didn't appear to be anything I could tear off the walls, floor, or ceiling I could use on the door. Then I heard the sound of a motor. Were my attackers coming back to beat and question me? If they planned to kill me, they could have done that earlier. What was this all about? I reached for my PUAI to contact the world outside and brought a smashed and useless mass of crumpled electronics from my pocket. My attackers, whomever they might be, had been quite thorough.

Men's voices sounded outside. I began kicking the door to get their attention, shouting for help between kicks.

"Someone's in there," said one startled voice.

"I'm trapped in here!" I shouted. "Can you open the door?"

"How'd you get in there with a locked door?"

"I was attacked, knocked out, and dumped in here last night. I have no idea who did it or why. Is the door locked out there?"

"With a big padlock," was the reply.

"Call the police, please," I pleaded. "I've been injured—lost some blood and don't may be badly hurt."

The sound of a phone call to 911 was a great relief and comfort.

An hour later I was being interviewed by Detective Karl Reston from a hospital bed in Lutheran Hospital, my head cleaned and bandaged and a few other cuts and abrasions patched up.

"You say you were attacked in a room in the Regency Hotel?"

"Yes, and I am worried about the lady, Mara Singleton, who was with me."

"Maybe she was a hooker, and you were set up for a robbery. That's not likely here, but it has happened."

"Impossible! Mara is a scientist at CDI. She's a colleague and a longtime friend. You must find her."

"We asked officers to check your story at the Regency right now. They'll report to me here as soon as they find anything. The Regency is a first-class hotel. They rarely cause us any problems, especially the kind you told us about. Hang on. I'm getting a call."

I watched as Officer Reston conferred with the men at the hotel. He was using the old cell phone system. IBIs were not yet in use by the police.

"They report there is no record of a Mara Singleton ever checking in. They checked the room that you claim she was in, and it's quite clean. It hasn't been occupied for at least two days. How do you explain that?"

"I can't. She arrived at the airport yesterday morning after a flight from Mexico City. She rented a Toyota from AVIS at the airport, came to CDI where we had lunch. After we left CDI, I went with her to the Regency and stayed with her as she checked in. I went up to her room with her and watched as she unpacked her things and placed them in drawers. She was planning to stay at the hotel for at least three weeks. Our company made all the arrangements."

After another lengthy cell phone exchange, Reston came back. "Everything you say—at least most of it—has been confirmed. CDI did make that reservation, and it was for one Mara Singleton. She was on the plane from Mexico City, and she did rent a Toyota from AVIS. They reported she changed her plans, returned the rental car last night, and caught an early morning flight back to Mexico City. She spent the night at a hotel near the airport."

"That's not possible! Something is wrong here. I'm a serious-minded engineer and worked at CDI for five years. I am not subject to hallucinations or flights of imagination. My record is impeccable. I know what I described to you happened."

"Well, Mr. Moon, that may all be true, but we are bound by facts we can verify, and those facts do not confirm your story. Fact is, they quite effectively refute it."

"Well, someone is messing with all of us big time, and I'd like to know why. As a matter of fact, I can quite accurately verify my story. I need another PUAI to replace the one my attacker demolished, and I can download records of most of what I told you." As I said it, I realized I could do no such thing. Both Mara's and my PUAIs had been turned off since shortly after she arrived. There would be no data recorded from that time on. The only data available would merely confirm the records Reston reported.

"I suggest you rest and take time to heal. That was one nasty knock on the head you took, and it might have muddled your memory. In the mean time, we'll contact your Ms. Singleton in

Mexico City and listen to her story. I've got to go back to work." As he walked out the door, Reston turned and faced me, a small grin softened his stony demeanor. "I don't think you're crazy. There is certainly more to this than appears on the surface. There is one powerful fact that adds credibility to what you told me."

"What's that?" I asked a bit sarcastically.

"That knock on the head you received, and you in that locked storage room. That's quite real and obvious. You didn't imagine that. So don't think my mind is closed on the subject, or that I don't believe you. Give me some more evidence. I'll listen."

My opinion of Officer Reston took a huge leap upward. That was the most encouraging thing that happened since the blow to my herad. Now I had work to do. The nurse informed me I was to remain hospitalized for the weekend and would be released on Monday. I had other plans. It took me thirty minutes to find my clothes, dress, and sneak down the service stairs to the first floor. I squared my shoulders and marched straight across the lobby and out into the parking lot, hoping my bandaged head and bloody clothes would not give me away. When I walked back to the Regency to retrieve my car from the parking lot, I walked through their lobby to see if any of the people I remembered from yesterday were there. No luck!

As I reached my car, I realized there were no keys in my pocket. A quick reach under the side and I retrieved the magnetic box containing spare keys to both my car and my apartment. I mentally patted myself on the back for such genius and headed for home. After changing my bloody clothes and checking my bandages, I grabbed the keys to my lab and headed for CDI.

Once inside my lab, I grabbed my spare PUAI from its charger on my desk and turned it on. *Mara! Mara!* My mind cued, searching for hers. Nothing! Wherever she was, she was off-u. I spent the rest of the day trying to make sense of what was going on with little success. Hell, I didn't even eat, I was so upset.

It was early evening when *Moon! Are you there?* came into my head. Another mind was on-u and linked. It was Vivek, the Italian member of our training group from a year ago. I was not in the mood for tech talk, but tried to keep that thought out of my mind. Piloto was a bit sensitive and easily hurt, even by what I considered the most innocent of thoughts.

What's up, man? I haven't heard a peep from you for months.

I've been doing training on advanced uses of the IBI since we completed our project. They made me head of our training program, not that I wanted it, but it does carry a nice increase in pay.

Congrats! You deserved a break. We both know how hard you worked on that project.

Thanks, I appreciate your thoughts, but that's not what I contacted you about.

As his thoughts flooded my mind, I was astonished. *I realize that now. It's Mara? She left CDI and went to work for Solomon Rachid in Pakistan. I find that hard to believe.*

Some rapid mental communication and my recent experience with Mara, the knock on the head, his source of the information on Mara, and our speculations about what this all meant was shared. We also shared that something was definitely wrong. We spent the better part of an hour linked mentally, sharing and speculating before we broke our contact promising to keep in touch.

Reflecting on what I learned from Vivek was sobering. I downloaded the TV news report from Pakistan, less than an hour old. There was Mara, with Rachid beside her, announcing she had left CDI and was joining Rachid's research group to further development of advanced IBI communication devices. She was definitely not herself. She appeared listless, heavily sedated and, I thought, a bit roughed up. Her speech was slow, deliberate, and brief. She was not there of her own volition. Rachid, an evil radical and enemy of all progressive nations, hated the Chinese and Americans and could never convince Mara to go to work for him willingly.

My next call, not IBI but cellular, was to my friend, Leo, at the Riverwalk Grille. After a few greetings, Leo saved me when he asked, "Who was that gorgeous little lady you had with you last night? She is sure something."

"Leo, you have no idea how comforting it is to hear you say that. Someday I'll tell you why, but for now, please know I will be forever grateful for your words."

"Moon? I always thought you were a bit strange. That confirms it." I could tell he was smiling and pulling my chain. "I also realized you two seemed to be a lot more than co workers. Something is going on between you. Am I right?"

"Right on, Leo. You are very observant. Do me a favor and keep that under your hat, will you? Don't let it be known to anyone else—that's anyone, please!"

"Mum's the word, friend. You can count on old Leo."

"There is one person you can share that with—if he ever asks about it."

"Who's that?"

"Lieutenant Reston, a Fort Wayne Police detective. Feel free to tell him about your experience but do so only in private."

"I know Reston. He brings his wife here frequently. He's an okay guy."

"That he is, my friend. I'd better return to work."

Reston! I thought. *I must talk to him and soon!* With that, I cued a call to Reston's home number and waited.

"Okay, Moon. What is it? Aren't you supposed to be in the hospital?" Reston's voice was definitely in the bothered state.

"I think you had better come to the lab and talk to me. I not only found a reliable witness to confirm my story but have a good idea what is going on."

"This had better be good, Moon. Don't you realize it's after ten on a Saturday night? I don't like wild-goose chases and this certainly smells like one to me."

My emphatic "It's not!"

This was greeted by a loud "Shit!" followed by "Okay! I'll give you a listen, but it had better be good."

In half an hour, Reston sat with me at my desk at CDI. After a short phone conversation with Leo and a view of the news reports about Mara, Reston was convinced and definitely on my side. He dispatched crime scene investigators to the hotel, AVIS, and the airport with instructions to "lean as hard as is necessary on anyone who might know anything about this little caper."

"Isn't this federal?" I asked. "Aren't the feds always brought in on kidnapping?"

"True enough, but first of all, there were several crimes committed in my jurisdiction, or did you forget the knot on your head?"

"Not at all. It still throbs."

"Okay then. Second, we don't have enough evidence that a kidnaping took place, and until that happens, I can't call in the feds. As soon as we obtain such evidence, I'll call them in personally. and third, this may be an international situation where I can't be of much help. Hell! At this point I wouldn't know who to notify. Would it be the United States, Mexico, or Pakistan?"

"I see what you mean."

"So let's deal with what we learned—here and now—the things we can legally investigate."

Reston's phone clicked as he was talking.

"Good work, Ramon. Don't leave until you question everyone possible."

Reston turned to me. "It seemed someone paid the night clerk at the hotel an enormous sum to remove all records of your friend's stay. Apparently, the lady walked out with two men while another two carried you out the service entrance, all to be forgotten and records obliterated in exchange for a large amount of money—several thousand dollars in fact. Ramon passed this information on to the boys who'll be calling on AVIS in the morning. They will use it to pry the truth out of the AVIS people."

"That sure makes me feel better. I knew I wasn't crazy."

Stilling walked in. "Moon, what are you doing here? I heard you were in the hospital, that you were mugged? Who is this?"

"This is Lieutenant Reston, a detective from the Fort Wayne Police. He's investigating the attack and the disappearance of Mara Singleton."

"She jumped ship yesterday. Went to Pakistan and joined that sleaze bag Solomon Rachid when she was supposed to be here. You helped arrange her supposed visit here, didn't you?"

"Yes!"

Stilling's face flushed with anger. "After she left here she hopped a plane to Pakistan early the next morning?"

"She was kidnaped. She didn't go willingly," I protested.

"How could you think that? In her press conference an hour ago, she said she chose to go."

"We were together all of yesterday until someone knocked me out and dragged her away last night. Believe me, she did not go willingly."

Reston piped in, "He's right about that. We confirmed he knows what he's talking about."

"Incredible! Incredible!" Stilling repeated. "Is anyone else at CDI aware of this?"

"Not that I know of. I didn't tell anyone—other than Reston here and Vivek Piloto in Italy. Oops!"

"I'd better inform Dr. Huer in Dalian right away," Stilling said as he rushed for his office and the secure phone.

"That should stir things up a bit for our friends in Pakistan," Reston said, smiling.

"I hope it doesn't put Mara in more danger than she is already."

Reston's response was not reassuring. "I doubt it will. but it could put international pressure on Rachid to give her back."

"That son of a bitch won't yield to international pressure. His puffed-up ego wouldn't allow it. No, he'll play this one out to the bitter end whatever his game."

"What could he want with her anyway? Do you have any idea?"

"Not at this point. I have no clue other than it must be something to do with the IBI system and our training program. What it might be specifically is anyone's guess."

"I'd better head for home. I told the missus I didn't think I would be long, and I wouldn't want to disappoint her. besides, there's not much we can do until Monday anyway."

"Yeah, I guess you're right, I'll soon be headed for home myself."

It wasn't more than two minutes after Reston left that Stilling burst into my lab, talking excitedly. "Dr. Huer wants us to do something about this!"

"Yeah? What?"

"It's dangerous, and he won't order you to do it, but he thinks you are the only one who could pull off her rescue."

"Rescue Mara? Me?"

"That's right, you!"

"What makes that genius think I can do it, or would try to? That's a dangerous game he's talking about. Solomon Rachid is no pansy. He plays for keeps. He kills people for fun."

"Exactly!"

"What do you mean, exactly?"

"Dr. Huer says you are young, strong, clever, ambitious, and in love with Mara Singleton, strong enough motivation."

"How could he possibly know that?"

"He's the inventor of the IBI system. He certainly knows a lot about the people working in his organization? He never for a moment believed Mara went there willingly. He understood your experience the moment I related it to him. He's sure you two are in love."

"Stilling, you amaze me. I think I would like to try that crazy idea. I had some Ranger training when I was in the military and I do keep myself in fairly decent shape. How does Dr. Huer propose I win at this undertaking?"

"First of all, I know you don't care much for me. You think I'm a jerk and not very sharp."

"Stilling? Don't say those things. You've already gone way up in my estimation. I know I seriously misjudged you."

"Don't apologize, Moon. We haven't the time for anything but getting you prepared and off to Pakistan. You'll fly commercial, and that first flight leaves early in the morning. There's lots you don't know that you must learn in the few hours left."

"Oh?"

"Yes!" Stilling was emphatic, excited, and unlike any other persona of his I had experienced. "You need to learn a lot, including how to use the latest military IBI unit which I plan to implant in your skull in the next ten minutes."

When I caught the six o'clock plane for Detroit, I was as steeped in new information and technology as could be completed in seven hours. My spare PUAI, still working properly, was in my pocket, but that was only as a ruse. The new military system, miniaturized to the size of a short length of pencil lead, was inside my skull, shielded by a new technique to be invisible to all kinds of indirect examinations including X-ray, sound, MRI, and several other sophisticated scanning systems. It used, but did not compromise, the existing IBI system already in use. The screen for this unit was my eyes. It appeared somewhat like the visual display used by fighter jets of a few decades ago. I focused on either the display or on the usual visual field beyond.

With a thought, I used the Ultranet normally or as a background to the MI-1 system which would override my PUAI in all situations. There was one other neat little feature. The MI-1 could communicate with all of the new IBI inserts, giving me selective access to the thoughts of those within about fifteen feet even when their PUAIs were shut off and without their knowledge. To sharpen my skills, I practiced doing this during the flights to Detroit and then New York. From New York to Pakistan, I slept most of the time, knowing that might be my only sleep for several days. My cover, sent out over a secure network operated by Rachid, was that I was coming to join Mara because I was so in love. They knew the truth about that, and we were counting on it to at least get us into his compound. From then on, I was on my own.

Oh yes. CDI equipped me with a new simple secret weapon, a pen with an air-pressure-fired bamboo dart that immobilized an average man in about two-tenths of a second. Crude but effective, it held six darts invisible to X-rays.

So equipped, I stepped off the plane in Karachi where I was arrested by Pakistan special military police. They took me to an interrogation room from hell, emptied my pockets, and took away all they found along with the small suitcase containing my clothes and toiletries. The questioning of the two black-clothed interrogators was neither gentle nor considerate. When I explained that I came to Pakistan to work for Solomon Rachid, they laughed.

"Who do you think we work for, American? We are part of Rachid's private army—his VM guard. He would like to know why you came, and we will soon be finding out."

As he pulled his arm back to strike me, another man wearing the same uniform as my tormentors came in and stopped him. "This is Mr. Leon Moon of the USA. He is to be the guest of Dr. Rachid and, as such, is not to be harmed, but protected from any who might wish him harm." Turning to me, he bowed. "I'm so sorry, Mr. Moon. My men made a foolish mistake and will be punished accordingly. Please follow me."

What he didn't know was that I knew his thoughts as clear as a bell. He obviously was using a CDI IBI implant system. His thoughts conveyed a far different picture from his words. *Count one for the good guys,* I thought as he handed me back my belongings and led me to where I was whisked off in one of three white SUVs.

An hour's bumpy ride and we arrived at what appeared to be a large fortress built back against a sheer stone cliff in the mountains. We waited as the huge gate swung open far enough for us to drive into a large, walled-in enclosure of at least twenty acres. We drove to the front of a rather impressive stone building with many carvings of people and animals atop low walls and in front of higher walls. It all appeared ancient. Once inside the large wooden doors, it was another world.

It was like a campus of modern, multistoried office buildings anywhere in the United States. The rows of windows apparently served offices and laboratories in what I realized was Rachid's main research facility. I was ushered directly into one of the smaller buildings and into a lavishly decorated reception room. We waited for but a moment until a neatly dressed woman in Western garb invited me to follow her.

"I am Rachel, Dr. Rachid's special assistant," she announced in flawless English with little accent as she motioned me toward a large ornate brass door which slid silently into the wall. "Dr. Rachid will see you now."

The room beyond the door was stark white, including the furniture, drapes, and carpet. Behind a rather modest white desk sat Solomon Rachid in a white lab smock over white pants and shirt. Seated beside his desk was Mara, also dressed completely in white.

"Come in, Mr. Moon, and welcome to our research facility," Rachid said quietly with a smooth, almost liquid voice. "I believe you know Ms. Singleton. How fortunate for us you decided to join our group. That is why you are here, I am told."

The MI-1 gave him a perfect reading of Mara's thoughts, but Rachid's were somehow blocked. Perhaps he did not use IBI implants although that seemed unlikely. Mara's mind fairly screamed at him in alarm. He could not link with her since he kept his PUAI turned off, closing his mind to unwanted intrusions.

"Yes, I thought since Mara chose to join you, I would like to do so as well, depending on your offer of course."

"Of course, of course," came from his narrow lips with a tone of sarcasm. "I understand you two are in love. The loyal lover coming to protect his loved one. How touching. Foolish, but quite admirable."

"Moon, you shouldn't be here. This madman now has us both," Mara almost cried as she said it. Her eyes were so terribly sad and her thoughts were more sad and terrified.

"Why is my coming so foolish? I have much to offer. You might consider it a ransom to recover, my dear lady. You should consider it."

"Why, Moon? I now hold you both. I find no compelling reason to release either of you for any reason. I hold two of the top IBI people in the world. Either of you would do my bidding to keep the other alive."

"True, but what if I told you that if one of us dies, the other will die instantly as well."

A sudden jolt of intense mental activity told me I had struck a nerve. This unblocked his mind to mine for a few seconds, long enough for me to understand what he planned and several other interesting items. It was obvious he knew nothing about the MI-1. He thought my mind was blocked because my PUAI was turned off. Advantage mine.

"And how do you intend to carry out such a feat?"

"That's for me to know and you not to understand."

"A foolish statement, young man. Perhaps I will incinerate you and see what happens."

"You'll not do that until you know why I'm here and what I intend to do."

"How can you be so sure? This little game does intrigue me, so perhaps I will let you live, at least for a few days while my associates extract what they can from you. Then I **will** incinerate you."

I had enough. I leaned over his desk, spoke sharply as to emphasize a point. I hit him dead center in the forehead with one of the bamboo darts from my pen directly from my pocket. He folded like a wilted plant. I pulled the dart from his forehead, grabbed his ID badge, and called for Rachel.

As she entered, I pointed to Rachid and said, "You'd better call a doctor. Dr. Rachid has collapsed from some sort of attack."

Her mind revealed a mixture of thoughts that I had killed him and genuine concern that what I said was true. When she found a strong and regular pulse, she was relieved and decided indeed to call for a doctor. She was doubly reassured when neither of us made a move to leave.

"What should we do?" I asked. "Can we help?"

"Go to your quarters and wait for further instructions. Here's the doctor. Go! Go!" Rachel was quite confused, and her thoughts betrayed her.

"Let's go," I urged Mara as I took her hand and headed for the door. "Where are your quarters?" I asked as quietly as possible.

"Down this way! But why do you want to go there? If you're thinking about escape, that's the wrong place to go."

"Walk naturally. I can't explain now, and turning on my PUAI would be a disaster, so trust me. I know what I'm doing."

"All right, Moon. and I do trust you."

"Take out your PUAI and drop it on the floor, now!"

As soon as it hit the floor, I ground it into a pulp with my heel. "Now they won't be able to track us. The GPS in my PUAI has been disabled, so they can't track me either."

"There are security cameras all over the place. They'll still know where we are."

"I'm counting on that. I know there is a heliport near here. Do you know where it is and how we can go there?"

"It's right at the end of the hall where my room is located."

"Great! That will make it easy."

"There are several guards always on duty, and the helicopter is locked down. It is released only when Rachid is planning to use it."

"He plans to use it in about ten minutes, or did before I zapped him."

"How do you know that?"

"I'll explain later. Here, pin this on under your blouse."

"What's that?"

"It's Rachid's ID badge. I yanked it off his coat as soon as he collapsed. I'm counting on it to give us access to that helicopter."

"How do you expect to fly it? Do you know how to fly one?"

"Flew several different types when I was in the military. This one can't be too difficult. but first we need to be inside your room."

"Why so?"

"We leave your ID badge there, and they'll think that's where you are. I doubt they will check. Rachid's ID should take care of getting you and me to the chopper. After that, it's prayer time."

As soon as we entered Mara's room, she dumped her ID badge on the bed, grabbed a long white coat, and we headed for the door. As we closed it behind us, we heard the announcement. "All guests, please stay in your quarters until notified it is safe to move about. There has been a security breach. Any guest found outside their quarters before the all-clear is sounded will be terminated."

"Well, the fats in the fire for sure," I remarked as we hurried toward the heliport.

"What?"

"It's an old Hoosier saying meaning there is no turning back."

"You can say that again . . . There's the stairs to the heliport. I wonder where the guards are. There are always two of them by the entrance to the stairs."

"My guess is they are all up on the roof guarding the helicopter, and the door at the top of the stairs will be locked. Let's go," I said, taking her hand and sprinting to the stairway and up the stairs to the door.

"There are at least six guards on the other side of that locked door. What can we do?"

"Stand next to the opening side of the door and try not to show your face. Hopefully they will rely on their ID scanner and not check you out too thoroughly. After all, you are now the big boss."

When we were positioned by the door, I began pounding on it and shouting, "Guards! I'm here for my trip. Open the door quickly and go down to guard the bottom of the stairs. Whoever caused the alarm may try to come up here."

Immediately four of the six unlocked the door, burst through, and headed down the stairs. The ruse worked. "Now, dear one, head straight for the chopper and climb in. I'll deal with the other two guards."

By the time Mara reached the chopper, I had locked the door. One of the guards opened the door and helped Mara inside as I held my breath. As he closed the door, the other guard approached me. The tiny bamboo dart folded him to the deck.

I called to the other guard, "Help! Your fellow here passed out." A few steps in this direction and he joined his buddy on the deck. They would be out for several hours.

Climbing into the chopper, I took a quick check of the instruments. Controls were fairly standard. *I can fly this bird if I can start it.* I thought. As soon as I grasped the yoke, a voice startled me, "Voice print command please."

"Shit!" I uttered out loud. "This damned bird requires a voice print to start. Now what do we do." Then it hit me. Mustering all the mental power I possessed, I thought clearly, *Start engines!*

Immediately the starting sequence began, and as the rotors gained speed, the voice said, "Have a successful trip!" Rachid had a mental override to the starting lock.

"Moon, you're a genius!" I remarked as we lifted off and headed for India a few hundred miles away. Mara beamed.

"We're not out of the woods yet. This chopper does at best about two hundred. That's at least an hour and a half to friendly skies. Pakistan has jets that can cover that distance in less than a third of that time. Oh yes, toss that ID out. We don't want them using that to track us."

As soon as the ID was dropped, I changed, heading far to the east. I explained to Mara, "That will take us longer to reach India, but anyone chasing us will assume we were continuing on our previous heading and spend most of their search efforts in that area. By the time they figure out what we did, we should be safe and sound." That is if the chopper itself doesn't use a GPS, a probability I didn't share with Mara.

About forty miles from safety, our luck ran out as a jet fighter blew past us at high speed. Before he made his turn for another pass and a kill, I dropped down on the deck and began following a riverbed that snaked through the mountains toward India.

It was chancy, but not doing it was suicide. On his next pass, the jet fired a missile that missed by at least fifty feet and slammed into a nearby mountain side.

"My guess is the next missile he fires will be a heat seeker. I'll play hell avoiding that."

After two more misses, it was obvious he had no heat-seeking missiles mounted. We were in luck, at least for the moment. Seeing a narrow canyon leading off toward the south, I took a chance and dove for it. With luck it would be a shorter route to safety. Wrong choice. The canyon wandered about, narrowed dangerously, and ended at a sheer cliff. Up and over was all I could do. Our luck changed as the jet flew under our sudden change of direction and plowed directly into the cliff. At his speed, he couldn't turn as sharply as we and paid the price. We were safe once more, at least for the moment.

Back up to higher altitude, we headed directly south toward India, less than ten miles away. Unfortunately, these jets would pursue us on into India in spite of the border. This too, I neglected to tell Mara. No need to alarm her.

My welcome words "We are now over India" were greeted with a sudden lurch as a pair of jets passed a few feet above us and hit us with their backwash. It almost turned us upside down, dropping us at least five hundred feet before I regained control.

"Another one like that and we'll be kissing those mountains below us," I warned Mara.

"Aren't we over India? Aren't they supposed to stay in Pakistan?"

"I'm afraid those pilots don't concern themselves too much with borders. I don't want to alarm you, but we don't have many options left. The terrain is flattening out, which means there are no deep canyons for us to fly in. If we fly too close to the surface, they can hit us with their backwash and knock us into the ground. If we fly too high, they can take us out with missiles or those old-fashioned guns they carry.

"I'm going to fly backward for a while. Then I can see them coming and avoid their attack by dropping or veering sharply. At the speeds they're flying, it's hard to change directions quickly. Watch for them, high and to the left toward the sun. That's where they're most likely to start their attack. I'm experiencing enough problems keeping from flying backward into the ground, since I can't see where we're going."

"There they are!" Mara exclaimed, pointing exactly where I said they would be coming from.

We watched as the tiny black dots grew larger and larger, coming straight at us. I planned to spin and dive for the ground at the last minute, or when I spotted missile exhaust trails. Unexpectedly, the jets turned and headed away from us. The reason soon showed itself as four jets with clearly Indian markings flew by about a thousand feet above us and directly toward the Pakistanis.

In less than half an hour, two Indian helicopters guided us to a safe landing at a military airport while the four jets flew past in an obvious salute maneuver. We were back among friends.

We were surprised when greeted by a large "Welcome CDI" banner above the terminal plaza entrance.

When the base commander greeted us by name, he added, "Thanks to the Ultranet and the old Internet, we were able to follow your exploits with interest since you took off from Rachid's compound. That was a daring rescue, Mr. Moon."

"We were lucky."

"Lucky and clever. You'll be interested to know that those were not actual Pakistani jets trying to destroy you. Rachid has been supporting a breakaway rebel military that has quite a bit of captured Pakistani equipment including four jet fighters. Your escape caused them to reveal themselves and their base. As a result, the real Pakistan military can now attack that previously unknown base and close it down. The same action also provided the Pakistan government with a valid reason to put Rachid out of business, permanently."

I looked at Mara and grinned.

Color Me Purple

Scene: a suburban bathroom in the morning. Darryl, fiftyish, is staring in the mirror and having an involved conversation with himself.

DARRYL. I'm purple! Wow! I know this is a crazy dream, but purple? A nice shade of orange wouldn't be bad or light blue or pale green, but purple, a bright purple face. It's my face all right, but purple. My hands are purple. Okay, I'll go along with the dream. Let's see. My eyes are still green, and the whites are still white. My tongue is purple, but my teeth are still white. Okay, greyish yellow, but my hair is definitely white. Ah, you handsome dude. Even purple, you're gorgeous. I wonder what my wife will think? I'll check to see if she's purple too.

(He leaves the bathroom, glances at his sleeping wife then returns, examines himself, and continues talking under his breath.)

Nope, her soft sleeping face is like always. I think I'll let her sleep 'til I figure this out. I don't seem to be dreaming, but this can't be for real. Ouch! Pinching hurts. Nothing changed, so I'm obviously not dreaming. Let's take these PJs off and see what color the rest of me is.

Yikes! Purple chest, purple legs, purple feet, and purple—well, you know, purple everything. This can't be for real . . . can it? If I'm dreaming, it's convincing. Was I poisoned at that dinner last night? I feel fine, but I'm beginning to be a bit irritated. Did those guys spike my dinner with some kind of dye? I'll kill 'em if they did. I'll take a quick shower and see if it'll wash off.

(He turns on the water, steps into the shower, and begins scrubbing vigorously.)

Damn! If it's a dye, it's a permanent dye. Waterproof too. The palms of my hands and bottoms of my feet are purple. Pale purple, but purple. Maybe it's just on the surface. I know. I'll try that abrasive loofah sponge.

(He scrubs rapidly on his arm with the loofah sponge.)

No luck. It doesn't lighten in the slightest. What will Jenny think when she wakes up? And the kids? They'll all be waking in a few minutes.

JENNY, *his wife, calls from the bedroom.* Darryl? Are you taking a shower? You took one last night, or did you forget?

DARRYL, *a bit startled.* Yeah! I musta forgot. Well, you can't be too clean. (*Then to himself*) What will I do when she sees me? I'll bet she faints dead away. (*Now aloud to Jenny.*) Are you . . . getting up?

JENNY, *sarcastically.* Of course, idiot. In case you've forgotten, I must get up and go to work. If you made more money, I wouldn't need to work. When are you going to ask for a raise, Darryl?

DARRYL, Not now . . . uh, not until we receive the next quarterly performance review anyway. (*Then to himself*) She'll be in here in a moment, then things will be exciting.

JENNY, *walking into the bathroom.* What are you standing there naked for? At least put on your underwear.

DARRYL, *looking worried.* Uh . . . don't you see anything peculiar?

JENNY, *in a joking tone.* You're always peculiar. Especially when you're naked.

DARRYL, *to himself.* What's going on here? No reaction at all and she looked straight at me. (*Aloud*) Don't you see anything different about me?

JENNY, *genuinely concerned.* Well . . . is it your potbelly? It seems a bit smaller this morning. Have you been dieting? That's wonderful. Maybe by summer you can reduce it down so you don't show that dunlop problem.

DARRYL, *quizzically.* Dunlop problem?

JENNY, *complaining.* Yeah! You know. Your belly dunlop over your belt. You had such a neat body when we first married.

DARRYL, *a bit hurt.* Is it that bad? . . . and no, I haven't been dieting.

JENNY, *lecturing.* Well yes! It's not like it used to be and you should be dieting.

DARRYL, *aggravated.* That's not what I'm asking about. (*Then to himself*) Maybe she's ignoring it in hopes it will go away. (*Aloud*) I mean my skin. Isn't it different?

JENNY, *in a joking tone then concerned then aggravated again.* It's the same old pasty skin to me. You know, you should go to one of those tanning parlors and be tanned. You are so much better looking when you're tan. Why are you staring at yourself so intently?

DARRYL, *defensively.* Okay! Okay!

JENNY, *questioning.* What's taking you so long to dress? And why are you examining your hands that way.

DARRYL, *explaining.* I'm getting dressed, and in what way am I examining my hands?

JENNY, *sarcastic again.* You're looking at them as if you'd never seen them before. You didn't polish your nails, did you?

DARRYL, *matter-of-factly.* No! Of course not. They seem a bit strange to me. Like they're discolored or something.

JENNY, *concerned and in motherly tone.* Let me see . . . They aren't a bit discolored as far as I can tell. You're imagining things. Why don't you go start breakfast. The kids will be up soon, and I must leave early.

DARRYL, *patronizing.* Okay! As soon as I finish dressing. *Then to himself as he goes to the kitchen.* What the hell is wrong with my eyes? Nothing else is purple. Not in the slightest. The hallway is normal. The kitchen is normal, and the appliances are still stark white. Boy, is my hand purple against the frig.

(His son, Jerry, enters the kitchen.)
JERRY. Hi, Dad! What's up?

DARRYL, Hi, Jer.

(Jerry is fifteen and has mouth to match.)
JERRY. What's the matter with you? You look strange.

DARRYL, *to himself.* At least he notices. *(Aloud)* How do you mean, strange. *(To himself again)* Now I'll find some answers.

JERRY, *almost concerned.* You seem so worried . . . or surprised. Like someone startled you or something.

DARRYL. Is that all?

JERRY, *still untypically concerned.* Well . . . yes. You do have a strange look on your face . . . like Mom did yesterday when I dropped her bowling ball right behind her and scared her out of her wits. She had that same startled look on her face. That is until she realized I was the culprit who scared her. Then she like wanted to kill me.

DARRYL, *in parenting mode.* Jerry, you ought to stop scaring people like that. Some day you'll do that to the wrong person and you'll wish you hadn't.

JERRY, *back to know-it-all teen again.* Ha! What could happen?

DARRYL, *still in parenting mode.* The wrong person might become angry and beat the tar out of you. I'm surprised Mom didn't at least backhand you.

JERRY, *typically.* She wouldn't do that. It was only a joke.

DARRYL, *seriously to himself.* A joke! Are they all playing a joke on me? Jerry may be the culprit, with the rest of the family in on it. Should I play along or call them on it now, or at breakfast.

DONNA, *ten years old, enters the room.* Hi, Daddy!

DARRYL, *lovingly.* Good morning, pumpkin. How about a kiss?

DONNA, *concerned.* Sure, Daddy! (*smack*) What's wrong? Are you mad at me?

DARRYL, *sweetly.* Of course not. What made you ask such a thing?

DONNA, *almost pouty.* You seem angry, that's all.

JERRY, *typically.* He's not angry, Donna, scared or surprised or somethin' like that, but not angry. He sure is out of it this morning.

DONNA, *concerned.* You and Mommy didn't fight, did you?

DARRYL, *solemnly.* Your Mommy and I never fight. We discuss things, that's all.

JENNY, *coming into the kitchen.* What's this about your father and me fighting? We don't fight and you know it.

DONNA, *questioning.* Then why does Dad seem so strange?

JENNY, *in command mode.* He seems normal to me. You kids, set the table—now! I'm in a hurry this morning. Honey, will you grab the cereal and bowls? I'll get the milk and juice. Cooperation—that will get things done in a hurry.

DARRYL, *muses to himself.* If this is a joke, it's a damned good one. They couldn't act this normally with me all purple. It's like I'm the only one that sees it. I'd better call in sick and go see a doctor. I'm apt to crack up if this continues.

JENNY, *as mother superior.* Darryl, you'd better hurry yourself. You know you scheduled that important meeting with Mr. Herkimer at nine, and you know what a stickler he is about being on time.

DARRYL, *startled, gets up, speaks then thinks to himself.* Holy cow, thanks. I had forgotten all about that meeting. (*To himself*) That should be interesting. If I look purple to Herkimer, he'll fire me on the spot. Damn! I sure wish I knew what's going on. Let's see . . . I've got roughly an hour and a half. Unless I'm the only one who sees it, my purple face should cause some interesting responses on the bus ride to work.

- ☺ -

DARRYL, *muses to himself, walks into the office and up to the reception desk.* No one seemed to pay him any attention on the bus or here in the office. I'll check in with Glynda. (*To Glynda*) Good morning, Glynda. Is Mr. Herkimer in his office? We are to meet in about five minutes.

GLYNDA, *the master receptionist.* No, he's waiting for you in that little conference room at the end of the hall. He was there when I came in. See him there sitting with his back to the door beyond the table?

DARRYL, *seriously.* Yeah. That's funny. Not like him.

GLYNDA, *surprised.* He wouldn't turn around when he said good morning as I popped my head in to greet him. Told me to leave and not let anyone in but you.

DARRYL, *worried, then talks to himself.* I'd best be cautious when I go in. That is strange. It isn't good for me. This is supposed to be an important meeting and he's already acting strangely.

MR. HERKIMER, *worried.* That you, Darryl?

DARRYL, *solemnly.* Yes, sir.

MR. HERKIMER, *worried, but still the boss*. Take a seat at the table, and we'll talk.

DARRYL, *incredulously*. Like this? I mean with your back to me?

MR. HERKIMER, *definitely in command*. That's right. I'm testing out a new theory for talking with employees. It's nothing personal.

DARRYL, *to himself, surprised*. Holy cow! He doesn't realize it, but I can see the reflection of his face in the window on the other side of the room. It's as purple as mine. (*Then to Herkimer in a commanding voice*) Sir, I think you ought to take a close look at me.

MR. HERKIMER, *startled*. No way! This new method doesn't allow it.

DARRYL, *straightforward*. Mr. Herkimer, my face is as purple as yours.

MR. HERKIMER, *incredulous*. What are you talking about, Darryl? Whose face is purple?

DARRYL, *straight talking*. It's true, sir. That's how I woke up this morning. With purple skin—all over. I'll come around in front of you so you can see.

MR. HERKIMER, *startled, still wary*. Damn it, Darryl. Stay right where you are.

DARRYL, *convincingly*. No one else in the family commented on anything unusual at breakfast, and on the bus, no one paid any attention to me. I tell you, you appear normal to everyone. except for me that is, and I'll bet I am purple to you. Take a close look. You can see my reflection in the window and I can see yours.

MR. HERKIMER, *startled and then amazed*. Well, I'll be. You're right. Come around in front of me so I can see you better.

DARRYL, *straight talk again*. Okay. What do you think is going on? (*Then to himself*) That usual florid face of his is a really bright purple with darker purple blotches where he usually has red ones. At least I'm not the only one.

MR. HERKIMER, *explaining*. I don't know. When I got up and looked in the mirror it was the shock of a lifetime. Fortunately, Ethel is away, so I got dressed and drove down early before anyone else came in. You're the first person I've shown my face to. I didn't see another single soul like this, all the way downtown. Everyone seemed normal. Now you. Any ideas?

DARRYL, *knowingly*. No, but it's obvious regular people see us as normal, so we don't need to sneak around hiding our skin.

MR. HERKIMER, *relieved*. That's a relief. It's also a huge relief to realize I'm not the only one. What do you think happened to us?

DARRYL, *more confidently*. I can think of several ideas now that I find you have the same problem. It must be something to do with our eyes.

MR. HERKIMER. How's that possible?

DARRYL, It's only logical. We both see ourselves and each other as purple, and no one else does. It's much more likely that our eyes see us as purple than everyone else seeing us as normal when we actually are purple. The latter is highly unlikely.

MR. HERKIMER. Why don't we see some other things as purple then? If it's our eyes, surely we'd see something else as purple when it's not. Wouldn't we?

DARRYL, *now in his element, explaining*. Not necessarily, particularly if the same thing was in our skin. Sorta like things that fluoresce in ultraviolet light.

MR. HERKIMER, *impressed*. Darryl, how do you know all this? I never knew you understood chemistry or other science. You're a lot smarter than I gave you credit for being.

DARRYL, *pleased*. Thank you, sir. Now we need to figure out what the two of us have done the same that created this effect.

MR. HERKIMER. I wonder if we're not the only ones.

DARRYL, What do you mean?

MR. HERKIMER. Let's walk through the plant and see if there are any other purple people. We can round them up and use their help.

DARRYL, *smiling broadly*. Good idea.

MR. HERKIMER, *turning and heading for the outer office*. Let's go.

DARRYL, (*to himself while peering about at all the faces.*) I can't see a single purple face in the whole office. Maybe Mr. Herkimer can see some. (*To Herkimer*) There's none in the office that I can see. What about you?

MR. HERKIMER, *disappointed*. Me either. Let's walk through the plant. There may be some among the two hundred odd people on the shift.

DARRYL, *after they walked through the plant*. Do you see any? I don't see a one.

MR. HERKIMER, *turning back toward the office*. Let's check the research lab.

DARRYL, *as they walk into the lab*. Where is everyone? John, Ken, and Jan don't seem to be around.

MR. HERKIMER, *to David, the lab manager*. Marilyn isn't here either. David, where is everyone? Are you and Penny the only ones here?

DAVID, *explaining*. The four who are missing all called in sick this morning. They were the four that were working with you two on that new systemic insect repellant last week. What's going on?

MR. HERKIMER, *a light goes on in his head*. Darryl, are you thinking what I'm thinking?

DARRYL, *as things click into place*. Right with you, Mr. H. I'll bet they stayed home because they're purple too.

DAVID, *surprised*. What do you mean, They're purple too?

MR. HERKIMER, *laughing*. It's a little joke between Darryl and me.

DARRYL, *thinking quickly*. Yeah! We were wondering what it would feel like to wake up and be purple.

DAVID, *shaking his head in disbelief*. Weird, weird. You guys are really weird.

MR. HERKIMER, *as they head for the office*. Let's go call our missing lab workers and see if they can answer some of our questions.

DARRYL, *knowingly as they walk together:* I'll bet that's it. Somehow that repellant affected our eyes and our skin. I'll bet we surprise the others when we ask if they're purple. That has to be it.

- ☺ -

Darryl's bathroom some three weeks later. Darryl gazes intently at his face in the mirror, talking to himself.

DARRYL. Finally, after almost three weeks, the purple is beginning to fade. It's blotchy on my face, and my chest is almost back to normal. I don't know if I'll ever tell Jenny. She wouldn't believe me anyway.

JENNY, *walking into the bathroom.* Darryl! Are you still staring at your face in the mirror? Honestly, I don't know what's gotten into you these past few weeks. You were never so vain before.

DARRYL, *smiling broadly in satisfaction.* Sorry, honey. A few of the guys at work developed a rash because of some of the chemicals we've been using. I keep checking to see if I've got it.

JENNY, *matter-of-factly.* Well, do you?

DARRYL, *smiling and pleased with himself.* No. Everything seems to be okay.

JENNY, *relieved.* Thank goodness. I wouldn't want anything to interfere with your new job. That big raise will sure make things better around here. I wonder why Herkimer promoted you before your review. and such a big promotion.

DARRYL, *smiling broadly in satisfaction at his clever response.* I haven't the slightest idea. Maybe it's because he turned purple.

JENNY, *sarcastically.* Yeah! Right!

Two Letters

Alonzo and Stephanie were high school sweethearts in Cleveland Ohio, They were the most popular couple in their school and had many friends. So it was quite natural that they married not long after their graduation. Alonzo, who became interested in working with wood in shop class at school, started working as an apprentice carpenter to his father as soon as he became eligible for the carpenter apprentice program. Soon after he started, they were married. While he was an apprentice, Stephanie went to secretarial school and soon had a job as a secretary for a small local business. They were happy, successful and in love.

After about three years they had saved enough for a down payment for a small home near her parents in a lower middle class neighbor hood on the west side. It wasn't too long after they moved into their new house that Stephanie announced, "Guess what, Alonzo, I'm pregnant."

Alonzo was not happy. "Why did this happen when we've taken on the responsibility of a home?"

Stephanie's head slumped as the tears blossomed and crawled down her cheeks. "I'm sorry. I expected you to be happy at the news."

"Well - - - I am, sort of. but it's gonna make things tough around here when you stop workin' and we lose your paycheck. I don't know how we'll manage."

"That won't be for at least six months. We'll just save up."

"And give up the idea of that new car we were considering." He replied gloomily.

"When I told mom she said we could use the crib and baby bed my sis has in storage so we won't be required to pay for that. We'll be OK. She is also giving me her old sewing machine."

"Big deal! We still need living room furniture. That bare room always bothers me."

Stephanie smiled and her face brightened. "You'll earn your carpenter ticket soon—about the time the baby gets here, then your pay alone should equal both our present incomes."

Alonzo leaned back in his chair, his face relaxing as the tension subsided. "That's right. I can ask for some overtime work to help out."

"Now you're thinkin'! Imagine how wonderful—our own little baby."

"I can build him some cabinets and shelves for his room, and a youth bed when he gets a bit older. Yeah! It'll be fun."

"Hold on there Mr Spade. How do you know it won't be a girl?"

"Well, I guess a girl would be OK. They're cute and pretty, but a boy—we would play ball together, do all those guy things together."

Alonzo got his way. They had a son and named him Gregory after his uncle. A year later they had a girl, Selma, and two years after that another girl named Velma. They had to wait almost five years before being able to afford that "new" car and it was a used Ford station wagon with about thirty thousand miles on it.

During the next year Alonzo and his dad joined forces and started their own contracting firm, Joseph Spade and Son, and started building houses. During the next ten years the children grew and the business expanded. In fact, Alonzo and his dad became modestly wealthy. They both built rather expensive new houses in an upscale suburb and their business sported a classy new building to house their trucks and equipment.

The children did quite well in their new schools. Alonzo became quite an athlete and Velma, a bright young girl, was a top student. Things went smoothly for a while until Selma began running with the wrong crowd of wealthy trouble makers. When she was fifteen Selma became pregnant.

Her attitude, "All the other girls were doing it. So what's the big deal? I can bring it up OK."

Stephanie and Alonzo were soon arguing about whether she should abort the bay. Alonzo was for it, Stephanie against. They were greeted with a nasty response from Selma.

"I will not abort this damned kid. He's mine and nobody but me will make that decision, so shut up about it."

"How are you going to handle it? Is your mother going to give up her new job to stay home and bring up **your** kid?"

Stephanie bristled. "Don't you talk like that to my daughter. Of course we will help, do whatever we can. That's our grandchild you know."

Alonzo stomped out of the house and headed for the local bar, an action he would take increasingly as the tension and conflict in his home grew and expanded involving the other two children. Mother and baby moved into a spare room and stayed. The baby was a boy they named Fred after his father. The father, a senior about to graduate first promised to marry Selma and provide for the boy. That soon evaporated as he denied all responsibility and moved far away to go to college. It took a great deal of persuasion to convince Selma to go back to school. Never much of a student, she went back reluctantly and did poorly.

Alonzo, now a regular at the local bar, was drinking "with his buddies" more and more. This led to arguments with both Stephanie and Greg. Both of them had to pick Alonzo up at the bar whenever he became too drunk to drive. The year Stephanie turned forty-five, she could handle no more. She threw Alonzo out of the house and filed for divorce. Alonzo was emotionally devastated as he still loved Stephanie. By the time the divorce was final Alonzo had moved into an apartment near his business. That same year Alonzo's dad, Joseph, died of a heart attack leaving the contracting business to Alonzo. It was more than he could handle so he sold it to two brothers and stayed on as a carpenter. Alonzo was fifty and a recovering alcoholic.

Stephanie tried several times to bring herself to reconcile with Alonzo. Each time she was afraid things would go back to the way they were. This was true even after she learned Alonzo was no longer drinking. She couldn't bring herself to stop hating him for what he had become. Alonzo Jr, finally reconciled with his dad who had watched his college and then professional football career from a respectful distance. Alonzo adored his children. They were reconciled before Greg retired from pro ball, so Alonzo Senior was able to attend a number of games as his son's guest. Velma, always by her mother's side, never reconciled or met with her father in spite of his frequent efforts. Selma never reconciled with anyone. Two failed marriages and drugs were defining her life.

As the years passed, Stephanie, by now a bitter woman, cultivated her anger with Alonzo, blaming him for all the family's woes. On the other hand, Alonzo's longing and love for his wife grew. Afraid of her reaction, he never contacted her though he did drive past her home frequently and went to the library where she worked to view her while remaining unseen.

One day Alonzo awoke and found himself in the hospital, the victim of a serious heart attack. He was seventy. As he lay in bed he decided to write Stephanie and tell her how much he still loved her. He wrote a full page letter saying how sorry he was for what he had done and asking her forgiveness. He also begged her to come to see him before he died. His letter was mailed on a Tuesday.

The previous week Stephanie had an especially hostile meeting with Selma who was, as always, asking for money. Fresh off that encounter, Stephanie vented her pent up frustration and anger at Alonzo in a hate letter she mailed to his apartment. Friday she received Alonzo's letter which she first threw in the trash. After some time, she retrieved the letter and read it. All the hate she had cultivated for so many years left in an instant. The love she knew when they were young returned in a flash and rushed back to overcome her heart. In a gush of tears she hurried to the hospital to try to see Alonzo and retrieve her angry letter before he read it.

Rushing up to the desk she asked breathlessly, "I'm Stephanie Spade. I learned my husband has had a heart attack and is here."

The nurse checked and announced, "Yes he is here in intensive care. Dr. Bowman will be out to see you in a few minutes."

"Can't I see my husband? It's important."

"Not until Dr. Bowman can speak with you. He knows you're here and will be with you in a few minutes. There's a small conference room right here across the hall. Please wait for Dr. Bowman there."

Stephanie walked across the hall and sat down in the tiny room. After about fifteen minutes Dr. Bowman entered the room.

"Mrs. Spade?"

"Yes."

"I'm Dr. Bowman from ICU. I've been caring for your husband."

"How is he? Can I see him?"

"I'm terribly sorry, but Mr. Spade passed away several hours ago."

Stephanie burst out in uncontrollable sobs and finally managed to ask, "How did it happen?"

"His heart attack was a major one. He barely made it to the hospital. He lived several days longer than we expected him to. Didn't you know he was here?"

"No, we were divorced for more than twenty years. I received this letter from him only this afternoon and I rushed right over."

"Such a shame. He seemed such a kind gentle man, always spoke highly of you and of his children, three I believe."

"Yes, he always loved our children."

Dr. Bowman struggled for a while trying to remove something from his coat pocket. Finally he retrieved a crumpled piece of paper "Incidentally, here is a letter he received. It was clutched in his hand when we found him."

The End of the Beginning of the End??

In the beginning—or was it really the end? Maybe it was the beginning of the end, or was it the end of the beginning? Or even the beginning of the end of the beginning—of the end? Damn! It's confusing. Anyway, she was there, as was he. At least—I thought he and she were there. I smelled her fragrance, or was it his breath? Of course, it could hardly be his breath since she—or was it he? —anyway, we don't take breaths. We simply breathe through our skin. Was it another one like her—and him. I couldn't see a thing, but that's not surprising since I have no eyes or organs with which to see. Oh, I can sense light—and lots of other electromagnetic energy—it's that I sense it, like I do radiant heat, all over my body. I feel a general direction of the source. I know to go the other way when it gets too strong. Sometimes that's hard to do.

You see, I have no legs, or arms for that matter, so I can't run away. She doesn't either, but he does move around. I'm on his and her trail again. I can taste that she and he were here—recently. Oh the passion of it all, the wonderful feeling of touching skin against skin. We are covered with skin, which, in fact covers our entire bodies. We do have mouths, no teeth, but mouths, soft mouths with which we ingest all that wonderful stuff. We also grow tiny claws or bristles along the last third of our body. They let us hold on to our homes when creatures try to pull us out.

Then there's the touching, the wonderful sensual pleasure of merging our skin with each other and sharing bodily fluids. It is an ecstacy so delicious that we risk our lives to enjoy the sharing. Leaving the relative safety of our homes, we venture out in search of each other and that wonderful sensual, sexual sharing.

That's when the monsters often attack. Things with claws, or teeth, or large gaping mouths, or beaks, or—well, all manner of horrors they employ to snatch us up or pull us from our homes and eat us. That's why at the slightest sound, the slightest vibration, we retreat into our homes, deep into our homes where it's safe, where the claws or teeth or mouths or beaks cannot reach us. We hear the slightest sound the monsters make, even without ears. We feel the vibrations in the air and through the earth around our bodies. That's how we know the monsters are out there. When they are, we only feel safe when we are alone and deep within our homes. Of course, we are not safe there either. Some of the monsters pursue us in our homes, destroying them with their claws and teeth and pulling us out to be eaten. Oh, the horror of it all.

But I digress. I venture cautiously from my home because it is still. The night is so beautifully quiet and gloriously damp. Her scent, or is it his, wafts through the moist air. I taste it with my skin and the excitement grows. Suddenly we touch, barely at first, a taste, a growing sensuous feeling. We move slowly over each other, melding more and more of our skin together. Finally we are in full sexual embrace, my he and her she, her he and my she. Ecstacy oh ecstacy—mutual orgasm—exchange of bodily fluids—it goes on for hours. Finally and reluctantly we part and withdraw into our separate homes. The promise of a new family now rests within both of us. After several days a capsule containing our precious infants is cast off. In a few weeks our new family will set out to eat, grow, build a home, and love as we did to keep the race going.

Once again—in the beginning—or was it really the end? Maybe it was the beginning of the end, or even the end of the beginning? Or it could be the beginning of the end of the beginning—of the end?

Do you know who or what I am?

❇   ❇   ❇

HINT 1 - Aw c'mon you guys. Keep fishing. You'll remember me.

HINT 2 - I am recognized as one of the most common and widespread critters on the globe. Among all creatures, I am exactly half way between the least complex and the most complex. One of the most successful and vital creatures on the earth, we populate all but the most severe ecologies. We range in size from less than a centimeter long to over four meters. We're an alien creature that lives right in your back yard—front too. There are more than 2,700 species worldwide and we come in red, white, pink, blue, grey and green.

Answer - You will know me if you are fishermen. We are often hunted and used by small boys. That is the horror of being a fishworm, earthworm or angleworm, from the word, *angle*, for to fish. Among the annelids, we earthworms are special because we are super-streamlined, stripped-down, no-nonsense, highly evolved critters.

Check out these sites:

http://www.backyardnature.net/earthwrm.htm

http://www.kidcyber.com.au/topics/worms.htm

❇   ❇   ❇

Each worm "eats" his/her way through the soil making burrows that are their "homes." These burrows can be several feet deep. Most, but not all species come to the surface at night to "mate" with the nearest member of the same species. They try to keep the rear segments of their body in their burrows so they can withdraw when danger threatens. Toads, frogs, salamanders, and small rodents are their main nighttime predators, while robins, flickers, and blue jays forage for them during the day. They are the main food source for moles, the only predator that digs them out.

Examine a section of lawn at night almost anywhere and you will see "night crawlers" stretched out of their burrows, their bodies "stuck" together mating or else alone, searching for a mate. Examine any earthworm and you will find a fleshy "ring" covering numerous segments. This egg sac is slightly larger than the worm's body and of a different color. Once the eggs are fertilized, the worm backs its body out of the sac leaving a small ball of flesh to protect the eggs and keep them moist until they hatch. A careful examination of soil in early summer will often produce several of these tiny balls of flesh.

They are fascinating animals most people know little about.

✳   ✳   ✳

ARE EARTHWORMS IMPORTANT?

The actions and results of what earthworms do, certainly is not simple in ecological terms. The naturalist Charles Darwin, after making a careful study of them, wrote this:

"...it may be doubted if there are any other animals which played such an important part in the history of the world as these lowly organized creatures."

"History of the world," he said!

One important thing that earthworms do is to plow the soil by tunneling through it. Their tunnels provide the soil with passageways through which air and water can circulate, and that's important because soil microorganisms and plant roots need air and water like we do. Without some kind of plowing, soil becomes compacted, air and water can't circulate in it, and plant roots can't penetrate it.

One study showed that each year on an acre (0.4 hectare) of average cultivated land, 16,000 pounds (7200 kg) of soil pass through earthworm guts and are deposited atop the soil -- 30,000 pounds (13,500 kg) in really wormy soil! Charles Darwin himself calculated that if all the worm excreta resulting from ten years of worm work on one acre of soil were spread over that acre, it would be two inches thick (5.08 cm).

This is something we should appreciate because earthworm droppings -- called castings when deposited atop the ground -- are rich in nitrogen, calcium, magnesium, and phosphorus, and these are all-important nutrients for healthy, prospering ecosystems. In your own backyard you might be able to confirm that grass around earthworm burrows grows taller and greener than grass a few inches away.

Sea Cliff

He had a lifelong weakness for controlling things and people, but none of that mattered anymore. The vultures were outside, already fighting over the best morsels. He hadn't moved or spoken in weeks but, as she reached over to touch the artery pulsing in his hand, his eyes flashed open and he said, "What the hell are you doing with my hand. That hurt."

She jumped back. Lines of startled concern mapped her face. "Thank God. You've come to. I'm so sorry. I didn't know you were back with us."

"What do you mean by back with us? And who in hell are you?"

"Addy, I'm Lois, your wife. Don't you remember? You've been in a coma, haven't moved, spoken, or opened your eyes in several weeks. Ever since you took that terrible fall."

"I fell? How? Where? What happened?"

"We were hiking the trail by the sea cliff. You were right in front of me when you tripped over that tree root and plunged off the cliff."

"What cliff? I don't remember any trail or cliff. Not one by the sea. There are certainly no sea cliffs in Denver."

"You were lying on the rocks. I thought you were dead. Our friends, Sam and Georgia, were nearby on the trail. Georgia ran for help while Sam climbed down and shouted that you were alive."

"Sam? Georgia? None of my friends are named Sam or Georgia. No, not with those names. Who are they . . . and who are you? I don't know you. That's for certain."

"My God, Addy, that fall brought on amnesia, or messed up your memory. I'm Lois, your wife. and what's that about Denver? We live in Capitola on the Pacific."

"Impossible. My Lois died in a plane crash that I survived years ago. That was right after we moved to Denver."

"Addy, you are out of your mind. I'm going to call the day nurse or the doctor. They should be able to find out what's going on here. Something's wrong."

She called the nurse and told her, "Call doctor Kline. Tell him that Adam Cizneros is awake and talking. He is making no sense at all."

After hanging up the nurse said, "They're sending a psychiatric specialist right over, they say she is quite an expert for one so young."

"That's all I need, a nut doctor." He hears an especially loud vocal exchange from the back yard. "What's all that commotion outside? All that arguing and loud voices?"

"That's your three partners, arguing about who's in control of your company. I doubt those vultures will be happy to see you awake."

"I bought those lousy partners out years ago. I hope this nut doctor is a sane, rational person who can tell me what's been going on?"

With that he tried to sit up but discovered he had no strength and slumped back on the bed, nearly falling off.

"Damn it Adam, don't try to move without help. You're bound to be weak as a newborn after lying there for so long. The doctor should be here in less than fifteen minutes. Maybe she can make some sense out of what you are saying."

"I am beginning to understand something about the sea cliff. There was a trail Lois and I used to hike in the park not far from that little house in Capitola. It did pass along a high cliff, right on the shore."

"That's the one. That's where you fell. Right now you are in our bedroom in our little house in Capitola."

"That's nonsense. Impossible. That was years ago, when I still had those partners you say are out in the back yard arguing. Although that's like them, always arguing. That's why I bought them out and got rid of them. Things went much smoother from then on. but that's all ancient history, as is my Lois."

"Well, I'm your wife, Lois, and I am not ancient history. As you can see, I'm solid flesh and blood. Touch me if you doubt it. You're here, and barely out of a coma. That's absolutely for certain."

"I don't understand. You and all this . . . the house . . . everything, are from the distant past. Yes, I do remember more now. My head seems to be clearing. Things . . . memories . . . Sam and Georgia . . . the business . . . I'm beginning to remember. Still, something is badly out of whack. It's like I've gone back years into the past, a long-gone past. Yet it's impossible. I remember my Lois was killed in plane crash shortly after takeoff from Denver in April of 2000, yet here you are."

"Addy, it must be because of the fall. You probably hit your head and that brought on all these odd memories. You'll be all right in a day or so. I know it."

"Was all this a dream? No, that's impossible. . . . Yet . . . I'm remembering more about the house . . . and those three idiots out in the back yard. As soon as I can move about, I'm going to buy them out. I . . . quick, bring me a mirror."

"What for, dear? You are a mess."

"I want to check something out, please. It's important."

Lois stepped over to the dresser and came back with a large hand mirror. "Here, see for yourself."

Adam looked in the mirror and let out a gasp. "My God! That can't be me. My hair is black . . . and I am . . . so young."

"You're thirty-five, Addy, and we've been married for twelve years. You remember our wedding, don't you."

Adam dropped the mirror on the bed, his eyes glassy and staring straight at the ceiling. One of his partners walked into the room. After a quick glance at Adam he turned toward Lois.

"I wonder if he'll every come out of that coma?"

"Oh, he's already out of it, Ed. Now he's suffering some weird sort of amnesia. Thinks I died ten years ago, right after we moved to Denver of all places."

"Really? When did this happen? Have you called the doctor."

"They're sending a psychiatric specialist over. She should be able to give us some answers."

Ed swivelled toward the bed and leaned over toward Adam. "How you doin' ole buddy? What's this business about Lois being dead? She seems pretty lively to me."

When Adam continued staring at the ceiling, Ed waved his hand in front of his eyes. "Are you sure he came out of that coma? He isn't reacting at all now." Ed waved his hand again with no response. Lois ran to the bed.

"Addy! Don't mess with us."

Silence.

"Addy, please, this is not funny." Then to Ed, "I wonder if he slipped back into the coma. He was awake earlier. The nurse and I both spoke with him. except for thinking I was killed in a plane crash ten years ago, he seemed fairly normal."

"Well, the jerk sure isn't normal. Check out that glassy eyed stare. It's scary."

Suddenly Adam turned his head, looked directly at Lois and said, "Get him out of here before I explode. . . Now!"

"Come on Adam, I was checking on you to see if you were coming around. What are you so pissed about, anyway?"

"Go! . . . Now!"

With that, Ed beat a hasty retreat out the door.

"Don't be so nasty, Addy. Ed was expressing his concern about you."

"Concern my ass. I remember. He and his brotherwere stealing from me for years. I know, I know, I'm simply imagining all this . . . but I'm not. I can't be."

"I hope that doctor gets here soon. I'm beginning to worry about you. All this must be a dream. A dream brought on and intensified while you were in that coma."

"You're probably right, Lois. Things are beginning to fall into place. It's hard to do, but I'm putting all those new memories, or whatever they are . . . I'm putting them in proper perspective, as dreams. Still, it all seemed so unbelievably real. I remember marrying a doctor that I met in the hospital where I was recovering from serious injuries I suffered in the crash that killed Lois. Her name was Sarah, Dr. Sarah Andros."

As he finished speaking, the doctor walked in the room. "I'm Dr. Sarah Andros. Did I here someone mention my name?"

Suagus and the Chetawk

Suagus snapped the laser lariat over the horns of the bull chetawk, pulled it tight, and dug his heels in for the expected battle. When the chetawk stood and stared at him, Suagus was flabbergasted. He yanked on the lariat several times finally pulling the chetawk over on its back. Still it made no effort to free itself, or move. It simply lay there staring at him. At twice his weight and with three short blunt horns facing forward as its only weapons, it seemed a poor match for the muscular Merlaner. It had no teeth to speak of because its food was the soft, leafy vegetation of Preator and its four feet were without claws or hooves. What were its weapons, and what could Manch have meant when he warned him to avoid these creatures? This one seemed harmless enough, docile and almost pathetic. He wondered how they had survived predation.

Merlaners are hunters who love battling and subduing strange new creatures on other worlds, and they are good at it. Since it seemed no threat, Suagus decided to release the chetawk and search for a more capable adversary, maybe a cassading or gerlew, both dangerous predators. He pressed the release on the handle of the lariat and it disappeared. As soon as the laser let go of the chetawk, it rolled to its feet. Then Suagus registered a furry blur and that was all he remembered.

He awoke in a medical facility, immobile and in considerable pain. The first thing he recognized was Manch's face staring at him intently. When Manch realized he was awake he spat out, "You stupid fool! I warned you to stay away from chetawks. You are lucky one of the searcher craft pilots spotted you and what happened or you'd be dead."

"What happened? All I remember was a blur after I released the damned lariat."

"Why didn't you do at least a little research before challenging a new creature. I warned you to stay away from them. "Those chetawks are unbelievably tough and deadly critters."

"Manch, you know it's the surprise of the unknown that drives our hunt. That's the whole point of hunting, overcoming the challenge of the unknown. Some people climb rocks, some people race rambots, we hunt."

"It's a stupid useless game as far as I'm concerned. Inconceivable danger with little or no valid compensation. Did you know you were dead when they brought you in here? The impact of the chetawk striking your chest pulverized your ribs, collapsed your lungs and shut down your heart. It's a miracle you survived. You can't know it was six weeks ago you were brought in here."

"Six weeks? I've been out for six weeks?"

"Yes, and during that six weeks we returned to Earth with what was left of your body. You're in the Dixon Medical Center in Denver, hooked up to a Kessy life support system. You've been hooked up to the Kessy since we picked you up and you'll remain so for at least another eight weeks. Did yo realize you are not breathing."

"Now that you mention it. How is it I can talk?"

"Don't you know anything about the Kessy?"

"Not much, just that it does some amazing things."

"Right now it's providing everything, full life support. It's connected to your neural net and does everything your body can't. Among other functions, it will provide your voice until your nervous system is rebuilt and you can again control your speech. Your entire chest has to be rebuilt, heart, lungs, nerves, circulation system, everything. It's in process. They're putting you back together one cell at a time."

"How come I still hurt?"

"Because you deserve to hurt! Maybe next time you'll heed at least some warnings. You were so badly damaged they must keep your pain network active to help find where all the damage is and how bad."

That's not very comforting, Manch."

"You don't need comforting. You need pain and discomfort to tell you not to do stupid things."

"You don't understand. It's what we do."

"You'd better find something else to do. It will be a long time before you heal and the pain goes away."

"OK! OK! Tell me, what happened? How did that chetawk do me so much damage?"

"Now you want to know about chetawks. It's a little late isn't it? You shut me up when I tried to warn you. Now you're all ears."

"C'mon Manch."

"All right. Long before you became a Merlaner you took marine biology didn't you?"

"So?"

"Do you recall a little ocean predator called the peacock mantis shrimp?"

"That's the little devil with the ultra high speed club that breaks shells, isn't it?"

"Right on. Do you remember how it developed so much power and was so fast?

"Yeah! it had a set of latches and tendons that were set by leveraged muscles storing a enormous amount of energy in a specialized spring. When the catch is released the tremendous energy stored in the tendons snaps their greatly enlarged and modified claw or hammer forward at unbelievable acceleration. This blow can smash the shell of most crustaceans and stun them into immobility. What's that got to do with the chetawk?"

"There is a similar mechanism in their hind legs that enables them to jump at incredible speed and over huge distances. They have been clocked at an unbelievable acceleration to over ten meters per second almost instantaneously. It's a defense mechanism as they are not predators. They aim themselves at a predator and let fly. When those three blunt horns hit any creature it is almost always killed by the blow. Most predators and many other creatures learn to avoid chetawks."

"Aren't the chetawks damaged when they attack? I would think that hitting anything with that much force with their heads would at least give them a serious headache."

"They possess an unusual bone structure, much like that of a turtle. Their ribs are fused into a solid cylindrical shell beneath that loose skin. Before they jump, they lock their skulls into their shell. As soon as they jump they tuck all four legs into their shell and by the time they hit, they become a rock solid single piece, a virtual missile. They walk away unscathed, at least the one that popped you did."

"Why couldn't you approach them from behind? They would be vulnerable from behind."

"I can read your mind. You're thinking about how to hunt and attack one when you are healthy, aren't you? Well forget it."

"You didn't answer my question. How about attacking them from behind?"

"Were you aware where their eyes were?"

"Yeah! Right on the top of their heads, on those little stalks."

"Their eyes give them 360 degree vision so you can't sneak up on them unobserved. They turn those eyes on stalks to face any perceived threat."

"Yeah! I seem to remember he always faced me. Then when I roped him and pulled him sideways, he didn't move. He finally fell over and lay there, docile as a lamb."

"That's another of their little tricks, playing possum. That usually causes their attacker to let down their guard. As soon as that happens they position themselves for a strike and POW!"

"That's about what happened. When I released the lariat he rolled onto his feet and turned toward me. That's the last I remember."

"Since I'm quite certain you are going to try again once you recover I suggest you do a thorough study of the chetawk before you attempt anything. There are two other little tricks they have in their repertoire that are effective and pose real dangers."

"Oh? And what would those be?"

"I assume the chetawk rolled on its back when you restrained him with your lariat?"

"Yeah! And those weird eyes on the stalks followed me. He moved so when he lay on his back they protruded on the side of his head."

"And what about his hind legs?"

"What about them?"

"He pulled them up tight against his body. Should a cassading attack it would have to go directly over those hind legs to reach the chetawk's soft underbelly, then, POW! Those hind legs that sent him hurtling at you would hit the cassading and fling it hundreds of meters in the air. By the time it landed, the cassading would be dead from the blow of those hind feet."

"Aren't there any predators that can take down a chetawk?"

"Packs of gerlews are known to attack and kill a chetawk on occasion, but then they usually lose at least one member of the pack. Then there's another thing. In addition to aiming themselves as a missile, they can cover lots of ground quickly."

"How?"

"The same muscle/tendon system they use to become a missile can also be used as an escape system. They lean back at about a forty five degree angle and let fly those hind legs. They fly 150 meters or more with their heads and legs locked in place. The hit the ground head first and then tumble until they regain their footing. They are back on their feet in about a minute. That's quite effective in getting away from any predator and especially a pack of gerlews. It also works to move them quickly in any direction."

"They sound like a real challenge. I wonder how I managed to place my lariat on him in the first place?"

"There are a number of other relatively harmless herbivores on the planet. A lot more of them than predators. He didn't see you as a threat until you lassoed him."

"Makes sense. I'll plan and execute my attack carefully."

"Well, you'll have plenty of time. Another eight weeks in the Kessy and after that, at least three or four months in rehab. You'll need a lot of conditioning to get in shape for any strenuous activity. Remember, almost your entire insides are being rebuilt."

"That long? I'll go nuts."

"Hell, you're already nuts. That's what brought you in here in the first place."

Manch had underestimated the recovery time. It was more than a year before Suagus was ready to face another challenge. It took several more months to arrange another Chetawk hunt on Preator. Once more his long time friend, Manch, organized and arranged for the hunt, "In spite of my misgivings." he commented.

Knowing what he did about the chetawks took most of the challenge out of the hunt. Still, there remained some unknown danger stirring his adrenalin. Each hunt was nearly identical. He would walk up to a chetawk, lasso it with his laser lariat, pull it over on its back, and bind it with a laser loop. Then as it lay helpless on its back he would walk a safe distance away before releasing the loop. The Chetawk would get up, shake itself, glance around, and then amble off as if nothing happened. Big deal. Several chetawks took that launch stance of forty-five degrees as if to jump at him, but then, because he stood so far away, they dropped down on all fours and ambled away, their eye stalks still focused on Saugus.

Challenge gone, he decided to return to the ship and consider another type of hunt. As he walked through the tall grass on his way he had a strange feeling. The hairs on the back of his neck stood at attention as his subliminal senses told him something was not right. He was being stalked. The hunter had become the hunted. From behind him and on both sides, he began hearing the swish of bodies moving through the tall grass. Almost imperceptible at first, he realized it kept growing. When he stopped to listen, the sound stopped. As soon as he started walking, the sound started again. It grew steadily louder and closed in.

Saugus took off at a run for a patch of forest ahead where he would be out of the tall grass and be able to see better behind. He would be able to see his stalkers. Before reaching the forest, he heard a new sound, a powerful thump, like something heavy hitting the ground. As he burst out of the grass, something crashed through the branches of the forest trees and hit the ground about fifteen meters in front of him with another loud thump. Several more egg-shaped grey bodies crashing to the ground around him. The objects unbundled and turned into a small herd of angry chetawks surrounding him.

He did not want a repeat of his last experience in the Kessy, so before any of the chetawks could aim themselves, he threw his laser lariat around a branch some ten meters up one of the trees, and retracted it, pulling him up and out of harms way, or so he thought. Several of the herd folded themselves into attack posture. The first one to let fly struck the branch above his head with such force the branch shattered and pieces pummeled him as they fell. He must climb higher up, much higher up.

He threw his lariat around a higher branch on the closest tree and pulled himself to a higher perch as two chetawks pulverized his previous foothold. Saugus knew he had to keep moving. Using his lariat, he pulled himself from tree to tree in the general direction of his pickup ship. He easily outdistanced the pursuing chetawks with their plodding walk. It wasn't long before the thump . . . crash of the chetawks told him they were using their jumps to catch him. He chose a zigzag path, making a sharp turn right, then left each time he heard a thump. This led him around the ship in a path he hoped the chetawks would not anticipate. He now had a much higher respect for intelligence of these creatures he once though stupid and a poor adversary.

As he approached the clearing where the ship waited he realized he had not heard any thumps for quite some time. Perhaps they had given up the chase. He pulled out his communicator and contacted Manch in the ship.

"Manch! Manch! Wake up my friend. I may need to get in the ship in a hurry."

"Saugus, you idiot, I don't know what you did, but there are about forty chetawks milling around the ship. They appear to be agitated, stomping their feet and shaking their heads. I'm assuming you are the cause of their anger."

"You didn't tell me they were pack animals. I thought the to be solitary herbivores. One at a time I can handle, but a whole herd? That's a different matter."

"I told you what I knew. I also told you to study all you could find out about them. You obviously did not take my advice."

"You forget. The thrill of the hunt is the unknown. If you knew everything about your intended prey it wouldn't be a real hunt."

"How do you intend to get to the ship through our guests out there?"

"I've been thinking about that. How much vegetation is there around the ship? You know, that leafy stuff chetawks are supposed to live on?"

"Well, there's nothing near the ship. The landing blast fried all of that. Let me check with the viewer."

While Manch looked around, Saugus began inspecting his position, searching for any cover where he might hide for an extended period. About a kilometer away a large, flat rock, the only interruption to the dead flat grass-covered plain, might provide a safe haven. He had run through a level wooded area. The rock appeared to be fairly flat with steep sides. Perhaps he would be safe and hidden on top of the rock, at least from any creature on the ground. Saugus began working his way through the forest toward the rock, an idea growing in his mind. His communicator sprang to life.

"I found one area of those leafy plants. It's rather small. I guess a bit more than a hectare. It's over toward you and about a kilometer north of your position. Right by that big rock. I'm sure you can see the rock."

"Yes, damn it, I see the rock. That's where I planed to hide 'til they got hungry and wondered off to feed. I'm working my way there as we speak."

"Well, I doubt they will be leaving soon. They don't appear to be interested in food. There's a small patch about thirty meters away and not one of them is looking in that direction."

"What's your fuel situation? Do you have enough to lift off and set down again, say right on top of that patch of vegetation over by the rock?"

"I don't know? That would be an expensive activity. We have plenty of fuel, but that would cut our safety factor for the trip home. Let me run a fuel analysis."

"If you have enough fuel, it would destroy their only nearby food supply and put the ship in a much better position for me to reach safely. They are herbivores, and my understanding is they will soon need to find something to eat"

"The fuel situation is this. If we make a perfect ascent and decent the first time, there's plenty of fuel. We could do that twice. but! And that's a big but . . . If anything goes wrong and we must make several tries, we won't have much wiggle room for a landing back home."

"Manch, if anyone could do a perfect job, it would be you. Let's try it. That would solve a whole lot of problems. The lift off blast would do a lot of damage to those critters, and that too will help."

"How soon can you make it to that rock?"

"A half hour if I go carefully. About ten minutes if I throw caution to the wind and run."

"In your shoes I'd run. It will be dark in less than two hours and I'd like to lift off for home before it gets too dark to see clearly."

"I thought you'd say that. I'm off."

With that Saugus took off on a steady lope so as to cover the intervening distance and still retain enough strength to climb the rock. Shortly after he took off, the ship sent off a blast that lifted it off the ground. Saugus did not expect that and still had a long way to run.

Manch called him on the com unit. "As soon as you started running, those critters all turned toward where you were moving and began hunching down in their take off position. I decided to mess them up so I did a slow burn lift off and will head toward the rock. With luck, I'll be there about the same time as you. The blast took out about half of them. The rest all folded up into their missile configuration and are presently lying on the ground where they lay after the blast. I'll let you know if they start moving."

Saugus was too busy running to respond. The forest began to thin out and about 200 meters from the rock he would run into the patch of fleshy plants so favored by the chetawks as food. He had no idea how difficult it would be to pass through these head-tall plants so he changed direction to skirt them and stay within the thinning forest. He could see the ship and its tail of flames blasting along about forty meters above ground kicking up a huge cloud of dust. *That should make it difficult for those damned critters to see anything,* he thought as he raced through the trees. Then his com unit broke silence.

"Saugus! Be careful. I checked and all of those folded up chetawk missiles are gone, nowhere to be seen. I plan on setting down right next to that rock on the edge of that patch of vegetation. Head for there if you can. As soon as I set down, I'll limber up the photon cannon in case we need it."

Two loud crashes in the nearby trees told him the chetawks had caught up with him. He stood close enough to feel the heat from the ship's engine blast. As he ran out into the open toward the rock, he saw a big problem. A steep gully ran through the patch of vegetation right in front of the rock. Dense vegetation hid the gully. He had to warn Manch. He grabbed his com unit while continuing to run.

"Manch! Manch! Come in! Trouble!"

Manch answered, "What's up?"

"There's a steep gully running through that patch of vegetation right between you and the rock. You cannot set down there."

"If I don't set down soon, we definitely will not have enough fuel. I'm going to try for the rock. It is flat and big enough."

As the ship lifted to go above the rock, Saugus ducked into a thick patch of the fleshy plants to shield himself from the blast. At the same time, a chetawk hit the ground near him and skidded to a stop no more than a meter away. Instinctively, Saugus threw a laser loop around him to bind him in the folded in condition. The chetawk remained helpless. He could not unfold, nor could he arm those powerful rear legs.

Suddenly the ship's blast stopped. Manch had landed atop the rock. Saugus released the lariat and ran the few meters to the rock wall and began searching for a place to climb up. He threw his lariat around a small tree growing precariously out of a crack in the rock and started pulling himself up. just as he reached the tree it pulled loose from the rock and he started to fall. Suddenly the tree stopped falling and then began pulling him up. March's lariat had found the tree as it pulled out. As soon as they reached the top of the rock they took off for the ship.

They ran for the ramp into the ship. Several loud thumps told them the chetawks had not finished with them. Fortunately it took at least a minute for the chetawks to unfold after they landed.

"Hit the dirt!" Manch shouted as he dove for the ground next to the ramp pulling Saugus with him. As they flattened on the rock, the roar of a photon cannon right above their heads preceded a brilliant blue-white flash and an ear-shattering CRACK!

"Okay! I think we can get up and enter the ship." Manch said proudly, holding his remote firing device up and waving it. "I aimed the photon cannons at the ground about fifteen meters out from the ramp figuring we might need some protection."

Saugus checked. Everything including the chetawks and a fair portion of the rock surface had been vaporized. "Let's go inside and tear out of here, NOW!"

"Aye Aye sir!" Manch said with a grin. "I hope you learned to leave chetawks alone." As soon as Manch closed the ramp, two loud bangs put an exclamation point to his words.

"Manch? I am convinced. Let's lift off before they figure a way to punch a hole in this baby."

They never knew it, but their blast off knocked more than fifty chetawks off of the rock.

Manch repeated what he said after Saugus' first experience hunting them, "Those chetawks are unbelievably tough and deadly critters, clever too, especially when they are in herds."

The Goo, the Ug, and the Badly

Ug shouted, "Remy, come, look," from his vantage point atop the rise in front of our camp. He stood waving with two of his four hands, urging me to come up the slope to see what he had seen.

I jogged up the hill, trying to attach the harness of Stan, my BADLY, as I ran.

"A human." Ug commanded as he pointed when I came near him.

"I can't see a damned thing."

"Near base of big zuppa tree, there. Another human. Ug."

I mentally turned on my android robot Stan's binoculars and checked in the indicated direction. I saw the guy Ug pointed to, only there were three of them, the range finder indicated almost four clicks. Handy gadgets, those head mounted binoculars. Their images fed directly to my optic nerves via the optic implant. Stan did a quick search of the universal database of facial recognition and I soon knew who those three were, independent prospectors, like me. They were competitors, and not legal or friendly ones, either.

Josh Jay, their leader and the brains of the group had crossed swords with me before. Stan gave me all the information he found in the BADLY database on the other two unknown to me. Lumpy Lucas and Jethro Dylan had records as hardened criminals, real bad dudes. These three would not play by the rules.

Josh tried to kill me more than once back on Apodia 5, and I'm sure things had not changed in the years since we last mixed it up. Back then I was technically just a little bit more legal than Josh. Still, I didn't rob and murder my competitors at every opportunity. Josh had ten or twelve kills on his record. Who knows how many others went unrecorded? Fortunately I wasn't one of them, although he tried several times. Still, I lost a member of my crew, missed two toes, and had a nick in my shoulder from our last battle. Josh lost a piece of his hip and his number one sidekick to my Galbo that time.

For obvious reasons they did not use a BADLY, in spite of the advantages it offered. Every BADLY had a legal recorder that could be used in court to convict its user of criminal activity. Stan gave me a tremendous advantage, but he made certain everything I did stayed legal. Stan would prevent my illegal actions and record everything I did to catch any slip up that crossed the legal line. That legal recorder was virtually indestructible, at least by the wearer.

189

BADLY is short for Body Android Defense Legal Yeoman. Some smart ass came up with that name for the robot/human interface system that enabled me to survive in some extremely hostile environments. It ties in wirelessly to the user's nervous system by use of six brain implants. Lots of guys don't like them because, well, each BADLY is an individual with an independent mind of its own. With its nerve connections, it can control your entire body, and override your own commands. This happens frequently in dangerous situations. I named my BADLY, Stan. I know he's a piece of high tech equipment, but he quickly became like a real person to me. Shortly after I acquired him, I started calling him Stan and it stuck.

"You know those?" Ug asked.

"Yep. Bad dudes. They'll try to kill us and steal our equipment. Let's head back to the crawler so I can dress." I had taken my weekly shower, courtesy of the crawler's water system, but hadn't yet put on my clothes. I sat hooking myself up to the BADLY, when Ug called me up the slope.

Ug, a local citizen of Argos 2, is my sidekick. Almost a pet, kinda like a dog on Earth, but quite a bit smarter, quicker, and with four hands with opposing thumbs. He has a limited vocabulary of English, and he peppered any conversation with *ugs*, thus his name.

"You want Ug hunt and kill?"

"No! I wouldn't want to take a chance to lose you. We'll avoid them. That shouldn't be hard with you and Stan on the lookout."

"They after gold too?"

"Gold, yes, but also platinum, palladium, and anything else of value they can steal."

"Why that stuff? Ug. Not good for anything."

"For some humans that **stuff** is worth a lot of money."

"What good money? Can't eat, can't drink, can't fight, can't make love, useless. Ug."

"Here, yes, but in my world and in most developed worlds it can be exchanged for all of those things and much more."

"You my pooga. Much power. Save Ug from goo worms with Galbo. I believe, but not understand money."

"That's why I'm here on Argus 2. I heard about a few, large deposits of precious metals to be found beneath certain types of rock outcrops. If I can find and recover one deposit, it will make me a wealthy man. I can live like a king."

"You like money, Ug like build grrruppa, big grrruppa."

"Boy, that's hard to pronounce. What the hell is a grrruppa anyway?"

"You call family or tribe. Ug call grrruppa."

"Whatever you say."

We folded up the shower platform and stowed it in the crawler, our lumbering transport. You could call it a king-sized RV/truck on tracks. Ug's four hands, each with three fingers and an opposing thumb made quick work of such tasks.

"Let's start the crawler and head away from those bastards. Hop aboard. We can head for that mountain range to the south. Prospecting should be good along those mountain streams."

As Ug hopped aboard he warned, "Lots of goo worms near those streams. Must be careful. Ug."

I ran the crawler in silent mode in hopes Josh and his men wouldn't hear us. Of course it's hard to keep a fifty-ton vehicle quiet while crawling through a dense forest, but at least silent mode ran the usually loud engine at a greatly reduced level. For insurance, I turned on Stan's scan mode and set it for any warm blooded life form near 100 kilos within three clicks. It showed nothing except Ug and me until I entered both of our ID scans. After that Stan would ignore our body scans. I thought my desired destination for Stan and then turned control of the crawler over to him. The heads up display showed up in my field of vision from inside my head. It took me quite a while to get used to those dancing symbols in my line of sight

I turned to Ug. "Remember how I found you?"

"Yep. Almost dead in worm goo."

"You stood up to your belly with all four feet stuck in that stuff."

"I know Humans kill us. You take out Galbo. I think you kill me. Ug. Then blast goo. Kill many goo worms. Dry up goo. Save Ug. You now my pooga. I protect with my life. Hunt food for you. You big pooga."

I laughed. "I think our relationship is a mutually beneficial arrangement, Don't you?"

"What that mean?"

"It means you do good for me, and I do good for you. We both do good for each other."

"Ug knows. Find you food. Point out dangers. You protect. Give me Galbo. Teach how use. Ug one big pooga like Remy. We do for each other, good. Ug."

"No truer words were ever spoken. I couldn't ask for a better buddy."

Soon after I gave him a Galbo blaster and taught him how to use it, I found Ug could aim and fire a Galbo quicker than any creature I had ever seen. He had amazing aim—he never missed. He could cut a zuppa fruit out of a tree at 50 meters without searing the tender skin of this delicious fruit, and then run and catch it before it hit the ground and smashed into mush. He always handed me the fruit since, like a dog, he is a pure predator. Ug had been my sidekick for almost a full year since I rescued him. A handy guy to have around on Argus 2, he excelled where life was somewhat reminiscent of the wild wild west of ancient American pioneer days, strange, lawless, dangerous, and full of surprises, especially for newcomers.

In a sudden and unexpected move, Stan turned the crawler to the left. We went about fifty meters and then resumed our previous heading. On our right a large reflective pool of goo spread out to at least a hectare. I'm fairly sure the crawler would bog down in the goo pond and we would then be digested. What a way to go. *Thanks, Stan*, flashed through my mind.

"Argos setting. Soon dark. Should stop. Camp now. Find high ground, away from goo worms."

"You're afraid of those critters. Aren't you?"

"Not afraid. Understand and avoid. Ug. Not stupid like before."

Stan had taken us a good deal east of where I suggested. The crawler headed toward a little rounded rocky hill half a click ahead.

"How's that hill for a place to camp?"

"Good. No goo worms there."

" I never thought to ask you, what did you do to be stuck in goo?"

"Chasing slartza not in grruppa. Try to mate. Ug."

"What's a slartza?"

"Slartza is female ready to mate."

"You chased a female you wanted to mate with when you got stuck in that goo? Passion makes males do stupid things," I said with a chuckle. "We're not so different, you and I."

"You chase slartza? Want to mate?"

"Like I said, we're not so different. You may have four arms and four legs, but only one . . . What do you call that thing you use to mate ?"

"Quorg."

I laughed. "We call ours a penis. It can get us into lots of trouble."

"Ug! Quorg make big trouble in grruppa. If pooga not approve, we no use. If we do, grruppa hurt much. Not fun."

"Why didn't you rejoin your pack?"

"Mated with slartza belong pooga. He find out. Pooga drive out of grruppa. Kill if ever come back. Remy now my pooga. Lot better."

"Well, I will let you use your quorg whenever you want."

"That no good. Remy has no slartza."

I had a good laugh over that one. It took us about half an hour to set up camp, a sleeping bag on the flat top of the crawler for me. Ug would climb a tree and settle on one of the lower branches. That got each of us above the ground away from a possible goo worm attack. Those little bastards are aggressive. They stay underground most of the day, but came out at night to mate and hunt. They caught lots of tiny critters by exuding goo on parts of their bodies and digesting them with that goo. When they worked together in considerable numbers they formed those goo ponds where they overpower and digest larger creatures.

Ug headed out into the woods to hunt for his dinner while I fixed my own from rations I carried in the crawler. He would be back before dark.

Just before dark, I finished eating when Stan's warning went off. It showed something moving, and heading our way. I used the call of a local critter hoping to warn Ug. Then I turned on our recon scan to see what we had. I spied three figures coming up the hill toward us. Stan indicated them to be human and about a click and a half away. They moved toward us at an easy jogging rate, following the path our crawler made earlier. If they kept up that pace they would be on us in about twenty minutes. Then they stopped and stared intently in our direction. Obviously they followed the path our crawler made through the brush. When their images winked out I realized they had turned on a device that scattered Stan's signal making them invisible to the scanner.

I grabbed a light and began running downhill and to my left as fast as I could while trying to remove Stan from my body. I knew I could communicate with my robot from as far as thirty meters. When I reached the position I wanted, I left Stan draped over a small bush and then moved off to the right, searching for a large tree to hide behind. When I doused my light, I could see nothing in the pitch black. They used some kind of light to see their way without revealing themselves, possibly IR, but that is easily detected using IR goggles. My guess would be far UV, not an easy light to see by, but the ionization of a powerful solar wind flooded the night sky of Argos 2 with it. I turned on Stan's UV detector and prayed the binoculars would work over the space between us. In the dim UV light I could see nothing moving in my extended field of vision. I turned up Stan's intensity. Still, nothing.

Then I spotted movement up in the trees. It was Ug, moving quietly through the branches at least twenty meters up. There was no mistaking those eight arms and legs. From the careful way he moved. I could tell he carried something quite large and heavy. As my UV sight improved, I could clearly see him trying to position himself directly above the path our crawler had created when we came up the hill earlier.

Josh's loud voice from behind me startled me, "Drop your weapons and don't move."

I turned and there was Josh about ten meters away with his Galbo aimed right at Stan. He didn't know my location, but homed in on Stan's UV signal. He looked in Stan's direction through a huge set of bugeyed lenses strapped to his head. Crude, but effective. At the sound of Josh's voice the other two came lumbering up the path toward us. Ug dropped his heavy object which flattened one of them noisily. At the sound, Josh whirled around and fired at the loud thump sound cutting what remained of Jethro in two by mistake. Lumpy ran back the way he had come.

Josh returned his attention to Stan and began firing. Stan has one neat feature. It is an energy shield system that uses the energy of any weapon firing on him to redirect all energy away from his parts. The result of a Galbo blast is a huge shower of brilliant sparks, much of it heading back to the source in Josh's hand. While the Galbo is immune to its own energy, the hand holding it is not. Josh lost a portion of his hand and writhed in pain on the ground. I raised my Galbo to put him out of his misery, but my finger wouldn't close on the trigger. Stan's voice in my head said, *it is illegal to kill an unarmed enemy unless there is imminent fatal danger.* At twenty meters and beyond, Stan was still in control.

 I turned to run over and disarm Josh. He still had one good hand and I wanted to remove his weapons while his wound occupied his full attenion. The instant I moved, a brilliant light flooded the scene. Lumpy had a search light. His following Galbo blast cut a big section out of the tree I had just abandoned. Another sizzled above me as I flattened my body against the ground. A loud thump followed by darkness and then silence with no further blasts from Lumpy's Galbo, and I knew Ug's primitive, but effective weapon had found its mark.

All the activity or possibly my hitting the ground so hard, turned my UV off. I couldn't see a thing, but I could hear Josh moving. By the time my UV came back on line, I could no longer find him anywhere in my field of vision. I could hear him moving away through the brush off to my left. He was trying to go back to the path. *Keep going that direction Josh. You'll be in for a surprise.* I thought.

Ug lowered himself out of a nearby tree carrying another of those heavy objects. "Remy OK?" he asked.

"Yes, thanks to you. What the hell is that anyway?"

"Whamp nut. Grow big on trunk of whamp tree. Ug use to kill food. Work on enemy too."

I lifted the basketball size nut by its stem. It resembled a pumpkin and had to weigh at least twenty kilos. It had a hard and rough surface, like the surface of a concrete block.

"That makes some weapon: primitive, but effective. It worked this time, thank you."

"Ug learn about whamp nut long time ago. Use to kill food."

"Our friend is headed for that huge goo pond we skirted yesterday. Hopefully he'll stumble into it."

"Smell much blood. He hurt bad. Goo worms got him."

"How the hell do you see? It's pitch black. I must use Stan's UV to see anything."

"Ug see in night. Eyes grow big. Light all around."

"You evolved far UV sight. I'll bet you see with your eyes what I see with Stan's UV only much better."

"Yep. Eyes grow big. See at night. Use to hunt food. Ug."

I retrieved Stan from the bush and strapped him on as I headed back to the crawler. A quick search with the scanner indicated nothing. Josh still had his hiding device turned on.

Ug headed back down the crawler path. "Get weapons and other stuff," he said as he cantered off.

About fifteen minutes later the unmistakable fzzzzt, fzzzzt of repeated Galbo blasts came from the distance. I thought Ug had run into Josh. My fears eased as Ug came walking up the path dragging what appeared to be a large sack.

"Josh caught in goo." Ug said as he dumped the sack at my feet. One of their jackets tied up made the sack. In it I found four Galbos, two sets of big-eyed goggles and several pieces of electronic equipment, all covered with blood. I was particularly interested in the two obvious data boxes.

"I wonder if he'll escape?" I said to Ug as the distant sounds of the Galbo continued.

"Big goo pond. Josh done for."

"I don't know about that. He's a tough hombre. I'll wager he had an a-pack kit he slapped on his hand to stop the pain and the bleeding. If anyone could cut themselves out of goo with a Galbo, Josh could. That's how I got you loose, remember?"

"Ug remembers. Goo pond much smaller than this one. Many goo worms here. They get Josh for sure."

"I wouldn't bet on it."

Suddenly the sounds of the Galbo ceased. "Goo worms got him." Ug said grinning.

A few fzzzzts farther away in the distance told us Josh still fought the goo. A few more from still farther away and I thought Josh had escaped the pond.

It was still the middle of the night and I felt beat. "I'm gonna climb in the sack and grab some more Zs. Can you stand watch in case our friend heads back this way?"

"Sure. Ug climb in tree. Like the night. Sleep tomorrow. You sleep now."

 I'll bet no more than two minutes elapsed after I climbed up on top of the crawler and into my sleeping bag I fell asleep.

I awoke to the fzzzzt of a Galbo nearby, and sat up quickly in broad daylight. I grabbed my own weapon and prepared for battle. A flock of four winged kaloo birds flew by the crawler in a panic. I realized it was Ug hunting his favorite food and relaxed. These critters are a local version of the Road Runners of the American southwest. Noisy, excitable, and unpredictable, they can administer a painful bite with their catlike mouth full of needle sharp teeth that sits atop a long neck. More than once I've seen them dig up goo worms with their long powerful legs, grab an end with their wicked mouth, and pull them out of their burrows like a robin does an earthworm.

It wasn't long before Ug showed up, a headless, eviscerated kaloo in each of the lower two of his four hands. He held them up proudly, "Ug got food for several days. Good eating."

"Stick them in the cooler. They'll last longer."

"Ug stick **yours** in cooler. Like mine ripe."

For an instant, I visualized Ug consuming a ripe kaloo and it almost turned my stomach. "If your kaloo gets ripe, please eat away from me. I don't think I could handle it close up."

"Ug forget. You like . . . What you call food not ripe?"

"Fresh."

"You like fresh meat, OK?"

"Definitely. I think we had better go back to what we came here for. These food discussions don't add any profits to pay for this little expedition."

"Search for useless metals again?"

"That's what I'm here for. I'll tell Stan to take us to those mountains to the south."

In about ten minutes we had packed up and left on our way. Stan homed in on our destination so we leaned back and relaxed as the crawler ate its way through thick underbrush and around obstacles like trees and an occasional boulder.

"We should be able to be there before dark. Then we can fire up the metal detectors to run while we sleep. By morning we may be rich."

"Rather hunt slartza."

"What if I said I could buy you a hundred slartza if we find enough of those metals?"

"You do that?"

"Sure, why not."

"How do?"

"I use the money we get for those useless metals to buy you many power stacks for your Galbos. You become really big pooga. Kill all . . . What do you call yourself? Slartza is female, what is male?"

"You say male, Ug say artza. Artza hunt for slartza ready to mate. Use quorg. Much pleasure."

"I hear you and understand. Anyhow you can kill all artza and take their slartzas. Then you will have many slartzas."

"Cannot do."

"Why not?"

"Other pooga hear. Hunt, kill Ug. Throw in goo worm pool."

"How can they do that? You can use your Galbo, they can't."

"Last night. Lumpy use Galbo. Ug kill. Kill Jethro too. He use Galbo."

"I see your point. Amazing! Tell me, how does a *pooga* become a *pooga* and form his grruppa?"

"Not easy. Find young gee want leave her grruppa, go with new pooga. Start you call family. We call grrruppa. Hard to say in English. Gee now slartza. Help find other gee to join new grrruppa. Take long time to grow to be like old grrruppa."

"What's a gee?"

"Gee is female not mated. Not slartza"

"What do you call yourselves, all artza, slartza and pooga in all packs? Like we call ourselves people or humans."

"Grrrup."

"Boy, that is hard to pronounce. So you are all, grrrup. You told me why your Pooga drove you out of your grrruppa, but what about your life before that?"

Ug grow up in grrruppa like all young artza, stay with mother in grrruppa. Many friends. Maybe thirty or fifty in grruppa. Hunt together, sleep together. Life good. Then guorg grow big. Ug try mate with slartza. Pooga angry. Chase Ug. Try to kill. Ug run away. Pooga catch many artza like Ug. Hurt quorg bad. Quarg no more grow big. Artza no mate. All pleasure gone. We call prud. Prud stay always with same grrruppa."

"I see. That's a lot like what we call a gelding among horses on Earth. They cannot mate but stay with the herd. Herd is another word for grrruppa or pack. What about the slartza? They don't mate with their fathers, or do they?"

"No. Pooga trade young gees with other poogas from other grrruppas. Pooga soon mate with gee. Gee then slartza. Slartza always belong some pooga."

"I think I understand, but how do you convince slartza to join a new grrruppa? You must steal them from someone, don't you?"

"Some pooga treat slartza bad. Slartza run away. Sometimes find new pooga. Must go far away. Ug meet young slartza that way. We mate many times. Move away, but not far enough. Angry pooga find slartza with baby while Ug hunting. Ug come home. Both dead. Ug wild angry. That pooga with big grrruppa. Too many for Ug."

"Sorry to hear that. What did you do then?"

"Chase other slartza from same grrruppa. Get caught in goo. Remy save."

"So you had just lost your mate and your baby when I found you. You must have been sad, and angry."

"Ug hurt inside. Slartza warm and helpful. Baby sweet. Now all gone."

"Wow. I never dreamed you could be so sad. Why didn't you ever tell me?"

"Hurt too much to talk. Now plan revenge. Big revenge. Feel better inside."

"Oh? What are you planning to do?"

"Ug stay with Remy until Remy find metal and leave. Then hunt bad pooga. Bad pooga not afraid of Ug. Doesn't know about Galbos. Ug sneak up. Kill sentinels with Galbo. Pooga come see what happening. Cut off quorg with tight Galbo blast. Pooga now prud. Ug take over grrruppa. New pooga. Big pooga. Biggest pooga. Ug now top pooga all places. Treat all grrrup good. Use quorg with many slartza. Much pleasure. Many new babies. All thanks Remy."

"That's some plan. I sure hope you pull it off. When the time comes, maybe I can help."

"No. Ug must do alone. Remy come help celebrate after Ug new pooga."

"I understand. I do. I'll stay out of your way. I'll also stay around to help celebrate with you. I'd like to meet your new grrruppa."

"Remy one smart pooga. Good friend."

"That goes both ways, my friend."

Late afternoon we made camp a ways up in the mountains on a rocky outcropping. I set up the metals scanner to search for deposits then went about cooking part of the kaloo for my dinner. Ug took his up the only nearby tree to eat and scan the countryside.

When I read the results of the metals scanner I let out a yell. "Holy shit, what a find."

Ug scampered down out of the tree and ran to me. "What Remy find?"

"Check this scan. We are sitting almost on top of a large deposit of precious metals. I can't believe we found this much so quickly."

Stan's thoughts interrupted me. *Why do you think I took you up here? I found that metal from at least fifty clicks back. Did you forget I know what you are after?*

Stan, I forgot about you being in my head. I thought. *I'm sorry. I don't think I'll ever get used to you being there. You are quiet for a long time, then, click, you're right there, in my head.*

No need to be sorry. I hold no emotional attachment to any of this, just instructions. I suggest you become busy with the mining equipment immediately. Josh could be back here and find you, or be lying in wait for you between here and the space port. I would project that he will bring reinforcements with him.

Yes, but we plan on placing any metal we find in orbit directly from here. Once it's on its way Josh can do nothing about it. Our claim tags and ID information will be aboard the cargo capsule so no one can steal it.

And what will you do with your person between then and when you haul in the capsule from your ship? All that ID info will be useless to you if you are dead. I'm sure Josh has plans for just such a scenario. He may try here, but more likely while you are returning to the space port. That's when you will be most vulnerable.

if you hadn't kept me from killing him, we wouldn't need to worry now, would we?

There are rules and protocols I can't let you break or avoid. You know that.

Yeah, but I don't like them or agree with them.

After enduring my long silence, Ug stared at me strangely. "Why you no talk? How you get metal?"

"Sorry Ug, I am thinking about the best way to extract it. Since it is so concentrated we can simply drill a hole down to it, and pump it out."

"Ug no understand."

"Well old buddy, we will soon become miners. It's all mostly automated anyway. You can help me take the tools out and setup. OK?"

"You say. Ug do."

It took several hours for us to take out and set up the drilling rig. Before long the drill was grinding its way through the soft rock toward our prize under Stan's guidance. We pumped the drilling mud down and recycled it when it reached the surface. Our almost magic mud separated from everything else in the shale shaker and then recycled. The several sieves in the shaker sorted everything that came up in the mud into various storage containers by particle size. We could see what we drilled through by examining the material that came out of the shaker. I checked it every hour or so. Down to 160 meters it remained unchanged. Then we hit hard rock. The time it took to drill a given distance doubled. Stan reminded me he had predicted this.

It took four days of constant drilling to hit pay dirt, literally. After we hit hard rock we had to change drill heads much more frequently and this added to the time. The sound of the drill changed . Stan informed me the drill had entered into the deposit, as if I didn't already know from the sound and the bright yellow pieces of metal that began showing up in the shaker outputs.

"Time to change the drill head." I told Ug, who then helped me pull the drill pipe.

Using slips to hold the pipe as each section was removed, we attached a grinder head to a long section of flexible drill pipe and put the whole shebang back down into the hole.

Down in the deposit, the grinder ate its way through the mother lode. All of the shaker output pans filled with almost pure metal, soft, yellow metal, mostly gold. We took the metal shavings from the shaker, washed, and put them in a press that turned them into almost solid blocks. As fast as one came out of the press, Ug picked it up and placed it in the storage capsule of the orbiter.

It took us nine hours to pull up and pack all the metal we could pack in the capsule. The total weight that the capsule rocket could put in orbit, about ten tons, limited our take. As soon as it reached the weight limit, we sealed everything up on the rocket, leveled the launch platform, and launched the rocket. I smiled as my fortune lifted off, arced gracefully to the west, and went out of sight. I hoped I would be seeing it in about a month.

We put almost a hundred more twelve kilogram blocks inside the crawler. That's more than a ton and Stan's advice said that would be the maximum the crawler could carry. I could leave all of the drilling equipment and take more gold, but our agreement said we must leave nothing behind. We pulled all the drill pipe, lowered the tower, and stowed everything in the crawler. We plugged the hole, cleaned up the campsite, and headed for the space port. It would take at least four days going north to reach the port.

Late in the second day, Stan's voice came in my head. *We have company, at least forty of them, and they are not human, but about the same mass as humans. They are about five clicks west of us and moving on a parallel course about as fast as we are moving. I'm fairly certain they are a pack of creatures like Ug.*

"Ug, I think we've found some of your grrrup. Stan says there are about forty of them and they are nearby. Maybe we should stop and be quiet until they are gone."

"No. Keep going, Ug go take look. If my enemy's grrruppa, this my chance. If not, I catch up easy. Ug much faster than crawler."

"How will we know?"

"Ug come and tell. Back in two, three hours."

"Good luck." I shouted as Ug took to the trees and headed west.

Stan kept track of Ug and the pack until an intervening hill blocked the scanner signal.

We lost contact, Stan's words came through clearly. *From the terrain ahead, we won't see them for at least two, maybe three hours. Then the hills flatten out all the way to the pass before the space port.*

With Stan controlling the crawler and picking his way through the dense forest of trees and underbrush, we moved rather slowly. Sometimes he had to back up to go through tight spots. Fortunately the fairly level ground stayed with us. We crawled out on an open plain that sloped gently up towards a hill where Stan saw for an instant a human blip.

Stan reported, *the grrruppa pacing us, is crossing this same plain about six clicks to our west. They are moving rapidly in single file, heading for the same low place between the hill and the mountains beyond as we are. At the pace they are maintaining, they will reach the wooded pass at least an hour before us. The space port is the other side of those mountains, no more than half an hour away. There is no more sign of any humans on my scanner.*

OK, Stan. What's the best plan?

Is there not an acoustical wave launcher aboard?

Hell I almost forgot we had that ancient weapon.

I suggest you raise the front turret and mount it facing forward. I can automate it to fire the instant we are fired upon by anything. That won't stop the first volley, but it will eliminate the source before the next shot, and do the same to any other weapon attack.

Even with the power assist, it took me almost fifteen minutes to muscle that heavy launcher out of its storage rack, onto the upper deck, and into the raised turret. Once I attached the heavy power cable and set up and tested the acoustic lens control, it was ready. The pass loomed less than a click away.

OK, Stan. Do you need to test it?

Once I complete the diagnostics, I will know if it's operable. I don't want to test it. We'll save that so it will be a surprise to them. My guess is they prepared a trap of some sort to stop the crawler, inside that forest ahead, right where the pass narrows. There is a high cliff to the right. That's where they will hit us. I'll take us well away from that cliff. They could blow it up and bury us under rock and dirt. Incidentally, that grrruppa? The individuals are all spread out through the forest in the pass. They are not moving. It seems like an ambush, but what for?

My mind raced. *What they hell are they doing there?*

The crawler rocked from a substantial blow.

Stan, what the hell was that?

They hit us with a blast from a large military Galbo cannon. No significant damage, but we won't be able to handle more than a few of those.

Did the launcher fire?

You surely felt the jolt. It fired at the same time the blast hit us. My guess is whoever operated that big Galbo is dead amongst the wreckage of his weapon. We will continue up through the pass. That grrruppa? They are all high up in the trees ahead and to our right. They certainly can move quickly through the trees.

if I had four hands and four feet, I could move quickly through the trees myself. I wonder what they are up to?

As we crested the pass and started down the other side, Stan stopped the crawler.

A creature is coming alongside. It's Ug. Stan said.

I opened the side hatch and there stood Ug with three more of his kind, obviously slartza.

"Remy. Ug now big pooga of big grrruppa. Revenge sweet. My slartza now. Big time happy."

"What about Josh and all his cohorts?'

"Many dead, include Josh. Others run away when big Galbo blow. Artza chase. Steal weapons, scare to hell. One stuck in goo pond. They never come back. Remy big pooga over all. Now every grrruppa know about Remy, and Ug."

"How'd you manage that against those guys and their Galbos."

"Ug secret weapon. Look!"

About fifty meters away in the woods lay one of our attackers impaled by a wooden spear as thick as my arm and as long as I am tall.

"How in hell do you throw a spear that heavy?"

"Look up."

At least fifteen meters up in the trees, four artzas worked at lashing two fair sized trees together. They stuck a big spear in a cup like device between the two trees.

"Now look at man."

As soon as I glanced at the dead man, Ug gave a signal. A loud twang from above and a second spear went through the man's body.

"That our secret weapon. Look up. See anything?"

I could only see tree branches and leaves.

A minute later he said, "Now look up."

When I checked again, the four were ready to fire another spear.

"Josh men never see us. Effective secret weapon."

We talked for about fifteen minutes. Ug told us his original plan worked like a charm.

"After pooga made prud, all grrruppa happy. Say he bad pooga. Hurt many in grrruppa. Ug new pooga. They say Ug good pooga. Make all happy. Ug quorg happy. Soon many babies."

After celebrating with the grrruppa for about two hours, I said goodby and headed through the pass down to the space port. Stan connected with security and my ship's crew of four soon loaded the metal bricks into our ship. After selling the crawler and contents to a local merchant, the total weight of the ship, including on board metal and the orbiting capsule with its stash, would be below max for our trip.

We lifted off smoothly and soon orbited tracking the capsule. Another four hours and we caught the capsule and stored it in the cargo bay. After we settled in stasis pods for the trip, Stan took over for the two month sleep on the trip back home.

✷   ✷   ✷

Torba, one of my ship's crew, awakened me rudely. He and Farley stood there holding Galbos aimed at my head.

"What the hell?"

Farley said, "Slight change in plans. We redirected the ship's destination to the Altos Transfer Station. We're docking there now. If you cooperate, we'll drop you off along with the two in the other stasis pods. Then we plan to head off into the sunset with all that gold."

Stan's words reassured me. *They don't know that as soon as they changed the destination I redirected it back to the original. We are docking at Earth Orbit Station One where the police will be waiting. Their Galbos? Totally harmless, I drained their power stacks. Have fun.*

"Thanks Stan," I said aloud.

It startled Torba. "Who's Stan? . . . I see. You're trying to distract me so you can jump me. Forget about it. I'm too sharp for you."

"Well asshole, go ahead down that exit ramp. The police are waiting to take you and Dumbo here off to the hoosgow. How do you like them apples?"

"I should blast you for being sassy with me. Shut up or I will."

"Go ahead, asshole. Shoot."

I laughed as they tried firing their Galbos and then ran down the open ramp into the waiting arms of half a dozen cops.

"You two doubled the share of that gold for your two buddies here. I'm sure they will be forever grateful to you." I shouted as the cops cuffed them. It's wonderful to see justice triumph.

I glanced back at the bound stacks of precious metals and thought, *My gloriously sexy Jeannie will be immensely happy, even considering my almost three year absence.*

That made me laugh and think of Ug and his quorg. My quorg and I would soon be immensely happy too.

A Bag of Marbles

My name is Charley Woods. I am past eighty and need to share this bizarre story from my youth. Since my grandson, George, revels in my stories, I am telling it to him. I am also providing a fantastic gift to go with my story and prove its veracity.

"George, I will tell you this story as I remember it. It happened more than seventy years ago when I was a boy about your age. Some of it is still difficult for me to believe, but I still keep the strange things I will be telling you about. I kept them hidden from the world until right at this moment. Many of the things I will describe may seem implausible, quite outlandish, even in today's highly technical world. So listen carefully"

"I will, Granddad. I love your stories."

✳   ✳   ✳

In July of 1937, when your granddad was ten, my parents took me to the Kosciusko County Fair for the first time. The county fairgrounds are in Warsaw, Indiana, about twelve miles from the tiny summer cottage on Lake Tippecanoe where I spent lazy summers as a boy.

The fair was an eye-opening experience for me. The midway and the rides were noisy and exciting with all the colors, booths, and barkers singing out the joys and excitement of their particular offering or ride. I loved watching the "mousey" game where a mouse, released from a can in the center of a table would run to and in one of the holes spaced around the edge of the table. The holes in the edge of the table centered in little squares in six colors plus white. The object was to place a bet on which color hole the mouse would select to run into. Six colored spots occupied each player's position at the counter running entirely around the booth. To play, you placed a coin on one or more of the colors. When the mouse ran down a hole, every spot matching the color of the hole won five coins like the one bet. If the mouse ran down a white hole, no one won except the booth owner. I stayed after I bet and lost the four pennies and the nickle I had in my pocket.

I hung around fascinated for at least an hour. While there I saw an unusual appearing boy standing near the corner of the booth. Something about his eyes and the way he moved attracted my attention. He seemed to be about my age and wore a floppy hat that hid his face. When I looked his way and directly into his eyes I realized he had been watching me. He turned his head down, and shuffled through the dirt as he walked away up the midway. About then my mom and dad walked up.

"Charley, Haven't you seen enough of that mouse game?" my dad asked with a grin. "Come along. We're going down to the church tent for some chicken and noodles."

"Aren't you about starved?" my mom asked. "You haven't had a thing since breakfast."

"OK, mom. I guess I am hungry now that you mention food." I felt terribly hungry, especially for the scrumptious chicken and noodles those church ladies made.

As we walked to the church tent at the end of the midway, The same boy who had been at the mousey booth stood staring at me. He probably fell in behind us as we walked and I didn't see him again until after we ate.

"Charley! Now don't you go back to the mouse booth again." My mom warned. "That's gambling and you know what your father and I think of gambling. It's an evil that can take you over and ruin your life."

I didn't see how a little game could ruin anyone's life, but I respected my parents and usually followed their directions.

"Can I go down to the barns and look at the animals after we eat?" I intended to ask for a quarter to go on some rides but thought my chances slim. The depression meant little money for non necessities and going to the fair cost us some of those. There would be little money for frivolous adventures, and I had already spent my entire allowance.

My dad turned to mom and said, "Mother, do you think it's all right? He's big enough to know what not to do. He's become quite a responsible young man." My father knew how to motivate me to want to behave well and please them. I didn't always do so. Still, it did create a powerful, positive force in my young life.

Mom smiled and gave me a hug and kiss. "Yes, you are growing up. Before we know it, you'll be a teen, and I hope you won't forget all we've taught you the way some boys do."

"Aw, mom"

"Now you run along, but be sure to meet us at the quilt display in one hour. That's three o'clock. Can you remember?"

"Sure mom." I said over my shoulder as I started for the animal pens at a run. I loved watching them, especially the pigs.

As I trotted toward the pigs, I caught sight of that same boy obviously following me. I wondered what he wanted, maybe a fight. Lots of boys our age looked for fights to prove—who knows what. I never wanted a fight, but when I had to fight, I fought to win.

After watching the pigs for at least fifteen minutes, I needed to head for an outhouse near the end of the midway. As I left the outhouse and walked around the back of the nearest booth, I almost ran into him. A bit smaller than I, if he wanted a fight with me he'd get the worst of it.

"What do you want? I've seen you following me. You lookin' for a fight?"

As I examined his face, It struck me how it was, well, different, especially his eyes. His dark blue eyes seemed too big for his face, much too big.

In an almost musical voice he responded. "Certainly not. I wanted to give you something to read."

He pressed a small brown leather bag into my hand. What appeared to be leather shoelaces tied it at the top. Soft and worn but sturdy, the bag appeared well used. I studied him carefully. Not only did he appear different, but so did his clothes. He spoke haltingly in his musical voice, almost as if reading from a book in class. I stood there staring at him, spellbound.

"Please read these and keep them for me. Some day I may be able to come back to retrieve them from you, so take care of them. It may be a long time before I come for them, probably never, but who knows?" He spoke directly, keeping his eyes glued to mine as he did. His presence seemed so friendly yet distant at the same time. The unusual sound of his voice and his strange appearance struck me as friendly.

We stood gazing silently at each other for several minutes until he turned and walked away. I felt intensely curious as I watched him head down the midway and disappear into the crowd. I stood there almost frozen for several minutes before I decided to check the contents of the bag. I sat on a packing case by the nearby booth and untied the plain bow knot that held the bag closed. When I poured the contents into my hand, seven marbles rolled out into my palm.

The marbles were quite unusual, large and quite clear without the swirls of color in my other marbles. Though they appeared to be clear, each had a pale tint of the six basic colors. The larger one was perfectly clear, no tint of any kind. Each one seemed to glisten in the sunlight. Something on their surfaces almost sparkled. They each had a gem-like, glistening quality, hard to describe. As I sat examining them, I wondered what he meant when he said, "something to read." How can you *read* a marble? Maybe I had misunderstood what he meant.

As I started to replace the marbles, I realized it held something else. Reaching in, I pulled out what seemed like the frame for a pair of eyeglasses, a frame with no lenses. Made of a black metal, I found them to be quite strong in spite of how thin and fragile they seemed. Then it dawned on me, the marbles would fit into the lens "holders" perfectly. The right side was enough bigger than the left to hold the clear marble while the left seemed about right to hold the six colored ones. Obviously the marbles fit in the frame so I plopped the clear one into the right frame and the blue one into the left. Then I hooked the ear pieces over my ears and looked through the marbles.

At first, the marbles merely distorted my vision so the midway booths appeared, distorted and fuzzy. Then, as the view started to clear up, I saw many tiny characters appearing. These characters could be oriental characters or pictograms, but at the same time appeared quite different. They had a gold color. I realized I saw what caused the glistening on the surface of the marbles. It was on the inside surface of the side of the marble away from my eyes. Then a view of the six colored marbles arranged in a row replaced the characters. They showed in the same order as a rainbow with the red on the left and the violet on the right. They seemed to hang in midair, outside in a rolling green meadow. Finally the red marble moved and headed straight for my left eye. When this repeated several times I realized it meant instructions. I should insert the red marble in the left eyepiece. When I removed the frame to insert the red marble, I spotted the tower clock above the midway and tents. I had barely enough time to meet my parents, so I dropped the marbles and frame into the bag, closed and tied it, stuck it into my pocket, and headed for the quilt barn at a run. I could investigate this strange bag of marbles later when we went home.

As we drove home, I decided I would keep the experience of the strange boy and the bag of marbles secret for the time being. At least until I figured out what the strange marbles were, how they worked, and what it all meant. Of course, a ten-year-old can only go so far before he must ask someone. In spite of this I knew these strange marbles and the glasses frame were not common objects. For this reason, I would deal with them unaided until I found valid answers.

Our little cottage had a small, stark attic reachable through a trap door in the ceiling of the only closet in the place. With rafters far too low for me to stand, I had to bend over to keep from striking the roof rafters. A few floorboards lay on top of the ceiling joists, so one wouldn't step through the ceiling of the room below. My father used the place as storage of things like curtain rods and poles and a few boxes of things wrapped in newspapers. Three small blocks of wood had been nailed to the inside of the closet door frame to provide purchase for the feet of those seeking entry to this forbidding domain. In spite of the difficulty of staying on those blocks, I could scamper up into this place and be hidden from everyone, a perfect secret hideout for a small boy. Recently my father had installed a light with a switch. I no longer needed to bring a flashlight to be able to see in the windowless space.

Monday after my father had returned to our home in Ohio, my sister came to pick up my mother and other sister to go to town shopping. When I said I didn't want to go with them mom said, "Promise me you won't take the boat out while we're gone. and stay on our landing. I don't want you going over to Black's or the pit."

"Sure mom, I'll stay here or go down to play with Herc and Paul. I promise." I had serious, secretive plans for their time away.

"There's sandwich makings in the ice box for your lunch, but don't drink your sister's pop. Make some Kool-aide if you want. There are grape and cherry packets there on the shelf." My mother gave me the pleasure of doing for myself. A terrific mother, she didn't hover or over protect like the mothers some of my friends had to endure.

As soon as they left, I grabbed the bag of marbles and a cushion from the couch and headed up to my hideout. I turned on the light, positioned the cushion against one of the vertical two-by-fours, and took out the bag. I dropped the clear marble into its holder and the red one into the one on the left and slipped the earpieces over my ears. My first view showed a fuzzy distortion of the roof rafters.

After a few moments the view cleared. Once more the strange gold characters appeared on the other side, inside of the marble. When I closed one eye and then the other, different sets of characters appeared in each eye. Yet when both opened, there was but one image where the gold characters hung in space. It was a bit like viewing those double photos with a stereoscope. Right before my eyes, the characters began shrinking and my entire field of vision filled with tiny gold characters seeming to hang in space.

The characters finally grew so small they merged into a scene, a beautiful scene of outdoors in a field or yard. I saw trees and bushes and mountains in the distance. Five people walked into my field of vision from behind me or so it seemed. They were so real I felt I could reach out and touch them. I seemed to be standing in the scene in stead of viewed it. After walking a short distance away, they turned to face me. The boy who had given me the marbles was one of them. Obviously talking to each other, I heard nothing. The scene showed a couple and three children, two girls and the boy. They appeared—well—different. Their clothes and movements seemed odd to me. They each had those same eyes as the boy. Other than that they could be a family like my own.

The woman pointed off to the left, and the scene shifted, rather like a movie or video camera panning a scene. As far as I could see my view had green fields, trees, bushes, and then the forest. I was, fascinated. Then I moved above the forest at some height, as if in an airplane flying. As the scene moved I realized I had seen no buildings or roads of any kind, nothing man made or artificial. Everything appeared wild, natural, and untouched. As the scene continued shifting I viewed lakes and rivers and several mountain ranges, rugged and spectacular with snow capped summits. Beyond the mountains there was an ocean or immense lake stretching to the horizon Next thing I knew, I descended to the field where I started. The family stood there, waiting.

They walked off toward a nearby clump of trees, motioning whatever or whoever took the moving picture to follow. Among the trees, we came upon an enormous rock that split open as we approached. Inside were two large metal sliding doors that opened to a dark green room. As soon as we entered, the doors shut and we stood waiting for several minutes. A diagram on the wall showed the rock and a shaft that descended from it to far below ground level. I realized it was an elevator—a different kind of elevator from those at my Dad's office or the department stores where mom often took me. It was quiet, and had no one operating it. The diagram indicated at least a dozen levels and the display showed our elevator stopped about halfway down the shaft.

The doors then opened into a lighted tunnel. At least I assumed it to be a tunnel. We obviously descended far below ground level. Everyone stepped into a small, open bus or cart that sat waiting by the elevator. The scene changed. We emerged from the tunnel into a vast lighted cavern with light green walls. This cavern, the only appropriate name for this enormous underground space, had finished walls, not the rough rock I had seen in a cavern we once visited. It was so immense it contained several buildings at least ten or twelve stories tall. I stood in a state of wonder that bordered on shock. I could not imagine a place like this existed.

At the far end of the tunnel a flat, vertical wall extended from the floor to the heights—the ceiling of the cavern. The little bus dropped us off right by the center of this wall. Then the wall split in the middle and began opening. The opening became a monstrous set of doors that could be opened and closed. The space beyond the doors seemed at least twice as large as the space on this side. In the center of the space stood a gigantic, square, white building, almost a cube, with no windows or openings of any kind in the walls. Then I realized it sat on many blocks, cubes about twice as tall as a man. Several stair cases lead from the ground up inside the building. Two wide ramps, one at each edge, lead up into the building. A truck of some sort carried a number of large unknown objects up one of the ramps into the building. None of this could ever be in any way familiar to me.

I felt a state of total wonderment, mesmerized at what I was seeing. Then we were climbing up one of the staircases and into the building. In a moment of temporary panic I reached behind me. The feel of the cushion and the two-by-four I found gave me assurance. All this was a picture I was viewing. We moved through corridors and rooms with people working using things unimaginable on desks and tables and fastened to the walls.

The view changed. I entered another building, walking down a grey hallway. Finally, we entered a large room, and faced a flat, barren wall of grey color. About twenty people occupied seats in the room. The family joined them and gazed at the grey wall.

At this point, the scene of the fields from my first viewing replaced the room. All but the red ball hung in mid air before my eyes. Then the red ball moved from behind me and into its position with the others, and the orange ball moved toward my left eye, an unmistakable message. I took the frames off and replaced the red ball with the orange. I placed the frame in front of my eyes as before. It took a few minutes for the scene to move through the gold characters into the room with the grey wall and the seated people.

A picture of the cavern with the strange white cube replaced the grey wall. We stared directly at the cube. It confused me terribly. Then the stairways and ramps retracted up into the building. All the people and machines that stood around and beneath the building disappeared and I could see that the towering doors were closed. All those in the room leaned forward in their seats as if awaiting something astounding to happen. Then the building disappeared, vanished. A cloud of dust and a few small papers flew about as if in a violent windstorm. I watched the papers slow and then gently flutter to the ground. At this moment the wall turned grey and the people all got up and left the room. I was dumbfounded. What did this all mean? How did those pictures appear? I was there but without sounds or feeling of any kind.

The scene before me changed drastically. The moon was in the sky with stars all around it. I realized it couldn't be the moon as it had blue sections with white whisps, and blotches of brown and green in strange irregular shapes. A large white patch covered one area. I guessed it had to be a planet like our earth. Then I saw the buildings, the blocks, hundreds of them stretched out in rows, hanging there in the sky with no support of any kind. New buildings appeared, one at a time at the end of one row. An incredible sight. Fortunately I had the open mind of a young boy. A Buck Rogers fan, I knew all about different worlds and such. Even so, the situation frightened and exhilarated me at the same time. An older person who knew such things could not possibly exist might go right out of their mind. All I could think was, *what's next?*

The scene moved rapidly toward the planet and past into darkness. Then a tiny light appeared in the center of my view and began growing in size. When near enough, I could see the object was a big hunk of grey rock slowly rotating. Roughly spherical but with an irregular surface of battered and chipped rock, the object seemed huge. Then the picture expanded to include both the planet and this rocky object which became extremely small, a point to be accurate. A dotted yellow line started from the object and moved in an arc directly to the planet. Touching the planet it created a huge, bright flash, an explosion of unimaginable force that almost blinded me. Then everything made sense. I remembered the buck Rogers book, "The Doom Comet" where the earth was nearly destroyed when a large comet passed nearby. The only difference? The reality. I watched a diagram of what had happened or will happen. I wondered, *why me?* My active imagination couldn't be playing tricks on me as there because of several real things: the boy, the marbles, the glasses, and the bag. Denial of these would be impossible. The six marbles once more appeared, the orange one changing places with the yellow. This time I removed both marbles and replaced them and the glasses in the pouch. I'd seen about all the marvels I could handle for the time being. The wonders in the yellow marble would wait. As I climbed down I heard Herc calling from the back yard. I stashed the bag of marbles in the back of my sock drawer and went out to the real world to see what Herc wanted.

"What's up?" I asked through the screen door.

My friend and playmate from the end of our lane, Hercules Pronger, stood on the walk, one hand on his hip, the other holding a large potato chip can. "Can you come out?"

"Sure! What's with the can as if I didn't know?"

"I thought we could go cricket huntin'. Maybe earn some money sellin' 'em to fishermen."

"I like the money idea, but we've about caught all the crickets there are around here."

"I found a new place for crickets, thousands of em. A place we never thought of before."

"Oh! Where's that?"

"You know the little cottage beside the channel to Little Tippy? The one sits all by itself?"

"Yeah, of course."

"Well, there's an old picnic ground right behind it. Runs north along the dug channel with the old, rickety bridge. Must be at least an acre of grass, soft fine grass, covering that picnic place. Walkin' through the grass I scared up tons of fat, black crickets. I found them when I went for a walk with my folks."

"I don't know, Herc. Mom's gone and she asked me not to take our boat out or go to the pit, and that's way the other side of the pit."

"Did she say you couldn't go out in our boat?"

"No—not really. She did tell me to stay on the landing though."

"I asked my mom. She said I could take our boat and that I could take you with me. She kinda likes you, you know."

"What about Paul? Isn't he around?"

"Na! He went home to Fort Wayne with his folks. Won't be back 'til Friday."

I wanted to go so badly. I could visualize those crickets jumping through the grass. Mom hadn't said I couldn't go out with Herc in their boat. That convinced me. "OK, I'll go. Let me write mom a note in case she comes back first."

I left a short note on the kitchen counter saying I was going out in the Pronger's boat, and she could check with Herc's mom if she wanted.

We had a very successful cricket hunt. We caught several hundred fat, black crickets chirping merrily from their prison in the chip can. At five cents a dozen we had a small fortune if we could sell them to local fishermen. Cricket sales would be our next chore.

By the end of the week we each had more than seventy cents in our pockets and enough crickets left for the weekend of fishing with my dad. He would be so proud. I had three weeks allowance I had earned myself. I thought about the marbles many times but there came no opportunity for a secret viewing so they stayed in my sock drawer. Friday I could wait no longer. The magic marbles held me in an overpowering draw so I thought of a plan. I gathered my treasure from my sock drawer and asked mom if I could go up to the road early to wait for my dad.

"Whatever do you want do go so early for. He won't be here for at least an hour and a half, maybe two?"

"I thought I might search for some of those *egg* stones in the gravel on the road while I waited." *Egg* stones as we called them, were dark-brown oval stones with bright yellow centers only visible if one broke the stones open. Though quite uncommon, all the kids collected them. I had three among my prized collection of odd things.

"Will you be careful of cars and stay out of the road? Keep to the sides of the road."

"Of course, Mom. They are never in the traveled part of the road anyhow. We always find them in the looser gravel on the shoulders." The little story I told my mom would mask my intent and protect my secret.

"All right then, but stay off the road. Some of those idiots go like sixty down the dirt road. If you hear one of those lamb-brained speeders commin' you get way outta their way, ya hear?"

"Sure Mom." I said reassuringly as I left the house making sure not to let the screen door slam to please her. As I ran down the lane I knew exactly where I would go. Where the lane met the road stood an old abandoned building that once housed a tiny store. I could climb into the doorway missing the door, and sit in the far corner of the floor. No one could see me there unless they came and looked in the doorway and I would surely hear them comin' first.

My fingers trembled with excitement as I slipped the yellow marble in place. A new scene appeared where I stood at a great height on what appeared like the same spot I had seen in the first marble. The view showed the same mountains, forests and intensely green fields I remembered. A brilliant white flash appeared the other side of the mountains and disappeared in an instant. Then a red glow almost like a sunset began expanding where the flash had been. The glow grew upward, bright orange, then yellow, then white objects rose above the mountains. There appeared hundreds, then thousands of these bright objects moving higher into the sky above the mountains. The sight was spectacularly beautiful but somehow ominous at the same time. Then the scene shifted to what appeared to be a much higher view. The brilliant objects rained down on the forest and fields which burst into flames and then disappeared in a brilliant orange-yellow cloud. A huge wall of turbulent water and foam flew over the mountains and engulfed the fiery cloud which turned white with moving spots of glowing red and orange.

Once more the scene shifted to a view of the entire planet. The scene resembled eerily some of the drawings I remembered from the book, "The Doom Comet." A grey haze punctuated here and there with small bright orange spots covered the entire planet. An arc of jagged mountain tops rose above the haze halfway across the visible face. Nothing else could be seen. Then the scene shifted far from the planet showing row upon row of those white buildings hanging in space. I could see millions of them stretching as far as I could see in every direction away from the planet. Comprehension of this as a reality was difficult, maddeningly so. Of course I wondered *what's next?* as the yellow ball exchanged places with the green one.

I placed the green marble in the eyepiece and looked. When the scene became clear I saw another blue, green, brown and white planet quite different from the first. From a resemblance to the globe sitting on the table in our living room at home I recognized our Earth. About twenty of those white cubes descended to the dark, shadow side toward what I knew was the Pacific ocean. Then I viewed one of the cubes up close as it settled into and beneath the dark water. What was happening was incredible yet unmistakable.

The scene change to what I realized was the inside of the cube. A long open area with eight cylindrical objects about twice the size of a Pullman railroad car or city streetcar filled the space except for an area on one end where an object that seemed to fit into the end of the cylinder sat on the floor. The object was round, a lens shaped disk at least a dozen feet high and about twice as wide as it was high. A large metal arm was attached to the top of the object and disappeared into the opening in the end of the cylinder. Quite obviously the disk fit into the end of the cylinder.

A number of people walked about on the floor near the object and through doorways in a wall running the length of the room flush with the openings to the cylinders beyond the wall. My imagination ran wild. Visions of Buck Rogers and Flash Gordon and their space ships filled my mind, but this was incredibly real, almost like I could reach out and touch them. The scene switched to the floor beside the disk where the boy and his family stood. I watched an opening appear in the side of the cylinder. The entire family walked into the lighted interior. The opening closed leaving no indication of where the opening had been. The arm began folding into the cylinder, lifting and turning the disk until it closed into the end of the cylinder.

There was a flurry of activity as doors closed over the disk and the end of the cylinder. People moved about watching brightly colored pictures in the wall, pictures that moved. After a short time the doors opened. The disk and cylinder were gone leaving only an empty metal tube the cylinder had fit tightly into. A small stream of water poured out of the tube and onto the floor. By this time the people had all moved down by the second cylinder and again the scene changed.

I was seeing the man and woman seated facing away from me toward what appeared like a movie screen on a flat wall directly in front of them. There was enough light so I could see them and recognize them as the boy's parents. Stars appeared on the screen as rivulets of water ran or were blown off the outside of the picture. I realized the screen was getting lighter. Then a picture of North America appeared, quite obviously taken from far above. Amazing and totally incomprehensible, but unmistakable, right in front of my eyes. The view was changing like with a zoom lens. First I could see most of the US, then the north central US. Lake Michigan got bigger and then disappeared as I watched Northern Indiana zoom up toward me. Then the view stopped. I recognized what I was seeing. It was our lake, Lake Tippecanoe, and I was close enough to pick out things I knew. The Tippecanoe Country Club, the dance hall, Patona Bay, the submerged islands in the east end, all were clearly recognizable. The time was winter as most of the surrounding lands were white with snow, my guess was early December as the lake was not frozen. It was amazing.

I was looking at our lake from close above and we were coming down. Everything was quite dark but there were lights here and there around the lake. All at once there were bubbles around the screen and I knew what happened. The ship was submerging in the lake in the deepest part off Silver Point across from the Country Club. To a ten year old SciFi fan, what was happening was obvious. These people were hiding their small craft in the 100+ foot depths of the lake. I assumed they would use the craft to go and come, at night when no one would see them. I was beginning to understand what was being shown, but why to me? When the green ball exchanged places with the blue in the view, I did the same with the real marbles.

The scene appearing next was absolutely impossible. First I was in the attic of our house, then with Herc in our back yard. He was asking me to go hunts for crickets. The camera or whatever device they used to take those photos seemed to be in my eyes. Everything I saw I had witnessed before: my friend Herc, hunting crickets, talking to mom, walking to the road and entering the little old store building. Everything in little snippits, from when I climbed into the attic right up to the present, everything.

I heard someone outside so I quickly removed the marbles and placed them in the bag. I had no sooner done so when a knock on the door brought my eyes up. There in the doorway stood the boy with the big eyes.

"Come with me," he said and motioned. "We must hurry."

When I hesitated after jumping down from the doorway he grabbed my hand, pulled, and again urged me to hurry.

"Why?" I asked, almost frightened. Where are we going?" He led me to a delivery van parked on the side of the road near the old store. The door opened and the man I assumed was his father jumped out.

"Charley, you must come with us. It is important."

"But, my parents always told me not to go with strangers."

The boy pulled gently on my hand. "If we wished you any harm we could simply take you. You experienced our capabilities. According to our laws you must come on your own, willingly. If you won't, we are forbidden to force you."

Something about his manner, his speech, seemed so honest, so sincere, I agreed and jumped into the truck. "My dad will be here in a while and I'll be in trouble if I'm not there." I said, pleading.

The man glanced back at me softly as he drove off. "It will be more than an hour until your dad arrives, by then we will bring you back here. I promise."

"How do you know?" I asked.

"Right this moment he is buying gasoline in a town called Ridgeville Corners in Ohio. He will take more than an hour and a half to come here."

I knew exactly where he stopped, at Ferd Bernfeld's station where we always stopped for gas. "How can you know? It's impossible!" I blurted out.

"We own and use many things beyond your understanding, those glass books for example. Surely what you read or as you would say, saw in them, can convince you we could know where your father is."

My SciFi mind adapted and understood. "I guess I understand—sorta. but where are we going now?"

"We're going to our home as you would describe, not far from here. We'll be there in about ten minutes."

We headed up the dirt road past the Henwoods' house toward Syracuse. Before we started to cross through the deep ravine, we turned off on the right on a narrow road I had never been aware of before. A narrow opening in a fence led to what appeared to be a small, grassy yard. We stopped after we entered the yard and the boy got out and reconnected the wire fence behind us. Then we drove across the grassy spot and down a steep, craggy path into the ravine stopping finally at the base of a vertical cliff about thirty feet high. They checked a little grey box the man took from his pocket and the cliff opened up like a silent doorway. We stepped inside and the door closed.

"Come this way." they urged as they started down a long flight of stairs in a dimly lighted tunnel. We went down more than a hundred steps before coming to another door. Once inside the place seemed like a modern house all lighted up with normal furniture, chairs, lamps, tables, and decorations. This could have been the inside of any new house in town except there were no windows. In place of window glass were grey panels like the big one I had seen they had on their planet. I assumed they could show pictures.

"Please take a seat." the boy said motioning to a chair. "My family will be out in a minute to talk with you and explain who we are, what we are doing, and how important it is you help us."

"I don't know what to say or do. This is all amazing to me and a bit frightening."

The rest of them came in and sat down near me. Then the woman spoke. Her smile and warm tone of voice were reassuring. "Please don't be afraid, Charley, I promise nothing bad or frightening is going to happen while you are here with us. You can call our son who gave you the books, John, as his name in our language would be hard for you to say. Please call me Mary, my husband Don, and our daughter's Lou and Jess."

Overcome with amazement I asked, "How was all this built? The tunnel, this place underground. Why are you hiding? Where did you all come from? You are all so—different."

Mary continued. "We will try to answer all of your questions, but first let me tell you about us and why we are here. By reading those books you know what happened to our home planet a few of your years ago."

I interrupted. "Yes but how did it work. I mean—you called those marbles books and said I should read them. They sure weren't like any books I've ever seen."

John spoke up. "When you read your printed books don't you see mental pictures of what is going on? Don't you seem to see what you are reading?"

I thought for a moment. "I see what you mean, but that's a whole lot different from the way I viewed those things in your books as you call them. To me they are like marbles, not books."

"Don't you remember seeing those gold colored characters before the pictures appeared?" John asked. "Those are our characters or maybe letters as you call them in your writing. When you see them, they bring those pictures or movies as you saw them up directly in your brain. It's complicated, similar to how your ears convert air compression variations to sounds you hear in your brain. Did you learn anything about that yet in school?"

"I don't think we've studied hearing much in school, but I read all about this in the book of knowledge. I sorta know what you mean. What you describe is like something straight out of Buck Rogers or Flash Gordon."

John laughed. "I saw some of your "Big Little, Buck Rogers" books. They're quite far from reality, but I can see the similarity."

"But what I'd like to know is what I asked before. What's all this about and how did it happen?"

Don spoke up. "We don't have a lot of time so I'll explain briefly. After the meteor destroyed our planet, we needed a new home, a planet as much like our old home as possible. Yours seemed an excellent prospect until we discovered advanced life forms had developed. We're here for a short stay of up to about two of your years. We need time to replenish our depleted energy stores. As soon as we complete loading our energy we will be on our way to try to find a new home."

"Couldn't you stay here?" I asked.

Lou smiled at her father. "My dad said there were already too many advanced life forms on this planet and there wasn't room for us. besides, do you remember how many of our ships as you call them you watched leaving our planet? Dad told me there were more than a thousand of our people in every one of those ships. In every one of those ships are several hundred small ships like the one our family used to come to your area. Our ship is hidden at the bottom of the lake where you live."

Don smiled at Lou as he told me, "When we left home we split up into thousands of small groups of twenty to fifty ships. Twenty-three of our ships came to your planet. We are searching this section of our galaxy to find a place suitable for all of us to live. A place where we wouldn't displace creatures even those of limited intelligence. It's one of our most powerful laws. Also, we'd like all of our people to be able to live on one planet once more. We'd like to make the place as much like the home we lost as possible. Should we find such a place we will call everyone so we can all head there and build a new home."

All kinds of questions flew through my mind. "I think I know what you mean—sorta. but energy? What kind of energy? Where can you find it and what do you do with it."

"Actually, we use electric energy. We store energy in what you might call batteries. Our powerful batteries can store tremendous amounts of power. Your best scientists would have a difficult time understanding our batteries and how they work. We go deep down in your Earth to where there is tremendous heat and convert this heat directly into electricity which we store in our batteries. All of this goes on in our ships as they sit on the ocean floor. It's where the internal heat of your planet is closest to the surface."

Something didn't seem to make sense to me. "That's interesting, but what does all this mean to me? Why am I here? I'm just a kid. There's nothing I can do for you, nothing!"

Don and his wife glanced at each other. Then Mary said, "There is something important we think only a boy like you can do for us, something simple and quite common that would be dangerous for us to do ourselves. This involves flying a kite. You can fly a kite, can't you?"

"I'm one of the best kite builders and flyers around. I've even won a few kite flying contests, but why couldn't you do that yourselves? Couldn't John do that for you?"

Mary bent down and looked me straight in the eyes. "Look at me, Charley. What do you see?"

"A nice lady with a nice family."

"Doesn't my face appear different to you? When you first saw John didn't you think he looked different from other boys, a lot different?"

"Well, yes. You all have those huge eyes, and you are, well different than most people."

"It's why we don't go out among you except in extreme emergencies. When we do, we try to hide our faces under a floppy hat, especially our eyes. You realized how different John appeared at the fair, didn't you? We took a big chance that day with all those people around. What do you think would happen if John had approached an adult like he did you?"

"I think I understand. An adult would be surprised and maybe make a big fuss. I only felt curious."

"An adult would call authorities, the police. How would John explain where his parents lived, or anything about himself. It could become an extremely dangerous situation for us, a tragic exposure. Who knows where it might lead?"

"Why? And what about this kite thing?"

Don picked up a small brown box with buttons and a grey square on the front. "You see this, Charley? This is a communicator, a kind of 2-way radio with which we can speak to our other people all over your world and sometimes on other worlds. We have three of these. They are necessary so we can stay in contact with our friends. We all help each other and receive instructions and news on these boxes. These are our only link to any of our people."

"Those are neat things." I said. "How do they work?"

"The important thing is now, none of them work. Two weeks ago we had a bad electrical storm, lots of lighting. We were transporting them from the ship to our home here when some downed power lines fell on our truck, right near your cottage."

"Yeah. I remember the storm. The thunder woke me up and I usually sleep through storms."

"Anyway, one of those broken power lines whipped around, broke out the rear window of the truck, and touched the stack of three communicators. It sent at least 7,200 volts of electricity through them and burned out the antenna system on all three units. We took one of them apart and tried to fix it, but the antenna signal amplifier had been burned out and we brought no replacement parts. We stretched out a wire and hooked it up to the fence to use as an antenna, but the signal was still too weak, We managed to hear a weak incoming signal to our receiver, but got no response to any outgoing signal which was too weak. I tried to figure out how to raise an antenna high enough to work when John suggested the kite. That's when we devised the plan to use John to find and contact a young boy, and here you are."

"Wow. Flying an antenna using a kite. That's smart. Where are we going to do this and when?"

"We will contact you to let you know, but now I had better take you back to where you will be meeting your dad. He should be arriving in about twenty minutes. I trust you can keep this to yourself?"

"I sure will, and I understand why, really, like something out of those SciFi stories I read. You can count on me. Uh, how will you let me know?"

"You know about the big stand of Sumac in the field across the road?"

"Yeah. My friends and I go there sometimes to dig for fish worms in the little gully running through the sumac."

"You said you flew kites. Do you have one here and do you ever fly it?"

"Yeah. I keep a neat box kite here which I fly up at the top of the hill beyond the patch of sumac."

"I don't think the hill will take us high enough, but we can walk from there up to the much higher hill this road crosses. Will it be OK? Will your mom let you?"

"I know it will work and Mom will let me."

"How about Monday at about ten"

"I'm sure it will be OK with Mom. I'll duck my sis though. She'll want to go with me if she sees my kite."

"Can you do that ?"

"Sure. I've done so before."

"Now we'd better take you back."

My dad arrived about ten minutes after I returned. After our greeting he asked, "Why are you so excited. You seem like you are ready to jump out of your skin. Some big surprise you're dying to tell me, but promised your mom you wouldn't? Some fresh cherry pies, maybe?"

"Nope. I'm thinkin' about goin' fishin'. I hear the bluegills are biting in the flats."

"Got any crickets?"

"A whole new bunch Herc and I caught. They're in the big can all ready to go."

"Make the boat ready while I kiss your mom, unpack, and change clothes. She might go with us."

It took almost an hour before we were all three out on the flats pullin' in bluegills. They were really bitin'. By the time we headed in before dark we had at least twenty of those hand sized beauties. They would be good eating over the weekend. All I could think about during the trip home was the space craft sitting on the bottom at the other end of the lake. We dumped our catch in the live box and headed in for dinner. Mom had fixed a plate of delicious fried bluegills I had caught a few days before. We ate them, corn on the cob and sliced tomatoes. Topped everything off with a piece of Mom's prize cherry pie with whipped cream on top.

After dinner Mom surprised me a bit. "Your son's had something bothering him since last week when we went to the fair. He says not, but I know my boy."

"Mom. I told you. Everything's fine. I caught us plenty of crickets and sold a bunch. I made almost three weeks' allowance."

Dad stared at me with a concerned face. "Whatever is bothering you, son, spit it out and off your chest. Your mother is never wrong about you."

"I don't have any idea what all the fuss is about. I'm fine."

"Did you have a falling out with Herc or Paul? Or the little girl staying at the Hackerd's cottage is the problem. You are a little sweet on her, aren't you? What's her name, Nancy, right?"

"Aw for gosh sakes. I'm gettin' on fine with all of them. Paul's at home in Fort Wayne, Herc's gonna take me for a ride in their boat and Nancy's comin' over to swim with me tomorrow afternoon. Everything's fine."

Mom wouldn't quit. "Charley, I know something's bothering you. I can tell. If you won't tell us what, we can't help."

Her words were the last straw. I didn't say a word, but left the table and ran out to the end of the pier where I often went to find some peace and quiet.

"Young man you come right back here to the table. You were not excused." my Dad called after me.

I would be in big trouble if I stayed out there so I walked back and sat down at the table trying to think up something to say.

"All right young man, out with it." Dad demanded.

I had to convince them. "There is absolutely nothing wrong, nothing's bothering me except you saying over and over something's bothering me. Do you want me to lie and tell you a made up story?"

They looked at each other, then Mom came over and put her arms around me. "Charley, I'm sorry." She turned to my dad and said, "We've both been pushin' him quite hard. I must be mistaken. Let's drop the whole thing."

"Thanks, Mom. I promise if anything's ever bothering me, I'll tell you." My fingers were crossed in my pocket, but it worked.

Monday morning took forever to come around. I grabbed my kite and string and told Mom about my kite flying.

"All by yourself?" she asked.

"Yep. I've done so many times before."

"Ok, but tell me where you'll be in case I need you."

"I'll be where I always am, on the hill on Tom's farm. I may walk up to the top of the hill by Henwood's. It's higher there and there's usually more wind."

"Can you hear me blow my whistle from way up there?"

"Mom, I can hear your whistle all the way down at the Kalorama grocery, farther away and with lots of woods in between."

"OK, I'll whistle for you when lunch is ready. Come right away when I whistle. Don't you dawdle."

John waited in the sumac when I got there. We walked up the hill, across the ridge through Tom's farm and up the road to the top of the hill. John's dad waited, partially hidden in some tall weeds by the road. We tied some fine reddish string to the bridle of my kite. The string filled the spool of an ordinary fishing reel.

"Using a reel is sure a clever idea. Are you sure the string's strong enough? It seems flimsy to me." I asked.

"Our string is plenty strong," John said. "There's a fine wire running through it to serve as our antenna. The string runs over to my dad's communicator and will let us fly the kite out there in the open while he remains hidden and tries to make contact. Could we have the parts sent to your mailbox? They are small, about the size of one of your quarters. This is the easiest way we could think of to send them here quickly and easily."

John held the kite up as I ran and launched it. In the brisk wind my kite climbed high into the sky. As I let out more string I asked John, "How will I explain this to my Mom? I don't often receive packages sent to me."

"Is there anything you could order and have sent to you?"

"I'll think of something." I said as I continued to let out string and the kite rose higher and higher.

John's dad called out, "I am receiving a confirming signal. They are connected with us."

I thought of something I had ordered before. "I can order a model airplane kit. The kit would be here in a week or ten days. How in the world would you be able to place those parts in the shipment?"

"Tell us what kind of model airplane kit you want. We'll do the rest." John's father told me.

"An Aeronca C-2 flying model. I've always wanted one of those. I saved enough to buy one."

"We'll gladly pay for the model and the shipping. Be careful when you open the box because those three antenna parts will be inside"

"How will I take them to you?"

"We'll know when the parts are delivered. Then John can meet you among the sumac trees like we did today. As soon as you have them, come to the sumac patch. John will be there. Now we must hurry home"

As soon as I got home I told my mom about a new friend I met while flying my kite.

"Mom, this morning I made a new friend while flying my kite. He lives up the road toward Syracuse. His whole family came while I was flying my kite."

"His whole family? He must be a very nice young man."

"Yes. His mom and dad are nice, and his sisters too. They are nice people."

"Sounds like it. I would like to visit with them."

"You know what, Mom? The Aeronca flying model I've always wanted? I told them about the C2 and they promised to send me one as a gift. Can you believe it?"

"Wonderful. They must be nice. and only after a couple of hours playing together too. They must realize what a fine young man you are."

"Yep. That's almost exactly what they said."

"It only goes to show you what nice people there are in our world."

I almost choked on her words, saying to myself, *and other worlds as well*.

*   *   *

Wednesday a week my model airplane arrived. I opened the box, removed the small package with the parts, and headed for the sumac patch. John was there waiting.

"Thank you so much for getting these parts for us. We've been out of touch with the others for four weeks. Now we can catch up on our search for a new home."

"Thank you for the neat model kit. I will start on it the first rainy day we have. We'll be working on models down in Paul's garage."

"I must rush home with these. How about we meet here late this afternoon and I can tell you the latest news?"

"Okay, I'll see you then."

*   *   *

About four I grabbed my kite and headed for the sumac patch.

"Off to fly your kite again?" Mom asked.

"Yep, We've had great wind recently so it is really fun and John will probably be there. He helps me start it up."

"I wish you would bring him to our house one day. I'd like to meet him."

"Maybe." I called to Mom as I took off running for the hill.

I walked into the sumac patch and found the whole family waiting for me. They told me some of their group had discovered a planet almost perfect for them and less than a hundred light years away from earth. Because they had been out of contact for so long they had to rush to get ready to leave. They would be leaving in their space ship early in the morning while it was still dark. There were hugs and teary goodbys all around until they reluctantly headed up the hill. Before they left, John handed me another pouch like the first one with those marbles, telling me they would teach me more about them I could experience in these new *books*. I trudged up the hill behind them, let my box kite fly in the breeze at the top while my friends disappeared over the big hill. I cried for a long time. I felt terribly sad. My adventure with people from another world was over, and I couldn't tell a soul about them. I flew my kite for a while then left the top of the hill and trudged sadly home.

Mom took one glance at my face. "Son, I don't know what's wrong, but you look as if you lost your best friend."

"I really did, Mom. John had to leave to go to his home. We became really good friends. Then this morning I found out he came from a long way off and had to leave right then to go home. He's from clear across the ocean and won't ever be back. He's a neat kid and yes, I am sad. We had such a short time together."

"I'm so sorry. You say he has already left?"

"Yes, Mom. The family left early this morning, before sunup."

"Where are you going now, son?"

"Oh, I don't know. Maybe I'll go back up to the hill and fly my kite once more. You never know whom you might meet."

"You miss your new friend don't you. He must be special."

"Yep." I said turning to hide the tears in my eyes. "See you later Mom."

✳   ✳   ✳

"Wow, Granddad, you told some story. How come you are telling me, now?"

"Well, George, you remind me so much of myself at your age, especially your imagination. You can reel off yarn after yarn for anyone who will listen. It's why we enjoy swapping yarns, you and I. I'm going to leave this old planet before too long and I had to tell someone my story."

"Yeah, but those yarns are made up. You told me this one is true."

"True as the sun shines and the sky is blue, at least blue some of the time. Young man, I can prove all of this to you with what I carry in these two pouches."

"Are those the pouches John gave you?"

"The very same. and now I'm passing them to you to do with what you want."

"What's in the books in the second bag? You never told me."

"Think of them as books you've not read. You'll see for yourself, won't you?"

"Not a hint?"

"Some wonders are best left for a personal discovery. You'll find out soon enough."

"Wow, Granddad. . . . Can I show them to my friends?"

"It's up to you, but I would think carefully before sharing with those who might be disturbed or wouldn't understand what they mean. You watch them first and then decide what to do with them. I will trust your judgement, like I did my own those many years I carried them. Until right now I never let another soul know about them, not one. Also, I never tired of viewing them. I seemed to learn something new each time, something I missed before. They were an unbelievable aid and comfort to me many times during my long life."

"Don't you wonder what happened to John and his family? Where this new world of theirs is and how they got along when they got there?"

"Many times. It's just the way life is. Sometimes you never learn the outcome of happenings you are part of. Those happenings make one a bit humble. Now, go find a special secret place where you can read those *books*, where no one will ever find you. Young boys always find such a place. I did. I won't ask about yours and don't you tell me."

"Thanks Granddad. You're the greatest"

"Maybe sixty or seventy years from now you'll be telling this story to your own grandson and passing on those *books*. Think of me when you do."

"I will, Granddad. I will."

www.ingramcontent.com/pod-product-compliance
Lightning Source LLC
Chambersburg PA
CBHW080821020726

47501CB00009B/2361